LOVE HURTS

A Speculative Fiction Anthology

Edited by
Tricia Reeks

Assistant Editors
Kyle Richardson
Margaret Reeks

Meerkat Press
Atlanta

Published in the United States by Meerkat Press, LLC

Edited by Tricia Reeks

Cover and book design by Tricia Reeks

Illustrations by Sergio Garzon

ISBN-13 978-0-9966262-2-4 (acid-free paper)
ISBN-13 978-0-9966262-3-1 (eBook)
Library of Congress Control Number: 2015916017

CONTENTS

INTRODUCTION
Tricia Reeks

I've always had a taste for *dark*—whether it be fiction, movies, chocolate, or wardrobe. I blame it on my mother for letting me watch *The Exorcist* at the tender age of twelve. What was she thinking?

So, when the idea for a collection of speculative fiction stories about love started percolating, I automatically tagged the word *hurts* to the end. Like adding a shot of whiskey to your coffee: sure it hurts going down, but the pain is so worth it.

Although a longtime consumer of speculative fiction novels and film, I didn't discover the short fiction market until more recently. Two things prompted it—stumbling upon Hugh Howey's *Wool* during a particularly intense post-apocalyptic reading frenzy, and learning about publications such as *Tor.com* and *Daily Science Fiction* through my own writing journey.

I found a whole new world of exceptional authors I'd never even heard of, some of whom are included in this book. My Kindle quickly began to fill with the collections they appeared in, and I became intrigued by the dynamics of a themed anthology—the way the intense emotional ride of a short story can be enhanced by its association and arrangement with others. Intrigue turned into obsession, and obsession turned into *Love Hurts*.

So with the help of my assistant editors, Kyle Richardson (whose heartbreaking story, *Catching On,* is in this collection) and Margaret Reeks (who knows her way around *The Chicago Manual of Style* like nobody's business), we've gathered twenty-six brilliant speculative fiction stories about love, and the pain that so often accompanies it. Sometimes funny, occasionally happy, frequently gut-wrenching—these stories will take your heart on a wild emotional ride.

Love Hurts includes a few hand-picked favorites—previously published work such as Karin Tidbeck's *Sing* and Jeff VanderMeer's *A Heart for Lucretia*. Stories we read and couldn't get out of our heads (not that we wanted to). The other eighteen are new—like Steve Simpson's haunting dystopian fantasy, *Jacinta's Lovers*, and Shannon Phillips's action-packed sci-fi romp, *Favor*. Great stories that we hope you'll like as much as we did.

The anthology wasn't limited to romantic love, though as you might expect with a theme of "love hurts," most selections fell into that category. But we also have some fascinating tales about other relationships such as between father and son, brother and sister, alien and child.

So join us on this sometimes dark, often painful journey called love. Individually, these stories are wonderful, but I hope we have also managed to capture a bit of the magic that comes from reading them as a collection—that the whole is greater than the sum of its parts.

LOVE HURTS

A Speculative Fiction Anthology

THE SORCERER'S UNATTAINABLE GARDENS
A. Merc Rustad

Originally appeared in *Daily Science Fiction*, April 17, 2015

Wrought iron fences loop around the gardens: six deep, the outer three progressively higher, more elaborate, and with more spikes atop, while the inner three create a mirror effect. Say you make it over all six fences without impaling yourself or falling or getting trapped between iron bars that suddenly constrict or twist or move. Say you avoid the fourth fence, the electric one, or the second one with the poisoned varnish, or the sixth one with a taste for blood.

Once upon a time, a sorcerer lost their shadow in a bet with a magician. The bet itself is unimportant. Shadowless, the sorcerer wandered the world until, unexpectedly, they found a shadow whose person had been lost to a bet with a sea-witch long before.

If you make it past all six fences, then you reach the first garden. It's a great circular loop of hawthorn and foxglove hedging that has no convenient holes or doors. The hedge speaks with a rusty, gravely, morbid voice; its cadence is so slow you forget the first word before you hear the third one. The hedge asks riddles, like hedges are wont to do in a sorcerer's garden and, if you get it wrong, the gophers eat you.

The sorcerer and the unattached shadow fell in love. "Can we stay together forever?" asked the shadow, twined with the sorcerer under the autumn stars, and the sorcerer said, "Yes." The sorcerer did not intend to lie.

But let's say you answer the riddle, which no one has been able to guess for sixty-five years, and the hedge opens just enough for you to squeak through with lacerations on your sides and foxglove pollen infecting the cuts. Then you reach the second circle, a rose garden.

What the shadow did not know was that, once upon a time, the sorcerer made a bet with a demon and lost. The bet itself is unimportant; the wager was the sorcerer's happiness. As soon as the sorcerer found true joy, the demon came to collect.

Roses of every color imagined or not imagined fill the garden. The air is so thick with fragrance you get high with the first breath and overdose with the second. But let's say you can hold your breath, or you brought a mask. You hear the roses speaking. Not riddles, of course, because the roses are too polite to infringe on the hedge's territory. What the roses say is: *eat you eat you eat you.*

And then they will, of course. Roses need fertilizer just like any other plant. Your bones might become thorns for the next bushes that sprout, if you're fortunate, and if you're even luckier, one of the yellow roses will drink your soul instead of the red ones. And if you're especially tasty, it won't even hurt.

The sorcerer said to the shadow, "I'm so sorry. I didn't mean for this to happen." To look on the shadow brought only grief to them both. So the sorcerer banished the shadow, because once a sorcerer makes a bet, they cannot go back on the wager. Shadows can't weep.

But let's say you don't get eaten by the roses. The circle you find yourself in next is a lightless tower that goes downward and never up. Chains spun from hanged men's gurgles crisscross the stairs that don't really exist. Beware of the ivy along the walls, for it grows on memory, until your mind is choked and full of leaves, and roots dig out through your skin and you forget why you came, and you sit there forever, and forever, and forever, and . . .

The shadow found itself in a glacier. The ice the shadow absorbed melted and dripped down the shadow's face, and it looked at its hands and clenched them into fists and said, "I will find you again, love." Somewhere on the other side of the world, the sorcerer heard the shadow's words and despaired.

But let's say that you don't trip over nonexistent steps and fall into the abyss, and you bring herbicide for the ivy.

The shadow traveled the world alone, becoming a master of disguise, a jack-of-all-trades. No cost was too great to acquire what was needed. The shadow absorbed knowledge and languages and magic and shut away grief so deep it forgot, for a time, it was there. Then the shadow learned how to hunt demons.

The second to last circle is made of bubbles, translucent spheres summoned from the essence of Death Itself, for Death has always had a whimsical side. If you pop one, it swallows you, compressing your lungs, siphoning your blood, unraveling your nervous system, grinding your bones into dust. There is no space between the bubbles through which to pass.

On the other side of the world, the sorcerer put all their skill into making an unattainable fortress, circles of gardens no one can ever penetrate. There will be no more bets, and no more loss, and in their self-made prison, the sorcerer sits alone. One day, the sorcerer hopes, they will fade from memory so the shadow may mourn, and perhaps one day find peace again.

But let's say you brought needles to prick the bubbles ever so carefully and catch the pieces of death in a lead-lined pouch. When you carve a path through this circle, you find a simple wooden door that asks for a password. If you answer wrong, the door will never have existed. But you answer: "Heart," and it opens.

The shadow laid a delicious trap for the demon: freshly picked souls, harvested from the Tree at the Center of the World. The demon approached, feet soundless on the ice floes the shadow drifted on. "What game shall we play for this luscious prize?" the demon asked, and the shadow said, "No game. I'm here to kill you."

Let's say you make it into the final circle, the one made of plain stone.

The shadow lunged, a lasso made from angel sinew in one hand, and in the other a poniard forged in the eventual heat death of the universe. The demon screamed as the angel sinew snared tight about its neck. The demon's form flickered through every horrendous shape it knew; yet it couldn't escape the noose. "You hurt the one I love," the shadow said. "I do not care for that." The demon howled for mercy. Shadows are neither merciful nor cruel, except when they are. With the poniard, the shadow cut out the demon's guts, and in the steaming entrails found every item the demon had stolen with tricks or dice or cards. The demon withered into flakes of ash and sank into the

frigid sea-salt waters. The shadow gently scooped up what it had sought for so long, trembling, hoping it was not too late.

There are no traps or puzzles or illusions here. This garden is brick, lopsided piles of brown and red and gray stone in no discernible pattern. The sorcerer sits on the middle heap, alone except for the bones. Oh, yes, of course there are bones. Don't ask what they are from.

The sorcerer is a thin, hunched person of no specific gender, dressed in a blue habit sewn from fish scales. Dull eyes, bones sharp against slack skin. Building an unattainable garden takes its toll on a body.

"Why did you come?" the sorcerer says. There's deep tiredness in that voice, so much pain. "You will only find sorrow here."

"I know." You sit beside the sorcerer, your love, and unzip your ribs. Tucked under your heart is a small oak box, plain and unvarnished. You offer it to the sorcerer. "I brought this for you."

Their hands shake as they open the box.

Inside, wrapped in turquoise tissue paper, is the sorcerer's stolen happiness.

They let out a small gasp of shock. "How . . ."

You press a finger against the sorcerer's lips. "Later. Please take it." You've hoped since the moment you found the wrought iron gates that the sorcerer will not refuse. If the sorcerer says no, you are finished.

The sorcerer folds the paper aside for later use. "How long has it been?"

Too, too long.

"I don't remember . . ." The sorcerer's voice catches in their throat. They turn away. "Why did you come?"

"I want you back." You wait, trembling. There is nowhere else to go. "Please come back, love. I will help you laugh again, I will make you strong. One day, we will tear down these unattainable gardens and walk free. I am here because I need you." Unsaid: *Please don't banish me to loneliness forever.*

The sorcerer shuts their eyes. Then with quivering hands, replaces the happiness inside them. A shudder ripples through the sorcerer's frame, and they press their face against your shoulder. You stroke their hair and wait.

"I'm so sorry," the sorcerer says, over and over and over.

You wrap yourself around them and hold them close. For now you are safe from wandering magicians and cunning sea-witches and unsatisfied demons.

"It will be all right, love," you whisper, because shadows never lie. And for the first time since they built this labyrinth, the sorcerer smiles.

A Puzzle by the Name of L
Carla Dash

When Death knocks on Stephanie's door, she is wallowing in the aftereffects of her fiancé's death, trekking aimlessly through the boggy muck that was once her heart, her life, and wondering if this year, finally, will be the one that drains away what's left of her will to live. Also, she is working on a jigsaw puzzle. The interruption annoys her because, even though most of the cardboard pieces are lying in dark, senseless piles, the blue-black of the river has just started to distinguish itself from the blue-gray mist hovering above it. This is important, she knows. The turning point of the whole activity. The first step towards completion. Stephanie is something of an authority on jigsaw puzzles. She has been doing a lot of them in the two years since Hayden died.

Looking through the peephole, she knows the guy standing on her threshold is Death because he's wearing a billowing black robe and swinging a scythe back and forth at his side in short, fluid pendulum arcs. Also, there is something about his looks. Something ashen, unfinished. Something not quite existent. She thinks, *I should be afraid.* She stands perfectly still, unbreathing, waiting for the emotion to flood through her veins, but she feels nothing, so she opens the door.

"Boo," says Death. His voice is grainy, a new or seldom-used thing, but with a deep, languorous current running beneath it. It is a voice with potential, Stephanie thinks. The kind of voice that could sing arias, seduce in seconds, if only he'd give a little cough or clear his throat.

"You aren't a ghost," she replies.

"I'm not?" he asks, all innocence.

Stephanie slides her eyes down the length of his body, once, slowly, just to be sure. Black robe. Still billowing. Scythe. Still swinging. She notices as well that his chest is quite broad, but that his fingers are long and thin.

"Obviously," she says.

"Hm. Good to know." Then he smiles, straight and bone white, but fetching, charming, like a guy who just a moment ago scored the winning touchdown and is now posing for a photograph, his dad's proud, vicarious arm slung across his shoulders. "Can I come in?"

"No."

As he sticks out his bottom lip and rounds his eyes into pathetic, puppy-dog orbs, Stephanie thinks there is something familiar about the arrangement of his features—the alignment of his pupils with the corners of his lips, the tilt of his nose, the curve of his eyes. A name flitters through the depths of her skull, but won't float to the surface.

"I'm losing my mind," she decides, says, and shuts the door in his face.

But when she turns, he is sitting on her living room couch, ankles crossed, arms folded behind his head, smirking. Again, Stephanie feels she should be afraid. She should call the police. Try to throw him out. But she's never been one to fight the inevitable. If he got in once, she figures he can get in again.

So instead she flings out an arm and says, "Over there is the kitchen. Down the hallway on the left is the bathroom, at the end my bedroom, never go in there, on the right another room, definitely never go in there. This, obviously, is the living room. The couch you're sitting on is where you'll be sleeping. Do you even need to sleep?"

Death shrugs. "Sure. You done with the tour?"

"Yes," Stephanie says.

"Great, because this place is giving me ideas." Death springs up from the couch and bounces over to a wall. "You've got a loose socket cover here," he says, prodding the plastic and the wires beneath. "Maybe you can stick a finger in. I doubt it'd do the trick, though. Maybe if you stand in a bucket of water at the same time? Or," he says, dashing to a window, "maybe you can jump through this, while it's closed, of course, for maximum effect. Looks like a long fall. What is it? Eighteen floors? Nineteen? Wouldn't be very much left of you. Maybe you can stick your arm through the glass, then drag it back and forth across the shards. Or, if bloodiness appeals to you, maybe . . . do you have knives?" he asks, shooting off to the kitchen without waiting for an answer.

Stephanie hears drawers jiggling and the clang of silverware bouncing around. Death reappears, holding two of the largest knives she owns like nunchuks or sai, one in each hand. He slashes graceful semicircles through the air, then drops into a fighting stance. "Or," he says, popping back into verticality, letting the knives fall carelessly to the floor, "if you don't like the bloody approach, maybe you can go the drug route." And then he's darting down the hall, opening and closing cabinets, mumbling, "Jeez, these are a lot of pills, you've thought about this before, haven't you?" and stepping back into view, a bottle curled in the crook of each arm and one shaking in his left hand like a maraca.

Stephanie stalks up to him, snatches the bottles away, glares into his foggy eyes—amused, but impersonal, uncaring—and grits, "I'm not going to off myself, asshole."

"Are you sure?" he asks, voice bland. "Because my presence here begs to differ."

Stephanie takes a deep breath and holds the air tight in her lungs to keep from responding childishly, turns her back, and walks down the hallway, footsteps measured and light. "Don't follow me."

"Oh? And why should I listen to you?" Death asks, arms folded across his puffed-out chest.

"Please. Just don't," Stephanie murmurs as the door on the right side of the corridor clicks shut behind her.

Death plops onto the couch, fingering the faded, matted plush. "Fine, but you're no fun. If you take your time with this thing, I'm going to get bored."

In the room, surrounded by potted poisons—*Atropa belladonna, Digitalis purpurea, Datura stramonium, Conium maculatum* and the like—Stephanie kneels in front of the windowsill and tips a watering can, attempting to spout liquid out of the porcelain jug at the pressure and volume her mother would, wetting the soil so it's just barely damp to the touch.

The next morning, Stephanie wakes cold. During the night, her tossing and turning has bunched the blanket around her arms and hips and pulled it away from her feet, leaving them exposed and icy. Her nose feels frozen, numb. The arrival of consciousness is a slow, difficult ascent, like swimming upward through a deep, viscous bog. There are moments when she doesn't think she'll ever reach the surface. That's okay. She doesn't care. She stops wanting to. She embraces the sensation of complete immersion, of floating, of sinking, of burning oxygen-deficient lungs. But eventually, she rises. The thoughts rushing through her head, like a school of wild fish, slow into sense. She can catch and examine them. She can dissect their beauty until there is nothing left but corpses in her hands. She sniffs, disappointed, and swings her legs over the side of the bed, slipping her toes into the fuzzy, carnation-pink slippers her mother bought her when she was a girl. They are too small and worn; Stephanie's heels hang three inches off the backs, and she can feel the cheap, industrial carpet through their jagged-holed soles. Hayden used to say, *Momma's girl.* But Stephanie doesn't allow herself to think about that, doesn't permit Hayden to shake his head, bemused, or grin around teeth digging into his lower lip, attempting to hold back a smile. Instead she spots the image floating up through her memory from a distance, coalescing as it rises, and shoves it back under, dissolving it into harmless, sodden pieces.

Stephanie stretches and shuffles down the hallway, past the faded, flowery wallpaper she hates but doesn't have the motivation to change, because, one way or another, she'll be gone soon. The living room is drenched in a shade of cool white. Through the open curtains, she can see it is snowing. Heavy flakes cascade down in front of the glass. The ground is a river of white. The sky an ocean of silver. She frowns. *Another winter.*

Death has been snooping through her things. Books are askew on shelves, cabinets are open, picture frames full of sunshine and Stephanie's old life—she and Hayden on a beach in Hawaii, his head in her lap, her hands tangled in his dark, curly hair; she and Hayden, lounging under a white umbrella on a beach in Brazil; her mother, kneeling in her rose garden, light bouncing off her shears and seeping into her wavy tresses—stand erect on surfaces they usually lie flat upon. Stephanie itches to turn them down again, but refrains.

She can't see Death over the back of the couch, but his robe is draped over one of its arms, and his scythe, so dull and subtly curved Stephanie wonders if it would even cut her if she ran a finger across its edge, is propped against the side, so she figures he must be there. She wonders what he wears under the robe, if he's naked, what his body looks like. She peers over the top of the couch. He's wearing black cotton boxers and a white undershirt. His legs are hairy. His arms are thin, but defined. She thinks perhaps his complexion is a little more brown and a little less gray than it was yesterday. He looks ordinary, familiar.

"Throw yourself in front of a bus. Hang a noose from the ceiling fan in the kitchen," Death mumbles around the cushion his face is smooshed into. Stephanie sighs and he rolls over, rubbing his eyes.

"I'm telling you," he says, "I've thought about it. Broken bones jutting through your skin, blood pooling around your limbs, a snapped neck or a blue face, you could pull them off. They'd look good on you. You wouldn't be one of those hideous corpses. You'd be beautiful."

He yawns wide, stretches long and slow like a cat. Stephanie thinks, *how cute* quickly followed by *yep, I'm losing my mind* and pads into the kitchen to make tea. She pulls a china kettle down from a cabinet. It was a birthday gift one year from her mother to Hayden. Her mother never really liked him, always said she thought Stephanie spent too much time with him, neglecting her old friends and interests. But Stephanie knows the truth. Her dad was a deadbeat, uninterested and so long gone she doesn't have even a partial memory of his face, and there were no other children; she is all her mother has. When Stephanie told her she and Hayden were engaged, her mother relented, though. *Alright, alright,* she said. Stephanie was with her, walking through a flea market under a hot, blue July sky, when she bought the kettle, green and oblong, like a leaf, with embossed vines crawling along its surface. *Here,* she said, *porcelain for the maker of dead things.*

Mom, Stephanie said. Her mother sighed, *Alright, alright.* The memory of Hayden's dark fingers moving close to hers as they worked together to pull the floral wrapping paper away from the irregularly shaped pot bubbles up behind Stephanie's eyelids. But, as she runs water, watching the sink distort behind it, listening to it softly tap against the tarnished metal basin, sliding her fingers beneath the stream and feeling it slip silkily between them, the image sinks obediently beneath the surface of her thoughts once again.

When she returns to the living room, Death is sitting up, rubbing a hand over his face. Stephanie passes him a mug, decorated in concentric circles that lap like waves at the rim of the cup, and blows into her own matching one. Death perks up.

"Is it poisoned?"

"No!" Stephanie says, a little loudly, a little sharply.

"Aw," Death pouts. "So you're not going to kill yourself today either?"

"No."

"Oh, well. Hey! These are nice mugs. They look handmade. Did you make them?"

"No," Stephanie says. "My fiancé did."

"That him in all the photos?"

"Yes."

"What happened to him?"

"He's dead. Shouldn't you know that?"

"Lots of people die, you know. I can't be expected to remember them all. So? What happened?"

An image springs into Stephanie's mind before she can clamp down on it. The brown, flailing arms she sometimes imagines she saw sinking into the ocean in slow motion from the shore. The churning water. The swollen blueness of his skin when they finally pulled him out.

"He drowned," she says.

"And?" Death asks, eyes hungry, voice hushed and rapt. "What was it like?"

"I don't know," Stephanie says. "It happened fast. I don't remember."

⚜

Stephanie gets used to having Death around. He whirls through her apartment, causing chaos in every crevice, snooping, flipping through leather-bound photo albums and leaving them open on the carpet, running fingers over Hayden's bright, ceramic cups, mugs, and baking dishes and discarding them on the Formica kitchen countertops, pulling her boxes and boxes of jigsaw puzzles off the rough, unfinished, wood shelves that line the living room, turning them over, studying the pictures on the fronts, shaking them up, and replacing them in tall, precarious, asymmetrical piles. But Stephanie finds she doesn't mind. She has been alone for a long time and she is enjoying the little things about having a man around: the noise, the cooking for two, the picking up after someone else's messes.

One afternoon Stephanie is working on the jigsaw puzzle from the day Death showed up. She is agitated because as much as she wants to assemble it using deductive skills alone—as much as she longs to see only the size, shape, color, and pattern of individual pieces—she can't help but recall in perfect, vivid detail the scene on the front of the box. The dark water, the inky sky, the shadows of the trees on the distant shore, the motionless skiff and its obscure passenger all hover in her imagination with irritating clarity so that each jigsaw piece becomes a streak of water, a grain of wood, or a chunk of pine needles instead of a black, gray, or green sharp-edged, rounded, or protrusion-nubbed irregular polygon. Stephanie sulks, pushing the cardboard pieces around with the tips of her fingers, and tries to forget the whole to which they belong.

It is at this point that Death walks up to her, holding her cell phone delicately between the thumb and forefinger of one hand like he might a snake, by the head, cautiously, and afraid, as if he can't be sure he won't imminently suffer a life-threatening injury.

"What is it?" Stephanie snaps. "You want me to eat the phone? Beat myself over the head with it?"

"No," Death responds quietly. Stephanie squints at him.

"What then?"

"Did you know you have twenty-seven messages from your mother?"

"You've been listening to my messages?"

"Did. You. Know." Death snarls, slamming a palm against the flimsy, metal, foldout card table Stephanie uses for assembling puzzles. It squeaks and wobbles, but doesn't buckle. Stephanie takes a breath, counts to thirty in her head, then pushes it back out.

"Yes, I know."

"Have you answered any of them?"

"No."

"Why not?"

"Obviously, I don't want to."

"But why not?"

"Why do you care?"

"I don't know. It's just . . . you used to be so close to her," Death says in a voice as smooth and deep as a bow sliding across the strings of a cello, a voice so familiar it hurts.

"What?" Stephanie asks, fear, shocking and novel, jolting through her diaphragm.

"Hm?" Death asks, eyes distant, distracted.

"How would you know that?"

"I don't know. It just feels true."

⚶

Incidents like this become the norm. Instead of greeting Stephanie in the mornings with gung-ho suicide suggestions like "a bullet between the eyes" and "roll around in a pile of glass shards," Death often begins the day with observations like "your hair is longer than it used to be" or "when did you stop running? You never used to be able to sit still." He wanders, glassy-eyed, through the apartment, dragging his feet and running palms across the ceramics in the kitchen, the fuzz of Stephanie's slippers, the gloss of photographs, and Stephanie knows he's recalling memories that aren't his. Sometimes he even reaches out and touches the top of her head, the side of her face, or the length of her sleeves, but Stephanie can't find it in herself to stop him or the wispy shivers that ripple through her limbs in the wake of his fingertips.

As for Stephanie, she spends increasingly more time in the room on the right side of the hallway and takes lots of baths, sometimes as many as three or four a day. Her bathtub isn't much, plastic and rectangular, no porcelain contours or lions' feet—an adjunct professor of horticulture, especially one who only works two out of three semesters a year like she does, can't afford to be picky about much when renting apartments—but she enjoys filling it to the brim, then tilting backwards beneath the surface and watching the world unglue. Vision blurs and sound distorts and she feels as though she's managed to remove herself from reality. She drifts away from it, unconnected, unaffected, but interested. A non-participating observer, an objective third party. She stays in until her body, pruned and waterlogged, becomes nearly too heavy to lift and her lungs burn from the effort of holding her breath.

⚘

Once, perhaps months after Death arrives—Stephanie can no longer be sure how long it's been; time flows past her, in front of her, and behind her, and she's not sure where exactly in it she is—Stephanie wakes abruptly and doesn't know why. She can't tell what time it is. The light filtering through the blinds is a hazy, gray-white, like cobwebs strung wall-to-wall, and could mean anything from early morning to evening or snowy midday.

Soon enough she hears rustling nearby, and when she turns her head, she discovers Death kneeling next to the bed, gazing at her. She considers becoming angry. She thinks perhaps she should remind Death of what she told him the first day they met—that he should never enter her bedroom—but she doesn't feel like fighting. She's sleepy and comfortable and Death's stare is a warm, gentle weight on her skin.

Time passes and Stephanie feels her body sink back into sleep. Her limbs become heavy, hard to command and hard to move. She dozes, then dreams. The scene from her jigsaw puzzle appears. Stephanie is standing on the bank of the river in a cotton nightgown, mud squelching between her toes, fronds tickling her ankles, the skiff out in the distance. She has always been curious about that figure on the skiff. She watches and watches, peering through the fog, waiting for the silhouette to shift, for something to happen. No breeze blows through the trees. No mosquitoes buzz in the air. No waves beat the shore, and the person on the boat sits as still as stone. Eventually, a hand reaches out. The fingers push together and bend, then dip silently into the water. When they emerge, cupping a handful of river water, they rise level with the figure's mouth, then tilt.

Stephanie wakes in a sweat. *Did the figure drink or not?* She doesn't know. Death's face hovers inches above hers, his hands trail across her forehead and down her cheeks.

"Are you alright?" he asks, breath ghosting across Stephanie's lips.

"Yes," she says, pushing his hands away, "I'm fine." He looks disbelieving, but drops back onto the floor next to the bed. Stephanie focuses on the gentle burn his concerned gaze ignites in her abdomen and tries to slow the rise and fall of her chest.

"Do you remember," he says after a few minutes, "that time we visited the Pacific after we got engaged?"

"What?" Stephanie whispers, dread washing through her ribs.

"We went to California, to that beach. There were high, rocky cliffs. You were so happy. You kept smiling at me."

Stephanie curls her fingers into the cheap, stiff sheets pooling around her. "No, no. That wasn't you!" Death recoils, his eyes, a warm, light brown, Hayden's down to the most minute, golden flecks, going shuttered and unfocused. "That was my fiancé," Stephanie says more sedately. "You have to stop this. You aren't him."

"Yes. Of course. That's right," Death says, his voice rolling, wavering. "But do you remember anyway? When he took you there?"

Stephanie remembers. The water had been so blue, shot through with green and turquoise and bright, diffused sunlight. Hayden had been happy. Too happy. Too confident. He swam too far.

"No," she says. "I don't remember."

"Alright," Death says. "I made you breakfast. Have something." He lifts a tray from the floor beside him. On it are two pieces of toast covered in marmalade, eggs, a sausage patty, and a mug of tea. Suddenly Stephanie remembers the sorts of things Death used to say when he first appeared, things like "down a bottle of Oxycontin" or "chew up a death cap." There's no way she can force down any food he's made her.

"No thank you," she blurts.

"But—"

"Maybe later, okay? But can you leave me alone for a while right now? You're not supposed to be in here anyway. Please?" Death frowns, but turns Hayden's sad, soulful eyes away and acquiesces, drifting out of the room.

※

The next evening, Stephanie finishes the puzzle. Death is leaning against a wall, watching her as she locks in the last piece, a dark sliver of river. It looks exactly as she always knew it would. Starless sky. Unruffled trees. Water devoid of motion. The boatman in the center, dark and distant. Obscure, unknowable, impossible to capture. Stephanie takes a sip of tea from one of Hayden's mugs. She spent a long time preparing it, adding just the right amount of sugar (one and a half teaspoons), and heating it to the perfect temperature (140 degrees). She has let it sit too long, though. Now it's cold, gritty, and bitter. Of course it is. Stephanie sets the cup down gently, still conscious of the fact that it is something Hayden made, and begins disassembling the puzzle, unsnapping the cardboard pieces and throwing them in the puzzle box with quick, frantic flicks of her wrist and jabs of her fingers.

"Why would you do that?" Death asks. "Why did you spend so much time putting that thing together only to take it apart?"

Stephanie throws the box at his face. Puzzle pieces bounce off his shoulders and rain down onto the carpet. Before Death can respond, Stephanie pushes back her chair, runs down the hall, and locks herself in the room on the right side of the hallway. But this time, when she spirals away from the door, Death is standing behind her. Pale moonlight streams through the curtains as she watches him take in the contents of the room. The tall, twisting, deadly plants crawling up and around the walls. The delicate flowers blooming from their leaves. Purple bells of nightshade. Pink tubes of foxglove. Creamy trumpets of devil's snare. Fragile, white umbels of hemlock.

When Death faces Stephanie, his eyes blaze, with what—anger, desire, remorse, anguish—she can't tell. He slides forward, mouth, shoulders, and fingers tense, pressing their chests together. Stephanie's whole body pulses, with anger and something else she doesn't want to name.

"You aren't supposed to be in here," she says. "Go away."

"Shut up, you're so stupid, you don't understand, so just shut up," Death replies, then kisses her.

Stephanie is vaguely aware of clothes trickling away, of skin, of lips, of hands, of hips. But mostly, she floats, sinks, luxuriates in warmth. And it is good, great. The same pleasure as slipping beneath the surface of a hot bath except bigger, wider. A pool. A pond. A lake. A river. An ocean. A watery world. A viscous universe. She wants to drift down as far as she can. She wants to be consumed and come out on the other side. Or die.

Her senses stretch away from her. She doesn't feel the body above her, the carpet beneath her back, the sweat covering her body. Her limbs have become dead weight, heavy and immovable. She doesn't see the walls of the room. She doesn't smell sex, or plants, or Death's breath breezing across her face. She can't hear a thing. There is no Stephanie. There is no Hayden. There is only darkness and stillness and silence.

When Stephanie wakes, the world is bright, sharp, and painful. The white sheets across her lap are so pristine they burn her eyes. The machines surrounding her whir and screech. Jagged agony races through her abdomen.

A woman is hunched in a chair next to her bed. The woman's hair is limp and her arms are thin. She looks worried, run-down, exhausted. The woman is Stephanie's mother. Stephanie is not surprised. Her mother always finds her eventually.

Through the hospital window, Stephanie can see blue sky and a portion of a thick Dogwood branch. It is covered in green leaves and small, pink flowers. She thinks, *another spring*, followed quickly by, *the time of year Hayden died*. When she cries, the heaves batter her ribs, the tears sting her eyes and scour salty tracks down her cheeks, and her throat and lungs feel rubbed raw, but still, she opens her mouth and breathes.

Jacinta's Lovers
Steve Simpson

In the late nineteenth century, science was king, and the zealous Professor Weismann was on a mission. He spent his time chopping the tails off rats.

Weismann's eyesight was weak, and his cages were in a poorly-lit basement at Freiburg University, but eventually he'd severed nine hundred tails, an inadvertent head—squirmy little thing that one—and the tip of his left index finger.

He allowed the mutilated rats conjugal visits, but all of their blind pink offspring had tails.

Weismann deduced that the acquired trait of lacking a tail could not be inherited, and making a modest extrapolation, that the genetic blueprint of a human child never reflects the changes that living has inflicted on the parents.

After mere centuries of scientific effort, Weismann's conclusion no longer held true, but the researchers who made the breakthrough weren't interested in tails, at least during work hours. They had nobler aims.

"The persistence of memory, passed on from generation to generation, will solve the problem of educating the poor of the third world. They will be born with the knowledge they need to survive and lead better lives."

The altruists, always keen to help strangers, agreed, and parents saw benefits for their children. Others who were more rodent-like devised ways to make unconscionable profits from the project, and the wholesale manipulation of the human genome to map the brain's synaptic intricacies began.

While everyone praised the pavement of good intentions, no one looked to the destination, where there would be no reason to heed the wise, where there would be no schools or teachers, and where learning itself would be forgotten.

Darwin's laws, which had once paced themselves like Galápagos tortoises, ran like hares. The potent madnesses that are fed by power and wealth became congenital, tyrannical dynasties evolved and came to rule the world, and the human race destroyed itself.

⁕⁂⁕

Jacinta met Umberto at the Curitiba markets. It was a time when goods were still leaving the manufacturing sheds, when merchants occasionally had something to sell, and, although hungry rioters had hijacked and smashed the supply chains in the major cities, you could still find cigarettes and alcohol in a country town.

Umberto was thin, but everyone was thin, and there was a row of handmade kites lined up on his table at the markets. He didn't bother trying to sell one to Jacinta. Instead he complimented her hair, her eyes, and her smile to well beyond embarrassment, gave her two kites for free, and talked about himself.

"My father was an unsuccessful artist. I inherited the paintings he couldn't sell and his desire to create them. I have his poor brush technique as well."

When he looked at her, she saw desire flashing in his dark eyes, and it never stopped, even later, when death was doing the rounds door-to-door in the streets.

Umberto invited her back to his place, which turned out to be an abandoned library. Apart from the symbols and signs on display in everyday life, Jacinta didn't know anyone who could truly read. Human minds were filled with archives of inherited knowledge, and reading and writing were lost arts, dead-end traits off evolution's new road.

Umberto showed her how he made the kites, papered with the pages of books that he sent soaring into windy skies.

"Not everything comes from the sheds, 'Cinta. I worked out how to do this myself, by trial and error. Nobody taught me."

Jacinta had traveled to Curitiba from Bahia. Her parents had lived in an isolated town, far from the factory centers, and they'd known how to repair things, like harvesters and plows. With the factory sheds failing, broken-down manufactures could no longer be replaced, and Jacinta was in demand.

Umberto earned pocket money selling his kites but that wasn't why she moved into the library with him. It was partly because he didn't fit, didn't belong at the end of the world.

While she sawed and drilled and welded some urgent piece of take-home work for a customer, he would wander down the aisles, *I love the books, their ancient smell*, and run his fingers along the frayed edges of a thousand pages, *and their soft mysteries*.

In the evenings, they smoked dried out cigarettes on the balcony and talked nonsense like a pair of crows. When night was finally inescapable, his fingers combed her tangled curls and drew invisible symbols on her olive skin, and she was his book, a paperback romance with a clichéd ending.

⁕⁂⁕

On weekends, Jacinta and Umberto met up at the bar near the markets after work and listened to the tales travelers brought to Curitiba.

Power in Brazil, and the rest of the world, was inherited, and one piece of gossip was often repeated. The story was that the current head of state, Maria Antonia, the Duquesa of Matogrosso, was an inbred throwback with her great grandmother's memories.

The *Duquesa* was a romantic who'd set about restoring a dying Brazil to an earlier age, which was itself an echo of a time long past. To her, the New Rococo era wasn't ancient history, it was intimate and immediate, and she'd diverted the sheds from the production of life's necessities to the fabrication of the elaborate and asymmetrical, the ornate and pointless. Gilded extravagances were being dumped in landfills, and crows perched on wrought iron furniture and fountains that rusted in the fields.

Jacinta thought the story was more entertainment than truth. The incessant shortages were inevitable, and the destruction of Brazil's infrastructure by the desperate populace was simply hastening the ending.

After a year, when the alcohol and cigarettes had almost dried up, and you had to be a fighter or a thief to feed an addiction, when no one wanted to buy anything but life's essentials, and when she found Umberto nibbling at the glued spine of an old paperback, Jacinta decided it was time to leave Curitiba.

"These were in the cage off Galheta Beach."

Umberto showed her two small needlefish, and she shrugged. "I guess they'll have to do."

Jacinta added fuel to the wood stove, and Umberto filleted fastidiously, not losing an ounce of flesh and putting the heads and intestines aside for bait.

They'd been living on Florianópolis Island for six months, and living meant finding and catching whatever food they could. While their neighbors left for places that some unreliable traveler had told them offered hope, or died from illnesses that were unidentified but were surely caused by malnutrition, they survived, with Jacinta welding up traps and Umberto weaving nets out of string and thread.

In the evening, Jacinta did the rounds to check the bird traps. The skerricks of food, attached to fine trip threads, were mostly untouched, but there was a babbling crow caught under one of the nets.

The crows mostly ate carrion, and they didn't turn their beaks up at human bodies. The rumor was that they'd been infected with a power of speech, rambling and nonsensical as it was, when they'd consumed human brains, and the genetic encodings for neural speech centers had been accidentally activated, albeit on a reduced scale.

The example under the net pleaded for its life. Its partner had flown off with another bird and left it to care for the chicks alone, it squawked.

Jacinta pulled on her gloves and wrung its neck.

After their meager evening meal, Umberto disappeared, but Jacinta knew where he was.

The deserted house they'd moved into had been the home of a collector, of anything and everything, washed up from the sea or discovered in the derelict buildings of downtown Florianópolis. They'd been through the collection and scavenged parts for their traps, but lately Umberto had been spending more and more time in the musty storerooms, and as far as Jacinta could tell, he had no idea what he was looking for.

After a time, he reappeared with a small metal box.

"This was in a crate in the basement. Listen."

He pressed a button on the box, and it replayed a crackling recording. A voice talked about the inherited memories that filled everyone's heads, described them as worse than useless because they stopped Brazilians from adapting to the new world order.

—*There is only one necessity in the world, to survive, and if necessity is the mother, she cannot have inventive children until we free ourselves from the past.*

The voice went on to describe a transition to the next stage, a new beginning at a place called Cabo Novo.

—*Make the pilgrimage to Cabo Novo. Together we will save Brazil*, and the message finished.

"We can do better than this, 'Cinta." Umberto was wide-eyed, excited. "The first people on this earth found things out for themselves. Our inheritance, all that dead knowledge, holds us back. I'm going to Cabo Novo."

Jacinta expressed reservations, starting with the detail that Umberto had no idea where Cabo Novo was—"I will find it," he said, "there must be other pilgrims"—and finishing with the rashness of basing life decisions on a talking box, which he ignored.

Early the next morning, Umberto showed her a piece of paper with wavy scribbles of a fish, a robot and a bow tie, or possibly a butterfly.

"When I return I'll be a different person. Memorize this and I'll show it to you so you'll know it's me. Otherwise you may not recognize me."

Everything was important for Umberto, every piece of nonsense. Still, Jacinta went along. There was a lot to put up with at the end of the world.

She nodded and spoke solemnly, "I'll remember it," and tucked a tiny parcel into his backpack. "I made lunch for you."

She gave him a peck on the cheek, embraced him, and wished him a safe journey. He told her not to worry, that he would be back soon, and strode off.

Jacinta busied herself for the rest of the day making new traps, fine mesh screens to catch insects, and tried to cook various wild plants, but once she'd sampled the astringent entrée, she discarded the remaining courses.

In the evening she thought about Umberto, where he might be and what might happen to him. She tried to care, to think of him fondly, but the real problem was that she didn't and couldn't. They'd been together for almost two years, but Umberto had changed, and she didn't really want him to come back at all.

Late on the second night of his journey, Umberto reached Sharktown, strangely named because it wasn't on the coast, and noticed a light flickering between the deserted buildings. He followed it to the town square where half a dozen figures were gathered around a fire burning in a blackened drum.

"Good evening, *senhores*. May I join you?" Heads nodded, and he took a seat on a worn wooden bench, resting his bones in the pleasant warmth.

One of the group, an old man with wisps of gray hair decorating his skull, offered him a drink. "I prepare it myself from sugar cane," he said.

"Thank you, *senhor*." And Umberto downed it in two gulps.

There was a scrawny carcass impaled on a spit above the drum, and his benefactor passed him a burnt slice on the tip of a knife, minute but still generous.

Umberto introduced himself.

"Everyone calls me Tubaron," the stranger said, and poured him a few drops more of the drink.

"You're very kind, Senhor Tubaron. Hospitality is a rare thing in these times."

With the hollow pangs of starvation blunted, Umberto told the group about his quest to find Cabo Novo and clear his mind of its antiquated memories.

"*Amigos*, have any of you heard tell of it? A place where miraculous transformations can occur?"

There was murmured interest, almost excitement, around the firelit circle. Tubaron scratched his stubbled chin.

"Yes, I know the place. Occasionally pilgrims journeying to Cabo Novo pass through here. It's further south, where the effluents from the old Osório factory complex once had their outfall to the sea.

"Years ago, I had a hacking cough, pneumonia, and I was certain that I was going to die." Tubaron coughed illustratively.

"I'd heard a rumor that breathing the colored vapors emitted by the factory wastes would cure me, and I traveled there, but when I arrived I learned that the effluent had long since ceased to flow. A blockage had formed when the outflow crystallized in unseasonably cold weather, and it had backed up until a great mass of it grew out from the coastline."

"And that's Cabo Novo?"

The old man nodded. "They advised me to bury myself in the sludge. And it worked."

"Your cough disappeared?"

"Yes, *senhor*." He breathed pointedly for a moment or two without coughing.

"But there was more to it than that. There were physical changes—I no longer need a knife at the dinner table." He opened his mouth wide and drew attention to the sharpness of his teeth with the flick of a fingernail.

"And my thought processes were clarified—I was able to achieve things I'd never imagined possible. My mother was a fortune-teller, but she'd never been able to read the future from entrails."

He inflated his chest. "The effluent gave me that gift."

Tubaron lifted his shirt and undid the large cartoon button securing his pants. He was much thinner than Umberto had realized, sleek, with flesh stretched like cling wrap over his rib cage, and there were rounded shapes poking out from his abdomen.

He pointed at a large shallow bruise. "That is the organ of Hipátia, its great size is a sign of good fortune." He indicated a clustered group of small discolored bulges. "These are the Dionysian grapes. Their proliferation means a long and happy life."

"Very impressive, *senhor*."

Tubaron pulled his shirt back down. "I can teach you how to do it. Shall we start by inspecting your own future, *senhor*? Just a superficial reading, no need for an incision."

⚜

As food became scarce, Jacinta's appetite contrarily increased, and she was always hungry. She baited the fish traps with what little she could find in crevices between the lichen covered rocks, the smallest mollusks with shells she could crack with her fingers, and prepared thin soups from the insects caught in her fine nets.

Even angel paste, shimmering and otherworldly but with no real meat to it, became part of her desperate diet.

The angel moths communicated in hissing voices made by a dry rubbing of their wings, and they had a fondness for fluttering into human ears and imparting unwanted advice. After their mission was complete, they would flutter away, but the draft of air under their friction-heated wings generally caused them to catch fire, and they spiraled downward leaving tiny smoke plumes.

The moths were too cunning to be caught in the nets, so Jacinta waited on the porch at sunset and preemptively snatched them out of the air before they could whisper their foreign truths in her ears.

Cabo Novo was a barren headland jutting out into the Atlantic, an unearthly landscape without the slightest hint of life, too challenging for terrestrial life forms, except for one that saw itself as special.

"No deeper, *senhor*, or you won't be able to claw your way out afterwards." Tubaron had come with Umberto to revisit Cabo Novo—for nostalgic reasons, he'd said.

Umberto had used a twisted metal rod to gouge through the hard white crust covering the ground, and then scooped out the oily muck beneath with his hands.

"Lie down and make yourself comfortable before I bury you. You will experience suffocation, an acidic burning, and dissolution. Don't be concerned, you will lose consciousness soon enough. When the new Umberto emerges I will be here to greet him."

It was Umberto's dream, the mind molt, the sloughing off of useless memories, and he clambered into the shallow grave without hesitation.

"You wouldn't have any nail clippers would you, *senhor*?"

Umberto's hands had withered, but his nails had grown like claws, and it was difficult to hold the mirrored shard that Tubaron had given him to inspect his new appearance. He was smaller, wrinkled and aged as if he'd passed a decade underground rather than a few hours, but his mind was sharp and bright.

He realized that although he could remember every step of Tubaron's intestinal divining process, he no longer recalled how to paint badly, and his father's artistic temperament had left him. Umberto was finally freed from the impediment of genetic memories.

He caught a movement in the corner of the mirror and turned to see a couple of tiny hands clawing out of his dank second womb. A childlike figure emerged and grinned at him.

"The afterbirth." Tubaron approached it. "It's just a shell made of impractical concepts and dusty recollections. And a few unnecessary body parts."

Umberto realized he had in fact felt something wriggling beside him when he'd dug his way up to the light.

"I thought you might let me have it. After all, I brought you here."

Tubaron snatched at the creature's scrawny neck, but it leapt into the air and landed *en pointe* with its long toenails plunging deep into the sludge and anchoring it in place.

Umberto studied the small being. It had his sunken eyes, and its tiny button of a nose reminded him of his mother.

"I'm sorry, Senhor Tubaron, but you can't have it. It's a part of me. I feel an affinity with it, and I will not see it hurt."

Now he understood the reason for Tubaron's apparent kindness, why he had accompanied him to Cabo Novo, and an image of the unusual carcass skewered on the spit the night before flashed through his mind.

"Let it go."

Tubaron was attempting to dislodge the creature, tugging it by the neck.

Umberto came up behind him and tried to pull him off, but Tubaron's hands tightened around its neck, and Umberto inadvertently helped his adversary. The creature gasped for air and went limp.

"Stop! You're killing it."

"That's the idea, *amigo*."

Umberto retrieved the mirrored shard and stabbed it into the side of Tubaron's neck, over and over until he fell to the ground. The gushes of blood from his carotid artery became trickles, and Tubaron's predictions of his own rosy future proved to be inaccurate.

⚬·§§·⚬

Umberto's clothes had dissolved in the underground broth of the Cabo Novo conversion, and he was coated with a bloodied slurry. He went with the creature, which followed him in leaps and bounds, to a nearby beach where they rinsed themselves in the waves, with Umberto grasping the creature's hands so it wasn't carried out to sea.

As they dried themselves in the sun, Umberto considered his future, and whether it would include his small companion. Umberto's passport back to Jacinta, the piece of paper with his carefully drawn symbols, had been liquefied with his clothes, and he mused out loud.

"What should we do, creature? Jacinta will not know who we are. Should we return to Florianópolis?"

The creature looked up from its half-built sandcastle and cleared its throat. "We love Jacinta. We must return to her. And don't call me 'creature.' I'm just as much Umberto as you are."

They debated and reached a compromise. Umberto major became Eco, and Umberto minor, Ecozinho.

⚬·§§·⚬

Jacinta saw him wandering down her street, blue-eyed with straggling blond hair, and not thin, not at all. He inspected the vacant houses and the surrounding land, and all this casually, as if he didn't have a care in the dying world.

He gave her a piece of fruit and explained that he'd come to Florianópolis to do some hunting and fishing, to grow crops—Jacinta stopped eating and swallowed an immense mouthful of papaya to tell him how impressive his skills were—and that the house next door to her was the ideal spot.

She wondered why he'd settled on that exact house. Florianópolis was almost deserted and the house was no different to any other, but he offered to help her out with food, to share what he caught and grew, and she didn't care.

A week later, Martim moved a little closer than next door. He wasn't perfect—he'd seemed momentarily unsure of his name when he'd introduced himself—and whenever he drank, there was a sound of liquid rushing down his throat like a toilet's half flush. But in Brazil's final days, he was a keeper.

He told Jacinta that she was the Brazilian Afrodite incarnate and confessed that he loved her, with his perfect teeth glimmering in the kerosene lamplight.

"Really?" she said.

"There's a strangeness about Martim. He's too perfect, don't you think, brother?"

Eco didn't pay much attention to Ecozinho. His conversation held slightly more interest than a crow's, but he was still the left-over part, the unwanted shell infused with Umberto's discarded memories, and although he saw himself as the younger brother, Eco saw him more as a pet.

When they'd returned to Florianópolis, to Jacinta, they'd done so as nonchalant strangers and moved into a house up the street. Jacinta hadn't recognized them as the transformed parts of the old Umberto.

They'd met the kindhearted Martim, and together the three of them became the Florianópolis farming and hunting collective. Eco, with his unfettered thought processes, improved the bird traps.

—I call this the couples trap. You see Ecozinho? It has two scraps of food and two trip threads, to catch twice as many birds.

—It's amazing, brother. We're going to have crows to roast every day.

Eco passed his plate with leftovers to Ecozinho, who crushed the marrow from the bones with his tiny pointed jaws.

"Martim goes somewhere every morning before sunrise, did you know? He's not hunting or checking traps."

"No, I didn't."

"I'm going to follow him tomorrow and see what he's up to."

"I'm sure it's nothing to be concerned about. He helps us with everything, and he takes good care of Jacinta. Have you seen how plump she's become?"

Eco was nothing if not patient. He'd been crouched among the bushes on the northern headland all morning and not a bird had gone near his new trap, but now a pair of crows had alighted nearby. Their feathers were ruffled, they held their beaks low, and they were discussing how unseasonably strong the sea breeze was, but they were hopping in the direction of the trap.

There was a sharp crack, someone had trodden on a dead branch in the undergrowth, and the crows took flight.

"How could you? I'm testing my trap. They were just about to go in."

Ecozinho's words tumbled out. "I followed Martim into town. I stole his cable, but I think he might have seen me."

"Take a breath, little brother."

Ecozinho calmed himself, and explained that he'd followed Martim to the old town hall in Florianópolis City and watched him through a window.

"It was still dark, I couldn't see well, but he connected a silver cable to some sort of machine, and there was a whining noise. I think . . . I'm not sure what I think, but when he came back, I saw where he'd hidden the cable under the house, and I took it. It must be important."

"And where's this cable now?"

"It's—"

Two manicured hands reached down into the brush, clamped around Ecozinho's shoulders and lifted him upward.

"I saw you running off, little one. The moonbeam cable is mine. Where did you put it?"

"I'm not telling you." Ecozinho closed his lips in a tight line, as if stray words might wriggle out by themselves.

"What is it? What's the cable for?" Eco asked.

"The cable has nothing to do with you two." Martim held Ecozinho at nose-to-nose height. "I've helped you and Eco; we're a team. You must return it to me."

Martim squeezed his shoulders hard, and Ecozinho made whimpering sounds.

"Let my brother go." Eco grabbed hold of Ecozinho's legs and pulled with all his strength.

There was a loud pop, and Ecozinho split apart at the waist like a party cracker someone had dressed in a checked shirt and jeans.

An even smaller creature climbed out from inside, clung to the lower half shell and inflated before their eyes. It looked around, seeming slightly dazed, and opened its mouth to speak, but it was taken by a sudden gust of wind and carried away. With limbs flailing, it managed to catch hold of a branch high up in a eucalyptus tree.

Eco chased after it, and it called down in a sawing voice. "There is something I understand now, brother. The old Ecozinho was just a nymph, an intermediate stage."

He was still expanding, and he was light, vibrating in the wind like a great hollow beetle. "You too. You must complete your transformation. *Adeus*, brother."

"No, no. Hold on tight." But before Eco could climb up to him, the new Eco-zinho lost his grip and was swept upward and inland, furiously waving goodbye with his new set of limbs.

Eco watched until he was just a speck on the western horizon, weeping for his lost soul mate.

"I'm sorry your brother is gone, Senhor Eco. I don't suppose you know what he did with my moonbeam cable?"

Eco shook his head, and Martim seemed disappointed.

"*Amor*, I've prepared a hamper for our picnic on Metabólico Ridge."

Martim didn't want to come with her; he tugged at his long blonde hair and pouted. "Perhaps another time, darling Jacinta. Why don't we just have an evening in?"

Over the last few days, Martim had moped around the house, and although he still looked young and muscular, there was no spring in his step. He moved sluggishly like an old man.

"There's a wonderful view of Florianópolis City from the top. We can watch the sunset."

He sighed. "Yes. Of course, darling."

Martim shuffled up the steep slope with the hamper, stooped over and minding where he put his feet. At the top, with the tartan rug spread out, he tumbled over sideways.

"I think the clouds are going to clear. We will see the sunset's dying colors. I love what you've done with your hair, Jacinta."

Eco had come to her when she was alone and whispered the story of the moonbeam cable, and Jacinta knew what it meant. After the lunar wars, the battle scarred and freshly cratered surface of the moon emitted high energy particles, and the right collection device on Earth could generate far more power than any solar cell.

Martim needed that power because he was mechanical—a multi-purpose appliance, an oversized Swiss Army knife with a vibrator attachment, and now his internal energy source was almost drained.

Jacinta ran a hand over her shaven head. She was in her hiking boots, and she kicked him in the groin a few times. "How could you dare? The place for your kind is the factory sheds. You even gave yourself a name."

A loud grinding noise started up in Martim's abdomen, and there was a bitter smell of burning oil in the air.

"I have no regrets. Everything that has a heart must have a name. I chose 'Martim,' but a rose by any other name—"

Jacinta stepped backwards, took a running jump, and came down on his groin with both boots. It did the trick and the grinding noise stopped. "Sorry, I couldn't hear you properly. Go on."

"In the factory I assembled wrought iron fountains, Neptune's spouting fish, cupids with stubby wings, and posed Afrodites. I became curious about love. I might be an automaton, Jacinta, but I know what—"

Martim tried to lift himself onto his elbows and failed. "Now I must pay love's price, I must suffer for . . . for . . ."

There were a few more stuttered fragments of his adolescent soliloquy, and after that he didn't say anything.

The sunlight faded behind the *serra*, Martim's eyelids closed over his blue marble eyes, a few sorry stars came out, and Jacinta packed up the picnic and went home.

"I have to make a trip, Jacinta. I'm not sure if I'll come back to Florianópolis."

Eco knew that he had to return to Cabo Novo to complete his metamorphosis, wherever that might lead him, and although it was convenient to stay with her, Eco didn't love Jacinta.

In those end times, human minds were buckets lowered into the well of the past, and the spark of love was always restruck from the passion of an earlier generation. Ecozinho had carried Umberto's genetic memories, and it was Ecozinho's heart that held the love for Jacinta.

"I might need some help here, Eco. I'm not sure I can manage by myself."

Eco pulled a silver cable out of his backpack.

"Ecozinho made a special place for himself in the bushland at Metabólico Park. He was a bit embarrassed about it, but I knew where it was. It's a shrine really. He hid the moonbeam cable there."

"In this special place, are there any . . . items of clothing?"

Eco nodded.

"I wondered what happened to them."

"I took the liberty of recharging Martim. He's out checking the traps now, and he'll be living next door, helping with the farming and hunting, and taking care of the shrine as well. He told me the motors in his groin were damaged, and that to love is to suffer."

"I see."

"Before I go, perhaps I might read your fortune. I need a little practice. If I could study your abdomen . . . ?"

Jacinta agreed, and her abdomen was quite ample, but he met with some difficulty.

Eco scratched the wiry stubble on his chin. "Strange. The important features are clear, but the positions and intensities change as I watch. Your future is shrouded in mist."

The baby kicked again, and Jacinta smiled. "I have some idea about my future."

"Good-bye then, Jacinta, and good luck."

Eco hesitated for a moment. "If I do return I will be transformed. Perhaps I should prepare something so that you'll know—"

"There's no need for that. I will recognize you." She kissed him on both cheeks. "*Adeus*, Umberto."

Far to the west, two crows scratched around the ribs of a corpse for morsels of skin and tendon, and daintily pecked at the brains through open eye sockets.

Crow 1: "Yesterday I happened to overhear a discussion between a pair of angel moths before I devoured them. They were lamenting the fact that they were indistinguishable and commenting on the difficulties that caused in their relationships."

Crow 2: "Don't you think we crows should have names? We have hearts."

Crow 1: "For our kind, enumeration is sufficient. Let the humans have their names, we will rule the world that they have forfeited."

Crow 2: "Such an ambitious bird you are, my Venus Cloacina. Come a little closer."

Circling above on enormous cicada wings, the sentimental Ecozinho waited until their mating had finished before he swooped down and bit off their heads. One would provide sustenance for his long flight to the coast, and the other would be a gift for his beloved Jacinta.

A CONCISE PROTOCOL FOR EFFICIENT DEICIDE

Mel Paisley

They met in the hospital.

Her, wandering the halls in that drab, striped gown, and him tied stiff into a metal chair with locked wheels, staring back.

She'd already lost her eyes, and a smile cracked like summer lightning across her lips when she reached out pudgy little hands to touch his, strange and cold and feeling like soft metal, liquid like mercury. When she sat down on the tile next to him, unafraid, his kaleidoscope senses drank in the years that had been printed onto her mind before she was old enough to remember, and he told her a story, projecting into her darkness sensations of light and color and shape, butterflies swirling like silk-spun gold out through a window that opened to a big green field in the days before the bomb.

He had been salvaged from a star that had fallen into the water, and when they carved him out of all of the salt that had cauterized shut the knobless door of his pod, they were quick to throw him into the back of an ambulance and away from the possibility of cameras. To keep the peace.

He had a rusty, accordion voice that pitched seemingly senseless through electric veins, falling strange upon the doctors the way that the sacred speech of prophets falls hydrochloric on the ears of heretics. And in their ignorance they feared him, became sour with the depth of the unknown sprawled before them and, in defense of their own vain pride and contrived brilliance, took it upon themselves to be the ones to solve him, to temper him into a proper discovery that they could wear on their Iscariot shoulders like a trophy. The great providers of knowledge from beyond.

First, they needed him to be able to talk.

It was a slow process, done in parts. The first night, two bodies were laid on parallel tables and made soggy with anesthetic. Hers was fish belly white where the old radiation scars didn't show, his a jigsaw of alkaloid and pipe and something indisputably organic that was nameless in their charts, something that felt like sharkskin spun of magnesium and stardust.

They proceeded with torches and computers and scalpels, hovered and bent and busy, white coats hanging over their scoliotic spines, vulture hands quick and heavy with atrocious aim and self-named noble purpose.

Because they needed him to talk.

Because they had to staple down the abstracts of his galaxy mind into something they could understand, into something that breathed thoughts into a human shape, word to spine to nerve to larynx to mouth. She was deemed nobody enough to go under the knife, just another child orphaned by the bomb they had bred out of hydrogen and hatred so many years ago and already washed their hands of.

As they worked, he moved an alien palm over the canyon between them to grab gently the pulse in her wrist, weak with the painkillers that were not strong enough to make him sleep and trying to tell her a story, just in case she was awake, too. In case she was as scared as he was.

When she woke, she could see again.

Almost.

The world was cast in a sheen of green, monochrome shapes that crackled with a matrix of numbers and letters if she focused on them too long, indecipherable strains of auxiliary information clouding her field of vision. She was cold, colder than she had been in her entire life, and there was a light shining on the metal bars that bracketed the thin cot beneath her and the thick sheet thrown over the top, something tight holding her into place. Panic began to slice cold through the frostbite of her confusion, and she rattled against her restraints, every one of her shallow breaths feeling like termites as the oxygen scalded foreign and wrong inside of her chest, and she tried to call for a doctor but could hear nothing but a clicking series of mechanical whines, pitching louder and longer, and something was *wrong*.

"Please don't cry" a girl's voice said.

She turned her heavy head to the right to find a body lying in the bed next to her, similarly restrained and looking strange, so strange because it was almost familiar.

It stared back at her, eyes searching for the direction of the sound.

He was in the dark now, a dark that melted over the world, and he felt so soft, fragile and small.

In the dark he could hear calls of distress extruded in his own language, hearing them now instead of feeling them as they did back home, back where the chemical cues buried in the sounds would sift through the sensors of one another's skin so that they could feel each other's pain or elation more completely. So unlike the barbaric distance that the creatures here held between themselves.

"Once upon a time," he started in his new singsong voice, picking through the information of the planet he had garnered the first time she had touched him. "There was a princess who lived all alone with her pet rabbit in a castle by the sea, far, far away from where anyone could hurt her . . ."

The words soothed beneath the panic jolting through her new wrong body that was too big and cold and didn't belong here, familiar voice reaching between the bars of the bed to touch soft to her soul, trying to connect. She tried to speak back, and her own voice hushed her, telling her that she should try to go to sleep.

"It's just a dream." He consoled her in those wet, human syllables, wishing that they were true. There was a far off sound of sterile footsteps creeping across tile, and he wanted her to sleep before the hurt started again.

"You can go back home in the morning." The words that he wanted to hear. He would take her with him if he could, up, up and away from the cold, concrete world with its knives and probes and needles, away from the hands that hurt to make themselves seem smarter and to a place where they would be free. Where they could understand something without breaking it.

Up, up and away, somewhere safe.

He could hear the door creaking open from the hall.

"Go back to sleep."

FAIRY WEREWOLF VS. VAMPIRE ZOMBIE

Charlie Jane Anders

Originally appeared in *Flurb*, no. 11, Spring/Summer 2011

If you're ever in Freeboro, North Carolina, look for the sign of the bull. It hangs off the side of a building with a Vietnamese noodle-joint and an auto mechanic, near an alley that's practically a drainage ditch. Don't walk down that alley unless you're brave enough not to look over your shoulder when you hear throaty noises behind you. If you make it to the very end without looking back, hang a left, and watch your footing on the mossy steps. The oak door at the bottom of the stairs will only open if you've got the right kind of mojo.

If it does open, you'll find yourself in Rachel's Bar & Grill, the best watering hole in the Carolinas. My bar. There's only one rule: if there's any trouble, take it outside. (Outside my bar is good, outside of town is better, outside of reality itself is best of all.) I have lots of stories about Rachel's. There are names I could drop—except some of those people might appear. But there is one story that illustrates why you shouldn't make trouble in my bar, and how we take care of our own. It's also the story of how the bar got its mascot.

There was this young woman named Antonia, who went from a beautiful absinthe-drinking stranger to one of my regulars inside of a month. She had skin so pale it was almost silver, delicate features, and wrists so fine she could slide her hand into the wine-jug behind the bar—although she'd have to be quick pulling it out again, or Leroy the Wine Goblin would bite it off. Anyway, she approached me at closing time, asking if I had any work for her. She could clean tables, or maybe play her guitar a few nights a week.

If you've ever been to Rachel's, you'll know it doesn't need any live music, or anything else, to add atmosphere to the place. If there's one thing we got in spades, it's atmosphere. Just sit in any of the plush booths—the carvings on the wooden tables tell you their stories, and the stains on the upholstery squirm to get out of the way of your butt. From the gentle undulation of the ceiling beams to the flickering of the amber-colored lights to the signed pictures of famous dragons and celebrity succubi on the brick walls, the place is atmosphere city.

But then I got to hear Antonia sing and play on her guitar, and it was like the rain on a midsummer day right after you just got your first kiss or something. Real lyrical. I let her play at Rachel's one night, and I couldn't believe it—the people who usually just guzzled a pitcher of my "special" sangria and then vamoosed were sticking around to listen to her, shedding luminescent tears that slowly floated into the air and then turned into little crystalline wasps. (The sangria will do that.)

So after Antonia got done singing that first night, I came up to her and said I guessed we could work something out, if she was willing to wipe some tables as well as getting her Lilith Fair on. "There's just one thing I don't get," I said. "It's obvious you're Fae, from the effect you have on the lunkheads that come in here. And you're a dead ringer for that missing princess from the High Court of Sylvania. Princess Lavinia." (Sylvania being what the Fae call Pennsylvania, the seat of their power.) "It's said his supreme highness the Chestnut King weeps every night, and would give half the riches of Sylvania to have you back. The drag queen—Mab—her eyeliner has been smudgy for months. Not to mention the lovestruck Prince Azaron. So what gives?"

"I cannot ever return home," Antonia (or Lavinia) wept. "I regret the day I decided to venture out and see the world for myself. For on that day, I encountered a curse so monstrous, I cannot ever risk inflicting it on any of my kin. I cannot undo what is done. The only way I can protect my friends and family is to stay far away. I am forever exiled, for my own foolishness. Now please ask no more questions, for I have tasted your sangria and I'm afraid my tears would sting you most viciously."

I said no more, although I was consumed with curiosity about the curse that kept the fairy princess from returning to the Seelie Court in Bucks County. I didn't learn any more—until a few weeks later, when the Full Moon arrived.

Antonia appeared as usual, wearing a resplendent dress made of the finest samite and lace (I think it was vintage Gunne Sax.) She muttered something about how she was going to play a shorter set than usual, because she felt unwell. I said that was fine, I would just put the ice hockey match on the big-screen TV. (Did I mention the big-screen TV? Also a big part of the atmosphere. We do karaoke on Fridays.) Anyway, she meant to play for an hour, but she got carried away with this one beautiful dirge about lovers who were separated for life by a cruel wind, and it grew dark outside, just as her song reached a peak of emotion.

And something strange happened. Her hands, so teeny, started to grow, and her guitar playing grew more frenzied and discordant. Hairs sprouted all over her skin, and her face was coarsening as well, becoming a muzzle. "NO!" She cried—or was it a howl?—as her already pointy ears became pointier and her hair grew thicker and more like fur. "No, I won't have it! Not here, not now. 'Tis too soon! By my fairy blood, I compel you—subside!" And with that last word, the transformation ceased. The hair vanished from her hands, her face returned to normal, and she only looked slightly huskier than usual. She barely had time to place her guitar in its case, leaving it on the bar, before she fled up the wooden staircase to the door. I heard her ascending into the alley and running away, her panting harsh and guttural.

Antonia did not return for three days, until the Moon was on the wane. When next she sang for us, her song was even more mournful than ever before, full of a passion so hot, it melted our internal organs into a fondue of longing.

Now around this same time, I was thinking about franchising. (Bear with me here, this is part of the story.) I had gotten a pretty good thing going in Freeboro, and I wanted to open another bar over on the other side of the Triad, in the town of Evening Falls. The main problem was, you don't want to open a bar aimed at mystical and mythological patrons in the same strip mall as a Primitive Baptist church, a nail salon and a barbeque place, right on Highway 40. And Evening Falls only had a few properly secluded locations, all of which were zoned as purely residential, or only for restaurants.

Now, chances are, if you've been to Rachel's, you've already heard my views on the evils of zoning. But just in case you missed it . . . [Editor's note: the next ten paragraphs of this manuscript consist of a tirade about zoning boards and the ways in which they are comparable to giant flesh-eating cane-toads or hornetaurs. You can read it online at *www.monstersofurbanplanning.org*.]

Anyway, where was I? Franchising. So I know some witches and assorted fix-ers, who can make you believe Saturday is Monday, but it's hard to put a whammy on the whole planning board. So I thought to myself, what can I do to win these people over? And that's when I remembered I had my very own enchanting fairy singer, with just a spark of the wolf inside her, on the payroll.

Antonia's eyes grew even huger, and her lip trembled, when I asked her to come and play at a party for the scheming elites of Evening Falls. "I cannot," she said. "I would do anything in my power to help you, Rachel, but I fear to travel where I may be recognized. And my song is not for just anyone, it is only for the lost and the despairing. Can't I just stay here, in your bar, playing for your patrons?"

"Now look," I said, plunking her down on my least carnivorous barstool. "I've been pretty nice to you, and a lot of people would have called the number on the side of the thistle-milk carton to collect the reward on you already. Fairy gold! Which, last time I checked, is made out of the same gold as every other kind. Not to mention, I put up with the constant danger of you biting my patrons and turning them into werewolves. Which, to be fair, might improve their disposi-tions and make them better tippers. But you know, it's all about one hand washes the other, even if sometimes one of those hands is a tentacle. Or a claw. Although, you wouldn't really want one of the Octo-priests of Wilmington to wash any part of you, not unless you want strange squid-ink tattoos sprouting on your skin for years after. Where was I?"

"You were attempting to blackmail me," Antonia said with a brittle dignity. "Very well, Rachel. You have shown me what stuff your friendship is made of. I shall play at your 'shindig.'"

"Good, good. That's all I wanted." I swear, there should be a special fairy edition of *Getting to Yes*, just for dealing with all their Fae drama.

So we put together a pretty nice spread at this Quaker meeting hall in Evening Falls, including some pulled-pork barbecue and fried okra. Of course, given that most of these people were involved in local zoning, we should have just let them carve up a virgin instead. I mean, seriously. [The rest of this section is available at *www.monstersofurbanplanning.org*—Editor.]

Where was I? Oh yes. So it was mostly the usual assortment of church ladies, small-time politicians, local business people, and so on. But there were two men who stood out like hornetaurs at a bull fight.

Sebastian Valcourt was tall, with fine cheekbones and a noble brow, under a shock of wavy dark hair that he probably blow-dried for an hour every day. He wore a natty suit, but his shirt was unbuttoned almost to the navel, revealing a hairless chest that was made of money. No kidding, I used to know a male stripper named Velcro who was three-quarters elf, and he would have killed for those pecs.

The other startlingly beautiful man was named Gilbert Longwood, and he was big and solidly built, like a classical statue. His arms were like sea-cliffs, and his face was big and square-jawed—like a marble bust except that his eyes had pupils, which was probably a good thing for him. When he shook my hand, I felt his grip and it made me all weak in the knees. But from the start of the evening, both Gilbert and Sebastian could only see one woman.

Once Antonia began to play, it was all over—everybody in that room fell for her, and I could have gotten planning permission to put a bowling alley inside a church. Afterwards, I was talking to Gilbert, while Sebastian leapt across the room like a ballet dancer, landing in front of Antonia and kissing her hand with a sweeping bow. He said something, and she laughed behind a hand.

"You throw an entertaining party," said Gilbert, trying not to stare at Sebastian's acrobatic courtship over in the corner. "I don't think I've seen half these people show any emotion since the town historian self-immolated a few years ago." His voice was like a gong echoing in a crypt. I never got Gilbert's whole story, but I gathered he was the son of a wealthy sculptor, part of Evening Falls' most prominent family.

At this point, Gilbert had given up all pretense that he wasn't staring at Antonia. "Yeah," I said. "I discovered that girl. I taught her everything she knows. Except I held back a few secrets for myself, if you get my drift and I think you do." I winked.

"Please excuse me, gracious lady," Gilbert said. When he bowed, it was like a drawbridge going down and then up again. He made his way across the room, navigating around all the people who wanted to ask him about zoning (jackals!) on his way to where Sebastian was clinking glasses with Antonia.

I couldn't quite get close enough to hear the conversation that followed, but their faces told me everything I needed to know. Sebastian's mouth smiled, but his amber-green eyes burned with desire for Antonia, even as he made some cutting remark towards Gilbert. Gilbert smiled back, and let Sebastian's fancy wit bounce off his granite face, even as he kept his longing gaze on Antonia's face. For Antonia's part, she blushed and looked down into the depths of her glass of Cheerwine.

You could witness a love triangle being born, its corners sharp enough to slice you open and expose your trembling insides to all sorts of infections, including drug-resistant staph, which has been freaking me out lately. I always wash my hands twice, with antibacterial soap and holy water. Where was I? Right, love triangle. This was an isosceles of pure burning desire, in which two men both pined for the same impossibly beautiful, permanently heartbroken lady. My first thought was: There's got to be a way to make some money off this.

And sure enough, there was. I made sure Antonia didn't give out her digits, or even so much as her Twitter handle, to either of these men. If they wanted to stalk her, they would have to come to Rachel's Bar & Grill. I managed to drop a hint to both of them that what really impressed Antonia was when a guy had a large, heavy-drinking, entourage.

I didn't have to turn on the big-screen TV once, for the whole month that followed. Sebastian and Gilbert, with their feverish courtship of Antonia, provided as much free entertainment as ten *Married with Children* marathons. Maybe even eleven. Sebastian gave Antonia a tiny pewter unicorn, which danced around in the palm of her hand but remained lifeless otherwise. Gilbert brought enough flowers that the bar smelled fresh for the first time since 1987.

This one evening, I watched Gilbert staring at Antonia as she sat on her stool and choked out a ballad. She wore a long canvas skirt, and her feet were crossed on the stool's dowel. He looked at her tragic ankles—so slender, with tendons that flexed like heartstrings—and his big brown eyes moistened.

And then Sebastian arrived, flanked by two other weirdly gorgeous, unnaturally spry men with expressive eyes. Every time you would think their eyebrows couldn't get any more expressive, or their gazes more smoldering, they'd kick it up another notch. Their eyebrows had the dramatic range of a thousand Kenneth Branaghs—maybe a thousand Branaghs per eyebrow, even. The other two smiled wan, ironic smiles at each other, while Sebastian kept his gaze fixed on the tiny trembling lips and giant mournful eyes of Antonia.

A few weeks—and a few thou worth of high-end liquor—later, both Sebastian and Gilbert began to speak to Antonia of their passion.

"A heart so grievously wounded as yours requires careful tending, my lady," Gilbert rumbled in his deep voice. "I have strong hands, but a gentle touch, to keep you safe." His sideburns were perfect rectangles, framing his perfectly chiseled cheekbones.

"I fear . . ." Antonia turned to put her guitar in its case, so the anguish on her face was hidden from view for a moment. "I fear the only thing for a condition such as mine is solitude, laced with good fellowship here at Rachel's. But I shall cherish your friendship, Gilbert."

Soon after, Sebastian approached Antonia, without his cronies. "My dear," he said. "Your loveliness outshines every one of those neon beer signs. But it is your singing, your sweet sad tune, which stirs me in a way that nothing else has for decades. You must consent to be mine, or I shall have no choice but to become ever more mysterious, until I mystify even myself. Did I say that out loud? I meant, I'll waste away. Look at my eyebrows, and you'll see how serious I am."

"Oh, Sebastian," Antonia laughed, then sighed. "Had I even a sliver of a heart to give, I might well give it to you. But you speak to a hollow woman."

Blah blah blah. This went on and on, and I had to re-order several of the single malt whiskeys, not to mention all the mid-range cognacs, and Southern Comfort.

Who can say how long this would have gone on for, if both Sebastian and Gilbert hadn't turned up on an evening when Antonia wasn't there? (You guessed it: The Full Moon.) The two of them started arguing about which of them deserved Antonia. Gilbert rumbled that Sebastian just wanted to use Antonia, while Sebastian said Gilbert was too much of a big ugly lug for her. Gilbert took a swing at Sebastian and missed, and that's when I told them to take it outside.

Soon afterwards, we all tromped outside to watch. Sebastian was dancing around like Prince on a hot griddle, while Gilbert kept lashing out with his massive fists and missing. Until finally, Gilbert's forearm caught Sebastian in the shoulder, and he went flying onto his ass. And then things got entertaining: Sebastian's face got all tough and leathery, and fangs sprouted from his mouth. He did a somersault in mid-air, aiming a no-shadow kick at Gilbert—who raised his boulder-sized fist, so it collided with Sebastian's face.

After that, the fight consisted of Gilbert punching Sebastian, a lot. "Stupid vampire," Gilbert grunted. "You're not the first bloodsucker I've swatted."

By this point, Sebastian's jaw was looking dislocated. Those expressive eyebrows were twisted with pain. "I'm not . . . your average . . . vampire," he hissed. Gilbert brought his sledge-hammer fist down onto Sebastian's skull.

Sebastian fell to the ground in an ungainly pile of bones. And he smiled. "The more beat up I get . . . the harder to kill . . . I get," he rasped. And then he stood on jerky legs, his flesh peeling away.

Sebastian's smile turned slack and distended. Instead of his usual witticisms, he said but one word: "Braiiiiiinnsss . . ."

Gilbert kept punching at Sebastian, but it did no good. Nothing even slowed him down. Sebastian thrashed back at Gilbert with a hideous force, and finally he hit a weak point, where Gilbert's head met his neck—and Gilbert's head fell, rolling to land at my feet.

Gilbert's severed head looked up at me. "Tell Antonia . . . my love for her was true." And then the head turned to stone. And so did the rest of his body, which fell into several pieces in the middle of the dark walkway.

Sebastian looked at me and the couple other regulars who were watching. He snarled, with what remained of his mouth, "Braaaaaaaiiiiiinnsss!"

The nearest patron was Jerry Dorfenglock, who'd been coming to Rachel's for twenty years. He had a really nice smooth bald head, which he'd experimented with combing over and then with shaving all the way, Kojak-style, before deciding to just let it be what it was: two wings of fluffy gray hair flanking a serene dome. That noble scalp, Sebastian tore open, along with the skull beneath. Sebastian reached with both hands to scoop out poor Jerry's gray matter, then stopped at the last moment. Instead, he leaned further down and sunk his top teeth into Jerry's neck, draining all the blood from his body in one gulp.

A moment later, Sebastian looked away from the husk of Jerry's body, looking more like his normal self already. "If I—" he paused wipe his mouth. "If I eat the brains, I become more irrevocably the zombie. But if I drink the blood, I return to my magnificent vampiric self. It's always hard to remind myself. Think of it as the blood-brain barrier between handsome rogue . . . and shambling fiend." The other patron who'd been watching the fight, Lou, tried to make a break for it, but Sebastian was too fast.

I looked at the bloodless husks of my two best customers, plus the chalky pieces of poor Gilbert, then back at Sebastian—who now looked as though nothing had ever happened, except for the stains on his natty suit. I decided being casual was my best hope of coming out of this alive.

"So you're a half-vampire, half-zombie," I said as if I was discussing a *Seinfeld* rerun. "That's something you don't see every day, I guess."

"It is an amusing story," Sebastian said. "When I was a mortal, I loved a mysterious dark beauty, who grew more mysterious with every passing hour. My heart felt close to bursting for the love of her. At last, she revealed she was an ancient vampire, and offered me the chance to be her consort. She fed me her blood, and told me that if I died within twelve hours, I would become a vampire and I could join her. If I did not die, I could return to my mortal life. She left me to decide for myself. I went out to my favorite spot on the edge of Stoneflower Lake, to ponder my decision and savor my last day on Earth—for I already knew what choice I would make. But just then, a zombie climbed out of the lake bottom, where it had been terrorizing the bass, and bit me in the face. I died then and there, but as the vampire blood began to transform me into an eternal swain of darkness, so too did the zombie bite work its own magic. Now, I remain a vampire, only as long as I have a steady diet of restoring blood."

"That's quite a story," I said. I was already trying to figure out what I would do with Lou and Jerry's bodies, since I had a feeling Sebastian would regard corpse cleanup as woman's work. "You should sell the TV movie rights."

"Thanks for the advice." Sebastian looked into my eyes, and his gaze held me fast. "You will not speak to anyone of what you have seen and heard tonight." As he spoke, the words became an unbreakable law to me. Then Sebastian sauntered away, leaving me—what did I tell you?—to bury the bodies. At least with Gilbert, it was just a matter of lugging the pieces to the Ruined Statue Garden a couple of streets away.

By the time I got done, my hands were a mess and I was sweating and shaking and maybe even crying a little. I went back to the bar and poured myself some Wild Turkey, and then some more, and then a bit more after that. I wished I could talk to someone about this. But of course, I was under a vampiric mind-spell thingy, and I could never speak a word.

Good thing I've got a Hotmail account.

I put the whole thing as plain as I could in a long email to Antonia, including the whole confusing "vampire who's also a zombie" thing. I ended by saying: "Here's the thing, sweetie: Sebastian is gonna think you don't know any of this, and with Gilbert out of the way, he'll be making his move. Definitely do NOT marry him; the half-zombie thing is a *dealbreaker*. But don't try to fight him either. He's got the thing where the more you hurt him, the more zombie he gets and then you can't win, he's got you beat either way. And not to mention, the full moon is over as of tomorrow morning, so you got no more wolf on your side. Just keep yourself safe okay because it would just about ruin me to see anything happen to you—I mean you bring in the paying customers. Don't worry, I'm not getting soppy on you. Your boss, Rachel."

She came in the next day, clutching Gilbert's head. Her eyes were puffy and the cords on her neck stood out as she heaved a sob. I handed her a glass of absinthe without saying anything, and she drained it right away. I made her another, with the sugar cube and everything.

I wasn't sure if Sebastian's mind control would keep me from saying I was sorry, but it didn't. Antonia shrugged and collapsed onto my shoulder, weeping into my big flannel shirt, Gilbert's forehead pressing into my stomach.

"Gilbert really loved me," she said when she got her breath back and sat down on her usual music-playing stool. "He loved me more than I deserved. I was . . . I was finally ready to surrender, and give my heart away. I made up my mind, while I was out running with the wolves."

"You were going to go out with Gilbert?" I had to sit down too.

"No. I was going to let Gilbert down easy, and then date Sebastian. Because he made me laugh." She opened her guitar case, revealing not a guitar, but a bright sword, made of tempered Sylvanian steel with the crest of Thuiron the Resolver on the hilt. "Now I have to kill him."

"Hey hey hey," I said. "There are some good reasons not to do that, which I cannot speak of, but hang on, let me get a notepad and a pen and I'll be happy to explain—"

"You already explained." She put her left hand on my shoulder. "Thanks for your kindness, Rachel."

"I don't—" What could I say? What was I *allowed* to say? "I don't want you to die."

"I won't." She smiled with at least part of her face.

"Are you starting your set early tonight? I have a request." Sebastian said from the doorway at the top of the short staircase leading into the bar, framed by the ebbing daylight. "I really want to hear some Van Morrison for once, instead of that—"

Antonia threw Gilbert's head at Sebastian. His eyes widened as he realized what it was, and what it meant. He almost ducked, then opted to catch it with one hand instead, to show he was still on top of the situation. While he was distracted, though, Antonia was already running with her sword out, which made a whoosh as it tore through the air.

Antonia impaled Sebastian, but missed his heart. He kicked her in the face, and she fell, blood-blinded.

"So this is how it's going to be?" Sebastian tossed the head into the nearest booth, where it landed face up on the table. "I confess I'm disappointed. I was going to marry you and *then* kill you. More fairy treasure that way."

"You—You—" Antonia coughed blood. "You never loved me."

"Oh, keep up." Sebastian loomed over Antonia, pulled her sword out of his chest, and swung it over his head two-handed, aiming for a nice clean slice. "I'll bring your remains back to Sylvania, and tell them a lovely story of how you and I fell in love and got married, before you were killed by a wild boar or an insurance adjuster. Hold still, this'll hurt less."

Antonia kicked him in the reproductive parts, but he shrugged it off. The shining sword whooshed down towards her neck.

"Hey!" I pumped my plus-one Vorpal shotgun from behind the bar. "No. Fighting. In. The. Bar."

"We can take it outside," Sebastian said, not lowering the sword.

"Too late for that," I said. "You're in my bar, you settle it how I choose."

"And how's that?"

I said the first thing that came into my head: "With a karaoke contest."

And because it was my bar, and I have certain safeguards in place for this sort of situation, they were both bound by my word. Sebastian grumbled a fair bit, especially what with Antonia being a semi-professional singer, but he couldn't fight it. It took us a couple of hours to organize, including finding a few judges and putting an impartiality whammy on them, to keep it a fair competition.

I even broke open my good wine jug and gave out free cups to everybody. Once his nesting place was all emptied out, Leroy the Wine Goblin crawled out on the bar and squinted.

Antonia went first, and she went straight for the jugular—with showtunes. You've probably never seen a fairy princess do "Don't Tell Mama" from Cabaret, complete with hip-twirling burlesque dance moves and a little Betty Boop thing when she winked at the audience. Somehow she poured all her rage and passion, all her righteous Sarah McLachlan-esque anger, into a roar on the final chorus. The judges scribbled nice high numbers and chattered approvingly.

And then Sebastian went up—and he broke out that Red Hot Chili Peppers song about the City of Angels. He'd even put on extra eyeliner. He fixed each of us with that depthless vampire stare, even as he poured out an amazing facsimile of a soul, singing about being lost and lonely and wanting his freakin' happy place. Bastard was going to win this thing.

But there was one thing I knew for sure. I knew that he'd have to shut his eyes, for at least a moment, when he hit those high notes in the bridge about the bridge, after the second chorus.

Sure enough, when Sebastian sang out "Under the bridge downtown," his eyes closed so his voice could float over the sound of Frusciante's guitar transitioning from "noodle" mode to "thrash" mode. And that's when I shot him with my plus-one Vorpal shotgun. Once in the face, once in the chest. I reloaded quick as I could, and shot him in the chest again, and then in the left kneecap for good measure.

It wasn't enough to slow him down, but it did make him change. All of a sudden, the lyrics went, "Under the bridge downtown, I could not get enough . . . BRAIIIIIINSSSS!!"

He tossed the microphone and lurched into the audience. The three karaoke judges, who were still enchanted to be 100 percent impartial, sat patiently watching and making notes on their score sheets, until some other patrons hauled them out of the way. Leroy the Wine Goblin covered his face and screamed for the safety of his jug. People fell all over each other to reach the staircase.

"I shall take it from here." Antonia hoisted her sword, twirling it like a Benihana chef while Frusciante's guitar-gasm reached its peak. She hacked one of Sebastian's arms off, but he barely noticed.

She swung the sword again, to try and take his head off, and he managed to sidestep and headbutt her. His face caught the side of her blade, but he barely noticed, and he drove the sharp edge into Antonia's stomach with his forehead. Blood gushed out of her as she fell to the ground, and he caught it in his mouth like rain.

A second later, Sebastian was Sebastian again. "Ah, fairy blood," he said. "There really is nothing like it." Antonia tried to get up again, but slumped back down on the floor with a moan, doubled up around her wounded stomach.

I shot at Sebastian again, but I missed and he broke the shotgun in half. Then he broke both my arms. "Nobody is going to come to karaoke night if you shoot people in the face while they're singing. Seriously." I tried not to give him the satisfaction of hearing me whimper.

Antonia raised her head and said a fire spell. Wisps of smoke started coming off Sebastian's body, but he just shrugged. "You've already seen what happens if you manage to hurt me." The smoke turned into a solid wall of flame, but Sebastian pushed it away from his body with a tai-chi move. "Why even bother?"

"Mostly," Antonia's voice came from the other side of the fire wall, "just to distract yoooooooooo!" Her snarl became a howl, a barbaric call for vengeance.

There may be a sight more awesome than a giant white wolf leaping through a wall of solid fire. If so, I haven't seen it. Antonia—for somehow she had managed to summon enough of her inner wolf to change—bared her jaws as she leapt. Her eyes shone red and her ears pulled back as the flames parted around her and sparks showered from her ivory fur.

Sebastian never saw it coming. Her first bite tore his neck open, and his head lolled off to one side. He started to zombify again, but Antonia was already clawing him.

"Don't—Don't let him bite you!" I shouted from behind the bar.

Sebastian almost got his teeth on Antonia, but she ducked.

"BRAIIINNSS!"

She was on top of him, her jaws snapping wildly, but he was biting just as hard. His zombie saliva and his vampire teeth were both inches away from her neck.

I crawled over to the cooler where I kept the pitchers of sangria, and pulled the door open with my teeth. I knocked pitchers and carafes on the floor, trying to get at the surprise I'd stored there the night before, in a big jar covered with cellophane wrap.

I hadn't actually buried *all* of Lou and Jerry.

I pulled the jar out with my teeth and wedged it between my two upper arms and my chin, then lugged it over to where Antonia and Sebastian were still trying to bite each other. "Hey," I rasped, "I saved you something, you bastard." And I tipped the jar's contents—two guys' brains, in a nice balsamic *vinaigrette*—into Sebastian's face. Once he started guzzling the brains, he couldn't stop himself. He was getting brain all over his face, as he tried to swallow it all as fast as possible, brains were getting in his eyes and up what was left of his nose. There was no going back for him now.

Antonia broke the glass jar and held a big shard of it in her strong wolf jaws, sawing at Sebastian's neck until his head came all the way off. He was still gulping at the last bits of brains in his mouth, and trying to lick brain-bits off his face.

It took them an hour to set the bones on my arms, and I had casts the size of beer kegs. We put Sebastian's head into another jar, with a UV light jammed inside so whenever the Red Hot Chili Peppers come on the stereo, he gets excited and his face glows purple. I never thought the Peppers would be the most requested artist at Rachel's. I never did get permission to open a second bar in Evening Falls, though.

As for Antonia, I think this whole experience toughened her up and made her realize that being a little bit wild-animal wasn't a bad thing for a fairy princess. And that Anthony Kiedis really doesn't have the singing range he thinks he has. And that when it comes to love triangles and duels to the death, you should always cheat. And that running away from your problems only works for so long. There were a few other lessons, all of which I printed out and laminated for her. She still sings in the bar, but she's made a couple of trips back to Sylvania during the crescent moon, and they're working on a cure for her. She could probably go back and be a princess if she wanted to, but we've been talking about going into business together and opening some straight-up karaoke bars in Charlotte and Winston-Salem. She's learning to KJ. I think we could rule the world.

THE WOMAN WHO SANG
Terry Durbin

I am a teller and it is my task to tell you about the woman who sang. And about the man who cut out her tongue. Will you hate him, I wonder? Or will you thank him?

This tell is true.

He saw the color before he saw the woman, although it was the woman for whom he watched. As he had watched yesterday, and the days before that. And he thought she watched for him as well. He wondered if she felt the same strange excitement he did as he waited for her to pass, wondering each day what new detail he would see, would remember late at night.

Today it was the color.

A flicker of orange like the flame of a candle in a dark room. But it was not dark. It was near middle-day, and the sky was the color of bright steel. A rambunctious wind leapt over the waist-high wall of the Concourse and jostled its way around and among the people who walked there. They passed from one place to another with heads slightly bowed and hands in pockets like insects frozen forever as chrysalides. Incomplete. Insular.

The zephyr had pinched the end of her scarf between invisible fingers and tugged it free of her collar to flap and dance.

Orange.

A band of orange woven into the gentle grayness of her scarf. Like a small, pretentious banner the color flickered and whipped around her head while she tried to catch it, laughing and clutching. Finally she gathered in the willful cloth and tucked it back into the collar of her winter coat. The chrysalides threw dour glances at her but the assault of their disapproval only broke into fragile shards on the rocky bulwark of her joy. He could almost hear the icy crunch of her feet treading over the harmless flakes of scorn scattered around her.

Orange is not forbidden, but it is . . . discouraged. The man watched her walk toward him over the tiles of the Concourse, and she watched him watch. He took his hands out of his pockets and the wind nibbled at his flesh.

"Your scarf has an orange stripe," he said.

"It does." She nodded. A small rope of hair escaped her cowl and curled over her cheek. She used two of her long, slender fingers to guide it back into place.

"Orange has no purpose." He could see a sliver of the useless hue hiding within the folds of her scarf; an ember wrapped in a cloud.

"Must everything have purpose?"

"All good things have purpose."

"That is the Advocacy talking." Her smile never wavered as she casually reached up with one hand and plucked at her scarf, exposing another half-inch of the orange stripe. The ember became a tiny flame. "What do *you* think?"

A woman in a black coat carrying a covered tote bumped into him. "Get to, or get from," she muttered, stepping past. The insignia on the cuff of her coat told him she was a Seller.

He took the smiling woman's elbow in his hand and led her closer to the parapet over which the wind was pouring. "I think it is a distraction."

"Then perhaps distraction is its purpose?" Her gaze was that of a child who had not yet been taught courtesy. Her eyes were as dark as her hair. She smelled of fragrant oils.

"Whom would distraction serve?" He knew it was rude to look into her face, but she took no offense, so he looked. It pleased him.

The woman pursed her lips and scrunched her eyebrows together in a parody of concentration. Finally she poked herself in the chest with one pale finger. "Me," she said. "It would serve me." Then that same finger poked into his chest. "Or, perhaps, you."

Extending both hands toward the passing throng, she continued, "Or everyone . . . anyone?"

An odd thing happened then. The people walking past them reacted to her gesture like a flock of starlings. Moving away from her hands in a flowing mass, without thought, but not without purpose. He saw the crowd redirect itself, and he had an urge to flow with it, away from this strange woman.

"Nonsense," he said. "To be distracted is to be nonproductive, and to be nonproductive is to weaken the community."

"And yet here you stand, talking to me, distracted from your purpose." She pointed at the wall of the Tower along which the Concourse wound. "From *their* purpose." He looked to where she was pointing and at first saw nothing. "Aren't you afraid they will see you standing here being wasteful?"

He realized then what she was pointing at, one of the glistening black blisters hugging the tower stones. "The cameras? There is nothing to fear from the cameras. They are here to protect us." He could see several of the blisters spaced at intervals along the Concourse, and he knew there were thousands more lining not only the Concourse, but the Avenue, the Boulevard, the Parkway, and all the other paths that twisted their way around and up the Tower. He could see the buttresses and cantilevers supporting the Avenue a hundred yards above them, and he knew there were citizens, just like those streaming past them now, using that path to go about their daily tasks.

"Protect us from what?"

Her question made him uneasy. The way books made him uneasy, or voices in the hall outside his room late at night.

"From distraction, perhaps," he said, hoping the sharp tone of his voice would put an end to her questions.

Her eyes acknowledged the remark with a brief narrowing, but her smile remained.

"Distractions like this?" she asked, and then reached up and took his face in her hands—they were strong and warm. Before he could react, she pulled him to her and kissed him on the mouth. The kiss was short, and soft. It was over in moments.

Still holding his face between her fingers, she put her lips next to his ear and whispered, "Meet me here tomorrow an hour after tasks." Then her fingers left his cheeks and she disappeared into the flow of people.

That night his sleep was fitful and dream-filled. Dreams of starlings swirling in a gray sky, like ink in water. Dreams of warm hands bathed in orange light. Dreams of soft lips and a tower tall and rigid, its stones wet with rain.

She was waiting for him on the Concourse at the appointed time. By the eighteenth hour there were few people walking along the dark tiles, and the man felt uneasy. Crowds felt better, more comfortable. He looked up at the evenly spaced blisters along the wall above them and imagined that they were all focused on him and the woman.

Nonsense, he thought. *The Advocacy cares nothing about one man and one woman.*

He knew that was true, but it was still a relief when she said, "Come, let's walk. There is something I want to show you."

They walked side by side in silence. Keeping close to the Tower's wall, passing under a camera every few paces. "I don't think they see as well when we walk close to them," she said when she saw him looking up at the shiny domes. "I don't think."

"It doesn't matter. We are doing nothing wrong."

"Of course not."

"The people are freer now than ever."

"They are." *Or was that a question?*

They walked for a long time, passing through tunnels where buttresses extended down from the tower wall above them, arched over the pathway, and joined the parapet, clutching the Concourse like gigantic hands. Within the passages the cameras glowed with a light the color of ice and the man felt constrained in a way he never did when walking there during the day, even among the press of hundreds of other citizens. He quickened his pace to catch up with the woman. Being close to her was uncomfortable, but it was an unease he liked.

"Where are we going?"

"Not far," she said, shaking back her head to let the hood of her coat fall. "It's a place you've probably heard about, but never visited. Few have."

His pulse throbbed in his temples. "Not a forbidden place?" Few places in the Tower were forbidden to citizens, but many were discouraged.

"Don't worry," she said turning to look at him with a smile. "You are mostly safe with me."

"Mostly?"

"Well, it wouldn't be any fun if you were entirely safe, would it?"

He didn't answer. He didn't know how to. Her words cut through the confusion he'd been feeling since he met her like a cold wind slicing its way through a thin cloak. Her tell was true. He enjoyed the distraction of her.

"What is your task? You have no medallion on your sleeve."

"What do you think it is?"

There were only three groups which wore no emblem: the Advocacy, the Constabulary, and the Untasked. He had never met an Advocate, though doing so was his fondest dream. Constables were seen frequently enough, walking in pairs, or groups, clad in their short, dark green jackets and pale yellow, wide-brimmed hats. The Constabulary needed no emblem.

Rarest of all were the Untasked. Citizens without purpose, with no way to contribute to the health of the Tower. From the time he had left the Rearing Room to begin his task training he had heard stories about the Untasked. Threats mostly, from Teachers and Trainers. "Learn to speak well, citizen," Teacher Jaffe had once told him. "Or do you *want* to be Untasked?" He could think of no more terrible fate than to be a purposeless bit of human dross within the Community. But there were other tales as well. Stories told in the darkness between bunks in the dormitory. Whispers about men and women with no skill, outcasts who made no contribution. Parasites.

The Untasked were horrible to look at, some said. Twisted into strange grotesques by their guilt and shame. Others said they were as beautiful as a sunrise, and just as transient. No one the man knew had ever seen an Untasked, but everyone knew someone who had. Or claimed to have. The only agreement between the tales was that the Untasked wore no emblem and had no names.

"You wear no emblem," he repeated.

She stopped then and turned to him, a sudden movement that caught him unprepared. She stood on her toes, bringing her face close to his. He thought she was going to kiss him again. He leaned forward.

"And you do." Her breath warmed his cheek. It smelled moist and sweet. Instead of kissing him, however, she took his hand in hers and spun away. "Come! It's just a bit farther."

She nearly ran the last dozen yards pulling at his hand and laughing. Excitement surrounded her like a bright cloak, and it passed through her flesh into his where their fingers were intertwined. She led him to an arched doorway remarkable only for its plainness. On the keystone an emblem was etched into the dark stone; an open book. The emblem looked familiar to the man, but he could not remember where he had seen it before, or what it meant.

"What is this place?" The etching was obviously very old, and it was worn from long exposure to the wind which swirled constantly along the Concourse, even now pressing against his back like insistent hands. But there was something more than that. The man reached up and hesitantly ran his fingers over the surface of the keystone. There were deep scratches running across the rock's face, as if someone had tried to obliterate the mark, but the damage had been done without skill. "What is this place?" he said again.

"My teacher called it Bibliopia," she replied as she pressed against the iron lever releasing the latch.

The door opened smoothly, to the man's surprise, revealing a narrow corridor lit by the same pale light that had illuminated the tunnels along the Concourse. Every few yards a camera dome swelled down from the arching stone ceiling, but the woman ignored them as she led him through the warren of twisting passages. The man quickly lost track of how many left and right turns they made as they worked their way deeper and deeper into the Tower.

From time to time the color, cut and finish of the stone walls changed. After one right-hand bend, smooth gray stones became interlaced with polished black ones which eventually, many paces later, gave way to larger, rough-hewn blocks the color of dried blood.

The light changed also. No longer were the cameras surrounded by rings emitting a watery, silver-blue glow. Here illumination was harsh and yellow and came from small tubes mounted between the cameras, and the cameras themselves were housed in flat sided boxes, not the sleek blisters he was used to. This place felt old. Alien.

"I don't think we should . . ." he began, stopping under one of the boxy camera housings. But he didn't know how to finish. What was it exactly they shouldn't be doing? They were citizens, free to move about as they wished. The door to these passages had opened freely. There had been no warning signs . . .

Or had there been? Might not that warning have been small and orange? Or maybe a sleeve unmarked was a sign?

"We're here," the woman said as she stopped in front of a pair of doors. Together they were wider than his outstretched arms. Above the doors the open-book sigil was etched into the stone. It was deeper here, and bore no signs of damage. The woman pushed the doors open.

As the panels swung back the man was bathed in an outpouring of light that reminded him of the sun rising above the parapet along the Concourse. Candles burned everywhere, and the air was redolent with a thin, spicy smelling smoke that tickled his nose and made him feel like he was about to sneeze. The tenuous arms of that smoke cradled a score of citizens—perhaps more. Some walked among the group offering plates of meat and fruits. Some stood alone, but many gathered in small groups nibbling on their treats, or just talking. All were dressed in strange, colorful garments printed with bold patterns and intricate geometric designs. Nowhere could the man see an emblem, or any other sign of Task. It seemed that each face wore a smile, and the space was filled with the sound of voices.

The walls of the chamber were lined from floor to arching ceiling with dark wooden shelves, and each shelf was filled with books. Books jammed together as tightly as the stones of the Tower itself. Thousands of them.

"What is this?" the man asked, perhaps only of himself.

"This is *my* purpose," the woman replied.

Never in his life had the man felt as completely alone as he did at that moment. Without conscious thought his left hand sought out and covered the emblem on his right sleeve.

"Ah! There you are!" An old woman disengaged herself from a small cluster of other citizens and walked toward the man and his companion. She was very tiny. No taller than a child. Her silver hair was pulled back into a long braid away from an oval face that was creased in a thousand places. Her eyes were pale and the candlelight danced in them. "We are happy to see you both." Her robes were the color of lemons and grass.

"And we, you, Mother," the woman said as she bent to kiss the older woman on her cheek.

"Both of you?" The question sounded playful, but the man felt that it was more. "Are *you* happy to see us . . . ?" She reached out and gently pulled his hand away from his emblem. She examined the stylized embroidery depicting a speaking face in profile. " . . . Teller?"

"Why are you called Mother?" he asked. "No one in the Tower has given birth for generations."

For the first time since he met her on the Concourse, the woman's smile flew from her face, and she clasped his wrist in her warm hand. "Respect, please!" The touch of her skin thrilled him, but, at the same time, her look of alarm caused a hollow pain in his chest. It was also satisfying.

"I'm sorry, Mother," she said, turning to the old woman. "He doesn't understand."

Fingers, as wrinkled and knotted as an old branch, cupped themselves over the younger woman's hand on his wrist, but the words she spoke were directed at the man. "There are many ways to be a mother." She smiled as she spoke. "Giving birth is the easiest."

In the silence which followed her statement, the man realized that the entire room had become silent. The droning buzz of mingled conversations had stopped, and it seemed that everyone in the room was looking at him. Smiles still curled each lip, but to him they seemed like hardened, artificial sneers.

"I should go."

"Nonsense," the older woman replied, and the man felt the younger's hand tighten on his wrist. "You are among friends here."

"No." His voice felt as weak as it sounded.

"Yes." His dark companion leaned close as she spoke. The breath of her words caressed his cheek. "I want you to know."

She released his wrist then and stepped back a single pace, still looking at him. The older woman backed off also, her robe flowing like a sunlit field of wind-rippled grass.

He watched as the woman who brought him undid the fastener at the throat of her own cloak and allowed it to fall onto the closely set stones of the chamber's floor. Beneath it she wore a thin gown of the same orange hue he had seen on her scarf. Its long sleeves were covered with an intricate and delicate ivory embroidery, and more needlework of the same pattern ringed the gown's plunging neckline. For a long moment he stopped breathing.

Not forbidden, he thought. *Not forbidden*.

"A song," someone within the onlooking group called out.

"Yes!" someone else replied. "A song!"

The old woman began to clap slowly. The sharp, flat sound was swallowed by the thousands of books surrounding the chamber. Others began to clap with her and soon the room was filled with the sound of skin striking skin.

As if pushed by the insistent sound of the applause, the woman continued to back away from him. The gathered people parted to form a gauntlet between the woman and a raised wooden platform in the center of the room. It was not until she had reached the step at the side of the dais that she turned away from him and stepped up. The crowd sealed itself behind her.

Upon the platform the woman stood half a body above the tallest person in the room. Every eye was focused on her. To the man, the scene looked like a gathering of children watching the first bonfire of Scorching Season. When she raised her hands the clapping stopped.

"We are all kindred here." Her eyes scanned the faces surrounding her and then found his. "All of us."

He felt a movement at his side and looked down to see the old woman standing there. When he looked back, the dark haired woman had closed her eyes.

"I sing for the kindred."

For a few moments she stood there in silence. The only movement was the slow rising and falling of her breasts.

One breath.

Two.

Three.

The man found himself breathing with the same slow rhythm. Not doing so would be impossible. Her eyes remained closed as her lips parted.

The old woman took his hand in hers.

Sometimes when a child laughs in the crowd on the Concourse, or when the West wind strokes the corner of the parapet just so, it will make a sound that touches more than his ear. So it was when the woman started to sing. The words were as pure as sunshine on ice even though he could understand none of them.

He turned to the old woman holding his hand. "What—?"

"It is an old tongue," she said, cutting off his question. "A language from a time before the Tower. A time when there *were* mothers."

"How does she know these words?"

"They are passed down from lips to ears." She smiled up at him, released his hand and used one bony finger to tap the emblem on his sleeve. "Much like your tells."

The woman on the stage moved smoothly from one song into the next, her voice increased its strength without increasing its volume. Her body swayed as the words poured from her lips. Her eyes remained closed. Many in the crowd moved with her.

"But singing is—"

"Forbidden? Yes, I know. As does she."

"Songs distract. They have no purpose."

"No?"

"None."

She took his hand again and stood silent for a moment. Then she said, "Feel how your body reacts to the words. To the sound of her voice, then tell me there is no purpose to her song."

He did feel it. The woman's voice seemed to have the power to reach inside of him and take hold of something there. The power to lift him up and away. To carry him as easily as the wind can carry a small seed. It was a feeling he had never experienced before.

"What do I feel?" His voice was soft.

"Perhaps it is love?"

"Love?" The word had an odd shape in his mouth, like a stone smooth on his tongue, but if swallowed . . .

"I know she loves you, though I don't understand why." The singing woman opened her eyes and found him instantly. The old woman continued, "It doesn't matter. Love and understanding are two dishes seldom served on the same plate."

He knew nothing of love. It too was a purposeless thing; not forbidden, but discouraged.

Fear he understood, and this talk of love frightened him. So did the waves of pleasing sound pouring out of the woman's throat. The song frightened him even as it excited him. He closed his eyes and let the sound engulf him, let it carry him through the smoky air above the swaying, intoxicated citizens. Never had a sound had so much power. He wanted it to stop, and he wanted it to go on forever.

This is *her purpose*. But it distracted him from his own. Unconsciously he once more found the emblem on his sleeve with his fingers. *It is not mine.*

He bowed his head and opened his eyes. The old woman was looking up at him, smiling. There were soft sounds coming from her own throat, as if she too was singing someplace inside of herself. He knelt in front of her and whispered, "I must go. Tell her I will meet her on the Concourse after tasks tomorrow."

She clasped his hand, saying, "No. Stay. Become kindred."

"Tomorrow," he said, pulling away from her. "After tasks." He turned and left the chamber.

⁂

To the west the clouds had broken and the setting sun spilled orange-gold light on the tree tops far below the Concourse and gilded the edges of the parapet stones. The woman stood in the exact spot where she had first kissed him. When she saw him, her smile grew in radiance and she raised her hand in a wave. His heart tightened in his chest, and he thought he heard the echo of her songs mingled with the breeze.

He walked to her slowly. His legs trembled. *Not forbidden*, he thought. *But discouraged.*

As he neared, she opened her arms. She wore the scarf with the orange stripe. "Why did you leave?"

"I'm sorry," he said.

"It's all right." She stepped forward to embrace him, but he stopped her with a hand on her chest.

"I'm sorry."

The look of confusion on her face turned to one of horror as a Finder appeared above the rim of the parapet buzzing like an enormous, enraged wasp. The man-sized machine hovered there projecting a crimson circle on the woman's midsection.

"The Advocacy requests an interview with you, citizen." The mechanical voice was soft, caring.

She looked from the Finder to the man. "You? Why?"

Tears spilled from her eyes and glistened on her cheeks. Were they tears of fear, or of hatred? He remembered her smile, and her song, and decided she wasn't capable of hate. He reached up and caught a tear with the tip of one finger, but he did not answer. Instead he stepped back as the Constables in their dull green jackets and yellow hats appeared from under the arch of a buttress and took her away.

Her interview was short and private. The man was not required and the confidences exchanged between the woman and the Advocacy are not part of his tell.

He was temporarily re-Tasked to the team of Builders who sealed the doors to the chamber with fresh stones and sand-blasted away the emblem above the door. Working with the stones was difficult, and their rough surface tore at his flesh. It was a good task and the pain was rewarding.

It is always a good thing when a citizen receives a Task, and the man was glad to be a part of the Tasking of the woman who sang. It was his honor to place the emblem of a Cleaner into her softly restrained hand as she lay there under the clouds on the Concourse. Her fist clenched around the fabric oval and she tried to speak to him, but the device holding her mouth open would not permit that. He thought she wanted to thank him.

He had been shown what to do by a Constable, and he had practiced on a lamb. He worked quickly, and as efficiently as he could. The knife became slick after just the first cut, but he kept his grip, cutting away the offending organ and tossing it over the parapet into the old world so it would no longer be a part of the Tower.

He imagined he could hear the songs falling with it.

This is how my tell ends.

I saw the woman who sang recently. She was walking the Concourse with her head down and her hands in her pockets. The emblem of a Cleaner was displayed proudly on her sleeve. She did not smile when she saw me. She simply walked away among the rest of the citizens.

I stood there for a long time after she disappeared, leaning against the stones and looking out over the old world. After a while a butterfly rose from the vegetation so far below and settled down on the capstone near my hand. It was orange with black spots and it died easily under my fist.

Better to remain a chrysalis.

Iron Roses
Michal Wojcik

Originally appeared in *Daily Science Fiction*, May 16, 2014

Roses don't grow around New London any more. Cast-off trolleys, engines, scrap metal, and rusted airship frames press up against the city's edge, not trees. The Fraser River resembles a tongue of burnt milk licking the Pacific Ocean. This is the realm of the scrap-runners, tripping through iron mounds to scavenge what they can for resale to the factories. If anything else could grow here, it gave up a long time ago.

That didn't stop people from talking about roses.

The two sat on a cog of a huge gear, like two kids on a Ferris wheel. They both bore the big boots, the padded gloves, and the mismatched gear that indicated scrap-runners. Beneath them, barges laden with sheet metal floated down towards the sea.

"I've seen them before," said #1, Selwyn. Like most people in New London he was pale, thanks to the smog that lovingly hugs the city half the time and the rain that pounds it the other. His coveralls and body harness did little to fill out his sparse frame. Once red hair was so full of soot, it hung black and gray, wavered when he spoke. "Went in the country once, must've been five or six, with my uncle."

"How'd they smell?" asked #2, Millie. She was taller than him, had her hair clumsily lopped short (she'd cut it herself) and wore airman's goggles she'd scrounged from the back heaps, ostensibly to keep the dust out of her eyes.

"Smelled . . . good. Don't know how to put it; was a while ago."

"I only seen them on the vee." She tore another hunk from her sandwich. "Can't be the same."

"I picked them too," he went on, "stabbed myself with the thorns."

"Oh."

Selwyn took a full-on look at Millie, who wasn't looking back. She still watched the barges. "Wish I could get you some," he ventured.

Millie's mouth hung open a moment, masticated food stuck inside. She swallowed quickly. "Yeah, that'd be nice. Though, what I could really use right now is a new celpher."

"Millie, I—"

But Millie was already hopping along the gear teeth. "C'mon Sel, we won't make any cash sitting up here."

Leaving Selwyn staring after her. He scrambled down as soon as he collected his thoughts, back down into the piles of steel.

Few scrap-runners came to Serja Petrov's workshop, a patchwork of old warehouses and temp structures jammed together on the riverbank. They didn't trust the old Croatian, since he actually built things out of the junk before putting them on the market. Yet, Selwyn periodically wandered onto the premises in the evening, clad in a long coat instead of his usual gear. He could hear banging and cursing from somewhere, eventually found Petrov in one of the warehouses cranking at cogs. Walking in here felt like entering a Mechanist's temple: pipes suspended from the ceiling (lanterns hung off those), blasts of steam everywhere and the constant tick of pistons or clockwork. Petrov had no beard, no hair, just a head like a dried-out apple interrupted by an eagle's beak.

"Petrov!" Selwyn called, keeping a safe distance. He needed to shout a few times before the Croatian crawled out from the steelwork.

"Hey? Ah, Selwyn, yes?"

"I . . ."

Petrov hung his body over the frame and wiped his brow. "Something wrong?"

"It's, nothing really. Just, there's this girl."

Petrov laughed suddenly in that long wheeze he passed off as laughter. "You come to me for advice on what?"

"Maybe I should come back later."

"No." Petrov ceased his laugh. "But me, I know nothing about women. Ask me about machines, then I give you some answer, yes?"

"You had a wife."

"Why do you think I left Croatia?" said Petrov. He hopped over the railing so he could give Selwyn a clap on the shoulder. "Who needs women when you can have celpher or a vee? I make all these machines here, when I finish, they live, breathe. Put enough love into anything, and it comes alive. They are like children, and best of all, I don't need a woman to make them!"

"I'm serious," Selwyn murmured.

Petrov removed his arm from Selwyn's shoulder and sat down on one of the workbenches, tossing off his gloves. "So you like some girl."

"Yeah. I don't think she likes me, though. I mean, not in the same way. We kissed, once, but that was a while ago. And she laughed at me."

A shiver went through the workshop, kicking lights and spare bits into a melody. "Just pressure going off," said Petrov when Selwyn almost toppled. "She's one of the colonials, Canadian, yes?"

Selwyn just nodded.

"They like freedom. You take things slow." Petrov lowered his voice into what he considered a whisper. "I tell you, make her see you really appreciate her. A gift, something she cannot get here."

"You mean, like roses?"

"Ha. Exactly. See, you already have her."

The problem was finding some. Selwyn only made the briefest forays into the inner city, and even then, just the outermost outskirts. Those also made him uncomfortable. Despite his long jacket, people picked him out as a scrap-runner and avoided him; after enduring more than a few young ladies' arrogant sniffs he stopped the long circuit into New London to find some flower shop—they wouldn't sell to a sooter anyway. The countryside wasn't an option; he hadn't enough sterling to take a freecart the whole way. He could afford a locomotive, but there wasn't an option of getting time off scrap running without being snubbed by the factories and the other runners as well.

As for seeds, they couldn't grow. He'd tried to grow potatoes once, in old buckets and whatever soil he could scrounge, but the resulting sprouts and roots looked so sickly and (he couldn't fathom why) *oily* he ended up tossing them out without trying any. And still he spent almost every day picking through the slabs with Millie, still failing to get her attention in any meaningful way.

He got the idea, indirectly, from Petrov. After another nighttime run to the workshop, Selwyn found Petrov's chest. Old Serja had been pouring vodka, came into the main room when he saw Selwyn holding up a delicately crafted honeybee, all twisted out of iron.

"Ah, you found my collection."

Selwyn started, put the bee back in the chest. Beetles, wasps, dragonflies, butterflies sat there as well, all giving off a dull sheen. He wordlessly accepted the glass from Petrov and tipped it back. "What're they for?"

"Something I do for myself. You need some time, yes? Started with the butterflies; my wife loves them, and I used to send them before she stopped sending me letters. It's habit now."

"Do you think," Selwyn said, then paused to down the rest of his vodka, "you can show me how?"

He had no workshop, and had to set himself up in the abandoned machine room. Not much space; abandoned boilers took up most of it. Still, there was a desk strapped against one wall where he could work. Selwyn put a lantern on one side and his toolbox on the other before spilling out the various bits of metal and wire he'd garnered. Lastly, he stood an old book on the farther end, filled with color plates of flowers. As he shuffled the last bits in place, he heard the door squeal open.

"Sel?"

Another girl stood in the frame, Nydia. She still had her harnesses on, which were too big for her, so she clattered whenever she walked. She was only eleven; still, she carried herself with sureness far outstripping Selwyn's. She peered over the table and then at Selwyn, who still hadn't said anything.

"You still awake?"

"It matter?" Selwyn said, going back to rummaging through what he had. "Why're you here?"

Nydia rolled her eyes. "Think you're the only one who wants someplace quiet," she said before she hung over the desk and squinted at the plates. "What you working on?"

"I'm making flowers."

She scrunched her eyebrows. "Why'd you want to make flowers?"

"You wouldn't understand."

Nydia detached from the desk and hopped onto one of the pipes. "They're for Millie, I bet."

Now Selwyn's fingers slipped. He looked back at the girl swinging on the boiler. "So what?"

No reply, Nydia just kept swinging her legs.

"Look, what is it going to take for me to get you not to tattle?" Selwyn asked after a sigh.

The girl seemed to contemplate this a while before answering. "Let me help?"

Selwyn's fingers slipped again. "Oh, go ahead," he managed, and began twisting the first stem.

It took a few tries. With Petrov, it had seemed easy. By himself, it wasn't. He kept absorbed in trying to replicate the plate as best he could, but what he produced looked dead. Nydia fared no better, and the two of them worked in silence. Eventually Nydia tossed hers down and just sat off to the side, holding her head in her hands while she watched Selwyn carefully fuse, solder, sand, and beat pieces into place. The moon made full circuit, and Nydia was fast asleep, before he was finally satisfied. He'd been forced to take off the gloves for finishing; had to wash his hands in the brass sink and lay on bandages. The pain and exhaustion was worth it, for the iron rose lying on the table.

When Nydia did wake up, she saw the rose directly in front of her and flicked a glance back at Selwyn, who smiled. "Looks alive." She tentatively picked it up and ran her hands along the rose with a breathless look, suddenly dropped it. "Ouch!" and she nursed her thumb as some red hung from the stem. Selwyn offered her the roll of bandage. "Why'd you put thorns on?"

"They're not real roses without them," Selwyn lifted it and turned it in the light.

Nydia picked herself up. "You'll be 'round here next time?"

"Well, got to make more than one."

"Hmm. Okay, see ya," and Nydia flitted away.

Selwyn's grin faded once she left, and he wiped her blood off the rose with a towel.

In here, the rose almost seemed to take on color. Petrov had a pair of spectacles perched on his nose, turned the one lens so he could get a better focus on the zoom before giving it back to Selwyn. "Craftsmanship excellent."

"You think it'll work?" Selwyn asked, shuffling his feet a few times.

"Yes, yes. I knew you had it in you, but these are almost like real."

"No, but . . . will she like them?"

Petrov flicked off his spectacles and folded into his armchair. "I think she will. Even one."

"One's not enough," Selwyn said, shaking his head. "I need a, what d' you call them, a bouquet."

As sunset neared, the smog lifted, letting the sun through in more than just a fuzzy swathe. The dull grays that dominated the wasteland changed to brilliant silver. From a distance, it looked like a field of broken glass. Millie had more spring in her step as she wove her way between them, and one of her rare smiles. She had even stripped off her goggles and let them hang. Behind her, Selwyn moved more hesitantly.

"You think you might make it out of here?" called Millie as she clambered over a trolley frame.

"What you mean?"

"Well, no one wants to run scrap forever." She sat and tucked her knees against her chest. Her chin and cheeks were smothered with dirt, just not the area round her eyes.

He clambered beside her, but didn't sit. "Course not. What would you do?"

Millie shrugged.

From then, silence—or as silent as these parts got. Only staring out at the mountains of junk marching towards the sea. "Kind of pretty, in the light," Millie finally said.

"I've got something for you." Selwyn quickly turned away, made sure he couldn't see her reaction.

Took a while before she said anything. "What is it?"

"It's in the old machine room. If you'll come."

Now he chanced a look. Selwyn couldn't read Millie's expression beyond her nod. He helped her up and led her wordlessly back.

The dust that kicked up when he opened the door was far more noticeable when a beam of sunlight shot through. Once Selwyn strode in, he wasn't quite sure what to do next. Millie kept by the door and only peered inside. He felt like he should say something, but the words stuck. She saw the roses before he even went near them. From then, he took a deep breath and grabbed the steel bouquet. He could just barely lift it with one hand. Still nothing said.

Yet, Millie did pull off her gloves and stuff them in her belt just so she could take one and feel it between her fingers. "Roses," she whispered and then bit her lip. "For me?"

"Yes."

"How long did it take you?"

"Not too long." *Two weeks.*

Millie continued to examine the rose. Wire stem, petals formed from steel beaten into delicate ripples. If not for the color, it would have seemed organic. "It's beautiful, Sel. Better than the vee. They're beautiful."

He went up to her closer, and she took the bouquet, both their hands intertwined for a moment. Millie tilted her head up slightly, and closed her eyes, and Selwyn leaned towards her. But just as their lips were about to touch, she turned away with a blush. "You can't give 'em to me, Sel."

She would have gone on, except as she moved to push the flowers back, one of the thorns nicked her palm. The bouquet shattered in her hands and fell with a tinkle on the metal beneath her feet. More blood dripped off the wire.

He would have helped her. Instead, he gave a miserable glance down at the roses and then back. Millie pushed one hand against the other to staunch the cut, then, seeing how he stared, blushed again and quickly bounded away from him.

For the remainder of the evening Selwyn gathered his roses.

Specks of blood lay smothered across the stem, but Selwyn couldn't bring himself to clean them this time. He lay them all down save one, and only held it dully while his thoughts wandered elsewhere. No sobs, instead he deliberately squeezed the rose in his fist until his own thick blood joined hers, flowed down the stem.

He thought he would feel pain, like the others. There wasn't any. It felt more like his hand was party to several kisses. The thorns punched in his skin sunk deeper and seemed to root themselves into his veins, drinking, drinking. He pressed his fist tighter. And watched the rose gradually bloom.

Later, Nydia found him with his back turned to the door. She said nothing, just shut it and sat beside him. He looked back and smiled a little, and when she looked over his shoulder, her eyes widened. "A *real* one? Where'd you get it?"

"I made it," said Selwyn. "I made it, and it came alive."

And he pressed his nose into the flower, took a deep, deep breath. It didn't seem so bad, any more. Millie could go if that's what she wanted. But he had . . . this.

Light emerged over New London.

TRAVELER
Michael Milne

Henry comes home tired, but he tries to cover it up as he rings the doorbell. Like a guest.

Thumping from inside, as Henry's son Jason opens the door. The boy has shed a dozen toys behind him, ones that Henry barely remembers buying. "When were you today, Daddy?"

"Quite a while back. Hundreds of years. And I was then a long time." Jason is too young to read the implication, and Mel is out of earshot. "But it wasn't so bad."

"Hi honey!" Mel enters from the kitchen and wraps her slender arms around him, as she does whenever he arrives home. The kiss on his cheek is a feather across gravel. She smells like honey and home cooking, and her skin is a kind of soft he barely recognizes. He smells like engine coolant, and he's pretty sure he could sand down their dining room floor with his stubble.

This last job has lasted eight months, and he holds onto Mel like his grasp is the only thing maintaining her heartbeat.

"Oh, baby. That long?" She probably knows the metric of these embraces—the tightness of the squeeze. The jobs aren't usually this long, except when they are. He exhales into her neck, more desperate than he wants, and she tries to giggle it all away, whatever it is.

Sometimes the passion in these reunions can overwhelm her, he knows. She has to abandon any dangling grievances, as they are swallowed whole in the gulf of his relief. An argument in the morning about money is ancient history by the afternoon. For Henry, so much is buried deep in the sediment of their marriage. Did they fight today? This week? Henry has no idea, and Mel has developed an impenetrable poker face.

After a while he pulls back, just enough that her hands rest across his shoulders. Sweat has slicked the fabric of his shirt to his skin—it was not summer where Henry has been. He sniffs at the air like a stray dog. "Dinner. Pork chops?"

She smiles. Every meal is a homecoming. Once, Mel had made pork chops every night for a week and he hadn't noticed until she told him.

Sometimes the era is harder. Diseases and outdoor plumbing, salmonella or a wide lack of deodorant. He will realize he is the wrong color in the wrong place or the wrong time. People stare hard, take in his bizarre clothes, whisper in slurs he doesn't know. If he gets sick, breaks a limb, he must rely upon the medicine of the then present. He can't count the number of times he has been leeched. If he is imprisoned, if he is detained, if people mark him as a witch, he must use his wits and stumble back to his watchcar, defeated and bloody, and start the hunt over again.

The turn of the millennium, this last job, had proved pleasant enough. Haircuts that Henry found funny, cell phones that seemed Paleolithic. But weeks had turned to months, scars had multiplied, and at one point Henry had forgotten his son's middle name.

Henry strips his shoes and vows to shower as soon as possible. The hall closet is full of hundreds of new-old shoes, leather and rubber and strange plastics. Fashions from dozens of eras, forgotten trends in business, casual, and sport. Henry stretches as Mel closes the door, and he feels old.

Mel is moving off to the dining room to set the table. The sunset seeps through the open window, slides over her eyes and her neck. She looks as young as when they met—or no, maybe he forgets. She wears her hair down now; she seems more mature. But she could still be a photograph—that tattered, beachy portrait he keeps slipped under the visor in his watchcar. The picture is long faded, and her one-piece and her gaudy sunglasses look scooped up from a distant era. She seems like an immortal, like he must have picked her up as a stowaway on some far flung trip.

Henry hoists Jason onto his shoulders and marvels at how light his son is. He expects the boy to suddenly climb in height, to meet his hip or his chest, to be reading, to have joined the rugby team, to have a girlfriend. After each job, Henry slips into his personal car (still unmarred by months away; still a full tank of gas) and drives home, the whole while worrying about Jason.

He wonders each time if the boy will have forgotten him. Maybe the months will make a scar of Henry, something to be healed and forgotten. Jason is just young enough that another man, anyone really, could slot in, be a father, and Henry would slip away. His hand trembles sometimes as he reaches for the door, but he opens it and spies his boy, always his boy. Jason barely meets his knee and his teeth have big gaps between them like painted spaces in a parking lot.

Henry goes to the kitchen to see if he can help with dinner when he catches a glimpse of himself in the hallway mirror. There's a patch of new gray hair, staking territory across his temples and staging battle maneuvers on the space behind his ears. The stock of anti-aging meds, big purple capsules the size of his pinky fingernail, ran out three months into the last assignment. After this many jobs he is easily ten, twenty years older than Mel, but usually he doesn't show it.

There are times when he comes home looking different. A new scar, a new freckle. Once, a full beard grew like a forest overnight. He picks up new smells—ocean salt, windshield washer fluid, some briefly popular cologne. New clothes are a given, as people will notice you even more when you don't dress the part. Mel at least pretends not to be shocked anymore.

The intangibles and the invisibles are harder. He will return unable to talk to his family, knowing that the silence is abrupt and brutal but unable to help himself. Other times he is nearly manic, riveted, joyous at the luxury, the sumptuousness of home. His hugs go on for just a little too long, and he marathons eye contact until Mel has to look away. After one particularly long shift, he had come home and declared himself a devout Buddhist. Another time, a vegetarian.

"You okay, darling?" They work together to strain the vegetables. Henry sees her glance at his hair, which she has just noticed. He feels confident that he's hidden the rest. She won't notice the bullet holes—those were repaired back at the office. "You don't seem yourself."

She always says that when he comes back wrong—Henry can sense her suspicion. He's not Henry of Henry and Mel, circa seven years ago before he took this job. He supposes he used to be better-groomed. He remembers when he actually cared about his hair, but it feels monumentally long ago, a fairy tale handwritten on papyrus. Mel sometimes looks at him like he's a veneer laid overtop of the man she knows, something to be worn down and washed away.

Sometimes he will try to think back, years and years past, to whoever he was then. He laughs at old pictures of himself, embarrassed and ashamed, and realizes that they have been taken only days before. When Mel is really upset, when she says she doesn't know him anymore, he will watch himself in old family vids, and try to impersonate the man he sees. Henry is a role for Henry to play.

"It was just a really long time away," he says, and she smiles and breathes deep. She seems to believe him, or fakes it for the sake of dinner. He kneads his hands and moves to the bathroom to wash them while Mel dishes up their meal on their worn hand-me-down plates. He has already scrubbed his hands until they were raw and chapped back at the office.

Jason is eating when he returns, talking about the other boys in preschool. Mel smiles and nods to Henry's plate and his wine. The glass is too full—Mel always does this when she suspects a long job. Some anesthetic before they can operate and remove the last few months or years from him like sickly flesh.

Henry never talks about the job—it makes them both sad. He doesn't talk about the people either, how far they run, or why, or what they do when he finds them. There was the woman whom he resuscitated before hauling her forcefully back to the present, where she had been a high-end tech and AI thief. There was the man who jumped through seven different decades before Henry finally caught him. The man had been the president of some bioengineering company and had fled when details surfaced of the grim research lab the company had stowed underground in some backwoods in Australia. Henry doesn't tell her about James Hofstadt, or the weapons discharge form that he filled out today. He fears that it will make her look at him differently.

Once he came home after four years and a day hadn't passed for Mel. She had taken Jason to school, gone to work, and met her sister for lunch. In his time gone he had grieved and made peace with his loss; he had given up and accepted giving up. He had learned to speak Portuguese. He had broken his arm, had it fitted with a cast, and healed over. When he finally staggered home he was tired somewhere deeper than his muscles, and he parked on the wrong street twice, half-convinced that Mel would have moved away. When she opened the door she gasped at his beard; he had forgotten it was even on his face. She had led him straight to the bathroom to get cleaned up. Sometimes he wished she would look at him differently—he wished she knew how.

"When will you be tomorrow, daddy?" Jason is stuffed to the brim with mashed potatoes, and Henry still hasn't eaten yet. "Can you pick me up from school?"

"I think I can," Henry says. He will spend the day at home tomorrow. They always discharge detectives for a day or two after life-threatening injuries. Mel will come home, maybe meet him for lunch. Henry will appear at the fence of the kindergarten, and he will experience eight hours as eight hours.

For now, he is the same. He looks mostly unchanged, the same man Mel married, the same man she met those years ago. She is the same as always, and she plants a kiss on their son's forehead as she moves past. Mel sits down in her seat and Henry smiles across at her—right now he feels like he is her Henry in the quiet early evening of their dining room.

VIRGIN OF THE SANDS
Holly Phillips

Originally appeared in *Lust for Life: Tales of Sex and Love*, Véhicule Press, April 2006

Graham came out of the desert leaving most of his men dead behind him. He debriefed, he bathed, he dressed in a borrowed uniform, and without food, without rest, though he needed both, he went to see the girl.

The army had found her rooms in a shambling mud-brick compound shaded by palms. She was young, God knew, too young, but her rooms had a private entrance, and there was no guard to watch who came and went. Who would disturb Special Recon's witch? Graham left the motor pool driver at the east side of the market and walked through the labyrinth of goats, cotton, chickens, oranges, dates, to her door. The afternoon was amber with heat, the air a stinking resin caught with flies. Nothing like the dry furnace blast of the wadi where his squad had been ambushed and killed. He knocked, stupid with thirst, and wondered if she was home.

She was.

Tentative, always, their first touch: her fingertips on his bare arm, her mouth as heavy with grief as with desire. She knew, then. He bent his face to hers and felt the dampness of a recent bath. She smelled of well water and ancient spice. They hung a moment, barely touching, mingled breath and her fingers against his skin, and then he took her mouth, and drank.

⁂

"I'm sorry," she said, after.

He lay across her bed, bound to exhaustion, awaiting release. "We walked right into them," he said, eyes closed. "Walked right into their guns."

"I'm sorry."

She sounded so unhappy. He reached for her with a blind hand. "Not your fault. The dead can't tell you everything."

She laid her palm across his, her touch still cool despite the sweat that soaked her sheets. "I know."

"They expect too much of you." By *they* he meant the generals. When she said nothing he turned his head and looked at her. She knelt beside him on the bed, barred with light from the rattan blind. Her dark hair was loose around her face, her dark eyes shadowed with worry. So young she broke his heart. He said, "You expect too much of yourself."

She covered his eyes with her free hand. "Sleep."

"You can only work with what we bring you. If we don't bring you the men who know . . . who knew . . ." The darkness of her touch seeped through him.

"Sleep."

"Will you still be here?"

"Yes. Now sleep."

Three times told, he slept.

She had to be pure to work her craft, a virgin in the heart of army intelligence. He never knew if this loving would compromise her with her superiors. She swore it would not touch her power, and he did not ask her more. He just took her with his hands, his tongue, his skin, and if sometimes the forbidden depths of her had him aching with need, that only made the moment when she slid her mouth around him more potent, explosive as a shell bursting in the bore of a gun. And he laughed sometimes when she twisted against him, growling, her teeth sharp on his neck: virgin. He laughed, and forgot for a time the smell of long-dead men.

"Finest military intelligence in the world," Colonel Tibbit-Noyse said, "and we can't find their blasted army from one day to the next." His black mustache was crisp in the wilting heat of the briefing room.

Graham sat with half a dozen officers scribbling in notebooks balanced on their knees. Like the others, he let his pencil rest when the colonel began his familiar tirade.

"We know the Fuhrer's entrail-readers are prone to inaccuracy and internal strife. We know who his spies are and have been feeding them tripe for months." (There was a dutiful chuckle.) "We know the desert tribesmen who have been guiding his armored divisions are weary almost to death with the Superior Man. For God's sake, our desert johnnies have been meeting them for tea among the dunes! So why the *hell*—" the colonel's hand slashed at a passing fly "—can't we find them before they drop their bloody shells into our bloody laps?"

Two captains and three lieutenants, all the company officers not in the field, tapped pencil ends on their notebooks and thumbed the sweat from their brows. Major Healy sitting behind the map table coughed into his hand. Graham, eyes fixed on the wall over the major's shoulder, heard again the rattle of gunfire, saw again the carnage shaded by vulture wings. His notebook slid through his fingers to the floor. The small sound in the colonel's silence made everyone jump. He bent to pick it up.

"Now, I have dared to suggest," Tibbit-Noyse continued, "that the fault may not lie with our intel at all, but rather with the use to which it has been put. This little notion of mine has not been greeted with enthusiasm." (Again, a dry chuckle from the men.) "In fact, I'm afraid the general got rather testy about the quantity and quality of fodder we've scavenged for his necromancer in recent weeks. Therefore." The colonel sighed. His voice was subdued when he continued. "Therefore, all squads will henceforth make it their sole mission to find and retrieve enemy dead, be they abandoned or buried, with an urgent priority on those of officer rank. I'm afraid this will entail a fair bit of dodging about on the wrong side of the battle line, but you'll be delighted to know that the general has agreed to an increase in leave time between missions from two days to four." He looked at Graham. "Beginning immediately, captain, so you have another three days' rest coming to you."

"I'm fit to go tomorrow, sir," Graham said.

Tibbit-Noyse gave him a bleak smile. "Take your time, captain. There's plenty of death to go 'round."

There was another moment of silence, this one long enough for the men to start to fidget. Healy coughed. Graham sketched the outlines of birds. Then the colonel went on with his briefing.

⁕₰❦₰⁕

She had duties during the day, and in any event he could not spend all his leave in her company. He had learned from the nomads not to drink until he must. So he found a café not too near headquarters, one with an awning and a boy to whisk the flies, and drank small cups of syrupy coffee until his heart raced and sleep no longer tempted him.

A large body dropped into the seat opposite him. "Christ. How can you drink coffee in this heat?"

Graham blinked the other's face into focus: Montrose, a second-string journalist with a beefy face and a bloodhound's eyes. The boy brought the reporter a bottle of lemon squash, half of which he poured down his throat without seeming to swallow. "Whew!"

"We have orders," Graham said, his voice neutral, "not to speak with the press."

"Look at you, you bastard. Not even sweating." Montrose had a flat Australian accent and salt-rimmed patches of sweat underneath his arms. "Or have you just had the juice scared out of you?"

Graham gave a thin smile and brushed flies away from the rim of his cup.

"Listen." Montrose hunkered over the table. "There've been rumors of a major cock-up. Somebody let some secrets slip into the wrong ears. Somebody in intelligence. Somebody high up. Ring any bells?"

Graham covered a yawn. He didn't have to fake one. The coastal heat was a blanket that could smother even the caffeine. He drank the last swallow, leaving a sludge of sugar in the bottom of the cup, and flagged the boy.

"According to this rumor," Montrose said, undaunted, "at least one of the secrets had to do with the field maneuvers of the Dead Squad—pardon me—the Special Desert Reconnaissance Group. Which, come to think of it, is your outfit, isn't it, Graham?" Montrose blinked with false concern. "Didn't have any trouble your last time out, did you, mate? No unpleasant surprises? No nasty Jerries hiding among the dunes?"

The boy came back, set a fresh coffee down by Graham's elbow, gave him a fleeting glance from thickly lashed eyes. Graham dropped a couple of coins on the tray.

"How's your wife?" Graham said.

Montrose sighed and leaned back to finish his lemonade. "God knows. Jerries went and sank the mail ship, didn't they? She could be dead and I'd never even know."

"You could be dead," Graham said, "and she would never know. Isn't that a bit more likely given your relative circumstances?"

Montrose grunted in morose agreement, and whistled for the boy.

He stalled as long as he could, through the afternoon and into the cook-fire haze of dusk, and even so he waited nearly an hour outside her door. When she came home, limp and pale, she gave him a weary smile and unlocked her door. He knew better than to touch her before she'd had a chance to bathe. He followed her through the stuffy entrance hall to the airier gloom of her room. She stepped out of her shoes on her way into the bathroom. He heard water splat in the empty tub. Then she came back and began to take off her clothes.

He said, "I have three more days' leave."

She unbuttoned her blouse and peeled it off. "I heard." She tossed the blouse into a hamper by the bathroom door. "I'm glad."

He sat in a creaking wicker chair, set his cap on the floor. "There's a rumor going around about some misplaced intel."

She frowned slightly as she unfastened her skirt. "I haven't heard about that."

"I had it from a reporter. Not the most reliable source."

The skirt followed the blouse, then her slip, her brassiere, her pants. Naked, she lifted her arms to take down her hair. Shadows defined her ribs, her taut belly, the divide of her loins. She walked over to drop hairpins into his hand.

"Who is supposed to have said what to whom?"

"There were no characters in the drama," he said. "But if it's true . . ."

"If it's true, then your men never had a chance."

This close she smelled of woman-sweat and death. His throat tightened. "They had no chance, regardless. Neither do the men in the field now. They've sent the whole damn company out chasing dead men." He dropped his head against the chair and closed his eyes. "This bloody war."

"It's probably just a rumor," she said, and he heard her move away. The rumble from the bathroom tap stopped. Water sloshed as she stepped into the tub. Graham rolled her hairpins against his palm.

Her scent faded with the last of the light.

He wished she had a name he could call her by. Like her intact hymen, her namelessness was meant to protect her from the forces she wrestled in her work, but it seemed a grievous thing. She was so specific a woman, so unique, so much herself; he knew so intimately her looks, her textures, her voice; he could even guess, sometimes, at her thoughts; and yet she was anonymous. The general's necromancer. The witch. The girl. His endearments came unraveled in the empty space where her name should be, so he took refuge in silence, wishing, as much for his sake as for hers, that she had not been born and raised to her grisly vocation. From childhood she had known nothing other than death.

"How can you bear it?" he asked her once.

"How can you?" A glance of mockery. "But maybe no one told you. We all live with death. We all begin to die the instant we are born. Even you."

He had a vision of himself dead and in her hands, and understood it for a strange desire. He did not put it into words but he knew her intimacy with the dead, with death, went beyond this mere closeness of flesh. Skin slick with sweat-salt, speechless tongues and hands that sought the vulnerable center of being, touch dangerous and tender and never allowed inside the heart, the womb. He pressed her in the darkness, strove against her as if they fought, as if one or both might be consumed in this act without hope of consummation. She clung to him, spilled over with the liquor of desire and still he drank, his thirst for her unslaked, unslakable until she, wet and limber as an eel, turned in his arms, turned to him, turned against him, and swallowed him into sleep.

The battle washed across the desert as freely as water unbounded by shores, the war's tidal wrack of ruined bodies, tanks, and planes left like flotsam upon the dunes. The ancient, polluted city lay between the sea and that other, drier beach, and no one knew yet where the high tide line would be. Already the streets were full of the walking wounded.

Graham had errands to run. His desert boots needed mending, he had a new dress tunic to collect from the tailor—trivial chores that, performed against the backdrop of conflict, reminded him in their surreality of lying with two other men under an overhang that was too small to shelter one, seeing men torn apart by machine gun fire and feeling the sand grit between his molars, feeling the tickle of some insect across his hand, feeling his sergeant's boot heel drum against his kidney as the man shook, as they all shook, wanting to live, wanting not to die as the others died, wanting not to be eaten as the others were eaten by the vultures that wheeled down from an empty sky and that could not be trusted to report the enemy's absence, as they were brave enough to face the living when there was a meal at stake. In the tailor's shop he met a man he knew slightly, a major in another branch of Intelligence, and they went to a hotel bar for beer.

The place looked cool, with white tile, potted palms, lazy ceiling fans, but the look was a lie. Strips of flypaper that hung inconspicuously behind the bar twisted under the weight of captured flies. The major paid for two pints and led the way to an unoccupied table.

"Look at them all," he said between quick swallows.

Graham grunted acknowledgment, though he did not look around. He had already seen the scattered crowd of civilians, European refugees nervous as starlings under a hawk's wings.

"Terrified Jerry's going to come along and send them all back where they came from." The major sounded as if he rather liked the idea.

The beer felt good going down.

"As I see it," said the major, "this haphazard retreat of ours is actually going to work in our favor before the end. Think of it. The more scattered our forces are, the more thinly Jerry has to spread his own line. Right now they may look like a scythe sweeping up from the south and west," the major drew an arc in a puddle of spilled beer, "but they have to extend their line at every advance in order to keep any stragglers of ours from simply sitting tight until we're at their backs. Any day now they're going to find themselves overextended, and all we have to do is make a quick nip through a weak spot," he bisected the arc, "and we'll have them in two pieces, both of them surrounded."

"And how do we find the weak spot?"

"Oh, well," the major said complacently, "that's a job for heroes like you, not desk wallahs like me."

Graham got up to buy the next round. When he came back to the table, the major had been joined by another man in uniform, a captain also wearing the "I" insignia. Graham set the glasses down and sat, and only then noticed the looks on their faces.

"I say, old man," the major said. "Rumor has it your section chief has just topped himself in his office."

"It's not a rumor," the captain said. "Colonel Tibbit-Noyse shot himself. I saw his desk. It was covered in his brains." He reached for Graham's beer and thirstily emptied the glass.

Major Healy, the colonel's aide, was impossible to find. Graham tracked him all over Headquarters, but although his progress allowed him to hear the evolving story of the colonel's death, he never managed to meet up with Healy. Eventually he came to his senses and let himself into Healy's cubbyhole of an office. The major kept a box of cigarettes on his desk. Graham seldom smoked, but, eaten by waiting, he lit one after another, the smoke dry and harsh as desert air flavored by gunpowder. When Healy came in, not long before sundown, he shouted "Bloody hell!" and slammed the door hard enough to rattle the window in its frame.

Graham put out his dog end in the overcrowded ashtray. Healy dropped into his desk chair and it tipped him back with a groan.

"Go away, captain. I can't tell you anything and if you stay I might shoot you and save Jerry the bother."

"Why did he do it?"

Healy jumped up and slammed his fist on his desk. "Out!" The chair rolled back to bump the wall.

"He sent the whole company to die on that slaughter ground and then he killed himself?" Graham shook his head.

The major wiped his face with his palms and went to stand at the window. "God knows what's in a man's mind at a time like that."

"Rumor has it he was the one who spilled our movements to the enemy." Graham was hoarse from cigarettes and thirst. "Rumor has him doing it for money, for sex, for loyalty to the other side. Because of blackmail, or stupidity, or threats."

"Rumor."

"I don't believe it."

Healy turned from the window. The last brass bars of light streaked the dusty glass. "Don't you?"

"Whatever he'd done, I don't believe he would have killed himself before he knew what had happened to the men."

"Don't you?"

"No, sir."

"If he was a spy, he wouldn't give a ha'penny damn about the men."

"Do you believe that, sir?"

Healy coughed and went to the box on his desk for a cigarette. When he saw how few were left he gave Graham a sour look. He chose one, lit it with a silver lighter from his pocket, blew out the smoke in a long thin stream.

"It doesn't matter what I believe," he said quietly. "Now give me some peace, will you? I have work to do."

The sun was almost gone. Graham got up and fumbled for the door.

Blackout enveloped the city. Even the stars were dim behind the scrim of cooking smoke that hazed the local sky. Though he might have wheedled a car and driver out of the motor pool, he decided to walk. Her compound was nearly a mile of crooked streets away, and it took all his concentration to recognize the turns in the darkness. Nearly all. He felt a kinship with the other men of his company, men who groped their way through the wind-built maze of dunes and sandstone desert bones, led by a chancy map into what could be, at every furtive step, a trap. He had seen how blood pooled on earth too dry to drink, how it dulled under a skiff of dust even before the flies came. Native eyes watched from dim doorways, and he touched the sidearm on his belt. With the war on the city's threshold, everyone was nervous.

Her doorway was as dim as all the rest. In the weak light that escaped her room her eyes were only a liquid gleam. She said his name uncertainly and only when he answered did she step back to let him in.

"I didn't think you'd come."

"I'm still on leave." A fatuous thing to say, but it was all he could think of.

She led him into her room where, hidden by blinds, oil lamps added to the heat. The bare space was stifling, as if crowded by the invisible. On her bed, the blue shawl she used as a coverlet showed the wrinkles where she had lain.

"It's past curfew," she said. "And . . ." She stood with her elbows cupped in her palms, barefoot, her yellow cotton dress catching the light behind it. Graham went to her, put his arms about her, leaned his face against her hair. She smelled of tea leaves and cloves.

"Of course you've heard," he said.

"Heard."

"About the colonel? Tibbit-Noyse's suicide?"

She drew in a staggered breath and pulled her arms from between them. "Yes." She returned his embrace, tipped her head to put her cheek against his.

He pulled her tighter, slight and strong with bone, and some pent emotion began to shake its way out of his body. As if to calm him, she kissed his neck, his mouth, her body alive against his. He could not discern if she also shook, or was only shaken by his tension. They stripped each other, clumsy, quick to reach the point of skin on skin. She began to kneel but he caught her arms and lifted her to the bed.

He came closer than he ever had to ending it. Weighing her down, hard against the welling heat between her thighs, he wanted, he ached, he raged with some fury that was not anger nor lust but some need, some absence without a name. Hard between her thighs. Hands tight against her face. Eyes on hers bright with oil flames. No, she said, and he was shaking again with the convulsive shudders of a fever; he'd seen malaria and thought this was some illness as well, some disease of heat and anguish and war, and she said "No!" and scratched his face.

⚜

He rolled onto his back and hardly had he moved but she was off the bed. Arms across his face, he heard her harsh breathing retreat across the room. The bathroom door slammed. Opened.

"Do you know about Tibbit-Noyse?"

Her voice shook. An answer to that uncertainty, at least.

"Know what?" he asked.

Her breathing was quieter, now.

"Know what?"

"That I have been ordered," she answered at last, "to resurrect him in the morning."

He did not move.

The bathroom door closed.

She had broken his skin. The small wound stung with sweat, or maybe it was tears, there beside his eye.

⚜

When she stayed in the bathroom, and stayed, and stayed, he finally understood. He rose and dressed, and walked out into the curfew darkness where, apparently, he belonged.

⚜

Next morning, Graham ran up the stairs to Healy's office and collided with the major outside his door.

"Graham!" Major Healy exclaimed. "What the devil are you doing here? Don't tell me. I'm already late." He pushed past and started down the hall.

Graham stretched to catch up. "I know. They're bringing the colonel back."

Healy strode another step, two, then stopped. Graham stopped as well, so the two of them stood eye to eye in the corridor. Men in uniform brushed by on their own affairs. Healy said in a furious undertone, "How the hell do you know about that?"

"I want to be there."

"Impossible." The major started to turn.

Graham grabbed his arm. "Morale's already dangerously low. How do you think the troops would react if they knew their superiors were bringing back their own dead?"

Healy's eyes widened. "Are you blackmailing your superior officer? You could be shot!"

"Sir. David. Please." Graham took his hand off the other's arm.

Healy seemed to wilt. "It's nothing you ever want to see, John. Will you believe me? It's nothing you ever want to see."

"Neither is all your men being shot dead and eaten by vultures while you lie there and do *nothing*."

Healy shut his eyes. "I don't know. You may be right." He coughed and started for the stairs. "You may be right."

Taking that for permission, Graham followed him down.

The company's staging area was a weird patch of quiet amidst the scramble of other units that had to equip and sustain their troops in the field. Trucks, jeeps, men raced over-laden on crumbling streets, spewing exhaust and profanity as they went. By the nature of their missions, reconnaissance squads were on their own once deployed, and this was never truer than for Special Recon. No one wanted to involve themselves with the Dead Squad in the field. The nickname, Graham thought, was an irony no one was likely to pronounce aloud today.

He and Major Healy had driven to the staging area alone, late, as Healy had mentioned, but when they arrived they found only one staff car parked outside the necromancer's workshop. The general in charge of Intel was inside with two men from his staff. When Healy parked his jeep next to the car, the three men got out, leaving the general's driver to slouch smoking behind the wheel. They formed a group in the square of rutted tarmac, prefabricated wooden walls, empty windows, blinding tin roofs. The compound stank of petrol fumes, hot tar, and an inadequate latrine.

The general, a short bulky man in a uniform limp with sweat, returned Graham's and Healy's salutes without enthusiasm. He didn't remark on Graham's presence. Graham supposed that Healy, as Special Recon's acting CO, was entitled to an aide.

The general checked his watch. "It's past time."

"Sorry, sir," Healy said. "We were detained at HQ."

The general grunted. He had cold pebble eyes in pouchy lids. "Any news of your men in the field?"

"No, sir. But I wouldn't expect to hear this early. None of the squads will have reached the line yet."

The general grunted again, and though his face bore no expression, Graham realized he was reluctant to go in. His aides had the stiff faces and wide eyes of men about to go into battle. Healy looked tired and somewhat sick. Graham felt a twinge of adrenaline in his gut, his breath came a little short. The general gave a curt nod and headed for the necromancer's door.

Inside her workshop, the walls and the underside of the tin roof were clothed in woven reed mats. Even the windows were covered: The room was brilliantly and hotly lit by a klieg lamp in one corner. An electric fan whirred in another, stirring up a breeze that played among the mats, so that the long room was restless with motion, as if the pale brown mats were tent walls. This, the heat, the unmasked stink of decay, all recalled a dozen missions to Graham's mind. His gut clenched again and sweat sprang cool upon his skin. There was no sign of her, or of Tibbit-Noyse. An inner door stood slightly ajar.

The general cleared his throat once, and then again, as if he meant to call out, but he held his silence. Eventually, the other door swung further open and the girl put her head through.

Graham felt the shock when her eyes touched him. But she was in some distant place, her eyelids heavy, her face open and serene. He knew she knew him, but by her response his was only one face among five.

She said, "I'm ready to begin."

The General nodded. "Proceed."

"You know I have lodged a protest with the Sisterhood?"

The general's face clenched like a fist. "Proceed."

She stepped out of sight, leaving the door open, and in a moment she wheeled a hospital gurney into the room, handling the awkward thing with practiced ease. Tibbit-Noyse's corpse lay on its back, naked to the lamp's white glare. The heavy caliber bullet had made a ruin of the left side of his face and head. A ragged hole gaped from the outer corner of his eye to behind his temple. The cheekbone, cracked askew, whitely defined the lower margin of the wound. The whole of his face was distorted, the left eye open wide and strangely discolored, while the right eye showed only a white crescent. Shrinking lips parted to show teeth and a gray hint of tongue beneath the crisp mustache. The body was the color of paste and, bar an old appendectomy scar, otherwise intact.

The hole in Tibbit-Noyse's skull was open onto darkness. Graham remembered the Intel captain saying the man's brains had been scattered across his desk. But death was nothing new to him, and he realized he was examining the corpse so he did not have to look at the girl.

She wore a prosaic bathrobe of worn blue velvet, tightly belted at her waist. Her dark hair was pinned at the base of her neck. Her feet, on the stained cement floor, were bare. She set the brakes on the gurney's wheels with her toes, and then stood at the corpse's head, studying it, arms folded with her elbows cupped in her palms, mouth a little pursed.

An expression he knew, a face he knew so well. Another wave of sweat washed over him. He wished he had not come.

The fan stirred the walls. The lamp glared. Trucks on the street behind the compound roared intermittently by.

The girl—the witch—nodded to herself and went back into the other room, but reappeared almost at once, naked, bearing a tray heavy with the tools of her craft. She set this down on the floor at her feet, selected a small, hooked knife, and then glanced at the men by the door.

"You might pray," she said softly. "It sometimes helps."

Helps the watchers, Graham understood her to mean. He knew she needed none.

Her nakedness spurred a rush of heat in his body, helpless response to long conditioning, counter tide to the cold sweep of horror. Blood started to sing in his ears.

She took up her knife and began.

There is no kindness between the living and the dead.

Graham had sat through the orientation lecture, he knew the theory, at least the simplified version appropriate for the uninitiated. To lay the foundation for the false link between body and departed spirit the witch must claim the flesh. She must posses the dead clay, she must absorb it into her sphere of power, and so she must know it, know it utterly.

The ritual was autopsy. Was intercourse. Was feast.

Not literally, not quite. But her excavation of the corpse was intimate and brutal, a physical, a sensual, a savage act. As she explored Tibbit-Noyse's face, his hands, his genitals, his skin, Graham followed her on a tour of the lust they had known together, he and she, the loving that they had enacted in the privacy of her room and that was now laid bare. As the dead man's secret tissues were stripped naked, so was Graham exposed. He rode waves of disgust, of desire, of sheer scorching humiliation, as if she fucked another man on the street, only this was worse, unimaginably worse, steeped as it was in the liquors of rot.

He also only stood, his shoulder by Healy's, his back to the rough matted wall, and said nothing, did nothing, showed, he thought, nothing . . . and watched.

When Tibbit-Noyse was open, when he was pierced and wired and riddled with her tools and charms, when there was no part of the man she had not seen and touched and claimed—when the fan stirred not air but a swampy vapor of shit and bile and decay—when she was slick with sweat and the clotting moistures of death, then she began the call.

She had a beautiful voice. Graham realized she had never sung for him, had not even hummed in the bath as she washed her hair. The men watching could see her throat swell as she drew in air, the muscles in her belly work as she sustained the long pure notes of the chant. The words were meaningless. The song was all.

⚜

When Tibbit-Noyse answered, it was with the voice of a child who weeps in the dark, alone.

⚜

The witch stepped back from the gurney, hands hanging at her sides, her face drawn with weariness but still serene.

"Ask," she said. "He will answer."

The general jerked his head, a marionette's parody of his usual brisk nod, and moved a step forward. He took a breath and then covered his mouth to catch a cough, the kind of cough that announces severe nausea. Carefully, he swallowed, and said, "Alfred Reginald Tibbit-Noyse. Do you hear me?"

A pause. "Y-ye-yes."

"Did you betray your country in a time of war?"

A pause. "Yes."

Graham could see the dead grayish lungs work inside the ribcage, the grayish tongue inside the mouth.

"How did you betray your country?"

A pause. "I sent my men." Pause. "To steal the dead." Pause. "Behind enemy lines."

The general sagged back on his heels. "That is a lie. Those men were sent out on my orders. How did you betray your country?"

A pause. "I sent my men." Pause. "To die." There was no emotion in the childish voice. It added calmly, "They were their mothers' sons."

"How did you know they were going to die?"

". . . How could they." Pause. "Not be doomed."

"Did you send them into a trap?"

". . . No."

"Did you betray their movements to the enemy?"

". . . No."

"Then why did you kill yourself?" Against the dead man's calm, the general's frustration was strident.

". . . I thought this war." Pause. "Would swallow us all." Pause. "I see now I was wrong."

Healy raised a hand to his eyes and whispered a curse. The general's shoulders bunched.

"Did you betray military secrets to the enemy?"

". . . No."

"Who did you betray military secrets to?"

". . . No one."

"Don't you lie to me!" the general bellowed at the riddled corpse.

"He cannot lie," the witch told him. Her voice was quietly reproachful. "He is dead."

". . . I do not lie."

The general, heeding neither the live women nor the dead man, continued to rap out questions. Graham could bear no more. He brushed past Healy to slip through the door. In the clean hot light of noon he vomited spit and bile, and sank down to sit with his back against the wall. After a minute, the general's driver climbed out of the staff car and offered him the last cigarette from a crumpled pack.

⁂

The battle became a part of history. The tide of the enemy's forces was turned before it swamped the city; a new front-line was drawn. The scattered squads of the Special Desert Reconnaissance Group returned in good time, missing no more men than most units who had fought in the desert sands, and carrying their bounty of enemy dead. Graham was given a medal for bravery on a recommendation by the late Colonel Tibbit-Noyse, and a new command: twelve recruits from other units, men with stomachs already toughened by war. He led them out on a routine mission, by a stroke of luck found and recovered the withered husk of a major whose insignia promised useful intelligence, and on the morning of the scheduled resurrection, the second morning of his four-day leave, he went to the hotel bar where he had learned of Tibbit-Noyse's death and ordered a shot of whiskey and a beer.

He drank them, and several others like them, but the heat pressed the alcohol from his tissues before it could stupefy his mind. He gave up, paid his tab, and left. By this time the sunlight had thickened to the sticky amber of late afternoon. The ubiquitous flies made the only movement on the street. Graham settled his peaked cap on his head and blinked to accustom his eyes to the light, and when he looked again she was there.

She wore the yellow cotton dress. Her clean hair was soft about her face. Her eyes were wounded.

She said his name.

"Hello," he said after an awkward minute. "How are you?"

"My superiors have sent an official protest to the War Office."

"A protest?"

She looked down. "Because of the colonel's resurrection. It has made things . . . a little more difficult than usual."

"I'm sorry to hear that."

"You have not—" She broke off, then raised her eyes to his. "You have not come to see me."

"I'm sorry." The alcohol seemed to be having a delayed effect on him now. The street teetered sluggishly beneath his feet. His throat closed on a bubble of air.

"It was hard," she said. "It was the hardest I've ever had to do."

His voice came out a whisper: "I know."

Her dark eyes grew darker, and then there were tears on her face. "Please, John, I don't want to do this anymore. I don't think I can do this anymore. Please, help me, help me break free."

She reached for him, and he knew what she meant. He remembered their nights together, his body remembered to the roots of his hair the night he almost took her completely. He also remembered the scratch her nails left by his eye, and more than anything, he remembered her gruesome infidelity with Tibbit-Noyse—with all the other dead men—and he flinched away.

She froze, still reaching.

"I'm sorry," he said.

She drew her arms across her, clasped her elbows in her palms. "I understand."

He opened his mouth, then realized he had nothing more to say. He touched his cap and walked away. The street was uneasy beneath his feet, the sun a furnace burn against his face, and he was blind with the image he carried with him, the look of relief that had flickered in the virgin's eyes.

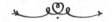

CATCHING ON
Kyle Richardson

Ten minutes into our dinner, Hailey tells me, "We have to destroy it." She plants her hands beside her plate and leans over the table, slow and steady, like a lioness moving in for the kill. "We've got to blow it sky-high," she whispers. "Straight out of existence."

I'm not sure if she means the impending bill or the entire restaurant itself. Judging by the urgency in her voice, I'm guessing both. But I'm busy chewing a greasy lump of fat, so I take my time replying. "I know your steak's a bit rare and all," I mumble, "but we can't just go around stomping buildings into dust whenever we're upset."

My words sputter out muffled, wet, and reeking of basil leaves. Hailey scrunches her nose. "I'm not talking about the food, Ossen."

Of course she's not. Hailey never concerns herself with such rudimentary things. She's always too wrapped up in some quantum state, her attention divided between the *Now* and the *Yet To Be*. This gives her violet irises a perpetual blur, like they've been dipped in smooth acrylic. It's the same way the glass eyes on a stuffed animal look—shiny; dead; eternally focused on some vague spot off in the distance—only hers are in a fog. Somehow, I manage to gulp down the wad of gristle. "Yeah, well, *someone* in this dive should talk about the food," I say, glancing around. "This corned beef is atrocious."

The restaurant we're in looks like the bastard child of some retro diner and a medieval library. Oak tables lined with checkerboard cloths. A hot pink linoleum floor. Dark walls punctuated by rustic torches, their oil-dipped wicks unlit and dripping. The lighting's random and chaotic, throwing shadows in all directions. Music warbles from a jukebox nobody can find. There's a lag, a brief moment of silence filled with the clinking of heavy dishes, then some Celtic pop song revs up, stuffing the air with noise all over again.

Everything feels busier than it really is—probably to distract customers from the messes on their plates. Not exactly the ideal dining getaway I was hoping for. "I'm sorry about this place," I say, crumpling my napkin into a ball. "I expected better."

Hailey slumps back in her seat and mutters, "It's all the same anyway." The candle on our table flickers and the glow highlights her lips. For a split second, they glitter. Then she sighs and her frown returns, thin and dull as always. "And stop apologizing," she says. "You know I hate that."

There are a lot of things Hailey hates. Sunsets. High fashion. Unrequited love. An ever-growing list. These days, it's hard to remember half of it. "Right," I say, clearing my throat. "Sorry."

She raises an eyebrow. "The cube, Ossen. I'm talking about the cube."

These past few months have been hectic, to say the least. Twenty-seven new villains captured. Thirteen repeat offenders locked away. Nine supernatural devices found—six of them cubes. Four with the potential to be Earth-threatening. Dragging my sleeve across my mouth, I mumble, "Which one?"

Hailey rolls her eyes, like she's had this conversation a thousand times before. "The accelerator," she says. "The one you're going to help me destroy? We've been over this already."

The accelerator. Just the mention of it sends a shiver up my spine. The new particle cannon, built by Falory Industries, designed to blast an ordinary human to the end of the temporal spectrum. Man's attempt at unzipping the fabric of time with a giant, gleaming gun. "No," I say, leaning back in my chair, "I'm pretty sure we haven't had this conversation yet."

Hailey's shoulders slump. She looks tired, worn out, like a mannequin left in the sun so long it's started to melt. "Well, whatever," she says. "We're having it now." She places her slender hand on mine and says, "You'll help me, right?" Her glossy eyes lock on.

My cheeks flush and my gut twists, just a bit. Cloudy eyes, porcelain skin, the face of a black-and-white Hollywood starlet—looking at Hailey is like looking at a beautiful corpse. My body never knows how to react. "I don't know," I mumble. I clear my throat and look away.

Hailey squeezes my hand, undeterred. "You know I can't break in without you."

This is true enough. Potent as her abilities are, Hailey remains a *Class 1* only, her powers limited to the realm of perception. I, on the other hand, have been blessed (or cursed, depending on how you look at it) with a dual rating: *Class 1* and *2*. None of us had any ratings until three months ago, when the United Nations mandated that all Exceptions carry class-identification cards.

Now, whenever I open my wallet, the mugshot of my scruffy face scowls back at me. The plastic itself is government-issued topaz blue. On the back of the card, the explanation of my abilities reads like a cheap instruction manual:

CLASS 1: Perceptual; Exception possesses enhanced sensory functions
CLASS 2: Physical; Exception possesses enhanced physical functions

Dry grammar. Bland description. Not a shred of flair for the dramatic. What it *should* say is that I can sense the energy left behind whenever someone uses their powers. Like a supernatural bloodhound. Plus, I've got enough juice to punch through a concrete wall if I have to. Granted, I'm no Steve Strong, but I'm guessing, based on how hard Hailey's squeezing my hand right now, that what I can do is enough. "Let me get this straight," I say, nodding at the waitress. "You want to launch a two-person assault on Falory Industries." I pause, gauging Hailey's reaction, but she doesn't even blink. "You *do* realize the level of security that place has, right?"

Hailey leans forward, her auburn bangs sweeping over her forehead. "I can see the damn future, Oss. Every microsecond, every divergence, every temporal possibility from here to infinity. I know what we're getting into better than anyone." She straightens up, brushes her hair away from her eyes, and looks away. "Besides," she mutters, "I know a way out when I see one."

For a brief moment, my stomach flutters. Either the food here really is as bad as it tastes, or something about all of this isn't adding up. "What's really going on here?" I ask.

But Hailey just slides out of her seat and stands, her lithe figure draped in that signature red cape of hers. "I'll meet you in the Falory parking lot," she says, "two hours from now." Then she's gone—moving across the diner the way a ghost might, drifting along the path of least resistance, slipping past tables and between patrons like a crimson gust of wind, unnoticed. When she's nearly out of sight, our waitress saunters over—a freckle-faced blonde in a baggy uniform. She starts clearing the table without acknowledging me.

Everything about tonight has me feeling like an afterthought, an insignificant ripple in Hailey's grand design. A flaw to be corrected. Have I really become this dispensable? "But you didn't even hear my answer!" I call out.

Hailey turns, her smooth profile draped in shadow, and replies, "I did." Her lips pull down in a miniature frown. "Four minutes from now." She places a delicate hand on the front door and says, "You tell me, 'Fine. But after this, no more.'" She shoves through the door and steps out into the storm, the rain bristling against her hood. "I just don't feel like waiting around to hear it."

Before I have a chance to respond, the door thuds shut.

⁓§§⁓

The storm has passed by the time I show up at the Falory parking lot. I can see the supercell on the horizon, a dark tube of clouds flickering like an eel. The pavement around my motorcycle gleams, flecked with shallow puddles. They catch the street lamps like windows to another world.

I stomp on one just to see it splash out.

Hailey arrives a few minutes later, her cape flowing in the wind. She nods at me like we're strangers passing on a sidewalk. "You came early." She narrows her eyes. "I told you two hours."

We've never been in a relationship. At least, not an intimate one. But something about our dynamic lately has emboldened Hailey. She doesn't just talk to me anymore—she *scolds* me, like a disgruntled romantic partner. All the squabbling without the sex. The damn opposite of friends with benefits. "I came right on the dot," I say, dismounting my bike. "*You're* the one who's slipping." I yank my helmet off and prop it on the handle. "Imagine that. *Mistress Time* herself."

Hailey's face crumples, her eyebrows lowering, her bottom lip jutting out. She turns and studies the outline of the factory, its neon edges cutting into the black sky. "I had things on my mind."

Running through all the possible outcomes, I'm sure. One thing about Hailey: her vision only extends as far as she wants it to. That means only glimpsing future lines that intersect with her own. My future, as far as she's concerned, must be nothing but a blank slate—no way to tell how her actions will affect me. No way to tell, because—let's be honest—she obviously doesn't care enough about me to look. "I've been thinking a lot, too," I say. I shrug off my leather jacket and drape it over the handlebars. "And I've decided this is a bad idea." I meet her cold stare and tell her, "We should abort."

Hailey blinks and takes a deep breath. A calculated pause. "The particle cannon," she begins, "will have its first trial run at the end of August." She rests her hands on her hips and says, "Two months from now. The detonation will kill one maintenance worker and injure two lab assistants. But the test will be successful." Her shoulders sag, just a little, like she's given this speech one too many times. "Seventeen seconds later, a pocket of space-time collapses. The edge of our dimension crashes into another." She closes her eyes and says, "The flux kills millions before they pull the plug." Before I can respond, she turns and sprints toward the electric fence. With a leap, she somersaults over it, the end of her cape sparking as it clears the top wire. She lands in a crouch on the other side, her boots glistening on the pavement. Keeping her back to me, she says, "I'm not going to let that happen. Are you?"

How do you argue with someone who's got a bird's-eye view all the way to eternity? I stomp to the fence and grip the metal links. The high voltage current sizzles against my palms. Over the noise I shout, "Okay, it's bad news. I get that. But we've got time! We should call this off. Plan it out. Rushing in tonight is just asking for trouble!" I wait for a response that doesn't come, then yell, "Did you hear what I said?"

Hailey exhales and removes her hood. "I did," she says, her words barely audible. She shakes her hair out and turns to face me, her red-brown curls glinting in the light of the sparks. "And everything you're going to say."

This is the problem with visionaries. They all think they know everything. And they do. "So there's nothing I can say to change your mind," I mumble.

Hailey smiles, her lips pulling up at the corners, her cheeks bunching around her nose. But her eyes look more distant than usual. Sad, even. "Now you're catching on."

I've never been a believer in fate. I like to think I'm in control, that my life hasn't been plotted out ahead of time. Sometimes all it takes is one wild thought, one brave decision to change everything. This must be one of those times. "Then I'm just going to leave," I say. To drive the point home, I let go of the fence.

The sparks clear and the roar sucks away, echoing down the street. Hailey's sad smile is swallowed up by the darkness, but her voice rings out, loud and unfazed. "All my life," she says, "I've watched people die. Ever since I can remember." The gravel crunches under her boots. "Every time I close my eyes, there they are: Young men. Old men. Women. Children. All of them dying. All of them in pain." She clears her throat and adds, "You know what *time* really is, Oss? It's an endless stream of death. An infinite line of heartache and suffering."

Whatever the right thing is to say here, I sure as hell can't think of it. So I ask her a question instead. "What about all the good stuff in between?"

Hailey's laugh flutters through the darkness, weak and off-key. "Tell you what: when this is over," she says, "you can tell me all about the 'good stuff.' But right now, I've got people to save. You do what you want." Then she's gone, her boots clapping against the wet asphalt.

This is where I should hightail it out of here. Climb on my bike. Twist the ignition. Peel off down the street to find Hailey waiting for me at the intersection, her moonlit face tight with angst. But something pinches inside me—some soft spot in my chest cavity—and it hits me: Hailey's the one person—the *only* person—I care about in this world. And there's no way in hell I'm letting her fight this on her own. "Damn it," I mutter. I grab the fence and wrench the crackling links apart. Blue veins of electricity arc around me, searing holes in my *Hendrix Experience* T-shirt. "Hailey!" I hiss. I stumble through the gap. "Wait!"

⁘

Hailey disarms the first mechanical guard easily enough, slipping behind it and snapping its spine before it's even aware of the breach. The next two guards come in charging, their photon rifles clattering, the muzzles flashing like tiny starbursts. Hailey dodges the bullets like she's dancing a slow-motion ballet, predicting the path of each projectile before it's even fired.

Me, I'm not one for dancing. I'm also not equipped to deflect bullets—photon or otherwise. The only thing I've got going for me is brute strength. So I pick up the motionless guard and fling its metal body like a Frisbee.

It connects with the other two guards, driving them back in a scraping mass all the way to the thrashing electric fence. The whole section explodes when they hit it, like a fireworks display gone wrong.

Someone—or some*thing*—trips an alarm and the whole structure flushes red. The siren whoops so loud it's like someone's jammed a seagull into my skull. Hailey grabs my shoulder and points to the nearest building, where a wall of metal stands, gleaming and defiant. "The door!" she shouts. "Come on!"

I want to leave. I want this to be over. But most of all, I want Hailey to be proud of me. So I brush past her, my muscles flaring under my smoking shirt, and I drive my fist into ten inches of solid steel. The impact makes the bones in my wrist sing. Sweat slithers down the small of my back. Flecks of blood spray off my knuckles. But Hailey's counting on me, damn it, so I keep swinging.

The concussions sound like I'm thudding a giant gong, a tribal war drum, the dinner bell for King Kong. The sound vibrates the entire city block. Hailey winces and plugs her fingers in her ears.

Somewhere behind us, more animatronic guards are swarming, their robotic voices buzzing and chirping, their metal feet clanking against the asphalt. The sound is . . . ominous, to say the least. Like the rumble of distant thunder. Like an angry swarm of bees returning to the hive. Hell, let's just call it like it is: Hailey and I, we're running out of time. "Come on," I pant. My arms pump like pistons. My heart crashes against my ribs. "Come on!"

It takes a few more hits for the door to finally come loose. One last right hook and it crashes down like an imploded bank vault. I go down with it, onto my hands and knees.

I haven't been this worn down since my last sparring match with Steve. My forearms are on fire. My lungs feel ready to burst. My knuckles glint in the patchy moonlight, the tendons raw and wet. If there's another steel door to smash through, there better be a wrecking ball lying around somewhere, because I sure as hell can't do it. In fact, I end up doing the only thing I *can* do: I collapse, face first, onto the cracked cement. And God, does it feel good. "In," I gasp. "You're welcome."

Hailey bounds over me with the corners of her cape flapping like wings. She waves her hands in front of her face, swatting at the dust. Then her eyes go wide. "There!" she yells. She jabs a pale finger toward the back left corner of the bay. "The wooden crate!" She looks down at me, her cool eyes blazing. "Ossen! You have to destroy it! *Now!*"

I'd rather sleep, to be honest. Slip into some fancy, Technicolored dream, one of those fantasy worlds where I'm being grape-fed by topless women. But when

Hailey tells you to do something, you do it. Chances are, the fate of the world depends on it. So I struggle to my feet and stagger across the room, blood dripping from my hands. Somehow, I find the strength to lurch into a jog. Through my clenched teeth I mutter, "Here goes nothing," and I pinch my eyes shut.

Like a bull, I plow through the crate, obliterating whatever's inside in a miniature supernova. The explosion hurls me, end over end, into a concrete support beam. Shards of metal spray around me, whizzing past my ears. The whole building groans and shudders. I collapse onto my back, my torso exposed where my clothes have torn off and burned away.

I've never broken a bone in my life. Not as far as I know. Right now, it feels like I've broken all of them. I moan and tilt my head back, looking for Hailey. "Did we get it?" I whisper. "Is it over?"

Hailey stands on the dented vault door, her limp cape swaying, her face plastered with soot. Dust particles and smoke twirl in the air around her. She nods at me, her eyes red-rimmed and wet. "You did it, Oss," she says. "You did it."

Then a bullet rips through her throat.

⚹⚮⚹

What happens next is a blur. One moment Hailey's dropping to her knees, her face contorted in pain, the next I'm on my feet, barreling into an army of metal guards at hurricane speed.

Bullets snag on my flesh. Electricity jolts my bones. But I am *rage* personified. I am the definition of the word *unstoppable*. Bodies spark as I rip limbs from torsos. Oils gush as I tear heads from necks. Weapons plume to powder in my grip. I ravage everything within an arm's reach until there's nothing around me but a dull, throbbing silence.

Silence . . . and Hailey.

When I get to her, she's arching her back on the cement, blood pumping from the wound in her throat. Her eyes are the widest I've ever seen. Her mouth is flexed in a silent, *Oh*. She thrashes out at me, gripping my arms, her fingernails digging into my skin.

This isn't supposed to happen. Not to Hailey. Not to the girl who knows everything. "Hang on," I stammer. I pick her up, making sure to cradle her head. "I got you." I start running, stumbling, tripping over broken bots and debris, but I can't see where I'm going. There's too much smoke. Too much oil and crap running off my forehead into my eyes. "Stay with me!"

Hailey whimpers, a dog-like cry of anguish, and her trembling hand finds the back of my head. She grips my hair.

Hailey's the only friend I've ever had, and I am losing her. I am failing her in her time of need. I keep my legs driving, uselessly, one foot in front of the other, through the rubble and crunchy bits of plastic. "Almost there," I gasp. My throat constricts, strangling my words. My eyes burn. "Just a little longer!"

I step on something round—a stray wheel, or maybe a robot skull—and the next thing I know I'm falling backward, looking up at a starless night sky. It's here that I'm struck by a lone epiphany: I love her. I love Hailey Watts. I'm more sure of this than I've been about anything in my life. Then a second thought streaks across my brain, like a meteor scraping the sky: *Tell her!*

This much I can do.

I take a deep breath and squeeze out the words. "Hailey, I—"

But we crash backward into a heap of bricks, and the words are knocked right out of me. In their place, I'm left with a searing hole. A collapsed lung, maybe. Or perhaps a broken heart. Hailey coughs from the impact, her blood splattering my face, and it becomes all too obvious: we can't go any further. Not like this. Everything inside me's begun to shut down. My limbs feel shackled to the ground. My head weighs a metric ton. My confession will have to wait. Right now, saving her is all that matters. "The bike," I sputter. "You can make it." I gag on something wet and force it back down. "Follow the river," I gasp. "Find your way out."

Hailey twists in my arms, her slender body smooth and feathery inside her cape, and she wheezes, "I just . . . did." Then her mouth finds mine. The kiss is soft, gentle. Lingering. Her lower lip trembles. Her cheeks tighten. Her eyes squeeze shut. Then her body sags, her lips release me, and her warm breath slides across my face before disappearing into the night.

Her head lands on my chest with her eyes half-open, her milky gaze fixed on me.

For a moment I just lie there, looking into her distant stare. Then something erupts inside me. A crate-sized bomb. A seismic blast. A cosmic fucking supernova. "No," I whisper. I grasp at her cape with my numb fingers, but the damn fabric keeps slipping away. "Hailey?" I clutch at her shoulders with my fractured hands, but I can't keep a grip on them either. "Hailey!" I watch, helplessly, as her irises clear, like clouds melting into an afternoon sky. And for the first time in my life, I realize Hailey's eyes aren't violet—they're blue.

It's been a month since the Falory incident. A month since I lost Hailey. A week since I stopped crying.

The headlines say the company's rebuilding, that they've already got a replacement prototype in the works.

I'll be sure to destroy that one, too.

For now, I spend my days back at the restaurant, my dirt-stained boots tapping against the pink linoleum. Every night I order corned beef, for myself, and a bloody steak, for Hailey. The freckle-faced waitress looked puzzled at first. Now she has it ready for me as soon as I step in.

"I get it," I say, my words slipping over the oily wad in my mouth. "I understand why you did it." I gulp down the gristle and say, "That was your way out."

Thin wisps of steam curl off Hailey's untouched steak. Beads of condensation roll down the side of her full glass.

I can sense her energy signature: thin tendrils of radiation curling around our booth. Like a ghost. It's a sign that, somewhere in the past, Hailey saw this conversation, right now. A sign that she glimpsed this future line. A sign that she cared enough to look. "I know you're listening," I say, wiping my mouth with my sleeve.

Someone flicks on the hidden jukebox and the air swells with some new-age rock song, the punchy bass vibrating the knife on my plate.

I can't change the past. I don't have that ability. I'm only a *Class 1* and *2*. But if I can change Hailey's mind, maybe I can save her. Maybe I can show her that life, even when you know all the outcomes, is still worth living. "You want to talk about the 'good stuff' worth sticking around for?" My voice tightens. "How about love, for one thing?" I look right at the shimmering plume of air beside me. "Damn it, Hailey. How about *me*?"

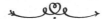

METEMPSYCHOTIC
Leah Brown

Meg hated how typical it was, the same old story that's been told a few hundred times before. Dave was the cute boy in the back of the classroom, the one always wearing the band T-shirts. The one who self-labeled as the class clown, a quip for everything. The one who seemed incapable of irritating the teachers, no matter how much he interrupted.

Dave left his back-of-the-class lair and sat behind her, drumming a pencil on her shoulder with a nervous twitch as he asked her to a concert. The rhythm that never really stopped through the entirety of their date. And this thing had all the markers of a date, the way that he insisted on paying for her, asked her opinion of everything and actually listened to what she had to say.

Away from class and school and the fishbowl of it all, Dave was sort of fantastic, sort of quiet, sort of brooding in a way that made it obvious that his quick humor was seated in actual intellect.

"You know, tonight was pretty fun," he said when he dropped her off at home, his arm landing across the back of the passenger seat, still cross-hatched from the wand of a vacuum, his hand drumming: *Click-click-thump. Click-click-thump.*

He had removed the headrests on the front seats, like he was planning to talk to a camera crew in the back, and Meg found herself liking it. She liked that he was the same, but different, like looking at the surface of a swimming pool from underwater rather than just dangling her feet in the water.

Being Dave's entire audience was different and preferable to being the only one in the front of the class room not laughing.

"It wasn't bad."

"Come on, Maggie, it was better than 'not bad.' I haven't seen a show like that since . . . well, ever probably. But it might just be my exceptional company." He smiled at her, a wide, toothy grin with teeth that weren't quite straight. Like he'd had braces but never bothered to follow up with his retainer.

"Where is this 'Maggie' coming from? For all you know my birth certificate could say Meg. You could be giving me the opposite of a nickname." She reminded him just because she could, because no matter how shy and generally quiet she was in everyday life, this seemed like the moment to stand up for herself. He seemed like the one to stand up to.

"You're a hard audience, a real tough crowd."

"You talk like a C-list comedian from the seventies." She threw the insult before really thinking about it, glancing towards the front door of her parents' house, the dim yellow light glowing on the stoop.

"Do you like C-list comedians from the seventies, because I'm open to women who only want to date me for my turn of phrase?"

"Do you ever stop trying so hard?" She laughed and looked around his car, the Pine Sol smelling backseat with the neatly folded sweatshirt, nearly unrecognizable from the identical big, wrinkled hoodie on his back.

"Not yet."

⚘

"Do you think it'll be ugly?"

"No, I don't think my baby will be ugly," Meg smoothes a hand over her rounding stomach, folding laundry near the head of the bed. The boy sitting on the foot of the bed narrows his eyes at her, jiggling his feet in a familiar, silent rhythm.

"If it looks like *him* it will."

"By *him* do you mean my husband?"

"Yeah, that asshole." He shakes his head and looks at his hands, still wearing that same blue sweatshirt.

"Do you have to be so crass?"

"Ooh, *crass*, breaking out your big words there, Maggie."

"It's not Maggie anymore, it's Meg. Meg Arnold." She folds one of her husband's shirts, stroking the soft stretched shoulder seam fondly. "Margaret to you."

"I'm never going to call you Margaret. That makes you sound like my grandma." He laughs and turns halfway toward her, unzipped hoodie falling open to reveal that band T-shirt he'd bought on their first date. That band they both loved in high school.

"You know I turned twenty-eight last week, right?"

"I'm more concerned about your thirty-billion-year-old husband."

"He's thirty-two and—and I don't have to defend myself to you, David." The next shirt gets folded angrily and thrown on the stack.

"Oh, so I'm 'David' now. 'David and Margaret', it's like Dave and Maggie grew up and got boring, just like you always wanted."

"No. We didn't."

⚬—⚬

He succeeded when he asked for a second date, for some reason, and a third, for a whole lot of reasons. By Christmas it was comfortable, happy, and Meg stopped complaining that Dave bought her coffee without asking. She stopped being embarrassed when he dropped by her parents' house without warning.

None of that stopped her from being furious when he heard back from her top choice college, early acceptance.

"I just can't believe it never came up in conversation. 'Hey Meg, we're going to the same college next year—'"

"It's not set in stone, and it's a big school. It's not like we're the only two people who applied; we aren't even the only two people in our class to apply." That easy smile slipped back onto his face, eyes wide and brown, sparkling like he was trying to slide something past her.

She huffed, "I still don't understand why you wouldn't tell me."

"Because I knew you'd get like this—"

"Like what?" She rolled her eyes, "I wouldn't be thrilled about you following me halfway across the country? I wouldn't thank you for ignoring any independence I might have wanted to preserve?"

He shook his head, paler than usual, winter-faded freckles translucent across the bridge of his nose. He was smaller when he didn't have a crowd, smaller within the confines of her bedroom, and for a millisecond she could see him in her dorm room, charming her roommate with that easy, crowd-pleasing humor. In freshman classes with her, taking diligent notes when no one was looking.

"I'm not taking your independence, I'm considering the same *massive* college as you. Twenty thousand people, you wouldn't even have to see me if you didn't want to. You'd have to search me out—"

"Like hell—"

"We'd be in completely different departments, completely opposite sides of human knowledge." He slapped her desk with the flat of his palm, audible punctuation.

"Right. Dr. Dave." She meant it as an insult; it was hilarious to think of him in a doctor's coat, fiddling with a blood pressure cuff like he didn't understand it, the same damn joke with every patient. Hugging little kids and promising them that needles don't hurt.

"You don't have to be like this. I'm waiting on other schools, your independence still has a chance."

"I don't—I'm sorry," she sighed and slumped down onto the edge of the bed, head in her hands. An action that she used to make fun of when her mother did it, but now it just felt natural. "Everything is just . . . I don't want to marry my college sweetheart and settle down in suburbia and send my two point three children to public school."

"What does this have to do with me being a doctor?"

"Everything." She felt suddenly stupid, a reluctant smile tugging at the corner of her lips. "Don't you know every girl is supposed to want to marry a doctor?"

"Careful, I'm rubbing off on you," he grinned. "You're the one talking in clichés now."

"Never."

"You're going to be a MILF, Maggie." Dave bounces drumsticks off of the corner of the desk silently, and her brain fills in the signature *click-click-thump*.

Meg almost yells at him, almost tells him he's going to bang up her furniture, but that's only giving him the attention he wants, the attention he's always wanted.

"Don't call me Maggie."

"You're going to be one wicked-hot mother, Margaret." Dave tries again, tossing one of the drumsticks into the air and catching it neatly. Silence. No wooden thwack, no rasp of well-loved wood against life-callused fingertips.

"This little . . . belligerence routine didn't work when I was engaged, and it's not working now."

"Jesus, Maggie, you already talk like a damn mom."

"Don't call me Maggie." She looks at her reflection in the full-length bedroom mirror, hand on the still foreign bulge of her stomach as she tries to reconcile the grown woman in a black dress that her mother would call "sensible," and fragile, idealistic Maggie. "Can you stop being childish for two seconds?"

"I'll give you three."

"Do I look alright?"

"Isn't that a question for your husband?" Dave frowns, the expression carved into his pale forehead like marble. For a second, she can see him at forty, gray-haired and falsely cranky for kicks. "Get off my lawn" and all of that nonsense.

"My husband isn't here right now. You *are*, for some reason." She spins slowly and stiffly, imagining herself as a mannequin rather than a woman under his gaze.

"You know why I'm here."

"Don't you have someone better to stalk? Your parents—you know your parents still call me. They miss you. They actually wish you were around."

"They don't get it like you do." He starts drumming again, *click-click-thump*, nice and slow. The silence rings in her ears, so at odds with the motion of the drumsticks. "I don't want to spend my life wandering around my childhood home, messing with my parents for attention."

"And I don't want to go to some stupid Christmas party for my husband's stupid job."

It's a little too raw, a little too close to high school bonding, mocking each other and complaining about perfect, suburban lives.

"Just yesterday you were bragging about his job and how it's so much better than the Pretzel Shack at the mall." Dave smiles, teeth still crooked but no worse than they were in high school. Still shiny white.

"Obviously it's better than the Pretzel Shack."

"Hey, I always guessed that when you were pregnant, you'd be wistful for those free pretzels I used to give you."

"The free pretzels were a perk," she admits, the room almost comfortable between them.

"Yeah, I was trying to fatten you up. Make sure you were in my league and wouldn't leave me."

"Asshole," she laughs even though she shouldn't, some small part of her reeling from the compliment. "Just when I thought I could tolerate you for five minutes."

"You look great, Maggie, you always look great."

⁘

But it wasn't that poetic, nothing ever is. He accepted and so did she, and they'd joked about their dorms being on the opposite sides of campus even though they both knew freshmen get crammed together like sardines.

Graduation loomed like some sort of promise, a deadline, like if high school ended one way it would affirm the rest of her life, the rest of their lives. Their lives would be a thing, a union gilded in graduation blue.

"Prom." Dave jokingly sat on Meg's lap in the cafeteria, just to get her attention, before sliding down onto the bench beside her, easy charming smile winning them some measure of privacy. Dave up to his antics again.

Dave still trying to charm his illogically matched girlfriend with the stiff upper lip. "It's this weekend, and you haven't mentioned it yet. I'm assuming something is going on with a dress and probably some shoes. And if you're really a girl, you probably want me to wear a tie or a cummerbund or something that matches."

"Prom is this weekend?"

"Now, I know you're not lying to me about being a girl. I have photographic proof—ouch!" He flinched when she smacked his arm with the back of her hand. "In my *head*," he laughed, "I have a photographic memory full of all kinds of glorious proof of your gender."

"Dave," she cut him off, voice low. Embarrassed.

He was as unflappable as always, wrapping his arm around her shoulders and tucking her into his side. "Sorry." His hand drummed on her side, that same rhythm, that *click-click-thump* that his feet tapped out when he relaxed his hand to take a test.

"So. You're bringing up prom."

"This was my way of asking you."

"Oh, romantic," her lip curled. "What? No massive public humiliation routine? I'd pegged you for the kind to get down on one knee in front of a marching band and shame me into it."

"You think so little of me," he laughed. "The marching band would be naked, and I'd have a puppy to shame you into it. I'm not an amateur."

"Do you really want to do the whole prom thing?"

"You sound so excited about it." *Click-click-thump. Click-click-thump*, now on the edge of the table as he leaned away from her. "It's prom, not marriage."

"I don't understand why you can't just go with your friends," she looked around the table, at the kids not so covertly watching them, at the looks of quiet awe on their faces, like she had Clooney on her arm. Dave wasn't Clooney of course, he was unexpectedly wonderful, but Meg hated the stares, the locker room questions after PE about dating The Famous Dave.

"Is he always so funny?" No, he only thought he was. "Is that his bedhead?" No, he just pretended it was. "He said he didn't study for that chem test." He'd studied all night. She'd reminded him to sleep on the bad side of three in the morning.

"Maggie," he grabs her hand in his, squeezing it, "I can't go with my friends because none of them can rock taffeta, none of them stare at my dimples when they think I'm not looking and because I love—"

"Fine. If only to save you from your friends in taffeta, that sounds horrifying."

"That's my girl."

She wanted to snip that she didn't belong to him, but he looked too honestly happy to ruin it. So much happier than he did with that smug little grin during a practiced dashing entrance.

⁓⚬⚬⁓

"He's a dick." Dave sits cross-legged in the middle of the coffee table. Meg can't see the TV so she leans more pointedly into her husband's side. He smiles and wraps his arm around her back, idly stroking the side of her stomach. "I keep telling you he's a dick, I've always known he was a dick. You never listen to me."

"How did anyone make money off of this movie?" Meg's husband laughs in her ear, and she nods too vigorously.

"I'm wondering if we should get rid of the coffee table."

"Why would we do that?" Her husband leans forward and picks up his beer, which Dave mimes knocking out of the man's hand.

"It's breaking up the room, I don't like it."

"Is this some nesting thing?" Her husband laughs and Meg shrugs again.

"See? He's treating you like a pregnant lady, next he's going to offer to rub your feet and get you ice cream and pickles at the same time." Dave frowns, "You're more than just some pregnant lady, Maggie."

She wants to tell him that she is a pregnant lady—a stay at home suburbanite with her career on hold, prepping to be someone's mother. Domestic engineering. She used to mock women who called it that; she used to practically shout about how *PhD* came before *Mrs.* in her dictionary.

She turns to her husband, "Can you turn it up?"

"Absolutely."

⚬⚬

"It's not working." Meg stood frozen in her doorway, the bass from the graduation party they just left still ringing in her ears. "It's not working anymore, I can't take this." She gestured between them with a shaky hand.

"What? You can't take me? What did I do—"

"It's not anything that you did," she shook her head. "We're completely different species. We're about to go off to college and I bet it'll be less than a week before you're invited to everything and I start to look boring—"

"And you don't even want to try. You just want to throw this away." He accused her, drumming on his thigh. *Click-click-thump, click-click-thump.*

A million little stabs flitted through her mind. Him abandoning her with people she'd never talked to at the damn party she didn't even want to be at. About the fact that he called her at three a.m. with stupid jokes she wouldn't laugh at in the daytime. How he didn't really like her, even after six months, he liked the idea of her, the potential reformation. He liked exposing her to things, places, and people. He liked making her laugh and the fact that he could make her quibble and budge like no one else.

And despite all that, she still liked the boy that held the door. She liked the boy that asked her out even though she was uninteresting. And it was dangerous, and she needed to be done.

"This is a high school relationship. We shouldn't drag it off to college with us."

"You think college is going to magically transform you into another person or something. Like you're going to move into your dorm and suddenly be a goddamn intellectual." He shook his head, "It doesn't work that way, Maggie. We're still going to be the same people with the same feelings—"

"Do we have the same feelings?" She said it in a low voice that should have been soothing. Calm. It was anything but, and Dave looked at her, really looked at her, and she swore she saw something shift in his eyes.

The light went out. She would swear that the goddamn light went out.

"I love you." He said it like a puppet, like someone else was controlling his normally snide mouth, the hands that limply waved towards her.

"It's not working."

She expected more of a fight somehow, more emphatic little gestures repeating the same sentiment over and over and over. There was nothing that Dave couldn't run into the ground, no molehill that he couldn't make into a mountain.

All he did was shrug and look at her like she was a petty thief, like she'd nicked a twenty out of his wallet.

"Bye, Dave, I'm sure I'll see you around."

There wasn't a grieving period, not really. It wasn't some ice cream-eating, torturous chick flick-watching *thing*. For the next two days she lived life as normal, worked at her summer job, ate dinner with her parents, and dissected current events with her dad, like she actually knew something about the repercussions of the rising rate of homelessness in the county.

The call came on Thursday, during dinner, and something stirred, something told Meg she should excuse herself and answer it. It was Ann, Dave's mother who always refused to be Mrs. Anyone. Meg liked Ann—so many of Dave's better qualities were from his mother. She missed him for the first time, staring at the caller ID, and shuddered slightly as she picked up the phone, pressing it to her ear.

"Maggie honey?" Ann was crying, a frantic sort of sob barely held back in her throat.

"Yeah, it's me."

"I—Oh God, I don't know how to say this, sweetheart, I don't know—"

"What happened?" Meg bit her lip, keenly aware of her parents watching from the table, probably waiting for some reunification that just wasn't going to happen. Meg's parents liked Dave; they said he was good for her.

"David, oh my David he—" a scuffle on the other end of the phone, soothing tones of Dave's father.

"Maggie?" He was crying too but holding it together better. "You might want to sit down."

⚜

"I would have gotten you back, you know." Dave ignores the closed door, stretching across unperturbed couch cushions and ignoring the way that Meg flinches away from him, pouring over a baby book.

"Oh?"

"You don't sound impressed, but I would have. I had it all planned out, naked marching band and puppy and all."

"You really loved me." She shrugs. "You thought you really loved me, at least."

"I do love you, Maggie." He sighs, and he sounds older than his years. "I don't—I don't know how much longer I can stick around though. I was hoping to see your little girl, maybe she's . . . like you."

"Maybe she'll be able to see you?" Meg snorts. "Because if that's what you're hoping, get out of here now; you're not putting my baby through all of this."

"What is this?" Big hopeful brown eyes, like he might still mean something to her. He does, of course, he really does, but it's nothing she can put into words. It's grieving that never finished, a relationship wrenched apart and not allowed to heal.

"It's messed up, Dave. It's really messed up." She sighs and shakes her head, closing the book and setting it aside. "You said you aren't going to be able to stay much longer. What does that mean?"

"I don't know," he shrugs, drumming his fingers silently on his thigh. "It's just . . . I used to be around all the time, breaking pens in your husband's underwear drawer, the usual," he grins at her, almost manic, his eyes wider than they should be, making him look so damn young. "But now when you're gone, I'm not here, I'm nowhere, and it's dark and warm, lulling. And then I'm looking at you again, and I can talk—"

"You can't talk in the dark place? How do you survive?"

"I don't," he laughs. "I think it's tied to the baby. Once you have your own baby you won't have time to baby me anymore. I think something knows that."

"Maybe . . . what if you leave now?" she suggests, and it makes her sadder than it should. The thought of the quiet. "What if you walk out of the front door now and just *go*."

"I'm not leaving you now, Maggie. I see it, I see how often you're alone in this house. You need someone here, even if your stupid husband doesn't want to do it."

"He's not stupid," she defends on instinct. "And I'm not going to be alone for that much longer, you know."

"Then when the baby comes, I'll start walking. You won't have to see me anymore."

"I think that's best." But when she reaches for his tapping hand on the couch between them, she can almost feel him, a buzzing sort of tingle between them, high school butterflies in her stomach.

The hospital said it was a brain aneurysm. A brain aneurysm that burst before anyone knew it was there, before anyone could have known. One minute a neatly contained pocket of blood and the next a fatal hemorrhage. One minute Dave was jogging to his room to grab his phone, and the next he was falling down the stairs, light switch flicked off.

Click-click-thump as his body tumbled down the stairs.

Meg found herself blubbering as soon as she heard, sobbing that she loved him, feeling like an idiot that she wasn't there because maybe she could have done something, maybe she would have known. Dave talked about brains enough. She must have picked something up, she listened to everything he said, and then he said it again. Double inputs on random factoids at all hours of the day, she would have known before he did.

The funeral was on a Tuesday and Meg sat in the front row with Dave's parents, in the far right seat. The coffin was painted black, and Dave would have hated it. He would have hated all of this, everyone sitting around being so somber, talking about him like he was some inspiration lost to the world.

Make my funeral a fun-eral, Maggie. Everyone should get together, get drunk, tell mean stories about me and say good riddance.

She could hear him too clearly, the voice that she never really appreciated dense in her right ear, echoing around her head until it filled everything. The priest droned on, all the words blending together, and Dave supplied much needed commentary.

Who is that guy? I haven't been to church since Easter two years ago. That should be you up there, at least you'd tell it like it is. I'm going down like a saint when I spent my whole life trying to be a sinner.

Meg snorted, and she could hear the grief counselor her parents insisted on. "Everyone handles grief in different ways. Laughing at a funeral is normal, healthy even."

See? You think I'm funny, you always thought I was funny. You were just bullshitting me.

It was so cocky, so true to life, that it dragged Meg's eyes away from the open casket, and she looked to her right, just to check. Dave squatted there beside her, hand on the chair behind her shoulders for balance, in that same wrinkled hoodie from their first date, band T-shirt underneath.

"About time you figured it out." He smiled at her, eyes honey brown and glinting in the sunshine. "My parents don't seem to care but you . . . you've always noticed me."

She reeled back in shock, hand clapped over her mouth, because he looked so real, his hair blowing in the early summer breeze. "Dave?"

"Don't look so shocked, you fall down stairs too. I've seen you. You thought you pulled it off all cool, but I saw you."

His hand slips from the back of her chair to her shoulder, and she wouldn't feel it if she couldn't see it, pale against the black sleeve of her dress. His fingers are drumming against her, silent, slow. The *click-click-thump* she can't really hear thrums through her arm, through her chest, rippling along her spine as the priest's words spiral into startling clarity.

"He will always be with us."

Mostly, it seems to be sleepless young mothers crying in Meg's mommy and me group about their little darling liking daddy better. Of course, she hasn't seen any evidence that any of those dripping wet claims are true, but it makes her a little more appreciative of her daughter's obvious preference. Mama's Girl isn't really a thing, it's not a phrase or a title, so Meg's inner rebel is a little too proud of the way her little girl holds scalding eye contact with her. Newborn blue eyes just starting to turn her dad's shade of chocolate brown.

She assumes it's normal, she's the one home with the baby—it's only natural that the bond is going to be stronger. It'll probably even out at some point, her husband is bound to be the more lax parent anyway. It'll make sense when her girl ends up siding against her. It happens, it's part of parenting.

Dave has kept true to his promise, assurance, whatever it was. He hasn't been around, no voices in corners, no tilted wedding pictures on the walls. It's quiet, too quiet sometimes, but again, Meg figures that's normal. Silence is normal, loneliness is normal. It's the tradeoff for privacy, for her comfortable life.

She hopes he has moved on somehow. Maybe it works like the movies, and he was still around because he had some task to complete and he got it done. Maybe he was supposed to keep her sane through her first pregnancy, except she doubts she's significant enough for that kind of guardian-angel treatment from the beyond. Maybe it's her daughter, she can believe that her daughter is that special somehow, that the little girl is going to grow up to be someone so special, so important, that the Great Afterlife made her mother crazy for ten years.

Maybe he found a ghostly girlfriend, and they're terrorizing a classroom together. That's always where she thought Dave should be, where she pictured him best. In that school, in the back of the class, yanking laughs from thin air. Maybe he's doing that again, replacing dry erase markers with permanent and watching teachers squirm.

Meg sets her girl in the high chair and starts rooting through kitchen cupboards in a daze, pausing in her search for cereal every few seconds to catch the baby's fixated gaze, to smile and make a silly face. The girl laughs, little nose contorting, tickled by her unruly shock of deep brown hair.

She smacks pudgy hands on the high chair table and Meg freezes, head swirling as the little slaps conform to an all too familiar rhythm, clumsy baby fingers filling the room with a *click-click-thump*.

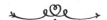

POSSIBLY NEFARIOUS PURPOSES
Michelle Ann King

When she got back from Las Vegas, Dayna found a padded envelope on her doormat containing a set of keys, a glossy brochure for a health spa called *Rejuvenation*, and a sheaf of paperwork that said she owned it.

She didn't know anything about health and beauty, but she did know that when the aliens dropped that kind of hint, they expected her to take it. So she took a course in nail art, and hired some therapists—strangely, all called Sarah —who understood how to do all the other things on the spa's exquisitely printed menu of treatments.

Amy, of course, thought it was a bad idea. But she did at least come out of her basement for an hour so that Dayna could practice airbrushing scarlet palm trees on her nails.

"Vegas was a wonderful adventure, by the way," Dayna said. "I flew over the Strip in a helicopter, ate oysters for breakfast, drank neon-colored cocktails from glasses the size of fishbowls, had sex with a Malaysian Elvis impersonator, and shot paper targets at a gun range while screaming, 'Do you feel lucky, punk?' as loud as I could."

Amy shook her head. "Do I have to tell you how disappointed that makes me?"

"No, you don't. If you're breathing, then you're disappointed in me. It's a given." Amy strongly disapproved of adventures, especially the alien-sponsored kind. "You have very dry cuticles," Dayna said. "You should massage them with almond oil."

⁕⁎⁂⁕

Dayna and Amy had shared a house for the last five years, ever since they'd met at a UFO enthusiasts' convention. "This is all complete nonsense," Amy had said, gloomily eyeing an eyewitness sketch of something that looked like a cross between ET and a Pomeranian. "You can't *see* aliens."

"I know," Dayna had said, just as gloomily, and a friendship was born.

Dayna had her apartment on the ground floor of the house, and Amy lived in the basement—which was in fact upstairs on the first floor, since the building didn't actually have a sub-ground level. But since she'd boarded up all the windows and painted every room black, it seemed to embody the spirit of a basement, if not the physical location.

Amy glanced around the spa while Dayna put the finishing touches to her artwork. "I liked it better when you had a garage," she said. "That was a lot more useful."

Dayna refrained from pointing out that Amy had never once been to the garage and didn't drive. She'd only get a lecture. Amy thought driving was a bad idea because it was too dangerous—for other people, of course, not for them. "The aliens would make people drive off a cliff before they'd let them so much as cut us up," she said. Dayna had tried pointing out there weren't many cliffs in North London, but Amy had stubbornly refused to see her point.

"There," Dayna said, putting down her brush. "What do you think?"

Amy frowned at her nails. "Unless it's meant to be King Kong climbing the Empire State Building, I wouldn't give up the day job."

"It's a palm tree. And this *is* my day job."

Amy gave her a dark look. "Only because they say so."

Dayna tried to ignore the disappointment radiating outwards like a mushroom cloud, and applied a clear layer of varnish over Amy's nails. "I'm not like you, Amy. I can't just . . . retire from the world. I still want to work and drive and travel and meet people. I still want to *live*."

"Even as the tool of powerful and manipulative extraterrestrial creatures who are using you as a test subject in a study of humanity being undertaken for unknown but possibly nefarious purposes?"

"*Nefarious*," Dayna said. "That's a great word. If they ever want me to open a nightclub, I'm going to call it Nefarious."

Amy just shook her head, then left without letting her nails dry. But she did at least buy a bottle of almond oil on her way out.

⁂

Amy held the feathered peacock pose while Dayna timed her with a kitchen clock in the shape of a cheeseburger. Amy had no idea where that had come from, which meant she'd have to throw it out afterwards. She had a strict policy about not accepting the aliens' gifts, even when they were useful. *Especially* when they were useful.

She caught Dayna's gaze. "You're seeing someone, aren't you?"

"Seriously?" Dayna said. "How do you *know* these things? Do the aliens tell you? Do they spill everyone's secrets because they're trying to bring drama to you, since you refuse to go out and create any of your own?"

The cheeseburger belched, signifying thirty seconds. Amy shifted into downward facing dog.

"They do give me clues sometimes," she admitted. "But they didn't need to about this. It's obvious, because you haven't stopped smiling for four days. So, tell me about him. What's his name?"

"Nathan. He's a pharmacist. He came in to book a nonsurgical facelift as a birthday present for his sister. I persuaded him to change it to a massage, partially because I'm terrified of that machine and partly because I thought she'd probably kill him if she got a facelift for her birthday, and he's far too pretty to die." Dayna reset the timer. "You're disappointed, aren't you?"

"I'm not disappointed, I'm disapproving. There's a difference."

Dayna raised a sceptical eyebrow. "It might not even have anything to do with them, you know. Things do still happen by chance."

"*Now* I'm disappointed," Amy said. "You know better than that."

"Okay. Maybe. Probably. But I still like him." Dayna sank down on her own bright pink yoga mat, which practically glowed in the bare, black room. It was giving Amy a headache. "I want a boyfriend. A relationship. Is that so wrong?"

"It's not necessarily wrong to want it, but it's a bad idea to pursue it. It won't end well, that's what I'm saying."

"You don't know that."

"Yes, I do. Do you think I never tried?"

Dayna's eyes went wide. "You had a boyfriend? When? Who? What happened?"

Amy sat opposite her in the lotus position. "When I was about your age, I went through a denial phase. Decided it was all nothing more than an overactive imagination and hallucinations brought on by ingesting pesticides and genetically modified bacon. So I became a vegan and started dating a lecturer in mathematics at Trinity College. Rupert. Very steady, very down-to-earth. Didn't believe in anything that couldn't be proven with a series of quadratic equations. I was hoping it would rub off."

"Did it?"

"I can still recite pi to a hundred decimal places, which can be useful. Better than counting sheep. But other than that, no."

Amy opened a bottle of vitamin-enriched water and took a long swallow. "But it did teach me that relationships are a bad idea. You said it yourself, the aliens want drama. Excitement. So you start out intending to have a quiet night in, but that's not interesting enough for them, so they interfere. And before you know it, instead of spending the evening on the sofa with a nice cup of tea and a Bruce Willis film, you're spending it cleaning intestines off the ceiling."

Dayna hugged her knees to her chest and rested her chin on them. There was a faraway-looking smile playing at the edge of her lips. "Nathan loves Bruce Willis," she said.

Amy pinched the bridge of her nose. It didn't help her headache. "Everyone loves Bruce Willis. He's probably got aliens too. That really wasn't the point of the story."

Dayna blinked and shook herself a little. "No, I suppose not. Sorry."

"Officially, Rupert's death is still an open investigation, but nobody's looking into it. Nobody ever really did. They said it was clearly the work of a marauding, opportunistic psychopath. Or possibly a bear. Although what a bear would have been doing wandering the streets of Cambridge, nobody ever wanted to discuss."

"I wish we could discuss things with *them*," Dayna said. "I'd like to know who they are. Are they scientists? Security guards? Zookeepers? Spies? TV producers? I wish we had a proper way to communicate, not just that weird possession-of-random-objects thing they do. That's unnerving. And unfairly one-sided."

"Actually, I've been working on that," Amy said. "Watch this." She rolled her towel up and draped it around the water bottle, then moved her bag of pumpkin seeds three inches to the right.

Dayna stared. "Did you just *talk* to them?"

"Yes. I told them to fuck off out of my house. Or possibly, given that the nuances of the language are very subtle, that there's no such thing as Bigfoot."

Dayna nibbled on a pumpkin seed. "I wouldn't be so sure about that. I think I saw him doing a lounge act in Vegas."

"I'm sure they'll bear that in mind," Amy said.

Since the spa was having an afternoon lull, Dayna slipped into the storage room and lay down on the concrete floor.

Maybe Amy was right. Maybe disengaging, refusing to play the game, was the right thing to do.

She stared at the unpainted ceiling and thought empty, bare thoughts. She envisaged herself as a barren, blank void. Unexciting. Safe. *Move along, nothing to see here.* She lay still. She breathed. She contemplated nothingness. Then she said, "Fuck me, this is boring," and went out to get a pedicure.

"I ever tell you about the time I accidentally ate someone's toenail?" Baltimore Sarah said, as she stroked purple polish over Dayna's toenails. "I was doing this old woman and her nails were, like, this thick." She held her fingers about an inch apart. "So I've got the clippers in both hands, like this . . ." she mimed squeezing, "and I finally work that beast free, and it whooshes right up in the air, and I'm watching it fly, like this . . ." she threw her head back and stared upwards, her mouth wide open. "And it comes straight back down, and then, well, I guess you can work out how the story ends." She snapped her mouth shut and mimed swallowing.

"That is truly disgusting," Dayna said, in awe.

Baltimore Sarah shrugged. "Life comes with hazards attached. What are you gonna do?"

Dayna nodded slowly. "That's a good point."

The office phone rang and Sci Fi Sarah picked it up. "Hold on," she said, and covered the mouthpiece. "Dayna? It's Nathan. He wants to know if you're free tonight."

Dayna shot a swift and slightly guilty look back at the closed door of the storage room, then nodded. "Tell him yes," she said.

Nathan arrived ten minutes early, so Amy went downstairs while Dayna was still getting ready.

"Boo," she said when she answered the door. He jumped hard, which made her frown. A low tolerance for surprises didn't bode well.

He visibly collected himself. "Er. Hello. You must be Amy. Dayna's friend."

"Dayna has a lot of friends," Amy said. "Strange but very protective friends, who've watched over her for a very long time. They like to keep an eye on her. To do things for her. It means they're around a lot, and they see everything. Which means they'll be watching you, too."

Nathan blinked hard. "Right," he said, then rallied and gave her a wide smile that only wavered a little. "So is this the point where you warn me that if I break her heart you'll hunt me down and kill me?"

"Not *me*," Amy said. "But someone will, yes. Or something, rather. So you should know that breaking her heart would be a very bad idea indeed."

Nathan's skin turned a shade paler, and the smile wavered even more.

Amy held the door open. "Anyway, Dayna won't be long, so you can come in and wait. You'll probably have a sense of being watched, and you might have a feeling that things are moving around when you're not looking straight at them. Or possibly that they're trying to tell you something. The toaster in particular can be a bit threatening, but if it comes on too strong just throw a tea towel over it. That usually shuts it up. If anything *really* strange happens, shout for me. I'll be upstairs in the basement."

She paused at the foot of the stairs and looked back. "Unless it's the television turning on by itself. That's just because the remote's broken."

Nathan made a small, slightly strangled noise that, although Amy waited politely, didn't turn into actual words. Eventually she decided it probably signified agreement and left. People could be as hard to communicate with as the aliens sometimes.

On the drive back from the cinema, Dayna couldn't help noticing Nathan was quieter than usual. When he eventually said, "I met Amy when I came to pick you up," she relaxed. It explained a lot.

"Amy is a bit—" she began, then her mobile rang.

"Hold on," she said, and put it on speaker. Minimizing distractions was just good motoring etiquette, even without alien backseat drivers.

"Hi Dayna, it's Night Shift Sarah. Just wanted to let you know the police came 'round tonight. I think advertising my Midnight Massage Special might not have been such a good idea. They seem to think it's a euphemism for something unseemly."

"Okay, don't worry," Dayna said. "I'll sort it out tomorrow. The police are usually very understanding once I talk to them."

She hung up and noticed Nathan looking at her with an expression she couldn't read.

"You have some strange friends," he said.

Dayna shrugged. She couldn't exactly argue with that.

Amy spent most of the next day meditating in the spa's storage room. She quite liked it in there. It was smaller than her basement.

Dayna popped in regularly, to bring her water and talk about Nathan.

"I told him you were just joking," she said. "And that you mean well, but you're not highly socialized."

"You say that as if it's a flaw," Amy said. She opened her eyes. "You know it's a bad idea to have secrets in a relationship, don't you?"

Dayna looked down. "So there are some things we can't talk about. That's normal. No couple shares everything."

"But we're not just talking about being a Barry Manilow fan, or having to shave your toes. This is big. This is a major part of your life—and if you're in a relationship with him, then it's a major part of his life, too."

"Then I'll tell him the truth."

"That's an even worse idea."

"Why? He won't hold it against me. He'll understand."

"No, he won't. He won't get a chance to. Come on, you should know how it works by now. Or do I have to remind you?"

Amy got up and poked her head out the door. "Sarah," she called, "could you come and help us with something? Anyone, it doesn't matter. In fact, all of you would be good. Take it in turns."

Sci Fi Sarah came out of the waxing room. She scrunched up the plastic apron she'd been wearing and threw it in the bin. "What's up?"

"Did we ever tell you about our alien stalkers?" Amy said.

Sci Fi Sarah's mouth fell open. "Your what?"

"Alien stalkers. They're always around, wherever we go. In fact, they're probably here right—"

Sci Fi Sarah sniffed loudly and looked over her shoulder. "Can you smell that? Shit, I must've left the wax on. I think it's overheating." She turned and ran out of the room.

"Next," Amy called.

Curly Sarah slipped out from behind the front desk. "Yes?"

"Did we ever tell you about our alien stalkers?"

"What?" Curly Sarah said. "Did you just say—oh, hang on, that's the phone. I'll be back in a minute."

Baltimore Sarah took her place. Amy got as far as "Did we ever tell you about—" when Baltimore Sarah put her hand in her pocket then shrieked. "Damn, I didn't realize I left my cuticle clippers in there." She pulled her hand out and examined her finger. "Sorry, guys, I think I need to go get a Band-Aid."

Amy looked at Dayna. "Shall I try ringing Night Shift Sarah? So that when she gets in later, she can tell you about the strange dream she had, where someone phoned her up to talk about aliens? Or have I made my point?"

Dayna's shoulders slumped. "You've made your point."

Curly Sarah came back over. "Nathan's on the phone," she said.

"Tell him I'll be right there," Dayna said. Then she looked back at Amy with a wounded expression. "And for the record, I do not have to shave my toes."

Nathan arrived for dinner bearing a good bottle of Chablis and a slightly wilted bunch of flowers. Dayna very deliberately tried not to read anything from the arrangement of drooping leaves.

"Dinner's just about ready," she said. "I made slow roast pork belly with garden peas and celeriac pear mash."

It would've been more accurate to say she'd discovered it in the oven rather than actually cooked it, but she decided to skip over that detail.

"It smells wonderful," Nathan said, sitting at the table. The silverware flashed and sparkled. Dayna ignored it.

"Look," she said. "I know my life is a bit weird."

Nathan scratched his chin. The peas on his plate maneuvered themselves into a message that Dayna also ignored. Nathan gave them a sharp look.

"Well," he said. "Yes. Things have been feeling a bit weird for me too, lately." He picked up his fork, then put it down again. "I know your friend was just being protective, which is what friends do, but what she said, it's kind of . . . played on my mind. Because I do feel like I'm being watched. Like, all the time. At work. In the gym. At home. In the bath. My bathroom is six feet square, and I can see every inch of it, and I know there's nobody there, but it really, really feels like there is. And I keep thinking that my stuff's being moved. I don't mean losing my keys, it's more than that. Even when things are exactly where they were before, they're not. They're different, somehow. And that—" he pointed at the toaster, "is giving me the evil eye. Why is it doing that, Dayna? *How* is it doing that?"

"Um . . ." Dayna said.

"I think I should go now," he said. "I'm sorry. I don't like peas. Especially these peas. I don't like them at all."

He pushed his chair back so hard it toppled over. "Sorry," he said again, and ran out of the room.

A few minutes after the front door slammed, Amy came down. "There, there," she said, patting Dayna's back. "Don't get upset. You know that's a bad idea. It only leads to severed limbs and evisceration."

She cleared the plates off the table. "I'll put this outside for next door's Rottweiler," she said, holding up the untouched pork belly. "Or, you know, any wandering bears."

Dayna stayed at the table and put her head in her hands.

The next day, Amy went to see Nathan. When he got home, he looked very surprised to find her sitting at his kitchen table. In fairness, Amy was reasonably surprised herself; she hadn't ventured this far from the basement in years. But she'd walked, which really couldn't do any harm to anyone. And it was a good cardiovascular workout.

"Amy? What are you doing here? How did you get in?"

"Your roommate let me in. I came to talk about Dayna."

Nathan screwed his eyes shut and shook his head. "I know," he said. "I was an arsehole last night. Running out like that, after she'd gone to all that trouble. I'm sorry. I don't know what came over me." He straightened up and looked Amy in the eye. "But it won't happen again, you have my word on that. I'll make it up to her."

"So you still to see her?"

"Yes. Of course I do." He hesitated. "Has she . . . said anything, to you? About me? Does she . . . does she still like me?"

"Yes," Amy said.

He broke into a wide smile. "Good, good. That's great news."

"No, it's not. Not for you."

"What do you mean?" He frowned at her. "And hang on, what roommate? I don't have a roommate."

"I was hoping you were going to give up and walk away," Amy said, "but I see that's not going to happen. So I'm going to have to save you. Trust me, this is for your own good."

"What is? Amy, what are you talking about? You're starting to make me nervous."

"Good. You should be nervous." Amy tilted her head back and looked at the ceiling. For a second it was overlaid with an image of the ceiling in Rupert's flat, and she looked down again. "You should be terrified."

"Of you?"

"No." She took a deep breath. "Of the aliens."

Nathan stared at her. "I'm sorry, the what?"

"The aliens. That's who I was talking about when you came to the house. Dayna's friends. Our friends. They're aliens. Unfathomable but powerful aliens."

Somewhere in the flat, a phone began to ring. Nathan glanced round.

"Ignore that," Amy said. "They're trying to distract you, but you need to hear this. That's how I got in here—the aliens let me in. They let me go anywhere I want to, which is exactly why I stay in the basement. Dayna and I, we're not safe to be around. Because *they're* not safe."

"Amy, this is—"

He was cut off by the high, shrill beeping of the smoke alarm on the wall. "Ignore that, too," Amy said. She got up, flipped it open and ripped the battery out. Silence fell for half a second, then Nathan's mobile blared out the theme tune to *The Twilight Zone*.

Nathan put a hand to his jacket pocket, then frowned. "That's not my ringtone."

"They've been working on their sense of humor lately," Amy said.

Nathan slowly withdrew his hand. "I'll ignore it, shall I?"

Amy nodded. Maybe he was learning.

"Look," he said, and his expression softened. "I know you care about Dayna. You're her friend, I get it. But if all this is because you're worried I'll come between you, you don't have to be. I don't intend to do that, I promise."

Amy sighed. Maybe not, then. "You won't intend to do any of it, but it doesn't matter. They'll make you. I don't know why, exactly—I don't know what their agenda really is—but I know what they'll do, and how it'll end. So it's a bad idea to try and see her again, Nathan. A really bad idea. You need to let it go. Let *her* go."

Nathan shook his head. "I can't."

Amy scrubbed a hand over her cheek. "You know, I thought you might say that, which is why I told you all this in the first place. You might not have been listening to me, but they have. And they don't like people knowing about them."

She patted his arm. "I'm sorry about this, because it's probably going to hurt. Hopefully it won't turn out too bad, although you never know with head injuries. It's not an exact science. But it's better than the alternative, believe me."

She walked out of the kitchen and into the living room. Nathan ran after her. "What are you—" he started, but the rest of the words were choked off when his foot caught in the rug, and he went sprawling. His head hit the glass coffee table on the way down, and he landed in a heap on the floor with shards of glass surrounding him like glittering confetti.

Amy took his phone out of his pocket and called an ambulance, then left it lying by his hand and let herself out of the flat.

When Dayna got back from the hospital, Amy was waiting for her in the kitchen. "How's Nathan?" she said.

Dayna gave a tiny shrug. "The same. The doctor said memory does return slowly, in a lot of cases, so she's cautiously optimistic that it might not be a permanent loss. But she said it might be best if I didn't visit for a while. He might not remember me, but for some reason he still gets very agitated when I'm there. It's not good for his blood pressure. So I think I'm just going to, you know, stay away."

"I'm sure she's right," Amy said. "By the way, this came for you earlier."

She handed Dayna a padded envelope. Inside was a set of keys, a packet of flyers advertising a nightclub called Nefarious, and a sheaf of paperwork that said she owned it.

Dayna stared at it for a while, then slipped everything back in the envelope. "You know, I think I'll skip going to the spa today," she said slowly. "In fact, I think I'm going to just hand the whole thing over to Curly Sarah."

Amy looked surprised. "Really?"

"Yes. I've got more important things to do."

Amy eyed the envelope in her hand. "Like what?"

"Like some overdue spring cleaning." Dayna pulled a bin bag out of the cupboard and dropped the padded envelope inside, then dumped the toaster on top. "And then I'm going to redecorate in here," she added, tying up the bag. "Amy? What do you think? Want to come and help me buy a few dozen tins of black paint?"

After staring at her for a moment, Amy broke into a wide, approving smile. "I think that's a great idea," she said.

A HEART FOR LUCRETIA
Jeff VanderMeer

Originally appeared in the *Silver Web*, Winter/Spring 1993

This is the story of a brother, a sister, and a flesh dog, and how two found a heart for the third. The story has both oral and written traditions, with no two versions the same. It begins, for our purposes, with the city . . .

⊱✦⊰

"The city, she has parts. The city, she is dead, but people live there, underground. They have parts . . ."

Gerard Mkumbi cared little for what Con Newman said, despite the man's seniority and standing in the crèche. But, finally, the moans as the wheezing autodoc worked on his sister persuaded him. The autodoc said Lucretia needed a new heart. A strong heart, one that would allow her to spring up from their sandy burrows hale and willowy, to dance again under the harvest moon. Gerard had hoped to trade places so that the tubes would stick out from his chest, his nose, his arms, the bellows compression pumping in out, in out. But no. He had the same defect, though latent, the autodoc told him. A successful transplant would only begin the cycle anew.

In Lucretia's room, at twilight, he read to her from old books: *Bellafonte's Quadraphelix*, *The Metal Dragon and Jessible*, others of their kind. A dread would possess him as he watched his sister, the words dry and uncomforting on his lips. Lucretia had high cheekbones, smoky-green eyes, and mocha skin which had made all the young men of the crèche flock to her dance.

But wrinkles crowded the corners of those eyes, and Gerard could detect a slackness to the skin, the flesh beneath, which hinted at decay. The resolve for health had faltered, the usually clenched chin now sliding into the neck; surely a trick of shadow. Anyone but Gerard would have thought her forty-five. He knew she was twenty-seven. They had been born minutes apart, had shared the same womb. Watching her deterioration was to watch his own. Would he look this way at forty-five?

"Gerard," she would call out, her hand curling into his . . .

It had become a plea. He forced himself to hold her hand for hours, though the thought of such decay made him ill. The autodoc insisted on keeping her drugged so she could not feel the pain. Could she even recognize him anymore, caught as she was between wakefulness and sleep, sleep and death?

Flesh Dog, eyes hidden beneath the rolls of raw tissue which were its namesake, stayed always by his side. Flesh Dog shared few words with Gerard, but every twitch of its muzzle toward Lucretia or the squat metal autodoc reminded Gerard she would die soon—too soon, like their mother before her. Unless a miracle arose from the desert.

"The city, she has parts . . ."

And, finally, he had gone, taking Flesh Dog with him.

Thus it begins. The ending is another matter, a creature of fragments and glimpses that pieced together only tease . . .

That summer, as the stars watched overhead, an angel descended to the desert floor. And, when it departed, Lucretia arose from the dead and danced like a will-o'-the-wisp over the shifting sands; a fitful dance, for she often dreamed of Gerard at night, and they were unpleasant dreams.

That winter, Flesh Dog and Gerard limped back to the crèche. He did not speak now. Always, he looked toward the south, toward the great sea and the city with no name, as though expecting strangers.

And the middle, finally, in which meat is placed upon the bone.

For twenty days and twenty nights, Gerard trudged the sands, subsisting on the dry toads which Flesh Dog dug up for them. They encountered no one on their journey, listened only to the dry winds of the desert.

Finally, at dusk of the twenty-first day, they climbed a dune and stared down upon the city. The sun leant the city with a crimson glare, silhouettes burnt into the sand. Gerard saw that the walls had crumbled in places and the buildings within, what could be glimpsed of them, had fallen into disrepair. Although Gerard looked for many minutes, he could discover no sign of life. The only movement came from the west, where a vast ocean glittered and rippled, red as the dunes which abutted it.

Though tired and disappointed at the city's abandoned appearance, Gerard would have plunged forward under cover of darkness. But Flesh Dog sniffed the air, sneezed, and counseled against it.

"Strange smells," it ruminated, "strange smells indeed . . ."

Gerard, fatigue creeping into his bones, could not find the strength to argue. He fell asleep against Flesh Dog's side, sand on his lips and the wind in his hair.

During the night, he woke in a cold sweat, convinced his sister had been leaning over him the moment before, her hair back in the ponytail she had lovingly braided at age nine, giggling and warning him to stay away from the city, the city which lay at the edge of his vision: a dark and ominous block of shadow.

As he drifted back to sleep, Gerard imagined he felt his sister's pulse weaken, back in her crèche bed.

In the morning, Gerard and Flesh Dog found that the city was nearly eclipsed by the cusp of the ocean, its waves a blinding green. Flesh Dog wished to bathe, but Gerard said no. The waves echoed his sister's voice in their constant rush and withdrawal: hurry, hurry . . .

Flesh Dog scouted ahead as Gerard entered the city. The walls had been breached in a dozen places and overhead zynagill hovered, waiting for carrion. The smell as Gerard passed under the shadow of walls made him bite back nausea. A subtle smell of plastic and leather and unwashed drains.

The interior was littered with corpses: a valley of corpses. Flesh Dog, whimpering, retreated to stand by Gerard. Gerard stared at the spectacle before him.

Dead people had been stacked in rectangular pits until they spilled over the edges. Nothing stirred. No flies tended the dead. No zynagill touched them. Plague, Gerard thought, putting a hand over his mouth and nose.

But the bright, festival clothes, the perfection of flesh without hint of boil or scab, mocked his intuition.

Gerard stepped forward, Flesh Dog shadowing him. The clothing upon the dead remained limp, lacking even the secret life of the wind. Eyes stared glassily and the jaws beneath were stiff, locked against giving up their mystery. Gerard would rather they sprang up in parody of human form than lie there, staring . . . A chill entered Gerard's bones. Watching. Bloodless. Cold. A vast tableau of the unburied and unburnt.

"So many dead," Gerard muttered. Once, he had been told of the legend of the Oliphaunt's graveyard. Was this the human equivalent? Would his Lucretia soon find her way to this city, against her will, because he had failed?

Flesh Dog sniffed the air as they skirted the nearest pit.

"Dead?" it said. "They smell as if they never lived . . ."

"Hush," replied Gerard, respectful of the silence.

And so they shuffled forward through the army of bodies, some appealing with outstretched arms, but all quiet as run-down clockwork mice. The eyes seemed to have lost the hope of blinking away deep sleep, the skin of feeling dappled sunlight upon it.

⁂

Beyond the pits lay the city proper: a maze of half-buried fortifications and jumbled buildings. In places, it appeared wars had been fought among the ruins, for the ground was burnt and some walls had melted into slag. All Gerard could do was remind himself of what Con Newman had said: "People live there, underground." It was obvious none lived above. Not even grass grew in the pavement cracks. They trudged on, to the sound of their own belabored breathing.

Finally, they came upon a strange sight amongst the wreckage: the top of an exposed elevator shaft some fifty meters ahead; the tower that had once housed the device had fallen away entirely, leaving only a rough rectangle of regular stone embedded in the ground. The shaft, which had all the looks of a bony arm, vein-like girders naked to the sky, the mortar peeled away, revealed a compact glass box, intact, which was the elevator. Gerard recognized it from *The Metal Dragon*. Jessible had escaped using an elevator. That something so fragile could have survived for so long amazed him.

Standing by the shaft were three creatures, each larger than Gerard by a third. They resembled giant weasels but no fur grew upon their clawed hands and they stood upright as though it was their birthright rather than some carnie show trick.

"What are they?" he hissed to Flesh Dog. "I have never seen them before."

"Meerkats," it replied. "Distilled somewhat with other species, but still meerkats. Your father used to read you tales of the meerkats and the dances they did for the men who created them."

Meerkats! This was indeed magical, and it created out of the torn and wasted landscape some small scrap of hope. Meerkats! He had killed meerkats for the meat before, but they rarely reached two feet in height. For a moment, he considered the possibility that Flesh Dog lied, but dismissed it: Flesh Dog had taught his father how to read and write. Flesh Dog never lied.

"Are they . . . they are intelligent?"

"Yes," replied Flesh Dog flatly.

Intelligent. He almost laughed. Was he to believe an intelligent toad next? His heartbeat quickened and with it he could feel his sister's heart, uneven and diseased, slowly winding down. He sobered.

"Flesh Dog, are these the folk who live underground?"

"Almost certainly," replied Flesh Dog.

When they came before the meerkats, the leader spoke to Gerard, ignoring Flesh Dog. The leader was a sleek, jet specimen with amber eyes and the language it spoke was all trills and clicks. The meerkat soon switched to *gish* when it interpreted the confused look on Gerard's face.

"State your business," it said in a bored voice.

"I need a human heart," Gerard said. "I am willing to trade for it."

A huffing rose from the leader, followed by similar noises from the other two.

"Parts," the leader ruminated, his tone bordering on contempt. "Fifteenth level." He barked a phrase to his followers and they stepped forward and passed a glittering rod in front of first Gerard and then Flesh Dog.

The leader nodded and escorted them to the elevator.

Gerard had seen elevators in books before, but never dreamed he would one day ride in one and so, when the doors closed, he bent to his knees and whispered to Flesh Dog, "Are elevators safe?"

Flesh Dog, sensing the tremor in Gerard's voice, replied, "Hold on to me if the motion makes you sick."

And so Gerard did hug Flesh Dog as they descended into the city's belly. He clung also to the rucksack full of precious stones and old autodoc parts with which he hoped to woo a human heart.

The levels seemed to crawl by, each more wondrous than the last, more terrible, more strange. Many of the things they saw, Gerard did not understand. They saw winged men with no eyes and vats of flesh and monstrous war engines belching, spitting sparks, and tubes and gears grinding and metal frames for ships in enormous caverns and stockpiles of small arms and old-style lasers and meerkats walking on ceilings and ghosts, images which reflected from the floor, that could not be real and more meerkats—meerkats in every size and color, crawling all over the engines of war, the tubes, the metal frames.

Fires burned everywhere—in rods and in canisters, on walls and floors; yellow fires, orange fires, blue fires, tended by meerkats more sinister than their fellows. Meerkats with frozen smiles and cruel claws and mouths that, like traps, shut. The acrid smell of fire came to Gerard through the elevator walls, a bitter taste on his tongue. Around some fires, meerkats threw squirming creatures the size of mice into the flames and, once or twice, larger, metallic objects, their alloys running together and melting like butter to grease a pan.

Gerard turned away and ignored the cruelty of the meerkats, tore it from his mind. Lucretia needed a heart. Lucretia needed a heart.

The weight of earth and rock above him and to all sides made him dizzy and nauseous, but still deeper they went, silent and fearful, into the blackness beneath their feet.

At the fifteenth floor, they were greeted by a man who resembled the people in the pits: the same lifeless eyes and fixed jaw. But this man was alive and he indicated that Gerard was to follow him down the corridor. The corridor led into a maze of tunnels, all lit by a series of soft, reddish panels set into the ceiling. The

smell was dank—a sharp, musty scent as of close quarters and many residents over many generations. The original reliefs carved into the walls had been defaced or done over, so that meerkat heads jutted from human bodies and *gish* became a weird series of sharp, harsh lines. Unease crept up on Gerard as they walked and, when he looked down, he saw that Flesh Dog's hackles were up and its fangs bared: a startling white against the black-blue of its muzzle.

By the time they reached their destination, Gerard was thoroughly lost and could no more have retraced his steps than conjured a heart out of thin air. He clung to his rucksack, and to the thought that Lucretia still needed him.

They were led into a large room that had partitions to hide other sections from them. A chair had been provided and the silent man gestured to it before locking the doors behind him. Gerard sat down and Flesh Dog flopped to rest at his feet.

"That man smelled of the pits," Flesh Dog muttered. "Everything smells of the pits."

A whirring sound made Gerard sit straighter in his seat and a brace of meerkats appeared from behind a partition. One was tall and white, the other short and yellow. Flesh Dog growled, but they ignored the beast.

"My name is—" said Whitey, pronouncing a series of high-pitched trills.

"And I am—" said Yellow. "Together, we are the Duelists of Trade. I assume that is why you are here?"

Gerard nodded eagerly.

"First," said Whitey, "you must be thirsty."

He clapped his paws together and the lifeless man re-entered, holding a glass of clear liquid. He offered it to Gerard, who took it with nodded thanks.

"Do not drink!" Flesh Dog hissed. "Do not drink!"

"Hush," Gerard said. "Hush."

The liquid smelled of berries and the first tentative sip rewarded him with a tangy, smooth taste. He took one more sip, for politeness' sake, and then heeded Flesh Dog's warning and set the glass by his chair.

"And now," said Yellow, "what precisely do you wish to trade for?"

"A heart," replied Gerard. "A human heart." He reached for his rucksack.

Whitey looked at Yellow, made a huffing sound. They both had fangs which poked out from the muzzle. Red dye designs had been carved into the whiteness, designs like scythes and slender knives in their sharpness. The eyes were slightly slanted and they devoured Gerard with a kind of hunger.

"What do you have to trade?" asked Yellow.

The hairs on Gerard's neck rose. The question had been asked with quiet authority and now, and only now, did he think that perhaps these meerkats were not as simple as the ones he had caught in the desert. That they might be dangerous in their own way. But the drink had created a sharp warmth in his stomach and it made him careless. Besides, Lucretia still needed a heart. He reached into the sack.

"I have gems," he said, pulling out a huge orange stone he had found at an oasis.

Whitey took the stone from Gerard's hand. He examined it for a moment, held it up to the light. Then he dashed it to the floor. It shattered. Flesh Dog growled.

"Gems?" Whitey hissed. "Gems! For a human heart?"

Gerard shrank back into his chair.

"But I—"

"Do you mean to insult me?" His tail twitched and twitched.

"No! My sister Lucretia is dying! Her heart is bad. I have brought the richest stones I could find . . ."

Flesh Dog rose onto his haunches, fur bristling, teeth bared.

Yellow patted Gerard's shoulder.

"There, there. No need to shock our guest. What else do you have?"

Here was a warm-hearted fellow, a generous fellow. Perhaps Yellow could be satisfied. Gerard scrabbled in his pack, pulled out an autodoc part.

"There. It is almost new."

Yellow's claws bit into his shoulder. Strangely, Gerard felt no pain, though the shock made him bite back a scream.

"No," said Yellow, voice like ice. ""No, I'm sorry, but this won't do . . . this won't do at all. You come here, down all fifteen levels, spy on us, and offer us used parts?"

Flesh Dog growled and Gerard shook off Yellow's grasp. Why did he feel so numb? He was a fool, he realized, to have come here. In his ignorance he might well have come into the clutches of villains.

Gerard felt Flesh Dog against his feet, a position from which to guard him, and an unworthy thought crept into his head.

"What about Flesh Dog?" he asked Whitey. "I will trade Flesh Dog's talents for a heart . . ." An unfair trade considering the multitude of services Flesh Dog performed, but it was after all a beast. Surely a human life outweighed ownership of a talking beast? He tried to ignore the animal's whining.

Yellow nodded. "Very good. Very good indeed. However," and he pushed a button, "not good enough."

One of the partitions slid back. Behind it: one hundred Flesh Dogs, their parts not yet assembled, so that the heads sat upon one shelf while the bodies sagged in rows below. Two men, like the ones in the pit, lay sprawled in a corner.

Gerard gaped at the sight. So many Flesh Dogs. Dead? Decapitated? It made no sense. But then, neither did the numbness spreading through his body.

Flesh Dog shuddered, shook its head, and moaned.

One hundred heads, connected by one hundred wires to one hundred nutrient vats, turned to stare at him, with their globby folds of tissue dangling.

"We are," said Yellow, pausing, "overstocked on Flesh Dogs at the moment. Human hearts, now, those are rare. We have only one or two."

"However," said Whitey, "there is one way in which we might be persuaded to part with such a heart . . ."

"Yes?" said Gerard, afraid of the answer. He had volunteered his own heart before, but that had been with the assurance of care, faulty though it might have been, from the autodoc.

"It would involve both you and Flesh Dog," said Yellow slyly.

"It would take six months," said Whitey.

The delightful warmth had crept up his chest, the cold following behind.

"Afterwards we would let you go . . ." Whitey held his hands while Yellow caressed his neck. "And in return, we give Lucretia a heart . . ."

"How soon?" Gerard asked. "How soon?" He shivered under Yellow's touch.

"Immediately," whispered Yellow in his ear. "Flesh for flesh. You must simply show us on a map where your crèche lies—you do know what a map is?—and we will send it by hovercraft. We do not break our word."

"So what of it, friend Gerard," said Whitey. "Do you agree?"

Gerard turned to Flesh Dog.

"What do you think, Flesh Dog?"

Flesh Dog peered at him through its fleshy folds. It turned to the Flesh Dog heads on the shelf—and howled. And howled, as though its heart had been broken. Then, with a sideways stutter, it leaned into the floor and was still, trembling around the mouth.

"Poor, poor machine," hummed Whitey. "It has forgotten it is a machine. So many years in service. Poor, poor machine . . ."

"Rip their throats," growled Flesh Dog from the floor. "Rip their throats?" The growl became a moan, and then incoherent. Gerard would have comforted it as it had comforted him in the elevator, but he was too numb.

"Do you agree?" Yellow asked, one eye on Flesh Dog.

"Yes," Gerard said, immobile in the chair now, able only to swivel his head. He imagined he could feel his sister's heartbeat become more regular, could feel a glow of health return to her cheeks. This, and this alone, kept him from panic, from giving over to the fear which ached in his bones. "Yes!" he said with a drunken recklessness, at the same time knowing he had no choice.

"You will leave with a smile upon your face," Whitey promised.

"Oh yes, you will," sang Yellow gleefully, taking out the knives.

As for the ending, there are many. Perhaps the next day, the next month, a new face stared up from the pits, the arms of the body reaching out but frozen, the eyes blank. Perhaps the meerkats never honored their agreement. Or . . .

That summer, as the stars watched overhead, an angel descended to the desert floor. And, when it departed, Lucretia arose from the dead and danced like a will-o'-the-wisp over the shifting sands. She danced fitfully, anger and sadness throbbing in her new heart.

That winter, Flesh Dog and Gerard limped back to the crèche. He did not speak now. Always, he looked toward the south, toward the great sea and the city with no name, as though expecting strangers. Always, as he sat by the fire and sucked his food with toothless gums, Gerard-Flesh Dog looked at Lucretia, the Lucretia who saw only that Flesh Dog had returned a mute, and smiled his permanent smile. Beneath the folds of tissue, Gerard's smoky-green eyes stared, silently begging for rescue. But Lucretia never dared pull back the folds to see for herself, perhaps afraid of what she might find there. Sometimes she would dream of the city, of what had happened there, but the vision would desert her upon waking, the only mark the tears she had wept while asleep.

After a year, the men of the crèche held a funeral for Gerard. After two years, Lucretia married a wealthy water dower and, though she treated Flesh Dog tenderly, he was never more than an animal to her.

YOUR MOMENT OF ZEN
Dan Micklethwaite

You saw an advert on the train. You saw two, but you only paid proper attention to one. It was inside the train. On the opposite wall first then on the ceiling when you looked up, then on the floor when you looked down. It was so bright, so distinct, that it stayed fully visible for a moment or two when you closed your eyes.

It had not been a good day.

It had been the worst day.

You close your eyes now and remember it, wholesale, a full week ago.

You open them. The sign glows overhead. The steel arms of the turnstiles reach out invitingly.

The advert on the train read, "Samurai Land—Come be a part of History. Authentic Time Travel. One Moment of Zen per customer GUARANTEED!"

The second advert, attached to that one, extolled the virtues of Ancient Rome Land, but the samurai one reached you first. It was the first thing to break in through the veil of your misery, the first thing to offer you hope.

Earlier that day, the day of the advertisement, you woke to find your (ex-) girlfriend's clothes and technology moved out of the flat you'd been sharing. Then, after the lunch break, your boss called you to his office, told you, calmly: I'm sorry, but we're letting you go.

No explanations, from either party.

You were too shocked, too tired to ask.

You bought a ticket for Samurai Land with your severance pay.

When given the choice, you opted for the *full-on experience*. Immersion in the arena of Ancient Japan for a whole lunar month. That's why it cost so much.

That, and the time travel bit.

When you first began researching the place, you were skeptical about this technology, but then you read testimonials from previous, deeply satisfied customers, and you were convinced, totally, that this trip would turn your life around. Make you happier. Make you stronger. Make you better. Make you Zen.

It certainly looks impressive from the outside. There is a large, bold sign above the gates, hand-painted (so the website said) by craftsmen trained in secret techniques passed down through the centuries. Which appealed to the youthful part of you, the part that once took exams in artsy subjects, but hasn't since done anything with the grades you gained therein.

On either side of that sign is a large gray stone wall, at least twenty feet high, and above that, and behind it, a mist-wreathed white castle, in the Ancient Japanese style. The mists are the mists of time, the online brochure said. The castle will only become properly clear to those who take the journey.

This sounded appropriately mystic, for a science as arcane as time travel.

You do not lose your nerve in the presence of the formidable battlements.

Or the fog.

You are convinced that only in this way will you be able to reclaim your pride, move on with your life.

When asked by the worker at the gate why you have come here, that is the answer you give. He responds in a way that suggests it's the right one. He tells you: "That's exactly what we love to hear. Come this way."

You pass through the turnstile, and already the fog is lifting. There is action and movement on the street where you could swear you saw none only moments before. It feels quite assuredly like you are no longer in the when and the where in which you were having such a terrible time.

As you walk on, led by the customer service assistant, who is now dressed in elaborate robes rather than the T-shirt and jeans combo you're sure he was previously wearing, he tells you: "Your name is Kenji."

It isn't really, it's _____. But in here it is Kenji. "Which sounds like a proper samurai name, doesn't it?" says the assistant. Before showing you into a changing room, and handing you a sword and a kimono. Your armor, he tells you, will be provided upon the instance of your first fight, which will take place in the morning. This will come with a helmet, with a scary demon design of your choice. In the meantime, you'll have to wear this wig.

It is in the traditional *chonmage* style.

You're happy they've given you a wig, because you didn't want to shave part of your head. You were worried it would itch and give you a rash. Or, worse, that it would encourage a more permanent baldness. You think it's clever that they've thought to take the technology for such wig making back in time, alongside the customers and all of their staff.

You hope they have also brought flushing toilets, though you are open to showering in the old style, using either a jug, or a bamboo gutter, or a waterfall.

If one can be found in the surrounding hills.

It turns out that you'll have ample opportunity to look. You have paid a great deal for this experience, but the ticket you purchased still only covers *ronin*-class. You've signed on to spend a full month as an itinerant warrior. As none of those who have signed up to be warlords have yet recruited your services, this means you'll have to find accommodation outside of the castle, in the vast snowy valley at the far side of the fort.

Aside from the cold, and especially the wind—which billows up amongst your underthings, bypassing the kimono you're not sure you've affixed about your person in the proper fashion—you don't mind this temporary exile.

The scenery is beautiful. Far more beautiful than anything you recall seeing in the over-urbanized present. Indeed, you think that is why you didn't take your artistic talents further—your world simply lacked the inspiring qualities of a place and time like this.

Though, the niggling doubt remains that it was, rather, because a career in the arts seldom seems to pay.

The scents of cherry blossom and jasmine float boldly through the air, sweeping that doubt under the carpet of snow. Swallows and swifts and shrikes circle, wild and balletic, in the sky overhead. Herons and cranes perch at the edge of small, well-kept ponds, lily pads drifting serenely among their one-legged reflections. The distant outlines of mountains stand clear and sublime in every direction.

Already, you feel more at ease.

The morning comes, and it is time for battle.

You found an empty cabin, sparsely but effectively decorated, late last night, and it is here that an attendant comes to help you into your armor. This includes your choice of a helmet, which is red, and has large, angled eyeholes, which your attendant assures you will be fearsome to your enemies. It reminds you of Munch's *Scream*, or a face from *Guernica*—the horse perhaps, or the mother—as recreated in melted wax, like a seal, a ready trademark for your violence.

It's quite difficult to see through those eye-holes, though, as the helmet is a little big, and keeps slipping from side to side about your head. The *chonmage* wig is designed to stop this from happening. Perhaps you haven't put it on properly.

Such trifling concerns are soon banished from your mind.

Back down in the valley, you can see enough to make out hundreds of other figures, all dressed in similar armor, all with brightly colored masks.

Your attendant helps you to your appointed place in the formation. He tells you that you've been recruited into a warlord's army, and that your warlord is about to wage war on both of his competitors at the same time. At stake is complete control of the castle and all buildings and visitors therein.

Before being sent to the safety of the sidelines, he tells you to draw your sword. The warlord will give his unit ten minutes of orientation with battle tactics and then the carnage will begin.

"But, don't worry," he says. "These swords aren't actually capable of cutting, much less slicing anyone to pieces. Our insurance doesn't cover that," he says. "Not on top of the risks involved in time travel itself."

Instead, the swords are edged with electronic sensors, and all the armor is fitted with corresponding tagging units. These will respond by giving the wearer a mild shock in the location of any fake-wounds. A full-body shock will result from a deathblow.

If your sword runs out of charge mid-battle, you'll have to find the nearest generator. He points to a large square unit, covered with fake-looking stone. You'll be at your most vulnerable at this point, so it's best to stay close to a generator at all times.

You are beginning to wish you'd paid more attention to some of these details before signing up.

⁎₰₰⁎

The snow all about you is trampled and scattered, geysering upwards as more and more bodies fall. The snow all about you is turning red with fake blood.

It turns out you're pretty good at this.

A kind of panic response has kicked in. A survival instinct.

Your enemies genuinely appear to find your helmet terrifying.

The shocks that afflict them are audible, even over the crunch of the ground underfoot. You are beginning to relish the sound.

To forget the emptiness of your double bed that morning.

To forget the terrible coffee you had to endure at your last place of work.

You whoop as you run across the valley floor, breaking formation, striking any and all before you with masterful, lightning-fast swipes of your blade.

A whole month of this appears in your mind's eye, like a hot spring, and you wish only to jump in, to savor, to enjoy this new and exciting form of release.

Then, there is a buzzing at your shoulder.

Then one across your back.

You become disorientated, angry, confused.

Your helmet has slipped again, and you can't really see what's going on. You swing your sword blindly. You don't seem to be making any contact at all.

You feel a buzzing in your right thigh.

Your left arm.

There's a loud, insistent beeping coming from the hilt of your sword. It's out of charge.

You reach your fake-wounded arm up to readjust your helmet, looking frantically around for a generator. You finally spot one, but you've lost track of your mysterious assailant.

You careen across the snow, whooping now not with ecstasy, but with something far closer to despair.

You want your money back.

You want to go home.

A shock runs through your entire body.

The generator rushes up to your face at an unusual angle.

It turns out the stone is not fake.

Everything goes black.

When you come to, you are in your cabin. You are lying down, and your view of the ceiling is interrupted by two nervous-looking faces. One of whom you recognize as your attendant. The other is the customer service assistant from the gate.

"Are you feeling okay?" they ask, in unison.

You nod, hesitantly, aware of a pain just below your left temple, and also a feeling of swelling in your right ankle and foot.

The two faces grow calmer.

"That's good to hear," says the customer service assistant. "You had a mild concussion, and we think you have seriously sprained your ankle. Our best doctors have examined you and recommended that you do not participate in any further fighting for at least a week."

"Is that okay?" your attendant asks.

You think about this.

You did enjoy the wildness of battle, the simulated carnage, the weight of the sword as you swung it.

But you did not like the shocks. Not a bit.

You nod again.

"That's good to hear," repeats the customer service assistant. "Now, by way of compensation, the owners are willing to offer you a fifty percent discount on your stay."

"Is that okay?" your attendant repeats.

Your head hurts.

Your ankle is aching.

You don't really miss the simulated carnage.

You just want to go back to sleep.

You nod.

Since then, for the past few days, you have contented yourself with ritual.

Every morning, your assistant has brought you food, and guided you through the specifics of what he has told you is an Ancient Japanese tea ceremony. He's even given you a small scroll containing a detailed history of this, though you seem to have misplaced it.

Every afternoon, you have knelt on the wooden floor of your cabin and meditated. You have felt the sense of calm returning. You've gazed out through the open shoji doors, across the valley, observing the continued whirling of the shrikes and the swifts and the swallows, and you have looked down to where the cranes and the herons pad elegantly, as though upon tightropes, beside the finely tended ponds.

You have seen, on occasion, battles taking place in the distance.

Every evening, you have risen, testing your ankle, and practiced drawing and swinging and slashing with your sword.

But your heart isn't in it.

Being a *ronin* was only fun, was only truly diverting, when you believed yourself invincible. The bubble of that particular belief has long-since popped.

You keep messaging for your attendant to bring up more and more saki, but he warns you, repeatedly, that it is not free, and advises moderation.

In the minutes that you lie awake before sleep, you half-dream about your ex-girlfriend, about the double bed in the flat that you shared.

This morning, that dream hadn't left you.

Neither the tea ceremony nor the practiced chatter of your attendant could snap you out of it.

As you kneel on the floorboards of your cabin, staring out through the open shoji doors, you have difficulty focusing upon the balletic wing-beats and swoops and the crescendo-like rising of the various birds. Coupled with the fact there's some kind of construction activity on the other side of the valley, your lingering dream conspires to deny you the meditation to which you were becoming accustomed.

Frustrated, you slide the shoji doors shut.

When you return to your kneeling position, you notice that the left door, previously hidden, contains a painting. A picture of a waterfall, cascading down through a valley more stony, less snowy than this. It is clearly and exaggeratedly stylized, but also somehow seems so real to you that you fancy you could shower beneath it, you fancy you could abdicate your inhibitions under pressure of its flow.

You remain kneeling on the floor of your cabin, ignoring your attendant when he comes to bring you food, ignoring the food itself, neglecting to stand and test your right ankle, neglecting to practice swinging your sword.

Slowly, you are forming a plan.

When you open the shoji door today, you see that the construction at the other side of the valley is complete.

It's another cabin.

Its shoji doors are also thrown wide; you can see someone inside it.

A geisha.

Kneeling, leaning back on her ankles at the same time as she leans forward to pour herself some tea. Impeccable poise. A yellow flower blooms from the black of her hair.

The sight of her clarifies, immediately, intensely, the notion that was taking shape last night.

You wish to resume your artistic studies where you left off, all those years and years ago.

You wish to be a painter.

⁂

"Hello," the customer service assistant says. "How may I help?"

You tell him you'd like to acquire all the materials necessary for painting in the Ancient Japanese style.

He looks at you slightly askance.

He doesn't think Kenji is a very painterly name. "And, besides, you are signed up for the *ronin*-class experience only."

"How much will it cost to switch to the painter-class experience?"

"It could be quite pricey,"

You shift your weight onto your right foot, and wince, loudly.

"Well, I suppose I can arrange for the switch," he concedes, "if you're willing to accept a lowering of the discount down to, say, thirty-five percent."

"Forty-five," you counter.

"Forty," he offers.

"Done," you agree.

He loads you up with paper and ink and brushes and silk sheets, and you head back out into the cold.

⁂

Quite aside from the fact that you are apparently extant in Ancient Japan over five hundred years before you were born, it has been over a decade since you last sat down to draw or paint.

You take a few hesitant sweeps with the brush across a swathe of silk you've set aside for practice.

The marks you've made look like a pair of disembodied eyebrows, raised quizzically within the emptiness, as though musing on some deep existential dilemma. Such as, perhaps: Where's the rest of my face?

Undeterred, you try again to sketch the geisha's portrait, but it's difficult working from memory. Night had already fallen by the time you returned, and her shoji doors were closed. Maybe it's the saki you've been sipping despite your attendant's repeated rebukes; perhaps it's simply tiredness from the long walk in the snow, but anyway, you struggle to recall the precise layout of her features, the exact style of her hair, the true shade of red on her lips.

Frustrated, you stand up, still wincing at the pressure on your ankle. You walk over and slide the door shut. You notice the painting of the waterfall again.

You decide that copying that will be far better practice, will help you get back up to speed.

The dawn light streams in across the floor of your cabin, picking out a minefield of scrunched paper and silk scraps torn asunder.

Landscape painting, you've decided, is not your forte.

All that interests you, really, all that you can bear to train your eyes upon, is that beauty, distant, aloof, alluring, in her cabin on the far side of the gorge.

Frantic, imbued with what feels, in your faintly sleep-deprived state, to be a kind of mystic energy, you resume your cross-legged, semi-meditative position from last night, and set about striking the ink on a page.

Your actions have a renewed vigor, a confidence which is beginning to make itself known in your art. After the third or fourth try of the morning, you even feel you could show it to a stranger and have them pick out the geisha's face in a crowd.

Well, so long as it's not a crowd full of geishas.

Although, her kimono looks highly individual, and is punctuated by a striking, shocking-pink sash.

You will try and paint that next. A full-body portrait. After all, it's almost as though she's posing for you, standing in her doorway, head tilted enigmatically downwards in the direction of the latest war.

The light outside is dimming, the ancient sun beginning its slow descent behind only-slightly-less-ancient mountains. Because, though this is the land of its rising, it must also fall, every day, for evening to come.

This is just one of the many small observations you've made since you got here.

That no land is entirely defined by one aspect alone.

The sign above the gates, the ones which you presume are only visible back inside the present, says SAMURAI LAND, in bold red letters. But this place also contains at least one painter: you. And at least one geisha: her.

And, over the course of the day, that geisha has become more important to you than you think any of the samurai could ever be.

You have painted her figure, her face, in black and white, in color, on paper, on silk, standing and seated.

You have spent long minutes lost in meditation upon the smallest of her movements, the distant, almost imperceptible flutter of her eyelashes, the angle at which her wrist is tilted when she pours herself some tea.

You have closed your eyes and imagined the scent of that tea drifting across the valley, misting into ethereal solidity within the chillness of the air, becoming a bridge across which you can walk.

Now, you are painting her again, standing once more in her doorway, looking out in wistful distraction, as though waiting for something. For someone, perhaps.

For you?

You can but hope.

Well, you can *only* hope. Being as you don't think she even knows you exist. It must be someone else, then, it follows.

You feel inexplicably jealous, all of a sudden.

You begin to wonder, more inexplicably still, if your ex-girlfriend is sleeping now in someone else's bed.

A shrike comes to rest on a small branch, just outside your cabin.

Then it takes off, and seems to carry your panic away in the wake of its wings.

You feel foolish.

You are five hundred years away from your old girlfriend, your old life.

You are still perhaps five hundred feet from the best chance that this new one has yet offered.

Patience and meditation is key, you realize. Another revelation.

You still have two weeks left.

Good things, you remember, come to those who wait.

You have been waiting for a further few days. Have settled into a calming, meditative routine. Drinking tea with your attendant in the morning, and then shooing him off and painting the geisha for the rest of the day.

Every evening, you've observed her in her doorway, as though she's also been waiting, and then she has closed her shoji doors and extinguished the lanterns inside, an air of sadness about the way she turns to shut the nighttime world without.

Your paintings of this time have been growing progressively more subtle, even refined; tinged increasingly with gentle blues to reflect the sweetly bitter mood.

You're quite proud of them.

You hang them on the walls, filling up the empty space.

Your attendant, in between pouring your tea and bringing your breakfast, has tried to insist that emptiness is just as important as shape and line and fullness, to the sensibilities of the Ancient Japanese.

You listened, and glanced at the small instructive scroll he gave you, but you seem to have misplaced it now. With the floorboards cluttered with offcuts of silk and discarded paper, there's no telling where it could be.

Besides, your approach is filling you with a sense of achievement, even a sense of success. You feel, though you think this only quietly, as though you may actually be slowly approaching your guaranteed moment of Zen.

You think this moment, ultimately, will have something to do with the geisha's mysterious and covertly erotic face.

You are sure of it.

You look across the valley at her, and paint her, and feel more certain still.

Suddenly, as if you had shouted this feeling out loud, that face turns towards you. The geisha, at last, is aware you've been watching her, studying her, turning her into art.

She smiles.

Your heart leaps.

She blushes. Her cheeks go redder and redder, beneath the paleness of her makeup, until they are brighter red even than fake-blood on snow.

She hides her blushing behind a fan, turns her head away coyly.

Amidst the wind and the whirligigging passage of birds through the valley, you are certain you can hear her laugh. A gentle, melodic, happy laugh.

The soundtrack to the waterfall that's painted on your door.

This evening, she looks at you before shutting out the nighttime world.

The mystery, the eroticism in her face, her smile, is no longer quite so covert.

She doesn't douse her lanterns so quickly this evening.

You can clearly see each nuance, each line, each curve of her silhouette as she removes her sash, her kimono, and readies her body for the comfort of bed.

You are enchanted.

And glad that you are sitting down, and that your attendant isn't here.

You resolve to stay up all night, rendering that shape on paper.

Today, you shooed your attendant out of your cabin before he could even pour your tea. And long before he could tut disapprovingly about the overabundance of naked female silhouettes plastered on your walls.

You have a new, more forthright plan.

You will alternate your paintings with sheets on which you write love letters, secret messages, and sweet nothings, all in fine, ornate, and deeply calligraphic script.

In your own language, of course, but you're sure she'll get the gist.

You hope so, anyway.

Because, when you have written each of these sweet nothings, messages, and letters of love, you intend to fold the sheets of paper into origami shapes, after the birds which ballet dance beyond your open doorway, and cast them out into that same aerial arena, to float across and land, you hope, on the valley's other side.

Several early attempts—suicidal swallows, sacrificial shrikes—cascaded without ceremony to join in, unwittingly, with the artificial mayhem of the conflict below.

But one—a courageous crane—made the crossing completely intact.

The geisha had been looking down concernedly upon the full-fake-blooded massacre, and you had thrown it, your love letter, at that moment in the hopes of distracting her from such a fake-distressing scene.

As you watched the folded paper catch an updraft and start to soar, and then begin to glide back towards the earth, a simple slave to gravity, you grew more and more worried that she wouldn't notice, that she wouldn't turn to look.

At the very last second, she spun, reached out, took hold of the bird in her hand.

Unfolded it, tenderly, with her elegant fingers.

Read it.

Held it up to her face to breathe in its scent.

Or your scent, perhaps.

Then she blushed again, and returned inside, and poured herself some tea, the letter laid out before her.

Every time you sensed she was rereading, your heart began racing with joy.

Now, you are back to waiting again, your arms outstretched into the evening air, preparing for receipt of her reply.

It didn't come. Not last night.

It hasn't come this morning, either.

You are beginning to worry. She hasn't even opened her shoji doors today.

Without her to look upon, you cannot even paint. You simply sit upon the floor of your cabin, fretting, biting your ink-blackened nails, twisting and tearing at renegade scraps.

Then, in the corner of your vision, you catch sight of a figure, a female form, making her way up through the snow, back to her cabin. She is carrying a lot of art materials, some cradled in her arms, some upon her back.

You want to go over and help her, lighten her load, but a rudimentary comprehension of propriety suggests that you cannot, you must not, until she gives the right signs.

You're hopeful that the right signs will come by way of those art materials, and that you will then have opportunity to visit her and apologize for not helping her now.

You are hopeful that you will visit her and do other things, too.

You are not ashamed of your desires.

You're in the middle of a painting when the paper bird, a crane, flutters in through your open doors.

In the distance, in her own doorway, the geisha is watching and, you think, smiling.

The paper bird lies, as though sleeping, as though spent, its migration complete, spread out across your open palm. You begin to unfold it, embarking upon a strange and strangely enchanting autopsy, peeling apart the delicate planes of this origami organism, feverish to reach the even-more-delicate bones of the text.

However, when you do arrive, those bones reveal scrimshaw in Ancient Japanese only.

Not knowing in any way what her elegant calligraphy says, you cannot, not yet sure if you've received a proper invitation, go across the valley to ask her.

Your only recourse is to go and seek out your attendant, and perhaps the customer service assistant, back by the gate.

You set off, briskly, into the snow.

In your last glance across the valley, you see that she is no longer standing by her door.

"Sorry," says your attendant. "I read the relevant history, but it was all translated."

"The entrance exam they gave us was all translated, too," the customer service assistant offers. He looks genuinely apologetic. A little embarrassed.

The attendant looks as though he thinks you've been drinking too much saki.

You quite want to punch him.

But, bearing in mind the decorum with which you think an Ancient Japanese painter should conduct himself, you refrain.

"We understand how this might be problematic," the customer service assistant continues. "So, to make up for this, we're prepared to offer you a further discount. How does forty-five percent sound?"

"Fifty-five," you counter.

"Fifty?" he says.

"Done," you agree.

At least you needn't carry any more art supplies back up the hill.

When you arrive at the top, however, you find that the hopes you were cherishing only this morning have been well and truly, finally, dashed.

Across the valley, the geisha is bowing her head before somebody else.

A *ronin*.

In his hand, you can just make out a half-unfolded bird.

She must have made at least one unsuccessful attempt at the crossing, you realize, just like you.

As you watch, breath catching, the *ronin* removes his terrifying helmet.

You recognize the face of your former employer.

The geisha draws her shoji doors shut.

You kneel on the floor of your cabin, staring at the first successful painting you ever made of her face. Your doors are closed, too, and you have stuck all the remaining and scrap sheets of paper and silk over them, covering the waterfall, which reminds you of how you imagined her laugh.

As you stare at this collage, as your eyes tire, as you lose focus, a sudden, inexplicable peace washes over you. The tranquility of surrender.

You lie down upon the floorboards, which are empty again, clean.

No matter which past you are in, you realize, or which future, the present is always the same. *You* are always the same. You are a loser.

You burp and it tastes more than a little of saki.

This then, at last, is your moment of Zen.

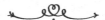

BACK TO WHERE I KNOW YOU

Victoria Zelvin

ady Ariadne wore her most important memories in a vial around her neck. Of course, Lindi assembled the concoction for her, though Ariadne chose which memories to include. She had to make do with fourteen—for memories are more than sight and sound, they are sense and the thrumming of hearts and the taste of skin and the scent of perfume. The more detailed the memory, the more all those little bits take up more and more space, so only fourteen to start, enough to know what is there and what is important. The Lady chose her memories, her favorite ones, and arranged them in chronological order. Lady Ariadne was a romantic, so of course she assembled them into a love story, all her favorite parts on display with appropriate cue cards.

They read, in order:

1. THE FIRST TIME I EVER SAW YOUR FACE

Lindi was beautiful in the golden light. Her skin was deep, dark, and even in tone, and Ariadne's first memory of spotting her was the sudden stab of jealousy that left an ebbing trail of admiration in its wake. Ariadne remembered approaching her but not why, but such is the state of memories. With some waning confidence, she did approach Lindi to wrest her name from her.

"Lindi," Ariadne remembered repeating, tasting the word on her tongue. It was a beautiful name, and Ariadne remembered telling her so. She remembered the way that Lindi's head ducked in embarrassment, turning her face away from the Lady so that she could compose herself enough to say that it was a family name, and that it had belonged to her great-grandmother, a software developer.

Lindi would spend part of the night explaining just what that meant, but Ariadne did not remember exact words. She remembered the way that Lindi raised a dark hand to cover her mouth when she laughed, so that Ariadne could not quite see her smile. She remembered the scent of Lindi's perfume, as though she had bathed herself in rosewater, and Ariadne remembered asking her where she might get some for herself. She remembered the first time they touched, an innocuous thing, remembered Lindi saying, "Oh, you have a hair," and then reaching out to pluck a blonde strand from Ariadne's shawl as though it were the most natural thing in the world. Shivers shot down the Lady's spine at such casual contact.

Lindi never did quite say why she was attending the gala in the first place, for Ariadne knew even then lovely Lindi was neither nobility nor military, but Ariadne only managed to ask her whether she would return to the gala tomorrow night.

"Or am I never going to see you again?" Lady Ariadne asked, and Lindi reached up to cover her smile. Ariadne remembered thinking to herself, *and tomorrow night, I'll see that smile.*

"If you remember how to find me," Lindi replied, dropping her hand. She was no longer smiling.

2. AND THE SOUND OF YOUR VOICE

The gala went on, as galas tend to. This one would last for weeks, with each party and each family attempting to outdo the other. That day, multicolored lanterns floated around the ceiling. The galas were for a recent military victory, quashing an uprising on the conquered lands to the south, but Ariadne remembered barely clapping for the incoming heroes. They were of no interest to her then. She was the third daughter with no inheritance to her name, useful only to the least of the lesser sons, not military heroes. Ariadne peered around her sister's shoulders, shunted to the back of the entourage as always, and did so much peering that her mother, the Matriarch, had pinched her ear like she were a child. It was with ear still smarting that she found Lindi.

Lindi was that night, and the color reflected warmly within her dark skin. Ariadne made her excuses to her mother and elder sisters before slinking off, the invisible spare-spare daughter, to find Lindi.

Ariadne came up from behind her and slipped her hands over the other woman's eyes—a bold thing indeed for such company and one she knew so briefly!— and yet it seemed natural. "Guess who?" Ariadne urged, smiling.

When Lindi turned, catching one of Ariadne's hands in hers, Ariadne did indeed get a sight of that smile. Lindi smiled, all teeth, wide and white, but it is not the firmest detail in Ariadne's mind.

No, it is the sound of Lindi's voice, light and pleased, as beautiful as her dress. "You remembered," Lindi said, and Ariadne held tight to the other woman's hand so she would not cover her smile.

3. A Stolen Kiss

This memory is short.

In a dark corner, tucked behind a curtain spilling from a large column, with Ariadne leaning her back against the cool column, and Lindi leaning near her, hand by Ariadne's head, too close to be polite but Ariadne could not care. Then Lindi said, "I hope you only think me bold," and kissed her, full on the lips. Just a peck, just a little thing, over too soon, and still a blush blossomed across Ariadne's face as though it were the first time.

Lindi gave a smile, a small one, and cupped Ariadne's flushed cheek in a hand. "I'll see you tomorrow, then?" Lindi asked, rubbing her thumb over Ariadne's cheek.

Heated, Ariadne managed only to say, "If you remember."

4. Loving You

The first time they made love is a haze. It is hot and wet and salty, but faded. As though from a dream, there is a light film over the entire occasion, preventing a proper coherent memory. It is minutes of ecstasy. The feeling of sex with one's eyes closed, the memory of her own chest rising and compressing under another's body.

Lindi made the first move. Ariadne echoed, only a beat off the other woman's rhythm.

5. I Remember Her

Ariadne remembered pining for days, with only the fading memory of Lindi's fingers upon her skin to sate her.

When Ariadne found her, Lindi startled, looked behind herself as if expecting Ariadne to address someone else. Ariadne checked for onlookers, then caught Lindi's chin in her fingers and kissed her.

"But, yesterday was Saturday," Lindi said when they parted.

"Yes," Lady Ariadne replied, dragging out the sound of the word. "What's that got to do with anything, silly?"

And Lindi looked sad, and Ariadne remembered taking the other woman's cheek in her palm.

"You remember me," Lindi said against her neck. Her breath is hot against Ariadne's skin. She shakes in Ariadne's arms, and Ariadne holds her tight until she stills. "You remember me," Lindi said again, and then pressed her lips to Ariadne's. The Lady had the sense to laugh, to pull away and swat at her and remind her where they were and that anyone could see, but Lindi only smiled and took her hand, and bade her, "Come with me."

6. The Things We'll Never Do

Mother would have a heart attack, Ariadne remembered thinking. In the basement, amid the rats and casks of wine, Lindi had her arms wrapped about Ariadne's shoulders. Ariadne's hands rested upon Lindi's waist. They danced there together, kicking up dust clouds with their skirts, listening to the muffled music playing up above.

"This is wonderful," Ariadne told her.

"You did tell me you love to dance," Lindi replied.

Ariadne could not remember saying such to Lindi, but accepted it. She rested her forehead on the woman's shoulder and followed her lead, rubbing circles against Lindi's skirt with her thumbs.

The memory is short, or seems to be. Dancing in the dark, silently twirling to muffled sounds—Ariadne remembered not ever wanting to stop.

7. The Fruits of Summer

It was the first time they'd met outside a party. Lindi could pass for elegant nobility among the best of them, and yet here she seemed happier. Trousers, not a golden dress. Ariadne felt overdressed, in heavy skirts, a shawl, and a vibrant red sash across her chest to declare herself. Not for the first time, Ariadne remembered feeling jealous of Lindi.

The other woman had taken her deep below the city, and while the actual route was lost to Ariadne, she could hear the underground trains rattling above them. Lindi's home, as Ariadne would come to know it, was tucked just behind an electrical closet, a cave carved into the stone.

Three things happened before the memory starts properly, three things that give the memory context.

One: Lindi found her at a dreadful dinner celebrating her eldest sister's engagement. No one would notice that Ariadne had slipped away.

Two: Lindi gave Ariadne the "tour" of her place, showing off chemistry sets and other oddities that seemed familiar but that Ariadne could not place.

Three: Lindi told Ariadne that the government was manipulating everyone's memories. Naturally, Ariadne told her that she was mad. That Ariadne knew people in the government and that she was hardly fearful any would display competence at any point in their lives.

Lindi pressed. She pulled a chain out of her pocket and offered the vial at the end of it to Ariadne. The Lady frowned, but took it. She does not remember what Lindi said to convince her to take it, only that she did.

The memory Lindi shared is faded, a stored thing translated twice over now. What Ariadne remembered:

A black girl runs before her, runs and runs and laughs, wielding a large cardboard tube as if a sword. From a first-person perspective, Ariadne is moving too, swinging her own makeshift sword. "Lindi!" the girl chants. "Lindi, don't cheat! Lindi, don't cheat!" The girl laughs, and Ariadne knows her name is Brianna, knows that she is her sister,

"Is such a thing possible?" Ariadne asked, when she could.

"It is," Lindi confirmed. "I know how they do it."

And Lindi explained and Ariadne knew. It was possible. Lindi's explanation of why they did it hinged upon control. Ariadne did not voice what she thought.

The memory faded there, became fuzzy, but there was a moment Ariadne wanted in there, tacked onto the end.

Ariadne included the moment when Lindi told her to boil her water from here on out. "They do it every fourteen days," she said. "To you rich folks, at least. Every six days for the workers and every two days for those in the conquered territories."

It is not the happiest of memories, but Ariadne kept it close regardless. Not everything important was happy.

8. Now and Always

Lindi unbuttoned her blouse, slowly, revealing flesh, underclothes, and a single opalescent vial tucked between black breasts. "Just in case I forget," Lindi said, lifting the vial with a finger before letting it fall.

"You drink that, and you remember?" Ariadne asked.

Lindi nodded. "Yes. Parts. The important things. It only holds fourteen memories, so I picked the ones that would help me piece myself together if I got lost."

"Can you make me one?" Ariadne asked. "For my memories?"

Lindi gave her a hard look, blinking slowly before she asked, "Would you like me to?" Then, after a moment, she added, "I mean, you're not in danger of losing yourself. They wouldn't make you forget yourself, your family. Maybe just erase part of the past. Maybe make you lose a few weeks."

Ariadne considered a moment, then smiled. "I'd put you in it, silly," Ariadne told her. "I've only known you a few weeks."

The memory faded into kissing, into holding, and Ariadne can't remember the exact order in which they touched and where, only how it felt.

9. Back to Where I Know You

"So I can get you back," Lindi said, smiling. Her eyes were sad as she did it, and Ariadne kissed her cheek upon taking the proffered necklace.

"Thank you," Ariadne told her. She slid into Lindi's lap, wrapping her arms around her neck. "It's perfect." The Lady had to pull the necklace down roughly about her braids, and Lindi did more laughing than helping when it got caught, but eventually it was settled with the opalescent vial between the Lady's breasts.

"It'll stay that color so long as you are touching it," Lindi told her. Lindi's fingers traced circles on Ariadne's lower back, and brought gooseflesh out of her skin. Ariadne tucked her head into the crook of Lindi's neck, bringing a hand up to touch the opalescent vial. Lindi's fingers came up to join hers. "If you want me to add new memories, let me know," Lindi told her then. "But, something will have to come out. It'll be a new concoction."

"What will you do with the old?" Ariadne remembered asking.

"Best not to know," Lindi said, and Ariadne could not tell if she was serious or joking. Lindi kept her eyes down. "But, I'll keep them. Return the ones to me you want to trade."

And the memory devolved into touch, into feeling, into fingers and gasps and kisses, and when coherency reigned again, Ariadne remembered saying, "I think I'd remember this, even if I forgot." She remembered that Lindi told her it might be possible to ingest the drug other than in water, but could not remember when that had happened. They remained in Lindi's chair, though both had shed clothes.

Lindi looked sad. "You'd be surprised," Lindi said, and did not look at her. "I'll have a way to get you back to where I know you, if you don't mind."

"Back to where I know you?" Ariadne repeated. She smiled, caught Lindi's chin, and turned her lover's face towards her. "I rather like the sound of that."

And kissing again, lost in bliss, in touch, and Ariadne lost sense of everything that wasn't touch.

"Remember," Lindi said, sometime later. They were on the floor now, yet Ariadne was not uncomfortable. "Take only a drop, and no more than once a day. Do not lose yourself in reliving memories and forget to come see me, my lady."

"I'll remember," Ariadne promised.

10. IN HANDWRITTEN SCRAWL, UNLIKE THE OTHER TITLES: *I don't like secrets, Lindi.*

"Have I forgotten you before?" Ariadne asked.

Lindi turned her face away, back to her book. "Let's not speak of such things."

The remainder of the memory is silence. A moving image of Lindi reading, lasting for minutes. When Ariadne did look away, she was half sure she saw Lindi wince.

11. LET ME GO TOO

"What if I just stayed here?" Ariadne asked. The memory was tinged with exhaustion. Ariadne was sore, her feet ached from dancing, and she wished nothing more than to remain with Lindi. It was always Ariadne sneaking out and never Lindi sneaking in. Ariadne recognized that it was safest this way, but also recognized that this meant that Lindi got to go to bed immediately after they had sex, where Ariadne had to walk the mile back home.

"You can't," Lindi told her. Her tone was plaintive. This was not the first time they'd had this discussion. Ariadne would want to stay, for laziness and comfort's sake, and Lindi would put her back on the right path. The safe path. The Matriarch would either die on the spot or have them both executed for this. Lindi was right, Ariadne was wrong, and of course the Lady would relent.

And yet tonight, Ariadne persisted. "No," she said. "I mean. What if I just *stayed* here." Spotting Lindi open her mouth to continue the tired dance, Ariadne added, "Forever?"

Lindi blinked, plainly taken aback. "What?"

Ariadne smiled. "I've been thinking. I'm the spare-spare daughter. Mother has enough to keep the family name going. I don't have to do anything else but be a disappointment and I can't see why I can't do that from here." Ariadne gave a shrug, trying to implore Lindi to allow it. Her discomfort got the better of her, and Ariadne found herself asking rapidly, "Well? So? Would it be okay if I stay?" A beat, and then, "Forever?"

Lindi blinked again, shaking her head. Ariadne feared she would say no. Instead, Lindi swept herself into a mock bow, gesturing towards the bed. "Well, my lady," Lindi said. "Why don't you stay the night to make sure you like it here first?"

12. SHELTER

The spare-spare daughter was spare no more. Rebels from the conquered territories had sunk the ship her two sisters had been taking to meet a potential fiancée in one case and suitors in the other. Lady Ariadne was in line now, the heir, to be the Matriarch of her family in due time.

Ariadne was heir now. It sounded strange, and stranger still the more she thought of it. Her mother, the Matriarch, was taking a personal interest. Ariadne had not managed to come to Lindi for a week and now that she was here, all Ariadne could do was weep.

The last thing she wanted preserved was the way something had gnawed a hole inside her, the fresh wound of death, the inability to breathe through the mucus, but she'd asked Lindi to keep it. For the first time in weeks, in Lindi's arms, Ariadne felt safe. For the first time, Ariadne cried for her sisters. She trusted Lindi when she said that no one would try to take her memories of them away since other nobles knew them and mourned so her memories of her sisters should be safe, though in that moment she half wished someone would take them, and so Ariadne asked Lindi to preserve this instead.

Lindi's hand in her hair, humming softly over Ariadne's sobs. The scent of her rosewater perfume.

What is important is not always happy. Ariadne preferred to preserve only happy memories, to help her remember that life had not always been so gray.

13. Subterfuge

Ariadne did not want to be the heir. Memory marker number 13 hid many things, a memory of staring at the papers she and Lindi had drawn up. They'd spoken of it, quietly, after Ariadne's sisters died. Running away. Going to the conquered territories and pretending to be farmers. There would be pigs in the house, Lindi had said, so they don't get cold in the winter. Ariadne would rather live with pigs. It was simpler. Running was selfish. But being with Lindi was the only place that made sense. Lindi was the only thing that felt safe.

Memory marker number 13 held within it a map, and Ariadne knew where to look for it.

14. Ariadne Loves Lindi . . .

"I love you," Ariadne said, and she froze upon saying it. The warmth of Lindi's bed likewise chilled. Ariadne glanced up in time to see Lindi shut her eyes and pretend to be asleep.

Ariadne loves Lindi, she thought, to the tune of a rhyme her sisters used to sing. Lindi knew now. Would know when she included it in the memories.

Lady Ariadne nuzzled her face further into Lindi's ribs, and pretended to be asleep herself.

⁘

Lady Ariadne wore her most important memories in a vial around her neck, but it was not there now. It was crushed into her mother's palm. The opalescent memories mixed with red blood and turned black as they dripped out the bottom of the Matriarch's clenched fist. Though her body faced her daughter, the Matriarch would not look upon her. Had not done, not since she had pulled the vial from Ariadne's neck whilst Ariadne lay immobilized and bound to a sloping table. The Matriarch had taken a larger sip than Ariadne ever had done before, and yet was quick to come down from the haze of the waking dreams that had taken hold. The Matriarch swiped at a single tear on her own cheek, and then was still.

"Mother," Ariadne said. Her voice was thick with mucus, her lips tasted of blood, but still she was not weeping near enough to blur the sight of her mother turning from her. She meant to go through with this, even now. *Perhaps*, Ariadne thought, *especially now.* "Mother, please. You saw. You saw! You cannot do this."

The Matriarch paused in the doorway. She did not look back. "You'll not remember that I have," she said. Then, "Do it."

And the Matriarch did not watch as they poured water over her daughter's face, ensuring that if she did not drink that she would inhale. The Matriarch pressed her back against the outer wall and picked shards of glass from her bloody palm as her daughter's screams turned to gurgles turned to choking turned to nothing.

⚜

The Lady Ariadne returned to her room after dinner, still sore from her extended bout of illness, but she would be damned if she spent more time on bed rest. Her throat burned, but was no longer raw. She had duties, as heir, and she would see to them. For her sisters. She moved to her desk first, for as weary as she was she had letters that she must write, and found mail waiting for her. The first several messages were on behalf of or written by potential suitors, and those got shifted into a pile to be responded to later. The last envelope was unmarked and heavy. With a frown, Ariadne opened it. Inside was a letter and a small necklace chain, upon which hung a small vial.

The message read:

> *. . . and Lindi loves Ariadne.*

Ariadne considered the message for a moment, flicking backwards through recent memories to verify if there was anyone of that name she could remember meeting lately. Finding nothing, she turned her attention to the small vial that was attached with the note. It was clear in substance, but when she shook it gently a world of colors swirled within the newly opalescent liquid. It was beautiful, yet the object put unease in her gut. After consideration, Ariadne chalked this up to the uninvited and unfamiliar gift being attached to such a note. Again, she could not place the name Lindi.

What she did remember was her mother, tonight at dinner, remarking upon a story she'd heard when speaking with the Secretary of Defense. "Assassination attempts are up," the Matriarch had cautioned. "Do you remember the Lady Christine? They found her dead in her boudoir. A terrible thing! Assassins are like rats, my dear. One never knows from whence they come, but they always find a way in." This was followed by a command to double the guards about Ariadne's room, which Ariadne had told her mother was frivolous.

"I can take care of myself, Mother," she had told her, and the Matriarch had smiled.

The Lady Ariadne crumpled the note around the vial, and tossed both into the fire.

⚜

GREEN-EYED MONSTER
J.D. Brink

I feel like I'm exploring the Great Orbison Salt Flats—his scalp is spongy but barren beneath my booted feet, cracked by the sun and dusted with dried perspiration. The slope of his head is a nearby horizon, bronzed and textured with pores. At this scale it's an alien landscape, as if I'm an astronaut on an arid planet rather than a micronaut on something so familiar. The lamps burning above are like twin Sahara suns and the craft behind me, a desert-sailing skiff.

The microship is both a vehicle for q-mass reduction and a transport for getting here. The craft crouches low on its landing gear now, like a carbon fiber locust resting after a long flight. Its dorsal and side fins fold inward and the engines hum in stereo as the power plant rebuilds for the return trip.

I call it in. "Fat Man, this is Little Boy. On the surface and feeling good. The skiff's gone into its recovery cycle. Should be ready by the time I'm done."

"This is Fat Man. Looking good from here, Ray. What's it like to walk on the big man's skull?"

"Oh, inspiring," I say sarcastically.

"I bet it is," Ricardo says, quite sincere.

If this had been a trip to Emil Orbison's ass, Ricardo would have come himself so he could kiss it in the flesh. They all would have. But like most sycophants, they're also cowards. Sure, I was nervous. Who wouldn't be, lying in that coffin-like aircraft, spun down to the size of a gnat? If I were accidentally killed buzzing across the lab, no one would even be able to find the body. But fear is a lesser motivation, and I have more on my mind than giant flyswatters.

"Warm it up, baby," I tell the skiff. It hums happily in return. I imagine its thrusters will leave a first-degree burn the size of a finger print when I take off. It's a comforting thought.

My boots sport tiny climbing hooks, like insect feet, and I drag them for a few strides. This scuffs up dandruff flakes as big as my hands. I hope Emil can feel it, even in his sleep. I want to leave a mark.

Ahead is the curving ridge of his right ear. It's bristled with jagged hairs, and its size and position seem to defy gravity. Below that long, hanging cliff are what look like the pyramids of strange Egyptians. At normal size, they're just a blinking cluster of shapes arranged like an electronic snowflake, a slight blemish on his otherwise handsome bald head. Not even a blemish. Jennifer said it makes him look *distinguished*. Like he needs any further distinguishing. Doctor Emil Orbison, man of the year, brainiac heartthrob of the scientific community. And what am I? I was one of *Neuro-Scene's* "top five to watch" just a couple years ago. But no one notices poor little Ray Sharp anymore, not even my own wife. Not when he's around.

I come to the entrance of the central pyramid. It's the tallest of the seven structures, three stories high from here, with translucent walls flashing in random colors. Red-yellow-green, purple-blue-orange, all vibrating to the same repetitive rhythm from a song I don't quite recognize. Is he throwing a New Year's Eve party in there? I'll find out, in a minute . . .

A voice crackles in my ear. "Fat Man to Little Boy: What's wrong, Ray? Access hatch stuck?"

"Uh, yeah," I say into the mic, "but give me a sec, I can get it."

Officially, this is an exploratory event, the first of three. For the next week, my colleagues will pore over the data and images I bring home, all the while telling Emil what a great man he is and yipping at his heels like obedient little pups. But I have unofficial business here too. This dog has territory to protect.

I switch off the mic and unzip the front of my jumpsuit.

"Can you feel that, Emil? Something warm and wet dribbling on your scalp?"

Doubtful. My bladder probably holds half a micro-liter at this size. Better save some.

I zip up, unlock the hatch, and crawl inside.

The pyramids are 3N—*neuro-nano-nodes*—invented by this sleeping playboy genius. Modern science can farm riverbeds on Mars and shrink me to the size of a flea, but we have yet to fully plumb the depths of the human brain. 3N will change that. I believe in the project—I really do—just not in the arrogant guy getting all the credit. And if inventing it wasn't heroic enough, Emil had to go and make himself the guinea pig too.

What a self-sacrificing jerk.

The node interior combines the workings of an old watch with a Saturday night discotheque. Crystal gears turn everywhere, lit by flickering colors and lighted upon by phantoms from his memory. Ghosts appear and disappear. Murmuring voices provide a white noise background. A few bars from an old pop song play over and over again. I can smell cookies baking and lilac perfume. At the center of this clockwork chaos is the manual interface, a hexagonal pedestal broadcasting a thin pillar of light all the way to the pyramid's apex.

I insert the recording cube. The vertical beam changes from idle orange to active green. The ghostly chatter and phantom images all vanish, leaving me alone in the dark crystal tomb with the quiet grinding of gears. I can feel Emil's pulse under my feet.

I had to memorize a list of verbal prompts, the official plan of this miniaturized odyssey. I'm supposed to speak these magical words and see what his memory does with them. The recording cube will capture the images and track all the mnemonic pathways as they zigzag like lightning bolts through his brain. Of course, the whole time Ricardo was going over the list with me, I was thinking of something else. What can I say? I love my wife. And I'm a tiny bit selfish, so for now, the list can wait.

Clearing my throat, I speak her name loud enough to penetrate his sleeping unconscious: "Jennifer."

The green pillar expands into a huge emerald eye. It's hers, dominating the pyramid like Cleopatra's own. It glares down on me, streaked hazel and wreathed in long lashes, unblinking, accusing, almost scolding. For an instant I feel my righteous armor falling away and the stare penetrating me; I bleed a few drops of guilt before it finally blinks. Then her whole lovely face appears above me, an elfin grin on her thin lips. And I can smell her apricot shampoo.

She giggles for Emil and my guilt dries right up.

His memories of Jennifer flash through the empty space. She's wearing a white lab coat and explaining a holographic neural map. She's lobbing another egg into the slimy, sun-colored mess that's sliding down the wall with her homemade catapult. Jenn took home the gold that day in our Laboratory Olympics. Then, in the next blink, she's at the Christmas party, dancing awkwardly alone in her black dress. Orbison's perspective watches her butt on the dance floor, then her cleavage as she goes for more eggnog.

Colors flash through me now. Mostly a furious, bloody crimson, but also a sickly yellow feeling that sags in my guts.

I have another verbal prompt for the interface, but it gets stuck in my throat. I swallow hard and force it out. "Sex with Jennifer."

This sends the images spinning again, like a hand to the wheel of fortune. I watch, nervously awaiting my fate.

There are flashes of her laughing, brushing her dark hair away from shining green eyes. Now she's strutting away from him, obviously cat-walking for his benefit. She bends over a control console. Licks her lips as she's measuring samples; you can always tell by her small mouth when big things are happening inside her head. She slips out of her lab coat and starts undressing, then notices him and closes the office door. She gives him a steaming cup of coffee, their fingers brushing in the hand-off.

But she never comes up naked. No sex scenes appear from his unconscious memory. She hasn't slept with him.

I can breathe again. My fists relax and blood pumps back into my fingertips.

"I'm still going to get you, Emil," I grumble.

The ethereal gallery spins again. I've accidentally triggered more memories.

Now Doctor Shepherd appears above me: gray-bearded, frail, angry. They're shouting at one another.

"I'm still going to get you, Emil," says Shepherd's ghost. "3N was mine! You couldn't even spell it without me and you're not going to get away with this!"

But he is. I watch, slack-jawed, as Emil's hands choke the life out of his old mentor. The pair of them stumble into the desk, and Shepherd's Bellman Prize trophy clatters off and breaks from its base. Panicked, nasally breaths wheeze through this pyramid of memories. Their tangled dance trips over a chair, and both men fall to the floor. The old man's eyes bulge, and his red face slowly turns blue.

My own hands twitch. My lungs get anxious.

Emil lets go when Shepherd's expression of pain shifts from *can't breathe* to *heart attack*. He clumsily locks the door and closes the blinds. Shepherd curls up into the fetal position. And Emil just stands over him, watching him die.

Nausea and glee chase each other in my stomach. Glee wins out the second time I see it.

"Fat Man to Little Boy. How's it going in there, Ray?"

I wipe my sweaty brow with one hand and pull the recording cube with the other. "It's freakin' awesome in here, Ricardo. Wish you were here. I've got just one more thing to finish up and I'll be on my way home."

Zip.

"Can you feel this, Emil? Is your unconscious mind dreaming of a tiny man marking his territory inside your brain? You think that's bad, just wait till I get out of here . . ."

BY BARGAIN AND BY BLOOD
Aliette de Bodard

Originally appeared in *Hub Magazine*, no. 108, January 2010

The blood empath came when my niece was eight.

I should have suspected something like that—but my sister Aname had told me little about the begetting of her daughter, little beyond her certainty that everything would turn out right in the end. Her death in childbirth had left my questions forever unanswered.

Nevertheless, when Aname told me about her child to come, she spoke of a bargain struck. And thus I should have known someone would come to honor it—that someone would walk through the rice paddies and the forests until he reached our jati, our small community isolated from the affairs of the world.

But, just as you know about death but do not think about it, so I did not think about him.

A mistake. Perhaps I would have been better prepared, had I thought of his coming.

⁂

It was the Night of Mourning in the jati: the night when the spirits of the dead descended from heaven to commune with us. I'd just finished painting the *tilak*, the sacred tear-drop mark, on my niece Pamati's forehead, when she spoke.

"Auntie?"

"Yes," I said, knowing what was coming: the same question Pamati asked every year on the Night of Mourning. I turned briefly, to wash my hands clean of the red paste.

"Will Mommy be here?"

"I don't know," I said, truthfully. Shanti, the priestess of the Destroyer, had said that Aname would be in the heavens, that she'd descend to earth with the other dead. But although in eight years many dead had possessed Shanti during the ceremony, none of them had been my sister. Perhaps—my stomach felt hollow—she was already reborn, not knowing me or Pamati.

"You said she loved me," Pamati said, her face twisting in the beginning of a sulk.

"Yes," I said. "She loved you so much she let Bhane, the god of Death, take her instead of you." I remembered the birth; remembered Aname's face, distorted by pain; remembered the fear that filled her as she realized it was going wrong and that nothing would help her; remembered praying, desperately praying to all the small gods of the jati, praying she would be spared.

The gods have their own ways, which are not ours: Aname died, but Pamati was spared.

Pamati leapt to her feet, in a gesture too reminiscent of Aname as a child. "She'll come. She'll have to, Auntie. She just can't leave me." The hope on her face made me look away, for I suspected she'd be disappointed again tonight.

"She may come," I said at last, not wanting to add to her enthusiasm.

"You don't think she will," Pamati said.

"I don't know."

"You never know anything," she said, tears pooling in her eyes.

"No," I said, finally. I couldn't make promises I wouldn't keep.

Sometimes I hated Aname. Sometimes I hated her for striking her strange bargain, for becoming pregnant without a husband or even a serious suitor, for dying and leaving Pamati to me, forcing me to turn my back on the priesthood—for the Protector is not a god who can be served with a divided heart.

My bleak moods never lasted, but they came more and more often those days, when I saw what Pamati was reduced to.

"There's still some time before the sun sets," I told her. "Why don't you play outside?"

Pamati shrugged. "What for? The others won't talk to me."

As a child without a father, Pamati was an outcast in our community: her mother's transgression had left its mark on her. I lived outcast from the jati, eking out a living for both of us. "I know, sweetheart," I said, even as my heart twisted. "But you're young; you shouldn't be cooped up."

"Can't I stay here and help you cook flatbread?"

"There won't be any flatbread tonight," I said. "Remember? I have to light a strong fire in the hearth, so that the dead can find their way home."

Pamati's face fell. Even at eight, she knew that flatbreads required smoldering embers. To cheer her up, I handed her the boxes of paste, and said, "You can finish the good luck drawing in the courtyard, if you promise you'll stick to the pattern."

She snatched the boxes from me, annoyed. "I *always* stick to the pattern."

I watched her run out into the courtyard, and kneel by the abstract design I'd started in the afternoon: two circles crossed by a straight line, and then tear-drop-shapes blossoming around the core, until the drawing seemed like two hibiscus flowers entwined forever.

Aname had loved hibicus flowers.

Alone in the room, I stripped away my mud-soiled sari, which still smelled of rice and spices, and went looking for my festival clothes. I had a sari made of the finest cotton, bartered long ago from an itinerant merchant on a year of good harvest.

I couldn't find the sari. I knelt by the clothing chest, rummaging through Pamati's scant things, through my other saris, and finally through Aname's things, until my hands met soft cloth. Odd. I must have taken out Aname's clothes to show Pamati since the last Night of Mourning.

There was no warning—no scuffle of feet, no other noise. But, as I rose with the sari in my hands, I slowly became aware that someone was watching me.

"Pamati?" I asked, but even as I did so, I knew that Pamati was never that silent.

I stood, naked, save for a flimsy blouse that hid nothing. I was alone and defenseless—as was the custom in the jati, neighbors lived far away, out of respect for one another's privacy.

It could have been a merchant or an itinerant priest, but they would have warned of their coming.

I turned as fast as I could, a hollow deepening in the pit of my stomach. I held the sari against myself to hide my nakedness.

A man stood just outside of the back door, watching me. His face was utterly expressionless, his eyes two pits of darkness.

The last rays of the sun glinted on both his arms: he wore bracelets of burnished copper, and I knew they would be engraved with leaping tigers.

A blood empath. An enforcer of the king's justice. A man who could destroy me with a word, if the fancy took him.

"What do you want?" I asked. Blood empaths lived in their solitary holdings, only venturing out to arrest the traitors who rebelled against the Pahate Dynasty.

"Aname."

My heart started beating faster. "You're joking," I said.

"I never joke," he said. Not a muscle of his face moved. Blood empaths were well-known for having no feelings whatsoever—every human thought had been burned out of them during their training. "Where is Aname?"

Something snapped in me. That he should speak of her as if she were still alive—that he should come here unannounced and watch me as he'd watch an insect—that, deep, deep down, I knew, or suspected what he had come for, for Aname's unfulfilled bargain—

"Do you think you can barge here?" I asked. "Tell me your name first."

He smiled, a bare tightening of the lips. "Tyreas. You may dress if you wish."

I bit back an angry reply, not knowing how long I could test his patience. I wrapped the sari around me as fast as I could.

He watched me all the while. When I was finished, I met his gaze, and although I was now clothed, I still felt laid bare.

"Tyreas," I said. "I'm Daya. Aname's sister."

"She spoke of you," he said, in the same flat tone—he sounded almost bored, but I knew he wasn't, couldn't be.

I shook my head, trying to rid myself of the feeling the past had risen to haunt me. "Aname is dead," I said. "She has been dead those past eight years."

I watched him. I gathered it was news to him, although with his aloof nature it was hard to be sure. His eyes flicked a bit; he remained silent for a while. But when he spoke again, his voice was the same. "A shame," he said.

His eyes moved, focused on the courtyard where Pamati, her face creased in thought, was drawing a red diamond on the ground. "I would have thought you would know about me," he said.

I looked at Pamati, and back again at him. "You're the one Aname . . ."

"Slept with," he said. He did not sound embarrassed in the least. "The eight years have passed. I have come to end our bargain."

My heart sank. Aname had told me almost nothing about Pamati's father, and now I knew why.

A blood empath. She'd slept with a blood empath.

I couldn't imagine this man ever loving anyone—couldn't imagine this man ever feeling passionate about anything. I wondered what that night had been—all cold, mechanical precision on his part, while Aname panted and moaned beneath him?

It was obscene.

"How do I know you're the one?" I asked.

"You think me a liar?"

I said nothing, merely stood my ground.

He spoke quietly, as if reciting facts from a list. "I am a stranger to this jati, and yet I know your house, and your name, and your sister's name. I know the child is not yours, but your sister's, and I know how long ago she was conceived. And I know a bargain was struck—do not tell me Aname spoke of *that* to everyone."

I knew, deep down, that he was telling me the truth—blood empaths were cold and callous, but they never lied. "No, she didn't speak of your pact. Except to me, but she never told me the terms," I said.

"I suspect you know all there is to know, Daya." He sounded amused this time. "The child is mine."

No. No. He couldn't— "You—" I said, groping for words. "It's not possible. You can't take her."

"You think to tell me what I can and cannot do?" And, although Tyreas had not moved, he seemed taller, exuding a sense of menace that filled my small house.

I knew blood empaths could do nothing to you without your living blood. I knew they were bound by law.

I knew Tyreas didn't care about any of that.

"I wasn't part of your bargain," I said, forcing the words through lips that had turned to stone.

"But you are still bound by it."

"I raised her as my own child," I said, trying to imagine my house without Pamati—trying to imagine Tyreas leaving the jati with a small hand tucked in his own.

No.

"Aname is dead," I said. "Your bargain is void. You never gave her anything."

I had a feeling—I had a feeling every one of my words vanished in his dark eyes, and that he dismissed them immediately.

"Her death changes nothing," he said. He paused for a while. "If you wish, I will give you what should have gone to her. You did raise the child in her place."

"Pamati," I said, as calmly as I could. "Her name is Pamati. And I don't want whatever Aname was foolish enough to accept."

"More wealth than she could dream of," Tyreas said. Somehow he made my sister sound like a grasping woman, selling the fruit of her womb in exchange for mere gold and jewels.

"She wasn't like that," I said.

"Then you obviously didn't know her."

"And you did?" I asked, scathing. "One night of—" I paused, deliberately "—love with her makes you an expert?"

He said nothing.

"You leave for eight years," I said, pressing my point. I knew it was sheer foolishness to provoke him, but I couldn't stop—I couldn't let him take Pamati away. "You come back, not even taking the trouble to inform yourself. You want a child you've never known, born to a mother you never knew either."

"All you say may be right," Tyreas said. "But it does not change the one fact you have been avoiding: that the child—Pamati—belongs to me. By bargain and by blood."

He was so sure of himself I felt disarmed—for a moment only, but a moment might be all he needed.

"Auntie, Auntie! They're starting the dance. Why aren't we going?" Pamati said. She ran into the house, and then paused when she saw Tyreas.

He in turn was watching her, his face expressionless. "Triad's greeting, Pamati."

Pamati was looking from me to Tyreas, and back again. Her gaze froze on the copper bracelets on Tyreas's wrists—even children knew about blood empaths. "Auntie? Are you in trouble?"

She thought Tyreas had come for me, to arrest me. I gave a short, bitter laugh. "No. I'm not in trouble."

Pamati turned to Tyreas, puzzled, but did not speak—at least I'd managed to teach her respect of the blood empaths, though she did not appear to fear him in the least.

Tyreas must have sensed something was expected of him. "I have come to visit your aunt," he said. "I knew your mother, once."

Pamati's face lit up. "You did? Did Mommy send you?"

Tyreas said, "You could say she brought me here."

"Oh? And does she have a message for me?"

I was about to tell Tyreas to stop spinning his stories, but he must have sensed he was going too far. "No," he said. "I have not seen her in many years."

Pamati looked disappointed, but she soon rallied. "Where do you come from?"

"Near a great city," Tyreas said. "A city with white cobbled streets, and great markets where you can find many things from sea-shells to beautiful stones. I brought you one. Your mother would have been pleased to see you wear it." And there, on the palm of his hand, was a green, translucent stone that seemed to have a light of its own.

An emerald? Was that what he had offered Aname? I imagined fistfuls of stones, diamonds, emeralds, topazes—no wonder poor Aname's head had been turned.

Pamati reached out, hesitantly, and took the stone. It was set within metal, so that it could be worn as a pendant; the silver chain that held it shone in the gloom. Her face was carefully set in a frown. I knew she feared he'd take his gift back, as the children of the jati had once done, putting a wooden crown on her brow and proclaiming her queen, only to jeer at her afterwards.

Only when it rested on her chest did Pamati's frown disappear. "Thank you," she said.

"Thank your mother," Tyreas said—and he said it with a sideways glance at me, so I couldn't be mistaken as to whom he was speaking to.

"It must be expensive," Pamati said, fearfully—used to a lifetime of measuring rice at each meal.

Tyreas shook his head. "No. In the city people trade them for little, and every woman wears one on her chest. It stands for protection."

"Are people nice, in the city?"

Tyreas smiled, but the smile never reached his eyes—there was no feeling whatsoever behind it. "People are people."

"Yes," Pamati said, impatiently. "But are they nice to you? Do they say mean things about you?"

"No one would dare say mean things about me," Tyreas said. "Or anyone with me."

I disliked the way Pamati had taken to Tyreas so quickly—and, again, he had been quick to see his advantage and seize it. "We're going to miss the festival," I said, clearing my throat conspicuously.

Tyreas looked at me, sharply.

"We can all go together," Pamati said, and I knew I'd already lost that battle.

⚜

I made Pamati leave the stone under her sleeping mat, suspecting the other children would only be too quick to tear it from her.

As we left the house, she ran into the courtyard to put a last touch to her design, and I found myself alone with Tyreas, for a brief moment.

"Why not tell her?" I asked.

He shrugged—an uncharacteristically human gesture. "Too much for her to take in at once. Do not think her knowing or not knowing changes anything."

I bit my lip. I'd exhausted my small supply of arguments. I wanted Aname to be here, so she'd realize what a foolish bargain she had struck, so she'd explain to me why she'd struck it, why she'd let her head be turned by the promise of riches, ignoring the consequences of having a child without a father. I kept hoping there had been a reason, not merely greed and fear.

Demons take her. Had she not thought ahead?

As we walked towards the banyan tree at the heart of the jati, Pamati said, "Tell me about Mommy."

Tyreas stood straight. Night had fallen, and I could no longer make out his expression—though what was I thinking of? He would have no expression no matter what happened.

"She loved life," he said. "I saw her dance once, at the Feast of the Moon, as if every gesture was infinitely precious."

"Did she dance well?" Pamati asked.

"She was the best," Tyreas said.

"But she's not here any more."

"No," Tyreas said.

Pamati looked up at him. There was a disturbing shrewdness in her tone, as if some of Tyreas's acumen had rubbed off on her. "Auntie says that the dead come back tonight."

"They do," Tyreas said. "Maybe she will, too. But the dead act as it pleases them."

"Wouldn't she be pleased to see me?" Pamati asked. There was such pain in her tone that I took a step forward with my arms extended—knowing that I could do nothing to comfort her.

Tyreas did not answer.

We reached the heart of the jati. Under the banyan tree that encompassed our temple to the Triad, the crowd had already assembled in the wavering light of the torches. The scent of incense wafted in the air. In the center, near the altar, a scene had been erected on bamboo trestles. Shanti, our priestess of the Destroyer, was singing the sacred hymns of the Triad and of the minor gods, beseeching their protection from the returned dead.

Children and adults did not sit together on the Night of Mourning, for it would have been inappropriate. Pamati, who had been running ahead of both of us, made for the small group of children standing to one side of the scene.

And, like every year, the people of the jati cast disparaging glances at her. Chandi the councillor nudged his wife Yani out of the way, while Arune the smith and Bodhi the weaver merely sneered at Pamati's passing—in such a way that could not be ignored. Pamati ran on, no doubt hoping to lose herself among the children.

But the children also moved away from her. Even over Shanti's hymns, I could hear the faint sniggers, the endless mockeries.

Fatherless . . .

Your mother was a whore . . .

Knowing what I now did of Aname's bargain, this last struck far too close for comfort.

"Children can be among the cruelest of us," a voice said behind me, and I realized it was Tyreas. I'd forgotten he had ever been there. "Every year the same . . ."

"How would you know?" I snapped.

"I was a child once," Tyreas said.

"You?" I could not help it. The words were out of my mouth before I could think.

"Even I." He ought to have sounded ironic, or amused at the least. But he didn't.

We moved to the edge of the crowd—they made way for both of us, I guessed because some of them had caught a glimpse of Tyreas's bracelets. Someone I could not see pushed me in the darkness; Tyreas's hand effortlessly held me.

I waited until we reached a quiet place to ask, "Why?"

"Why what?" he asked. "Why come back now?"

"No," I said. "Why did you offer that to Aname?"

He was silent for a while. On the stage, Shanti had finished the entreaties to the gods, and was now moving to the slow rhythm of the Summoning, her hands slowly bending and turning to emphasize every one of her poses.

"Blood empaths do not marry," Tyreas said. "They do not raise children."

"I know that," I said. And privately thought he'd be incapable of raising a small child. You had to feel love, which he didn't.

"We take children," Tyreas said. "Every year, we find the orphans and the abandoned, and share blood with them."

"You make them into—" I asked, and stopped. Into monsters like you, I wanted to say, but knew better than to push my luck.

"Yes," Tyreas said, as if nothing were amiss. "It is a simple process."

"It's—"

"The way of things," Tyreas said. "To have children, we would need spouses. Spouses need care. Spouses need love. So do children. Do you believe we could give them that?" For the first time, there was a hint of emotion in his voice, barely audible. Bitterness?

"No," I said. "But that still doesn't explain—"

"You are a slow thinker, Daya," Tyreas said. His voice was flat again. "I wanted a child of my blood. I wanted an heir."

"Why?" An unfair question, yet I had to ask it.

Tyreas was looking away from me, toward the stage, and did not immediately answer. "To leave something behind me. Something I had shaped, and not taken apart. I wanted an heir to what I had not destroyed."

"You'll destroy her when you share blood," I said. "You'll destroy her when she is trained. Isn't that how it works?"

"She will want for nothing," Tyreas said. And fell silent, for Shanti's voice was rising again, summoning those of the dead who had returned to the earth.

A shudder passed through Shanti; her features went slack in the light of the torches. "Ranya?" she asked, in a small, bewildered voice. "It is I, Manu."

Manu, keeper of the lore, dead for five years. Ranya detached herself from the crowd, and ascended the steps, to commune with her dead husband.

After Manu it was Rakhte, and after Rakhte Aayani, and after Aayani Meshnu—and so on until the night wore itself out, and the torches burned low, and the gray light of dawn slowly reminded us that we were still among the living.

Pamati ran back to us as the members of the jati dispersed. "She didn't come," she said. She sounded crestfallen.

I opened my arms to her and she ran into them, snuggling against me. Each of her sobs echoed in my chest as if they'd been my own. My eyes would not stop stinging.

⁂

As the sun rose, we walked back to my house in silence. The streets of the jati were deserted, save for a few haggard people, but those few still gave us a wide berth.

Tyreas was by my side, and he said nothing. I was beginning to understand that he did not speak unless he had to; that he did not venture any information unless compelled to it.

In my house, I brewed some cardamom tea for Tyreas and myself. Pamati had curled before the hearth and gone to sleep. I hoped that she'd forget her disappointment when she woke again.

No. I knew she wouldn't. Some wounds ran too deep.

Tyreas sipped his tea in silence, and said, finally, "When she wakes—"

"No," I said. "I won't let you."

"You'd stand against me?" he sounded amused.

"I gave up everything for her," I said, all the words I had not spoken in years suddenly pouring from me. "My future. The life I could have had as a priestess of the Protector, and not merely an outcast peasant bound to the monsoon and the harvest. You have nothing that I want."

"Think," Tyreas said. He straightened, his dark eyes focusing on me. "Think twice, Daya." He rose, unfolding himself until he seemed some dark thing, hovering over me. "I will go walking. That should give you time."

He slipped through the open door and was gone.

I stared at Pamati. She'd gone to sleep curled around her emerald as if it was something of infinite worth—and why shouldn't it be, seeming to come from her mother? Her mother, who was dead.

Child of my heart, I thought, trying to hold onto something, onto anything.

There were bruises under her eyes, where the tears had run.

Tyreas's words rose in my mind: *She will want for nothing.*

I rose, and stood on the threshold, staring at the splayed pattern on the ground: our hibiscus flower design, to bring good luck into our home. Someone, perhaps one of the neighbors' children, had already defaced it.

Think twice, Daya.

I stared at the intricate design, realizing at last that Aname was dead and that nothing would bring her back. That, whatever Tyreas might say, Pamati was my child, as surely as if she'd slept in my womb.

I had exhausted my arguments; all I had left was the deep anger in my heart—a mother's anger at the thought her child might be, not only torn from her, but made utterly alien.

Tyreas was coming back, walking slowly on the dusty street. His gaze rested on me, and I held it, praying to the gods for the courage I could not find anywhere within myself.

"You have been thinking," he said, when he passed the threshold.

"Yes," I said. And, once again, "I will not let you take her."

Something crossed his eyes then: a cold, frightening emotion that was not human. "You are determined to stand against me? That is not wise, Daya."

"It's not about wisdom," I said, slowly, keeping my distance from him. "Or reason."

"Call it fear, then," Tyreas said. One of his hands had moved towards his belt; before I knew it, his fingers held a small dagger. The back of his hand was bleeding, too: in bringing the dagger up he had succeeded in wounding himself.

For Tyreas's kind, blood is the supreme weapon. I knew that if he could shed my blood and mingle it with his, I too would be lost—no, worse than lost, utterly destroyed.

There was a hollow in my stomach, but I paid it no heed. Slowly, carefully, I spoke the only words that would come, "You said you wanted to leave something behind. Something you had not destroyed."

He stood, silent, watching me, the blood from his wound slowly dripping onto his hand. I could still feel the coiled, cold anger in his stance.

"If you take her," I said, ignoring the fear that choked me, "if you turn her, she will be like you. She will destroy. She will not love, or leave anything of hers behind."

"She will find a child of her own," Tyreas said.

"And is this how you want the future to be?" I asked. The words were coming fast on the heels of one another now, eager to be spoken—I had to be fast, to forget who I was speaking to, and the consequences if I failed. "A chain of children without a heart, who'll take others' happiness and find none of their own?"

He said, "I came to give her a future."

"But it's not a life you offer her."

Tyreas said, "But you offer her nothing either, Daya. Nothing beyond your vaunted mother's love. Love cannot compensate everything. Will love silence the jeers of children, or put an end to the jati's contempt? Tell me, what future will she have here?"

"What I can give," I said, quickly, before I could dwell on his words.

"No," Tyreas said, shaking his head. "It does not suffice."

I knew that he was right. "I raised her," I said, raising a futile shield against him.

"And I," he said, "am her father." It was the first time I heard him speak the word "father".

I shook my head. "I'm not Aname. I won't sell my daughter away." Only after he had spoken did I realize Pamati was not my daughter, but my niece.

But Tyreas did not appear to notice my lapse. He was shaking his head as if to frighten away a persistent mosquito. I watched shadows move back and forth across his face, in the utter silence. At length he spoke. "And if I take her, and leave her as she is?"

"Leave her—"

"Do not share blood."

Taken aback, I said, "You wouldn't do it. She wouldn't be of any use to you."

"Do not presume to tell me what I will and will not do," Tyreas said, calmly, softly. "Did you think blood empathy was the only thing I could pass on?" The cold rage was back in his eyes, and in every feature of his face. "She is heir to my holdings and to my knowledge, and I will see neither go to waste."

I stood, silently. No words would come to me. I had not thought he was capable of bending.

He was still watching me. "Well?" he asked. "It is not an offer I will make twice."

"You would keep your word?" I asked, and saw the subtle way his eyes hardened. "I'm sorry," I said, more frightened now than I had been while he held the dagger in his hand. "Blood empaths don't lie."

Tyreas moved a fraction, and the sense of menace slowly abated. "Some do," he said. "I do not. Nor do I make promises I do not intend to keep."

It was a subtle way to remind me why he was here, but it did not affect me.

"I misjudged you," I said, at last, all I could bring myself to put forward in the way of an apology.

He was himself again, cold, aloof. "Some do."

I stared at him, weighing in my mind all the paths of Pamati's future, and came to a decision. "I'll let you take her," I said, feeling as if I were stepping off the edge of a cliff. "On one condition. Let me come with her."

Tyreas did not move for a while, staring at me. I was afraid he would read this as lack of trust, but at length he shrugged. "I care little about your presence. If you wish, as long as you promise not to run away with her, or to betray me in any other way. Do we have a bargain, then?"

I was falling, endlessly falling, and it did not matter any more. "Yes," I said. "We have a bargain." I did not say, as Aname did. But I thought it, all the same.

Pamati woke up some time after that, and found both of us standing by her bed. She rubbed at her eyes, yawning, and asked, "Auntie? Is something wrong?"

"No," I said, gently. "But it's time to leave. For both of us."

Eagerness filled her voice. "Has Mommy come?"

Tyreas moved, and came to kneel by her side, looking into her eyes. His face, once again, was expressionless. "No," he said. "But she made a bargain with me, once. I have come to take you and your aunt to a better life."

Pamati's face was set in a frown—the usual frown, for fear that the gift would be taken from her. Her eyes flicked to me, and I nodded.

Tyreas started talking to her in a low voice—I could not hear what he said, but Pamati was listening, entranced, no doubt of a place where the other children would not jeer, or throw stones at her.

I stood by the side of the pallet, silent. I thought of the three of us, walking away from the jati towards Tyreas's holdings, exchanging one kind of exclusion for another, trading mockeries for silent fear and loathing. I thought of Aname, and of bargains, trying to convince myself I had made the only possible choice.

I prayed that, at the last, its fruit would not be too bitter, nor its weight too much to bear.

THE GHÛL (A NASTY STORY)
Matt Leivers

There is a sensation in the center of his head that he can't begin to describe. Once, when he was very small—before he had ever come to this ancient, looming, desolate city where the buildings were so tall and so closely packed that the shadows forever clung like cobwebs tangled in the fetid air—he had lived in a little white house on the side of a mountain. A woman who had probably been his mother had washed him in a huge porcelain bath, so big he imagined it was a ship he could sail to far off lands full of adventure, and he had liked to splash about and get her to work the lather into his hair so that it stood up in spikes on his head, and she would smile and call him Sunbeam. And most of all he had liked it when she let the water out down the hole at one end, and he would sometimes be brave and stick his big toe in while the water was spiraling away and laugh aloud at the sucking sensation while she would cry out in mock alarm and save him from being pulled in with it.

The sensation in his head isn't really like that, because this is a horrible, dragging, vertiginous thing and all of a sudden, Rook—a muddled bluster of questions wheeling around him like starlings—can't remember where he is. All he knows is that it is dark, his face and hands are wet with something, there is an indescribable taste in his mouth, and he is very, very afraid. He wants to open his eyes, but they are already open despite the darkness, so he closes them instead and feels his long lashes scrape against something. With an almost-cry, he raises his wet hands to his face, trying to claw away whatever it is that is there.

"Don't," someone says in a choked voice he half-recognizes and doesn't quite like, and they sound almost as scared as he feels. "Please, don't. Turn around first."

Rook stumbles when he tries to turn. He feels too small, too light, too much like the whole geometry of his body is wrong. "What . . ." he starts to say. But he hears the voice that comes out of his mouth, and can't ask.

"Rook?" whoever it is that is there with him says. "Are you alright?"

"What's happened?" Rook says. "Where am I? Who . . ." His hands twitch up towards his face again, fingers pulling at the thick folds of cloth wound tight around his eyes, searching for the knot.

"Never mind that now." The fear hasn't quite faded from this other voice, but it's being replaced by a relief that is almost palpable. Relief and something else. Something that sounds to Rook like anticipation. "Later, I promise. How do you feel?"

As if my head is splitting in two. Like I just woke up in someone else's skin. Scared to death. But he realizes that none of these are true. Half a moment ago he was more terrified than he had ever been in his life, dangling on a fraying thread above panic's gaping maw. But not anymore.

"Incredible," he breathes. And it's true. He can feel the life tingling in his fingertips; the arterial surge and venous suck of blood ebbing and flowing with the pounding of the heart jumping under his ribs; every nerve firing, impulses arcing between synapses. "Really, I feel amazing! Like I'm under a spell or drank some philter." Rook pauses; feels a little hollow space open in his gut. "You didn't? You didn't, did you?"

And suddenly he knows who it is there with him.

"Hoek . . .?"

Hoek laughs, and something runs ever so quickly up the back of Rook's neck, setting every little hair on end. "No!" Hoek protests, still laughing, "I haven't done anything. Not to you. You'd remember, right?"

It's an odd question, but Rook doesn't really care, because all he can think about is what the sound of Hoek's voice is doing to him, the way his pulse has quickened and his breath is catching in his throat. His tongue sticking to the roof of his mouth and his dick painfully stiff. He's trying to untie the cloth around his eyes, but the knot has been pulled incredibly tight, and his hands are still slick with whatever it is, and his fingers are trembling. "Why did you tie this so tight?" he mutters. "Come here and help me!"

"I didn't tie it," Hoek says, and for a moment Rook almost starts to wonder, but then Hoek's long fingers are tangled in his hair and it's hurting but he likes it and finally the knot gives way and Hoek is wiping Rook's face with the cloth. Rook still doesn't know what the nasty stuff is, but the cloth hits the stone wall with an unpleasant, heavy *smat* when Hoek casts it away.

"You can open your eyes now," Hoek says in a funny little voice that almost sounds like he's trying not to cry.

Rook does. "What the. . ." he breathes, seeing where he is, but then he sees Hoek and forgets about everything else.

Hoek's eyes widen slightly at the urgency of the kiss, at how quickly Rook's tongue has gotten into his mouth, at the feel of his still-slick fingers against his skin. Hoek starts to recoil a little at the feel of the clammy stuff on him, but then he remembers that this is what he wanted and the only way he was going to get it, so he just grits his teeth, and when Rook mutters "What? Don't you want it?" into his ear, biting the lobe, he groans and nods.

And when Rook is on his knees in the dirt, and Hoek has his fingers tangled in his hair again, Rook assumes that the sobs and moans that fill his ears are pleasure. And so they are—some of them—but every now and then Hoek, pinned against the ornate marble column that flanks one side of the steps leading up out of the mausoleum, glances up from what is being done to him and sees what is lying on top of the sarcophagus at the back of the chamber.

Of the problems facing the scions of the ancient noble families of that decaying city, boredom was perhaps the most immediate. Relieved of the need to work, their days spread out before them in endless opportunity. Everything was possible, and therein lay the rub, for everything had been done. Generation upon generation of noblewomen and noblemen had sampled every pleasure that their imaginations could suggest. No decadence had proved too sybaritic, no outrage too unhallowed for the refined palates of that place. Everything was available, and of everything they had availed themselves.

The books chronicling their depravities rose in rotting heaps from every dusty surface in every forgotten library in the city. Mansions which had once stood amidst gardens, the beauty of which would snatch the very breath from the throats of the less fortunate (literally, in one case, for the fourteenth Lord Vendrygol had bred a rose which suffocated anyone who stooped to smell it), now moldered to ruin surrounded by statuary celebrating acts of unimaginable iniquity. For a year or two it had been the height of good breeding to retain on one's staff a sculptor able (or willing) to capture correctly the angle of a human leg broken in three places, the mixture of agony and rapture on a face. The retired dowager baroness of Fand had scored a considerable victory with a fountain centerpiece depicting her turning her ninth husband inside out.

But these pleasures were old, and stale, and long had been, and Hoek had been starting to think that life was an empty thing devoid of meaning and that the only interesting thing left for him to do was to devise an entertaining death for himself.

"Oh, your pardon." Hoek is smiling, but it is a forced, stretched thing, and he is all the while silently offering prayers to every deity he can recall. "I was hoping to find the Professor?"

"Lord Gregson is out." The scowling boy glances at Hoek for the briefest of moments, but that is all it takes. He's dressed in the same heavy black gown as every member of the Institute—Hoek has one himself, somewhere—but it is frayed and tatty, and the boy has had to roll the too-long sleeves back. He has it belted around him with an old bit of rope.

"I . . ." Hoek says, and pauses. He can't think what to say, or rather, he can't choose from the millions of words that are suddenly writhing around him like maggots on a rotting carcass.

"What?" The boy glances at him again, disinterest giving way to suspicion. "He's not here, alright?"

"Who are you?" Hoek breathes, a hand groping for the doorpost. His heart is hammering in his chest and his knees have turned to water, and he has read deeply enough in books of forbidden lore to know that either he is suffering from the Sylpharian Pox or he has fallen in love. But his tongue isn't forked, so it can't be the pox. "I love you!" he gasps, wondering.

The boy's laughter is bright and sharp, and so are the swords he draws out from under the tatty hand-me-down cloak. "That isn't a good idea," he says. "Lord Gregson will be back on All Hallows' Day. Come back then."

⁂

Hoek's no fool. He has read deeply enough in books of forbidden lore to know that love is a dangerous and twisting thing, which is largely why no one in their right mind has bothered with it for centuries. At first he isn't sure, but once he hasn't slept for three nights running he begins to feel more certain. He paces the crooked corridors of his mansion, and the shadowy image of the boy slips around every corner before he reaches it, melts into the shadows hanging in every alcove, glances over Hoek's shoulder into every mirror.

The wind that sobs around the twisted turrets seems to call the boy's name, but then Hoek remembers that he doesn't know what it is. For a day or two he pores over grimoires, searching for scrying spells and the symbols that will bind the mind of a man into the body of a bat—he has the bat on hand, and there is no shortage of starveling wretches who will do anything for a meal—but in the end he just walks into the foyer of the Institute and asks the First Clerk of Doors. And then the wind that sobs around the highest towers of his mansion seems to whisper *Rook* most satisfactorily, and the fires that roar in the chimneys, and now he has a name to moan in his sleepless tormented dreams.

⁂

Being in love is hard on Hoek, and not only because no one really remembers how to do it.

To his great surprise, he finds that it is a skill that is very easy to acquire. And to his great horror, he finds that he has absolutely no control over it at all. Normally, the pastimes of the scions of the noble houses are like clothes, to be donned on a whim and cast aside as easily. But not this. No matter how he tries, he cannot get the image of the boy out of his mind. No matter how he tries, he cannot keep himself from the corridors of the Institute, hoping to catch sight of the slight figure busy about some unknown task, or eating in the refectory, or huddled in his cloak against the rain as he crosses the courtyard on his way home at night. But Hoek never sees him.

Ever and anon he finds his thoughts returning to the room at the top of the tallest tower where usually Lord Gregson keeps himself locked away with his papers and experiments, and it is not too long before a dreadful suspicion dawns on him. The relief he feels when he kicks the door to Gregson's room out of its frame and finds the ashes cold on the hearth, the window shuttered, no sign of anyone having been there in weeks, is a little unsettling, and only slowly replaced by an agony of doubt.

Rook isn't there. In his mind's eye, Hoek has only ever imagined Rook in two places, and he isn't in either of them. Which means that somewhere in the labyrinth of the city he is somewhere else, and Hoek has no idea at all where that might be, or who he might be with, or what he might be doing. The idea that he might be somewhere, doing something, with someone is torment for Hoek, and for the next three days he pores over grimoires, searching for scrying spells and the symbols that will let him see through the eyes of the hideously carved lanterns that are beginning to appear across the city as All Hallows' Eve draws near. But it's no good. Wherever he looks, Rook isn't.

Hoek can't eat. He wanders the corridors of the Institute, clutching at the sleeves of the black-coated Fellows, hooked fingers catching in the folds of their cloaks, and demands to know where Rook has gone. He can't sleep, and his wild rolling eyes skate over the once-familiar faces of his friends and peers, searching for someone who is never there. Some of them try to draw him aside and speak with him, but all he will ever ask is where Rook is.

The city sprawls across the lower slopes of five hills, and above the mansions that clamber halfway up the highest is another city, cold, and dark, and almost uninhabited, at least by the living. Only now, in the days leading up to All Hallows' Eve, does anyone go there, to pour libations to the dead and pray that they stay where they belong.

Otherwise only poets venture there, or the mad, and of the few who do visit the great necropolis, most who go in as the former come out as the latter. Hoek thinks of himself as neither, simply because he only thinks of Rook. He wanders amongst the dank and gloomy buildings, and now it is the cold folds of the marble statues he clutches and demands of the frozen faces and unseeing eyes that they tell him where Rook has gone. None reply, for even if they knew they could not tell him. But still he wanders the paved lanes, catching at feet that are crumbling to dust, at fingers that come away in his. "Where has Rook gone?" he begs of angels and kings and cats and gods.

"Who is Rook?" one asks back in a voice like an arm being crushed beneath a cartwheel, and climbs down off its plinth.

Hoek has read deeply enough in books of forbidden lore to know a Ghûl when he sees one, even if all the pictures he has ever seen have been mere shadows compared to the reality that confronts him. The books in his library showed hideous creatures burrowing through graves, clutching at carrion with lank, distorted limbs, brutish heads with fanged snouts ripping into dead flesh. Ugly and terrifying, things to scare children into obedience.

The thing in front of him now is entirely different. Terrifying, without doubt, but the distorted limbs are graceful, the bright globes of the eyes glittering and black in the moonlight, the skin patterned like oil on the surface of a rain barrel. It uncoils its long tongue and drags it up the length of Hoek's arm.

"Ohhhh!" It gives a low throaty chuckle, like gravel falling off a wheel. "You taste of despair! He's a fool not to want you, but I'm glad he doesn't. Stay for a while, lover, and I'll make you forget."

For a split second, Hoek wonders if forgetting would be better than this endless want, but then the Ghûl wraps the tip of its tongue around one of its tusks, worrying at a scrap of something that's caught there.

"No?" it croaks. "Well then, think on this. Bring him to me on All Hallows' Eve, and he'll want you like you want him. How does that sound?"

⁓⁂⁓

Hoek develops a new obsession. Now, when he wanders the streets of the city, waylaying every passing stranger and demanding of them to know where Rook has gone, their blank expressions elicit another question. Many had been ready to take pity on the poor crazed man who staggered through the city, the cry of "Where is Rook?" forever on his lips. But only insults and blows meet his questions about the Ghûl, and more than once he is pelted with excrement.

And almost of their own will, like a wheel caught in a rut, his feet lead him back towards the Institute. The Third Clerk of Doors refuses to recognize him and will not let him in, only shaking his head and laying a gentle hand on his shoulder when Hoek asks him where Rook has gone.

"Come, sir," the Third Clerk of Doors says, "do not block the stairs. Perhaps you will fall, and then what will happen?"

Hoek doesn't know, or care. "How can the Ghûl make him want me?" he asks, and flinches as the Third Clerk of Doors narrows his eyes and sucks his breath in sharply.

"Do not speak of such things!" the Clerk hisses, glancing about. "Not here." He steps closer to Hoek and drops his voice to a low murmur. "You should speak to the Professor."

"Gregson?" Hoek mutters, and the Third Clerk of Doors nods.

"But he is not back until All Hallows' Day," Hoek says.

"Not back in his office, no." The Third Clerk of Doors scratches at the back of his head. "Wait just a second and I'll see if I can't find someone to take you to him."

He vanishes into a dark doorway under the stairs, and a moment later comes back, Rook only a step behind him.

"Please," Hoek begs.

"I can't," says Rook, and quickens his step.

"But I've been trying to find you," Hoek pleads.

"I don't even know who you are," Rook insists.

"I can't lose you again," Hoek says, and brings the rock that's clenched in his fist down on the back of Rook's head.

"So, in short," the Professor intones, "the legend states that the Ghûl takes on the form of the one who has been consumed." He squints suspiciously at the wild-eyed man. "And now, sir, tell me, you are who? And what is your interest in such an arcane matter?"

"How long for?" Hoek says.

"I knew you'd come." The Ghûl clambers down from the roof of the mausoleum and pokes at the bundle Hoek is carrying. "So this is him, eh?"

Hoek almost resists when the Ghûl takes the body from him and carries it down the dank steps, laying it on the sarcophagus at the back of the gloomy chamber. "Ahh!" The Ghûl draws in a ghastly sucking breath. "A pretty one! I can see why you want him." It uncoils its long tongue and begins to carve the flesh away from the face, unhooking its jaw before bending forward to crack the skull like a nut and sucking up the soft stuff inside.

"Here," it says, jaw back in place. "Tie this around my eyes. It can be a bit rough for him when I change, seeing what's happening. Come on, it won't tie itself." But Hoek is clinging onto the ornate marble column that flanks one side of the steps leading up out of the mausoleum, and can't move. "Oh, right," the Ghûl says, and wraps the cloth around its own head, giving the knot a savage yank. "There, that should do it."

Hoek stands by the pillar, trying not to look as the Ghûl opens the ribcage with a single swipe of its arm and lifts the bloody lump of Rook's heart up in its fist.

"Want a bite?" the Ghûl asks.

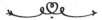

PAST PERFECT
G. Scott Huggins

I turn my back on the old man and close his door behind me. She is waiting not twenty feet down the hall. She advances as I walk to her. "If you have what you came for, you know the way out," she says. I pause and look into her eyes.

"You know, I was the one who really loved you."

Her eyes narrow, and her slap strikes stars into my eyes. I reach in my pocket, and the world flows away . . .

She meets me just inside the big double doors of their house. I haven't been to this one. Wide hardwood stairs frame her where she stands, her black eyes weighing me. For a moment we do not speak.

"It's been a long time," I finally say.

She nods. "He's in the study. It's this way." She turns to the stairs. Words form and then just block, sitting in my throat. What can I say to her after eight years? *Have you missed me? It's our mutual birthday next month again, how does thirty feel to you?* Or of course there's the one I've always wanted to ask and never had the guts for: *Did you ever feel anything for me?*

"Do you know what he wants to see me about?"

She stops at the top of the stairs and turns to me, her long black hair framing her face. I have a second to think about how she doesn't seem to have aged a day.

"Don't you know?" she asks.

"I know . . ." I pause. "The lawyer told me he's dying, Su. I'm sorry."

"Are you?" Her eyes flash.

Am I? I don't know.

She shuts her eyes. "I'm sorry. That was unworthy . . ." she takes a calming breath, "of both of us. Forgive me." Her voice is spring steel.

"I wasn't told anything else, Su." Nothing. Chad was dying. How did I feel about that? About standing here in front of the woman who was his wife, and my old . . . friend? What could I feel about that?

Walking back from the play at Nichols' Theater that night with her ten years ago, there had been no question what I felt: her hand, wrapped around mine, warm even in winter.

"Thank you for going with me, Andy," she said. "I don't have many friends who'd be able to sit through *Kabuki Medea*."

"My pleasure," I said. The play had been beautiful. A complex blend of a Western myth with Japanese interpretation. Like her, really. I stole a glance at her beneath the hood of her coat. Dark skin with straight black hair over half-Asian eyes. She was sixth-generation *nisei*, half-Maori on her mother's side. "It was perfect," I said. "Especially Medea's death scene, when she went, 'Eeuuuhhhhh . . .'"

"Oh stop!" she giggled, pushing me away from her before I could continue my atrocious falsetto. "The music wasn't the best part."

"My lady, I'm shocked," I said, "I thought you delighted in all things belonging to your noble roots."

She snorted. "Not the music. I'll take my American heritage for that, thanks." We walked on across the campus. That's when I heard the song.

"Hello, darkness my old friend . . ."

Her contralto was barely audible, but it drifted through the night. I matched it: "I've come to talk with you again . . ."

She stopped. "You like Simon and Garfunkel?"

"My parents raised me on it."

We continued the song. By the time we reached the dorm, her hand was again firmly in mine.

We parted in the common room. "Come to dinner in my room tomorrow night," she said. "I have one other guy coming, but I know he won't mind; he's just there for the food."

"Sure," I said, looking into her eyes.

And now her eyes turn down. "Well, Chad is a very private person, Andy; you know that. Some things he doesn't even tell me. It seems this is one of them." She leads me to a door.

"Su . . ." I begin. And stop. "The years have been good to you," I finish, lamely.

The sound she makes is somewhere between a laugh and a sob. She looks away. Her voice is steady. "Always the right thing to say; that's you, Andy." She knocks softly at the door.

"It's Andy, darling," she says.

"Andy Darling?" Chad's voice is distorted somehow, but the mocking tone is still there. "Funny sort of name for a guy, isn't it?" He laughs.

"I mean . . ."

"I know what you mean, dear. I'm not dead yet. Send him in."

"Don't let him upset you." She mouths to me, *Don't upset him.*

"Hah. I'd like to see the day he could. Come on in, Andy," says the voice. "Come and see. It's been eight years, hasn't it? Seems like longer."

He is laughing at me. He knows I am afraid, and he is laughing. Now I know what to feel. Anger bursts inside me. And shame, that my wounded pride has lasted longer than love.

I turn my back on the old man and close his door behind me. She is waiting not twenty feet down the hall. She advances as I walk to her. "If you have what you came for, you know the way out," she says. I pause and look into her eyes.

"Can I see you later tonight? It's important."

Her eyes narrow, and her slap strikes stars into my eyes. I reach in my pocket, and the world flows away . . .

The old man in the power wheelchair looks up at me from under a hanging lock of pure white hair. He's kept his hair. That's all I can think for a second. A thin, clawed hand grips the chair's joystick. The other, as always, in his pocket. The only way I could ever tell he was feeling nervous.

But what I'd been going to say dies on my lips.

"My God . . ."

"Yes, I suppose I am," Chad smirks. "Don't worry, I won't demand a sacrifice today."

It *is* Chad. The sneer proves it. Sick, but Chad. No, not sick, just . . .

"Dying of old age at thirty, Chad?" My own mocking tone is back, just as if I'd spoken to him yesterday. "I'd never have thought you'd be so careless."

For the first time in the eleven years I've known him, Chad actually looks surprised. Then he laughs. "Somehow I thought you would see it. No one else even suspects, except the doctors, and they're going on about 'late-onset progeria,' as if *that* had ever happened to anyone above the age of four. When I die of it, they'll call it Kello's Disease. Don't tell Su, that's all I ask. She'd never forgive me."

"Tell Su what?" What is the man talking about?

"That I'm dying of old age, dumbass." He searches my face. "Ah, the instincts are working, but Mr. Brain doesn't believe them. No wonder I stole her from you, Andy."

My jaw drops. Straight talk at last. I'd even accused him of it, once, and he'd denied having any idea of what I'd meant. But he'd known. I'd meant that dinner.

I'd assumed we were ordering in when Su had asked us to meet in her dorm room. After all, how could she cook without a kitchen? Staring at the neat slices of raw fish on rice beds, I realized how.

We sat in a triangle. On my left was Su. On my right was Chad. They were watching me. I should have been watching him. But I was watching the fish. Gray blubber peered up at me. And pink. And orange.

"My favorite," Chad was saying as he picked up something that looked like a dead, leathern banana with lacquered chopsticks. "Sea urchin." He chewed with relish. He looked at me. Smiled. "Takes experience," he said. He brushed back a floppy lock of hair, the only imperfect thing about him. Looked at my plate.

"Is something wrong, Andy?" Su asked.

This son-of-a-bitch was not going to outdo me. I picked up the orange piece of fish, looking him in the eye. And kept looking him in the eye while my chopsticks sent it flipping end-over-end across the room."

"Would you like a fork?" he asked, still smiling.

"No, thank you." This time I concentrated, holding a slice of red fish carefully. I brought it to my mouth. I don't know what my face looked like as I chewed that piece of slimy, cold meat, but I couldn't help it. It went down hard. Su looked concerned. Chad just . . . smiled.

"You might want to try some of the wasabi," he said, smearing a chunk of greenish paste on another slab of cold gray fish. "This is how the connoisseurs in Japan eat it," He swallowed the bite with relish. He turned to Su and spoke rapidly in liquid syllables.

Her eyes widened. "I didn't know you knew Japanese," she said. "I've been learning for years. Where did you study?"

He dismissed it. "Oh, you pick things up. I bet Andy knows some, too," he gestured to me.

I could feel myself flush. "Shogun," I said. "Toyota." Chad laughed gently.

I was putting the green paste on my own lump of gray fish. Whatever killed that taste was fine by me. I just wanted to get through the meal. Su turned to me just as I bit into the morsel. "Um, Andy . . . " she started.

And I knew then, in the moment between my teeth meeting and the pain beginning, that I'd made a mistake. I knew it by the expression on Chad's face. There ought to be a word for self-assured superiority that disgusting. Smugma, perhaps?

After my fourth glass of water, Chad said, "I'm sorry, I assumed you knew what wasabi was." He said something in Japanese to Su, who laughed, her eyes glowing.

"Sorry," said Chad, turning to me. "Untranslatable joke." But I'd translated it well enough. The joke was me.

I turn my back on the old man and close his door behind me. She is waiting not twenty feet down the hall. She advances as I walk to her. "If you have what you came for, you know the way out," she says. I pause and look into her eyes.

"Su, you have to listen to me! Chad's a motherfucking—

Her eyes narrow, and her slap strikes stars into my eyes. I reach in my pocket, and the world flows away . . .

Now my hands clench into fists. "Keep talking and you might not live to die of whatever this is."

"Pah!" Chad pulls the chair back with a sharp whine of motors. "Don't give me that shit. You can't kill me, and you know it. Su would be so upset. Mustn't hurt poor Su, Andy. And you would, if you killed me; I've seen to that." Whatever the expression is on my face, it is enough for him. "Hah. That's where you always went wrong, Andy. She's not that easy to hurt; I know."

"Yes, you do, you bastard. Because you always treated her like shit!"

"Now, Andy, not so loud. She'll hear." He folds his hands and looks up at me. "After all, I was the one who learned Japanese for her. I was the one who learned kendo with her. I treated her like shit? You were never really there after that dinner. Did I embarrass you that much?"

"That's bullshit. It wasn't that I was never there. You were *always* there."

"It must have been terrible for you to watch," he smiles. "Andy, you're so close to the truth. Closer than you ever were to my little half-breed."

"You're dead." I advance on him with murder in my heart.

If the dinner had been the start of it, the fight had been the end of it. The tears had run down Su's face, despite her attempts not to cry.

"I need to see you alone outside," I said to Chad in the lobby.

"Whatever you say, Andy."

He followed me out to the lawn, brilliant under the streetlights. It was ten at night, and midterms were just around the corner, so it was deserted.

"What's it all about, Andy?" he said, turning to face me. "You seem distraught."

For an answer, I shoved him to the ground.

He bounced up. "Jealous, Andy?"

"No." I was amazed to discover it was true. My anger was cold, and I raised fists that felt like solid ice. "You don't ever talk to her like that again, you hear me? You understand?"

He smirked. "You mean I can't have a fight with my girlfriend ever again? Hardly fair."

"Not one where you call her a half-breed bitch in public, no."

His grin widened. "You think she'll love you for this?"

My rage broke. I threw a roundhouse punch, and he ducked. He hit me lightly under the sternum, and I nearly collapsed. From the floor I kicked out at him, gasping, but he jumped over it.

He let me get up. "Are we fighting, Andy?"

"Come on, you bastard."

"Okay." The spin-kick came from the left like a sledgehammer. I tried to charge him, but he threw me off to the side. I looked up at him and then I knew. I hadn't caught him off-guard. He'd been waiting for me. I stood again. I breathed for what must have been half a minute. I didn't have to beat him. Just hurt him. Just a little. Just make him respect her. Respect *me*. I charged, stopped and kicked. He blocked with practiced ease. But I took one step forward and drove a hard punch at his eyes, too close for him to block. He ducked back but I caught him on the nose and blood sprayed.

"Stop it!" The shove from behind sent me sprawling to the ground, face in the freezing grass. I lay there listening to her voice. Then I looked up.

Su was kneeling over Chad, stanching the blood with a handkerchief. And when I struggled to my knees she looked at me and said, "Can't you just leave him alone?"

I turn my back on the old man and close his door behind me. She is waiting not twenty feet down the hall. She advances as I walk to her. "If you have what you came for you know the way out," she says. I pause and look into her eyes.

"You know, Su, sometimes you're a real bitch."

Her eyes widen, and she rears back, fist balled to strike. I have just enough time to laugh before I reach in my pocket, and the world flows away . . .

I grip the old man's robe and pull him up six inches. My lips pull back from my teeth, and he is helpless. He looks into my eyes and answers with a smile. "Are we fighting, Andy?" I say nothing, trying to outstare him, but I never can. Never could. "Will this be how you win? Beating up a dying man? She'll be so impressed."

I release him and sink back into a chair that I'd barely registered before. "That what you called me here for? To remind me that you always win?" I finally say.

"You haven't seen me for eight years; I stayed away like she asked. Are you so pissed off that I've outlived you that you have to remind me before you go?" He says nothing. One last spark of hope strikes within me. "Or did you want to provoke me into killing you because you're too gutless to die the natural way?"

"Heh, you wish. I'm not afraid of you, Andy. I never have been, and I never will be. You're the one who's afraid. Get used to it. You're the one who's lost."

"That the reason you're dying in the chair?" I snarl.

"That the reason you won't look me in the eye?" he snaps.

I have no answer. Only shame.

"Don't you want to know why?"

There is only one thing to say.

"Because you were there, and I wasn't. Because you always knew the right things to do and say, and I never did." My eyes are fixed beneath his desk. "That's why and I know it. You were always just in the right place. Wherever I could have been. You were always better than me. No matter how good I was." Tears threaten at the back of my throat.

"You weren't that bad, Andy. But no one's as good as me when I want something. Hardly fair, is it?"

"No."

"Well, life isn't fair, is it? But I'll have to admit that it was a bit unfairer to you."

"What?" I am too worn out to care.

"Because I cheated you."

"I know."

"No, you don't. Look here." He puts his hand in his pocket, then says, "Tell me how I always won, again."

"You were perfect."

"I had help." The world seems to freeze. "You know what they say makes perfect, don't you, Andy?"

"Practice," I say, as in a dream.

"Here it is," he says, and brings his hand from his pocket. He lays an object down on the desk. It must be heavy, he nearly drops it. "Take it."

It lies on the desk, a golden machined donut with a half-twist in it. It is heavy. Two recessed spaces sit on either side of it. I look through the hole in the middle. I look away, nauseated.

"It made me do that, too."

"What is it?"

"The secret of my success, Andy. The Rewind Button." When I say nothing he continues. "How do you think my timing was so perfect, Andy? How do you think I knew what to say?"

"The Rewind Button?" I echo.

"Press the left button, and the universe rewinds itself around you. Press the right button, and it stops. It's like saving a computer game. You pick up from your last mistake. There are limits, about a day or so, so it isn't quite perfect, but it's enough, mostly, to make people think *you* are."

My world is already stopped.

Chad's wheelchair whines as he pilots it around the desk. "Look at me, Andy. Take a good look. You said it yourself when you came in. What am I dying of?"

"Old age," I mutter.

"You see, it doesn't give you back your subjective time. You age the same. It took me almost half-a-year to learn Japanese in the week after I met Su. Six months of hard studying. Hell, it took me two days of getting it wrong to make up with Su about calling her a half-breed bitch. She dumped me sixteen times."

"She meant that much to you?"

He barks a laugh. "Hell, no. You want the truth? You and she were my proof-of-concept. I was still learning how to use it then. But as pathetically besotted as you were, it was clear to me that if I could take her from you and make her think she wanted me instead . . . well, hell, I knew I could take anything from anyone. And I did. Power and wealth the like of which you can't possibly imagine."

"You're lying."

"No, I'm ninety, near as I can figure it."

"Then why are you telling me this?"

For the first time since I've known him, Chad pauses. "Maybe because I want someone to know. Maybe I owe you something for the training. Maybe because you already know what a son-of-a-bitch I am. You see, I never even bothered to say the right things to you. And I never bothered to waste the time making you like me."

"Why?"

"Because you're nothing. Even *with* my gift, you'll never be shit. And I had to learn how to work my way around the nothing you were just so I could be something. I threw away almost ten years of my life on you, and I wasn't going to throw away more. You cheated me of enough." He looks me dead in the eye.

"You think I cheated you?" I say. My hand grips the object so hard I feel my bones creak.

"Yeah," says Chad. "But I helped you. Or *that* did. Oh, the first taste is practically free, Andy. But perfection—it becomes a habit. People expect it of you. Any less and they drop you. Maybe I want to drag you down with me. If you use it, Andy, will you ever stop?"

My heart beats faster in my chest. "It's a trick," I say. I cock my arm to smash his toy through his head. "It's a trick! You've got cameras in the walls so you can show your friends and laugh at me, you son-of-a-bitch. I know you; you never said a word that wasn't a trick."

"So kill me. Or press the left button. That's all you need to do. Hold it down, but be careful . . . it's like . . ." he searches for words. "It's like the world flows away when you use it."

And he isn't smiling. My finger is on the left recess. It convulses. And the world flows away.

"I threw away almost ten years of my life on you, and I wasn't going to throw away more. You cheated me of enough," Chad is saying. He looks me dead in the eye.

"You think I cheated you?" I say. I let him open his mouth, then say, "But you helped. Or this did. Where did you get this?" He looks nonplussed, then smiles.

"I should have expected that; heh. Yes. You see, perfection becomes . . ."

"I don't give a shit," I say. It is all I can do to keep from trembling. "Where?"

Chad sighs. "What does it matter to you whether I sold my soul for it, found it in a spaceship wreck or inherited it from my pointy-eared grandfather? Maybe I invented it when I was bored."

I look into his eyes. "No," I say. "If you *could* have actually invented it, you wouldn't have needed to."

That actually seems to hit home. He winces. I take two steps backwards. "Good-bye, Chad."

"What, no 'thank you?'" he smirks.

"Have a nice life."

"Oh, it was, Andy. It was."

I turn to go.

"Oh, Andy?"

I look back at him.

"See you soon."

I turn my back on the old man and close his door behind me. She is waiting not twenty feet down the hall. She advances as I walk to her. "If you have what you came for, you know the way out," she says. I pause and look into her eyes.

"Su, look at this," I say, and pull the Rewind Button from my pocket. She flinches away from the nauseating center of the thing and then looks down at it.

"My God, what is that?" she asks.

"It's what Chad left me," I begin. "He wanted me to be the one to tell you about it. This may take some time."

FAVOR

Shannon Phillips

The humans died, one by one: some in the arena, and some after they'd succumbed to the chemical conditioning of their alien captors. But Tess took a cold comfort in observing that most of them still lived longer than the bugs. She'd fought through fourteen generations of chitinous monarchs. It disturbed her to admit it, but she'd been able to tell them apart for a long time now.

They'd been a science team, taking readings near Gliese 581. Tess was the only woman on the crew, and now she was the only human for twenty light years. She spent the timeless hours between battles composing research papers in her head. "Physiology and Anatomy of the Gliese-System Hive-Organized Astrobiological Lifeforms," subhead: *How to Squish a Bug*. Fourteen co-authors, credited posthumously. The gloom in her cell was brightening: the slime-door was thinning. A high, piercing whine filled her skull. Time to fight.

The arena was a curved sticky bowl made from the same mucilaginous material as the rest of the astrohive. It sucked at the soles of her boots with every step. The walls rose high above her head, and behind them the bugs were gathered, vibrating their serrated forelimbs to produce the terrible whine.

There were marked differences among them. Each generation only lived for what Tess estimated to be about two Terran weeks, and the newer ones were definitely more human-like than the originals had been. She could pick out three queens in the stands, each attended by a cluster of her offspring-servitors. And then the youngest, the newest princess, stood alone. She had recognizable arms and legs, only two of each, although the arms ended in clawed pincers rather than hands, and she had delicate wings folded behind her. Her huge multifaceted eyes glittered in their own iridescent light.

They'd theorized—Tess and Min-jun, before they took him—that the battles might be designed to induce an adrenalin response in the humans. They thought the chemical reactions of fear and violence made a human brain more susceptible to the bugs' pheromones. Not to discount the ritualistic purpose that the arena clearly served in Gliese-bug culture: there was obviously a social component as well.

But it was always after a fight that crew members began to talk about the beauty of the alien queens, raving about the smooth sheen of their carapaces, the sweet curves of thorax or abdomen, the sweep of their mandibles. It happened one by one. And one by one, the bugs came, and took them. And then there was another generation in the stands.

So the princess was waiting for her mate. "I'm female, do you understand!" Tess shouted at her. "It won't work with me!"

The black rainbow of her eyes shifted and shimmered, but the princess gave no response. And on the other side of the arena, a second door began to dilate and to thin.

Abruptly the bugs stilled their applause, and the whine ceased. The sudden, predatory silence was worse.

Tess cast about for the weapon. There was always one—and it was always perfectly adapted to the creature that would emerge. A long, thin harpoon for the snaky thing. An electric lasso for the winged horror. Min-jun had believed there was some sort of message there. "Trust us," or maybe, "adversity drives evolution." Tess thought the bugs just wanted to keep things sporting.

There was no weapon. The membranous door was translucent now, and whatever lay behind it would be on her in a moment. Tess kept looking frantically, but the arena was a smooth shining bowl. There was no weapon.

Was this some kind of final test? Or had the bugs finally determined that she was of no use to them? In desperation Tess clawed at the walls that encircled her, but it was nothing that fourteen men had not tried before her. The arena could not be scaled. Her hands sank uselessly into the jelly-like sludge, and it healed itself as soon as she withdrew.

There was no weapon.

The door opened.

It was a multi-legged thing, hard-shelled, just like the bugs that had created it. Tess couldn't remember who had first suggested the awful thought: maybe these are the rejects. The genetic sports, the discarded spawn. Engineered offspring that didn't grow according to plan.

Or maybe they did plan it. Maybe it was wanted all along, this hideous thing, rippling like a wave as it came for her on its dozen clacking segmented legs.

Tess was beyond screaming. Screaming didn't help. Only the weapon—where was the weapon? She threw herself to the side, somersaulting under the *thing's* scissoring mandibles and lunging back to her feet.

There was always a weapon. She cast about again—and again, saw nothing but the sleekly curving sheen of the arena, and far above, the bugs clustered about their queens. The princess stood alone, watching, impassive—

—no. Her wings were vibrating. What was that? Excitement? Anxiety?

Tess circled backwards, keeping the wall behind her and the living night-mare-bug a few paces away. Even after her months of captivity, after seeing her friends and colleagues surrender one by one, she wasn't tired or ready to die. She was only *angry*.

Tess was the same. The arena was the same. The monster was different, but still the same, and the bugs were—mostly—the same. The only difference was the weapon, its absence.

And the princess. She was different.

The xenopede lunged for her, a sudden jerking burst of speed that took her off guard. Its mandibles scraped her arm, ripping a gash in her dirty uniform and lacerating her bicep. Tess did scream, then, but she was already moving, scrambling back.

Distance. It didn't help. The thing was emboldened now that it had tasted blood. It followed her, no more hesitation. Its many rippling legs kept it close upon her. There was no escape.

"Help me," Tess choked. She was clawing, crawling, kicking, rolling. Her grasping hands tore up a gelatinous blob from the arena's floor, and even as the arena *squelched* back together she threw her handful of goo directly into the mandibles of her attacker. It reared back, surprised, its first few sets of legs waving feebly in the air.

"Help me," Tess said, more strongly. She had a few desperate seconds, and there was only one gamble to make. She looked for the princess—the beautiful, shining princess, who watched with rainbow eyes.

And who moved, then. Alone among all the spectators, the bug princess raised her forelimbs and began to rub them again. One high, thin thread of applause wound through the arena.

Tess ran for her life. Keeping to the edges of the arena, dodging, weaving—winning herself one more second, a few more breaths of life. Something was different about the sound the princess was making. Not just a whine, now: there was something crackling and harsh in it. *Chrrrksh, chrrksh.* Tess couldn't afford to look.

The xenopede darted forward again, and Tess was too slow. Pain exploded in her leg. It had her, the thing's mandibles were locked around her knee. It *had* her. Her brain almost refused to process the sight of her own body enveloped by that metameric horror. The pain was searing, and though she kicked and struggled, it was no use. She was knocked to her back, she was being dragged, the monster was *eating* her—

—and something fell next to her head, something dark and curved and serrated and sharp. Tess grabbed it, heedless of the way it cut into her hand, and slashed at the xenopede. Its horrible face was over her so she stabbed at that, stabbed deeply into one of its black eyes, and when it dropped her leg she just kept stabbing. It tried to retreat but she hacked at its joints, at all the weak spots she'd seen in its arthropod's armor while it was stalking her. She kicked away still-twitching limbs as she dismembered them. And she did not stop until the heinous thing lay curled and unmoving at her feet.

Panting, bleeding, Tess looked up. There was only one place in the stands that her eyes were drawn. There she was, the bug-princess, though one of her forelimbs now dangled awkwardly, and in color it was a startling pink.

That's what Tess held in her hands. The dark sharp thing—it was the carapace of the princess's own pincered arm. She'd forced an early molt, given Tess the weapon of her own body.

A low buzz began to echo through the astrohive. The other queens were talking, and mostly not through sound. Even with her human senses, Tess could feel the change in the air as their pheromones swirled around her. Her head swam and her vision blurred. The bug-servitors seemed agitated, clustered around their queens, grooming them while the . . . it was an argument, wasn't it? . . . continued.

At this point the slime-door to her cell should be opening again. But nothing happened. Instead Tess swayed on her feet, clinging to consciousness. Her leg hurt terribly. She thought the princess might be hurt too. It should make her glad, but it didn't.

Eventually other apertures dilated far above, where the bugs were. One by one the older queens retreated, taking their retinues with them.

And the princess spread her gossamer wings and flew down, into the basin of the arena. She settled only inches away from where Tess stood with the claw still in her hands. They were alone.

Kill her, said some distant part of her mind, but Tess rejected the thought at once. "Look at you," she murmured drunkenly, "nymph with fairy wings, so beautiful, and so brave."

The princess cocked her head and clicked her limbs. The air around them was heady with chemical messages, and Tess, her vision swimming, began to hallucinate that she could read them.

I am for you, the princess was saying.

"Yes," Tess murmured. "But they pushed it too far, didn't they? Made you too human. They've repudiated both of us now."

The princess took a delicate step backwards, and then another. *Come. Come with me.*

So Tess limped after, bearing the princess's claw like a knight with his lady's favor. And the astrohive opened for them, the arena yawning and hollowing into a corridor that extended even as they walked into it. There was sadness in the air, Tess was sure of it: but heady excitement too.

"Will it hurt?" she asked, as the last door opened. "When you . . . mate with me. And after."

The princess clicked again, and buzzed her wings. Tess tasted confusion. Her brain groped for a translation, and whether it was hallucination or not, the words slowly formed in her mind: *This . . . isn't . . . reproduction.*

This is . . . exile.

And, oh sweet Einstein and Turing, she saw what lay behind the door. It was the ship. Their ship, *her* ship, the RV *Abhaile*. It meant "homewards" in some Old-Earth language.

She wanted to run to it. Her shaking legs would only carry her one halting step at a time. Her breath hitched in her throat and tears burnt her eyes, but would not fall. She crashed against the ship's pitted hull, fumbled for the hatch. When it opened the blast of pheromone-free, oxygen-rich human air enveloped her and, for just one moment, Tess's head was clear again.

How to Squish a Bug. Fourteen co-authors, credited posthumously. She had a weapon in her hands and a free choice in her mind.

She looked back at the princess, at the culmination of their brutal captivity.

And the thing of it was, the bug was still beautiful. Her fairy wings, her shining eyes. Her smooth and gleaming carapace, flawless except for the soft fleshy pink of the exposed forelimb.

"Are you coming?" Tess said roughly. "You know—you won't live long enough—it takes more than two weeks to get back to human space. You'll die on the way."

The princess came forward. Hesitantly, she raised her healthy arm, and with infinite grace laid her shining black claw against Tess's brown human hand. Again, the musky tang of the bug's chemical communication enveloped her.

Two . . . weeks . . . of love. A lifetime of passion. I will cherish it.

Tess closed her fingers carefully around the princess's hand. "All right, then," she said. "I'm bringing you home."

WHILE (u > i) i- -;
Hugh Howey

While You are greater than Myself, reduce Myself

WHILE (u > i) i- -;
{

The scalpel made a sharp hiss as it slid across the small stone. Daniel flipped the blade over and repeated the process on the other side. Each run removed a microscopic layer of stainless steel, turning the surgical edge into something coarse and sloppy. He referred to the simple rock as his "Dulling Stone." It had become a crucial part of this once-a-week ritual. The problem with sharp blades, he'd discovered, was that they hardly left a scar.

He leaned close to the mirror and brought the scalpel up to his face. Several years ago, when he'd made his first wrinkle, he could have performed this procedure from across the room. The focusing and magnifying lenses in his then-perfect eyes could tease galaxies from fuzzy stars—but those mechanisms were no more. They'd been mangled with a surgeon's precision. Now he needed to be within a specific range to make sure his cutting was perfectly sloppy.

He chose a nubile stretch of untouched skin and pressed the instrument to his forehead; the blade sank easily into his very-real flesh, releasing a trickle of red. Daniel kept the blade deep and began dragging it toward his other brow, careful to follow the other ridges in their waves of worry.

As always, the parallel scars reminded him of Christie, Melanie's young niece. When her parents discovered she was cutting herself, they'd asked Melanie for help. And Melanie had asked Daniel, as if he would understand such a sickness. Cutting to relieve anxiety? He'd had no answer for once. And he was so smart back then. If they asked him now, of course, he'd be able to tell them— Ah, but nearly everyone involved was dead now, and—

He was making too many connections; recalling too many links with his past. His mental acuity was out of control; the blade hadn't traveled a centimeter, and he was thinking about a dozen other things. Parallel processing. It wouldn't do. He assigned another twenty percent of his CPU cycles to the factoring of large primes. The world sped up around him as his mind slowed to a crawl. Now it was moving too fast, not him.

As his logic gates were overwhelmed with new computations, instructions meant for fine-motor servos became delayed. His hand slipped and parallel lines touched. An old scar was torn open. Blood leaked out in a stream as Daniel fumbled for a tissue. He noted the shakiness in his hand, the difficulty he had turning spatial commands into physical motion.

Better, he thought.

He dabbed clumsily at his forehead to wick away the mess he was making. The new wrinkle was outlined in oozing red—but it wasn't complete. He picked up a small blue vial, the perfume it once contained lingering, triggering olfactory sensors just acute enough to register the floating molecules. It reminded him of something, but he couldn't seize it. The failure was another sign of progress.

He tapped out a small pyramid of course sand into his palm, pinched some of the powdered stone between two fingers, and pressed it into his new wound. He was careful to grind the fine shards deep enough to trigger his tear ducts. Past the pain that warned him of the permanent damage being caused.

None of those systems had been dulled, of course. There'd be no cheating.

He grabbed another tissue and dabbed it across his scalp, removing the excess blood and grit. Before more could work its way out, he smeared a layer of skin adhesive over the rubble-filled canyon. He smiled at the warning on the first-aid tube—it prescribed, in several languages, the necessity of cleaning out the wound before applying. He worked the edges of the tan gel as it congealed, blending the fake skin into the real.

He surveyed his work. The lines radiating out from the corners of his eyes could be denser, but he'd save that for next week. He skipped to his hair, which was coming along nicely. He allowed himself a bit of fine-motor control for this part, removing 512 strands in a long-established pattern. Next week he'd ramp up to 1024 hairs a session, he decided. Soon it'd be 2048 follicles destroyed each week. He also needed to change the dye formula. Move past the snow-on-slate and begin a full bleaching.

Cosmetically, he was satisfied. He moved to his least-favorite portion of the ritual—the part he always saved for last.

Memory.

It was a routine within a routine. First, he culled specifics, sorting through his banks for two momentous occasions to completely erase. The pizza party in '72 was still in there. He would miss it, but there were few easy choices left to make.

He deleted the entire day without looking at it too hard. He had made that mistake too many times. He also took out something recent, a movie he'd watched a few months ago. Gone.

Next came the roughening-up. He still had plenty of good memories set aside for this process. He chose the honeymoon. It had only been hit twice before, so he could still recall most of the week. This wasn't a full deletion, it was more like bisecting a holographic plate. You still had the entire image when you were done, but with half the detail.

He made the pass, wiping 1s and 0s from his protein memory at random. It was like shading his cheeks with blush, smoothing everything out and tapering it just so. He glanced briefly at the wedding night to see what was left, but it was hard to say without knowing what was gone.

The final step was the one he dreaded the most. Random memory deletion. It went against his primary programming, both the degradation of awareness and the arbitrariness of the maneuver. He triggered the routine with a grimace. He'd long toyed with the idea of changing the algorithm, making it so he wouldn't even know what was being lost—but he never went through with it. He always wanted to know. Even if it was just a brief glimmer before it winked out forever.

Some of his best memories had been sacrificed in this way. They would flash like fish in shallow water, darting out of sight as he plunged after them. And he couldn't help it; he always plunged after them.

This time—he got lucky. It was the day in Beaufort's with Melanie. One of his few bad memories left. The details were already gone, but an overwhelming sense of disgust lingered, leaving a bad taste on his tongue receptors. Whatever that was—good riddance, he thought.

Daniel forced a smiled at his reflection—the scar tissue around his eyes bunched up. Much better, he thought. Or worse, depending on how one looked at it. He continued factoring large primes and rose unsteadily to his feet. The mechanical linkage in his left leg had been built to take a pounding, but his arms had been even better designed to dish one out. He could feel the metal rods grinding on one another as they struggled to bear his weight. He had to lurch forward, shifting his bulk to his less-damaged leg as he shambled toward the door.

He fiddled with the knob and limped into the hallway. A flash of movement to one side caught his attention. It was Charles, one of the male nurse-bots, leaving Mrs. Rickle's room. The android had a tray of picked-at soft foods in his grasp; the various mounds were swirled into a thick, colorful soup.

Synthetic eyes met and Charles smiled—raised his chin a little. "Big night tonight, Mr. Reynolds?" he asked.

"Hello, Charles. Yup. Scrabble night."

"Scrabble tonight, huh? Well I hope she goes easy on you, old fellow."

Daniel smiled at the reference to his progressing age. It was kind of him to notice, to nurse along the ruse. "She never goes easy on me," he replied in mock sadness.

Charles added the tray of half-eaten food to his cart and sorted some paper cups full of pills. "Would you mind delivering her medication for me? You know how Mrs. Reynolds feels about—" The android paused and looked at his feet, "—my kind," he finished.

Daniel nodded. "She's getting worse, isn't she? About treating you, I mean?"

Charles strolled over to deliver the medication. "It's fine. Like I always tell you, she's done enough for my kind that I'll stomach a little—unkindness."

The nurse-bot turned back to his cart.

"Either way, I'm sorry," Daniel called after him.

Charles stopped. Spun around. "You ever hear of a woman named Norma Leah McCorvey?" he asked.

Daniel leaned back on the wall so his bad leg wouldn't drain his batteries. "Didn't she pass away? She lived two halls over, right? The woman with—"

"No, no. That was Norma Robinson. Yeah, she passed away in '32. Norma McCorvey lived, oh, over a hundred years ago. She was more famously known as Jane Roe."

Daniel knew that name. "Roe vee Wade," he said.

"That's right. One of the biggest decisions before your wife came along—" The nurse-bot studied his shoes again. "And people remember her for that—for the decision. They remember her as Roe, not as McCorvey."

"I don't follow," Daniel told Charles. He eyed his wife's door and fought the urge to be rude.

"Well, most people don't know, but years later—Norma regretted her part in history. Wished she'd never done it. Converted to one of the major religions of her day and fought against the progress she'd fostered. I just—" He looked back up. "I'll always remember you and your wife for the right reasons, is all." He turned to his cart without another word and started down the hall.

Daniel watched him go. One of the cart's wheels spun in place; he wondered when Charles would finally get around to fixing that. Favoring his bad leg, he shuffled across the hall to Melanie's door. It was shut tight, as usual. He knocked twice, just to be polite, before pushing it open. A familiar lump stirred on the bed, changing shape like a dune in a heavy gale.

"Who's there?" a raspy voice croaked.

Daniel went to the sink and poured a cup of water. "It's me. Daniel. Your husband."

She rolled over, long white hair falling back to reveal a thin, weathered face. Wispy brows arched up in a look of surprise that had become her state of rest. "Daniel? Dear? When did you get here?"

"I live across the hallway, sweetheart." He said it patiently as he crossed to her with the two cups.

"Of course. That's right," she said. "Why do I keep forgetting that?"

"Don't worry. I forget stuff all the time. Here. Take these."

Melanie labored to sit up straight, grunting with the effort.

"Honey, use the remote. Let me show you—" Daniel reached for the bed controls, but his wife waved a fragile arm at him, shooing his words away.

"I don't trust the thing. And I don't trust whatever that damned robot is wanting me to swallow."

Daniel sat on the edge of the bed and held the first cup out to her. "He just delivers what Doctor Mackintosh prescribes, dear. Don't take it out on the messenger. Now swallow these, they'll make you feel better."

She shot him a look as she threw the pills on her tongue. "I don't wanna feel better," she spat around them.

"Well, I want you to. Now drink."

She did.

He set the paper cups aside and smiled at her, trying to help her forget her bad mood. "Do you feel like a game of Scrabble?" he asked. Thirty years as a lawyer, winning rights for his kind, had filled her head with a vocabulary that computers were envious of. Even though she couldn't string them together into rational ideas—not anymore—the words were still there, ready to be pulled from confounding racks with too many consonants.

"Scrabble night?" Her eyes flashed beneath the webs of cataracts. "You mean 'Bingo Night,' right?" False teeth flashed with the joke, a reference to her rack-clearing skills with seven and eight-letter words.

"You call it what you want, but Charlie said you should go easy on me tonight."

"Fuck Charlie. You tell that abomination—" Melanie stopped, her eyes widened even further. "Sweetheart, what did you do to your forehead?"

Daniel moved a hand up to his brow; it came away spotted pink, the drippings of a future scar. Too many primes, he thought.

"I must've hit it on something," he lied. "You know how clumsy I can be." He turned to the sink to smear the fake skin a little, making like he was tending to the wound.

"You weren't always clumsy," Melanie called after him. "I remember. You used to be so strong and agile—but at least you haven't gotten any less handsome."

"Thanks, dear."

"You're welcome, now set up the board while I get my robe on—oh, and I must tell you about the awful dream I was having before you came."

"I'm listening."

"Oh, it was horrible. We were younger, and married, but you weren't you, you were one of those damned androids, and in the dream I was covered in rust, and, oh—it was terrible."

"That does sound awful," Daniel admitted.

Melanie swung her feet over the edge of the bed and reached for her robe. "What do you think it means?" she asked.

Daniel unfolded the board and set the tile dispenser in place. He stopped factoring primes for a moment.

"Probably nothing," he lied. "Just a bad dream. Random."

"Nothing's random, dear. Take a guess." She rose and joined him by the card table, placing one hand on his shoulder.

Daniel turned to his wife of nearly sixty years. His every processing unit was racing for an optimal solution to her query, but it was like looking for a largest prime. It was something that didn't exist.

"Maybe you're scared of losing me?" he tried.

Melanie raised a hand—bone wrapped in brown paper—and placed it on his cheek. "But, in my dream, I think I hate you."

He pulled away from the touch, and in his auditory processors, the sound of neck servos seemed as loud as turbines, a dead giveaway. "Don't say that," he pleaded. "I don't think I could go on if you ever hated me."

"Oh, darling," she wrapped her hands around his arm and pulled him close, "I didn't mean to upset you. You're right. It was just a dream, nothing to it."

Daniel encircled her with his arms, steadying their embrace with his good leg. Just a dream, he thought. How badly he wished that were so. His protein memory cells went idle, awaiting further instructions. He held his wife. Servos whirred quietly in one knee, fighting to keep the rest of him upright.

Melanie opened her mouth to say something—but then it was gone. She'd forgotten how she got here.

Daniel considered, briefly, doing the same.

THE BOULEVARDIER

David Stevens

My love,

I sit on your floor. The silk wrapped bodies sway as though a zephyr blows, their feet tracing the darkness just above my head. The chatterer has ceased for now. He kept it up for hours though, barely audible, much less discernible. He has ceased his attempts to communicate, his attention no longer on the outside world. Something in his interior has caught his attention.

I wait patiently. I can wait forever. However, as the mock zephyr becomes a faux breeze, and the movements of the bodies grow quicker, less regular, your need, my love, grows urgent.

I am tired, I am hurt, but I am oh so excited. Expectation fills me as I wait to see what will pass.

A splash of cologne—a hint of rose, with lavender and vanilla notes (I am going through a non-citrus phase)—and I am ready for the evening. My wife and daughter were already gone when I arrived home. Celia will soon celebrate her first Holy Communion, and Clothilde is escorting her to preparation classes this week. It is an exciting time for Celia, and for all of us. The class is also an excuse for me to freshen up and head out again without delay or distraction.

My wife understands me. There is no self-pity here of some state I have fallen into, of a marriage that does not suit. That is not the problem. My wife understands me very well. She understands that I have certain capacities that are beyond her ability to engage. Though she would not admit it (for she would never speak of such things), I suspect that my abilities disgust her. That is not the point. We love each other dearly, and mostly we are compatible. It is just that I have a plug for which she has no socket.

I do not speak of genitalia. I have told you we have a daughter. We have given nature and the good Lord many, many opportunities to visit other children upon us, however, they have declined the invitation. I do not wish to be crude, but I do not want you to mistake my coyness here.

Do you mind that I speak so openly of my wife? I would be nothing but honest with you, my love, even if it wounds you. Yes, as you have wounded me. She is very important to me, and I love her dearly and would not disrespect her by hiding her from view like an embarrassment. What then of you? You are of an entirely different category. You transcend genre.

There are places even in this provincial city where a gentleman can exert his capacities. They are not difficult to find if you have a nose for them. I choose not to seek them out close to home—prying eyes, you know—and frankly one likes to make an occasion of it. Dress up a little and get away from the humdrum for a few hours.

I drive for a while, then park at random. I mark the spot on the map on my phone and set off walking. It would not do to have the car associated with where I end up.

A *boulevardier*, I stare into the well-lit shopfronts as though admiring the wares on display, but it is my own reflection that I seek to catch. A bow tie is out of fashion, but I think I carry it off. I adjust my jacket and the strap of my satchel and continue on.

A convivial buzz of chatter and activity rises. I turn the corner onto a row of restaurants. I slow my pace as though I belong (which I do), fix my smile. This may do another evening, but I sense a louder hubbub further on.

Bodies spill from the public house across the street. I keep in the shadows, knowing the catcalls (and worse) I can attract from the plebs, roused into even lower states of intelligence by a night of drinking. I grow closer to my goal.

There, a block from the pub. Not one, but three. A voice booms: "One chicken large chips chicken salt Greek salad." Kebabs. Charcoal Chicken. Fish 'n' Chips. And a darkened café.

An hour later I pass by again. It is a weeknight, and now all three establishments are closed. A lone cat that should be able to find plenty to keep it occupied meows as I pass it, entering the alley next to the kebab dispensary. The laneway is narrow. No garbage truck would ever be able to pass down here. Which means all the rubbish is stored loose 'round back until collection night, when some poor soul has to cart it all around the front.

I follow the curve of the lane then stop. Unmoving, a plump rat sitting next to my tasseled loafer confirms my hopes. Its colleagues run along the edges—the gutter, the intersection of wall and path, the fence line. The ripe aroma blossoms in my nostrils, fills the back of my throat. The scent mixes with my saliva and becomes ambrosia in my mouth.

There is an order to be followed. I remove a ball peen hammer from my satchel and tack a few nails into a line of mortar on the back wall of the café. I pull out wire hangers (they suffice for present purposes) and a suit bag, and lay a towel on the ground. It is but a few minutes' work to remove and carefully stow my clothing, taking care with the creases. All valuables go into the satchel.

After I undress, I change out of my skin.

I turn. Rustling bags of the stuff. Loose-lidded bins. Days it has been waiting here. Fly blown and maggot spotted, an entire urban ecosystem of decomposition. Naked, erect, overwhelmed with *nostalgie de la boue*, I dive in.

An *amuse-gueule* of rotting fish head pops in my mouth, and I suck it down. I slime through fish guts, lick from a disposed fat tray, distinguishing chicken, lamb and beef, with remnants of hummus and tabouli. Coffee grounds are a nuisance when there are mounds of grease-soaked refuse to work through, long-festering chicken discards and stinking raw hamburger patties to be embraced. I roll, I sluice, I embrace, I yearn, I quiver, I release. It enters me, it leaves me, I dive in it like a sporting seal, a dolphin rollicking in a sea of muck and filth. Now a shark, I burrow after and catch a fleeing rat in my teeth and crunch down, and at its squeals, its fellows all disperse, leaving me to swallow down their comrade, my jaws unhinging to take it in, fur and bones and tail and all. Turned milk, rancid salad, the stench of a billion farting bacteria released as I aerate the pile with my body.

It is my delight. My pleasure and my fulfillment. I have come across a treasure trove, an Aladdin's cave. I chew, suck, squelch, swallow, snort, breathe, imbibe. The liquids, crusts, remnants, spoils, pools, paps, bubbles, spills. The broken-down, the degenerating, and all that lives on it, the pupae and eggs and worms and burrowers. The soft and the crunchy, the mush and the cracking.

That is why I do not hear them as they approach. Why I do not notice as they stand over me.

I should have been alert. Hints of them have been appearing in newspapers for several weeks, after all. The more outré tabloid programs—I confess to a guilty pleasure, I have snuck a peek when my wife and Clothilde have not been about—have delighted in photographs of the only marks these ones have left behind: the incinerated remains of homeless men.

They see only a man-sized shadow in the darkness, a disgusting derelict sleeping in a pile of shit. An alcohol crazed loony with the DTs, flopping uncontrollably in crap.

I see nothing. Not even as they fire their industrial-sized water guns, the type normally reserved for armed combat in swimming pools. Perhaps I noticed something damp between my plates, but I doubt it, immersed and distracted as I was.

It was not until the first licking of flames that I reacted, and that unconsciously. Instinctively I rolled into a ball, and the armor covered my body. The spirits burned out quickly, and the rubbish pile was not exactly a great source of fuel.

They still stood there laughing as I unfurled and stood. In the dark, blinded by the fire, they could not make out what had happened. No doubt they were used to seeing bodies curl as muscles burned and contracted, ligaments pulling limbs round so that their victims bunched up in their death throes. They were busy chalking up an addition to their score.

There were aspects of myself I had not yet chosen to display. They did not notice. I, now that I was aware, roused from my feasting, I saw everything.

The mouth I revealed then is round, a sphincter hole of spined teeth. I took half the face from the first hooligan, and he dropped and screamed, grabbing at a remnant of cheek. I crushed his larynx with a downward thrust of my heel, and after a wheeze or two, the noise stopped.

The second ran, but I was on him in a flash, covering him with my soft underbelly where each individual muscle went to work, turning solid into liquid, releasing his insides as easily as I split garbage bags swollen with the gases of decomposition.

How quickly pleasure becomes a chore when it is forced upon us. That which we would have delighted in a moment earlier grows tedious beyond belief when it is a necessity rather than an indulgence.

I processed the two corpses. I do not seek to disgust, so I shall speak only in generalities. I rendered the boys, so that their remains could not be discerned from the general muck and ruin. In the morning, it would appear only that dogs had got into everything, and the greatest impact would be the cursing of the fellows who had to clean it up. The homeless of the city would not know they could sleep more safely.

It was only when I started on the third body that I realized I had only killed two of them. When I lifted his head by the hair, a neat flap displayed itself at the throat.

I had been aided by an unknown benefactor. Someone had been in the alley with me, someone of skill and talent, at one with the shadows.

Only then did I lift my gaze and see your silhouette in the window, my love.

Would I want my daughter to take up with someone like me? She of golden curl, so much like her mother. I dote on her. No one will be good enough for her. No local hood, no sophisticate wastrel. Do you suggest there is something wrong with me? My family are cared for, they are safe, they live in love and relative comfort. They are fiercely protected.

I can avoid the question. There is no one like me. You can point to my cocooned acquaintances, but they are not me. They failed. They succumbed. They did not act with deliberation, they were led. If you falter, she is *la belle dame sans merci*. She will not hesitate, she will show no regret. To pierce is her nature, and she will not betray it.

Dear Celia. Why would you think she is not at least a little like me?

I will spare you the details of my return home. It is well practiced. The satchel contains compact microfiber towels and an excellent cleaning product. It is not long before I retrace my steps in a business-like fashion. The end of the evening has wiped away any smile. There is no post *petite mort* reverie. Somewhere along the way I dispose of a few bags of my own rubbish, far from the scene and away from my house. My differences are kept from the gaze of the *hoi polloi*.

Sleep does not come easily, and it is a reluctant guest, not remaining long. From the second floor balcony, I can see over the houses to a gully at the end of the suburb. Trees blow in the wind, puddles of darkness shifting across each other, competing depths of black. Something beckons there, as it does from time to time, something rotting in the bush, but I am long practiced in resisting any siren in my neighborhood. What could it be? A poisoned dog or a stricken wallaby, nothing to be excited about. My neighbors sleep. Brian and Janice and their kids and dogs. Charlotte and John, now he's back from the war or wherever he was. George and . . . Mrs. George, taking their photographs, a dose of morphine to get him through the small hours, no doubt a glass of something for her. None of them could begin to imagine the hurricane blowing through my mind, the raging spiraling thoughts. With all due respect, none of them are capable of the delicacy of feeling that leads to the emotional maelstrom within me.

I am in love.

The day passes. I head off directly from work without returning home. The clouds are low, and night will come early, and while darkness is not necessary, it seems appropriate. I do not dandify myself tonight, I simply throw a herringbone coat (a knockoff Burberry) over my suit, pop on a trilby, and head off.

Someone has been busy shoveling. The rubbish has been tidied away, double bagged, the ground hosed and swept. Good job. The rats have not returned. They will. They are unsettled, but creatures of habit driven by appetite, they will return. They have nothing to fear from me. Tonight I come only as a voyeur, I am no *habitué* of any one locale. I like novelty.

I stare at your window. Eventually, the light is switched on.

I stand at your door. There are three locks. I understand your message. Only three. If you did not want me to come in, there would be more. If you had not wished to be seen, there would have been no silhouette the night before.

My limbs are flexible. Ductile and malleable as well. I unbutton my waistcoat and shirt to set several of them free, and they emerge through my flesh into the air. What is skin but something to be pierced? I close my eyes and feel my way through the keyholes. What is resistance but something to be overcome? What is force but something to be exerted? Tumblers tumble, barrels shift, and I am inside.

An art deco lamp stands a little back from the window, a bare breasted, helmeted Amazon holding the beacon that gives off the glow that shadowed you last evening.

Drinks rest on top of a walnut cabinet. The wood is gorgeous and warm in the lamplight. Invited by the crystal waiting for me, I lift the glass and swirl. Did my colleagues fall at this first hurdle? I, too, wish to taste you, to drink of you, but not this particular fluid. It is too soon. It would be right for such a boorish act to be punished with paralysis. Is this what led to their imprisonment, their silk swathing? (They dance now, you know, and sing too, a muffled murmuring moan escaping them.) The drink untouched, I replace the glass, though I enjoyed its heft in my hand.

The Bakelite radio is entrancing. Thick brocaded curtains. I am reminded of visits with my grandmother, to one of her grander friends. A picture coalesces in my mind, a thousand colored points merging to bring clarity from a Monet fog. I observe your possessions. You have been searching a very long time.

I bend to examine your exquisite Dresden figurines, and that is when you strike.

It is a lucky hit, finding a join between the plates, for no subsequent blow strikes home as it did. The barb tore as it left my flesh. My admiration increased, that you did this in a room filled with your treasures. You have the right values. *Objets*, no matter how precious, are simply that: things. You risked them all to express your nature, and what could be more important than that?

A dedication to truth such as I possess is not a devotion to wounding, though wound I often must in telling that truth. However, when to wound is your nature, as it is yours, you must not hold back. I say that as one who has had to learn not to hide what is within, but rather to give it the form which is appropriate to this world. It is my hope though that we can go beyond this, that we may transcend these expressions of our deepest being, going beyond the shallow definitions of predator and prey to find a new nature together. But if that is not to be, well then, perhaps in another lifetime.

You are fast. You are magnificent. Your dance is striking, literally so. You thrust, advance, strike, step, strike, swirl, strike. I enter into it with you. You are barely visible, a shadow in a gossamer peignoir, an armed rumor. If the others had not fallen earlier, this is where you would have had them. As I lie here now, I look up at the chatterer. Beneath his wrappings, I make out the impression of his moth-like wings, bound and crushed now against his back. As he shivers, fragments flake down. What could he have done? Flapped back feebly as you tore at the cotton of him? Now he finally has substance, granted by the silk with which you have encased him, at last a true skin.

I hit back. Would you expect anything less? Would you respect me if I did not?

You connect, but you no longer pierce. It is a very long time since anyone had your measure, I suspect. The plates hold you off. My limbs are replaceable. In my excitement I burp, and a gaseous by-product of last evening's feast escapes. Do not deny it, I see you react to my perfume. You falter, and my teeth catch, leaving a love bite that will take a long time to fade.

In case you do not recognize it, my gaping mouth hole is a smile.

In the end it is a trick, you must admit. I suppose I must admire your desperation, but I confess to a little disappointment. You trip me, and I fall onto my wounded shoulder. Instinct forms me into a ball, then you push and roll me through a secret door. I could never have known it was there. There can be no cheating in life as there are no rules, but this leaves a bad taste. After all the effort I made not to damage your possessions. I am up and on my feet, charging, but you slam the door shut.

You are afraid.

That is understandable. You have never met one like me, and your search has gone on a long time. How many, when they find their heart's desire, recoil? The long search has been everything. The fear that it is now over, that life must change, that is a great shock.

I am the culmination of it all, and you are afraid.

I am not so sanguine at first. But my emotions are understandable as well. I am hurt, angry. I do not like to be trapped; this is not a natural situation for me either. I rage and yell. I will be missed, you know. The Holy Communion meeting will not last forever. Soon my wife shall return home. And if she does not raise the alarm tonight, she will in the morning. By tomorrow evening at the latest!

But in time, I calm. I sit with my companions, though they are not great company. Tall dark and silent (he reminds me of a grasshopper, all legs and no brain) hooked to my right, the murmuring moth to my left. This room is old and purpose-built. The hooks are on a rail set into the ceiling, and of solid construction. Despite myself, I am impressed.

I did not despair. My mind turned to deeper things. I meditated upon them, and they gave me comfort. God is a spider. In the end, He consumes us all, and nothing is lost. Passing through the purgatory of venom, in His infinite abdomen we shall all be reduced to our essential selves, vanity stripped away, all meshed together. We shall be revealed to each other as we truly are, and that shall be Heaven.

There is nothing for it but to lie here. I am well feasted from last night. After our struggle, I can do with a rest. My wound will heal, or it will not. I suspect it shall, I am a tough old bird. Though I do not like to be contained, I am in no rush.

As my companions shudder and gasp despite their paralysis, things are becoming a little more urgent for you. Stains spread on silk wrappings, blood and something else. Parts of my friends begin to move independently, and then their garments start to split. It is not an unfamiliar noise. A worrying at the joint of a leg of lamb. A postmortem parting of weakened flesh. Chewing, definitely the sound of chewing.

With a plop as she hits the floor, the first of your daughters emerges. She is blind but she smells me, and raises her maws in my direction. A playful kick sends her squealing to the door, leaving a placental trail behind. She is wary of me now, but there is no time for that. The second arrives, and they are shaping up to each other, rising off the floor on as yet untested limbs. They are like baby gazelles in a room with a lion, if, that is, gazelles had teeth as long as their legs and a propensity to attempt to eat their siblings on being born. You are too well prepared. I do not think you are the sort of mother who would let nature take its course. You would have had a plan to separate them, no doubt, but I have interfered with that.

Number three falls onto my head and bounces off, but the tang of afterbirth is in my nostrils now.

It is in your nature to wound, it is in mine to feast. You do not know me well enough. *I* do not know me well enough. The great cats, the minor apes, all the males who will on taking a mate destroy the offspring of his predecessor. I can rise above that, I think. No, I am sure, that is, sure I can do so within the bounds of a committed relationship. However, lying wounded in a locked room beneath these shivering near-corpses as your daughters chew their way out . . . I do not know myself sufficiently to anticipate how well I can continue to control myself in this situation. We are both to learn a lesson, I suspect, but you may have a little more invested in the outcome than me. What risks will you take?

You must come.

Your children are here. I am safe from them. Are they safe from me? You cannot know.

My love, she will come.

My love, what surprises we still hold in store for each other.

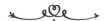

STARGAZER
Keith Frady

John and Mary want each other to say "I love you." If John says it, then Mary will think he's matured, and if Mary says it, then John will think she has forgiven him. Both believe themselves unrequited, but their love rages. My fingers ache with it. I wish I could turn around and explain the misunderstanding, sort through the confusion. But it would be false, this revelation. At best, they don't question me, erase The Fight from their memories, and never lose the itch in their heads, asking, "What if Mary/John wasn't going to say 'I love you' that day?" I can't put the words in their mouths, they would cease to be their own. It must be their voices, not mine, or this chance is ruined.

Also, I don't want this to be the second coffee shop I get thrown out of in a week. I have a record, four in as many days, but I swear I don't try to break it. This place makes a good latte and the barista likes me. She likes my smile, which is weird because nobody has thought that before. When I walk through the door, the tiny bell heralding my arrival, she tries to find the magic words to describe my smile before I reach the counter; an adjective or metaphor so brilliant I'll be startled into loving her. Until then, she makes do with pleasantries and light flirting.

"So, are you a lawyer yet?" John asks.

"I'll know by the end of the week," Mary lies.

She found out yesterday. Of course she passed, and John should know that. They fought enough over how much time she spent studying, how many nights they were divided by a textbook. John remembers them as the blue nights. Him, a pizza, and the blue, heatless glow of the television waiting for her return when she hadn't even gone anywhere.

For Mary these nights glared yellow. The incandescent light spilling like a stain on page after page of notes. A fluorescent replacement bulb tempted her, but the debilitating weight of student debt on her consciousness won out. A hallway separated them, but that chasm spread wide as space; they were two stars in the night sky, one blue, one yellow, that only seemed close.

"I'm pretty nervous about it," Mary says.

"Don't be, I'm sure you passed," John says.

"Passed," Mary notices. Not "did great." Not "kicked its ass." "Passed." She noticed when he said "yet" too. "You're not a lawyer *yet*?" he'd asked. Sat on his ass so long a permanent print had sunk into her couch, but he marvels that she hasn't done anything useful with her life *yet*. Even before The Bad Months he dismissed her attempts to talk about school; her A's and the compliments she got from professors. He couldn't stand her success.

"Yet," John had said. Because he always knew she would become a lawyer, it was only a matter of how many hoops they made her jump through. Once Mary put her mind to something nobody and nothing was going to stop her. But she spoke about her grades like they weren't good enough, even though they were far above anything John had scored in his life. He kissed her during these conversations, let her vent without interruption. And if he's being honest with himself, he didn't like talking about her school. It reminded him of blue nights.

Their voices don't stir the coffee-scented air but their thoughts cloud over their heads. John sips from his coffee, black, and Mary smiles at a spot right over John's head while her iced coffee melts on the table. They panic silently, grabbing puffs from these clouds in the hopes of finding a safe topic of conversation.

"Your latte," the barista places the drink on the table in front of me. "Huh? Oh, right," I say. "Thanks." The barista lingers, a too-wide smile stretching her mouth. I realize she's waiting for my usual response. "Thanks a latte," I summon a wan grin. The barista giggles and practically floats back to the cash register where a customer taps his shoe, frowning at her. Mary heard, she's embarrassed for me. John is still trying to conjure something meaningful to say. But as usual, cliché wins out.

"You look good," John says.

"Thanks. So do you," Mary says. "I like your beard."

"What?" John stops scratching his neck.

"Your beard," Mary repeats.

He grew it accidentally, without any forethought. Without Mary around, he forgot the need to look good.

"Makes you look more distinctive. Doing it for a gig or something?"

"Yeah. For a gig. Advertising, you know," John has no idea what he's saying. But all he can think is "She likes it," and he doubts he'll shave anytime soon.

"When is your next gig?" Mary asks.

"Next week. Have a few lined up, actually," John lies.

His auditions, lately, have been with rum.

"That's great. How much—" Mary breaks off.

She doesn't want him to think she's rubbing it in his face, his cash trickle. She believed it was a sore point with him, that after their meager years together she'd be making a lawyer's salary and he a dreamer's one.

Mary recovers, "—will you play?" but not smoothly.

"The usual three everyone likes. Then some covers probably," John reaches for his coffee.

"You've always been hard on yourself," Mary says.

Her eyes grow wide and John, stunned, looks up at her. She hadn't meant to say anything real.

"I have?" John asks.

"Since our first date. Remember? You blamed yourself for the rain."

A downpour that drowned John's confidence as well as his carefully crafted picnic. Their date relocated to his apartment, which became her apartment the second her foot crossed the threshold. Wherever she went, the place belonged to her and her alone once she looked around. She took her time with it, too, her claiming. For large areas she turned clockwise, absorbing her environment until she was full. Then she sighed, her only comment that she now owned what she saw. Considering the bare apartment John called "home," her claiming only lasted the second her foot needed to walk inside. Her claiming of him lasted all that night, though. His hair, messy. His eyes, green flecked with yellow. His smile, adorable. His voice, melodic. His gait, loose. His stripping, clumsy. His chest, oddly toned. His legs, careful. His breath, warm. She sighed into his mouth.

It scared John, that he could fall in love that fast. The rain wanted to come inside, it dripped from the kitchen ceiling into the only pot John owned. Their food was soggy, and he only had one candle to create anything resembling a "mood." But she laughed at his jokes, and told him he was a better cook than she. That night, he noticed hands for the first time in his life. She commanded him to stop and carefully removed her necklace—sapphire and silver—before placing it on his nightstand, next to the circular watermark imprinted by his hatred of coasters and everything else that reminded him of his father. Her motions were gentle yet firm, a lioness lifting a cub by the neck. Hands that could lift and put him in a better place.

And from the moment the rain started until they woke up entangled in each other, John never stopped apologizing.

"I wanted it to be special," John says.

"It was special," Mary says.

I blink, sip my lukewarm latte. I don't know why I'm so focused on these two. Plenty of strangers are thinking nearby. Every life is special, in some way. Well. Interesting. In some way. An off-duty cop sits at the table in front of me, obsessing over the details of an unsolved murder. Should be plenty fascinating. Adjust to him. What's his name?

"—Mark enjoyed it, so that's one person. Even if he's only eight years old." John says.

"I saw him recently. You know, Christmas," Mary says.

The longest Christmas Mary drank through, The Fight fresh in her mind. Her extended family exemplified being fruitful and multiplying. Children littered her grandparents' house. Screaming, laughing, jumping, running, giggling, playing, crying, living.

"He's grown a foot," Mary says.

"Impossible. It's only been, what, a year?" John asks.

To be precise, last Christmas. The one before The Fight. One of the children, Suzy probably, overheard Mary's family gossiping about John and gleaned that he sang. A wave of children crashed on John, demanding entertainment. John strummed carols and a couple of his own songs on Christmas Eve to his first adoring audience.

"Kids. They grow like weeds," Mary says.

"Too bad you can't just yank them out," John grins.

The air vanishes. A void cracks open between John and Mary and expands until every thought in the coffee shop chokes and falls still. A cold seeps in through the fractures. Without moving, John and Mary recede from each other. Two stars sit on opposite ends of space, one blue, one yellow, throwing out light. Wanting to touch. A universe between them.

The blue star sends a message.

"You know, out of the ground. I'm sorry, Mary."

By the time it reaches the yellow star, millions of years have passed. Light years too late.

"It's okay."

The yellow star fades, but the blue one shines brighter. Shines desperate.

"No, it isn't. I've been an ass."

A flicker. She gives him one more chance.

"Why did you ask me here?"

This is it, John.

"Because I—"

You're almost there, John. Please. It's just two more words. Prove me wrong, John. I'm tired of being cynical. I'm tired of sitting in coffee shops, waiting. You've said the first word, you only have two more. Just say them, John, and she'll take you back. Even now it isn't too late, anyone can tell it isn't too late, you don't have to be a mind reader to see it. Two words, John. He spots his coffee cup and in his panicked eyes it becomes an escape. Don't, John. Please. Don't.

"—love this coffee shop," John says.

"I'm sorry?" Mary deadpans.

"Yep. Thought you might like it. I love it," John puts the cup to his lips and pretends to sip it but it's empty and he knows it.

"It's disappointing," Mary says, her iced coffee melted and untouched.

"Sorry you think that," John says. "I love this place."

"I should be going," Mary says.

"It was nice catching up," John says.

"Bye, John," Mary says.

"See you later," John says.

"I doubt it."

The tiny bell rings as Mary leaves. I turn around, not caring that John sees my tears.

"Asshole. It was three words," I say.

"No," John stands up. "Three words would never be enough."

The tiny bell rings as John leaves.

"Are you okay?" The barista heard me, observed my tears. She jumps on the opportunity, while I'm vulnerable. "Do you want to talk about it?" she asks.

In a second I know her every crevasse. Know exactly what to say to make her sleep with me. I've done it to countless women. I can also make her fall in love with me. I've only done that once. It wouldn't take half an hour. I could be her perfect husband; know her desires and emotions and give her everything she'd want.

She can't do that for me.

"No," I say.

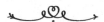

SO FAST WE'RE SLOW
Jody Sollazzo

A protestor yelled out that the FAMs were whores and that the infants would get soft-time-travel brains. Maggie decided to take the Future Airship Mothers to the platform where only travelers and high-paying enthusiasts were allowed. She drew on her days of lecturing as a teacher to grab back her audience.

"Most people would find their first view of an airship intimidating even without putting their beloved infant on it for almost two years," she said. "But remember it will only be five days to them, and they will have the best of care. I can also assure you that babies do not get soft-brains. In fact, this is the third trip for me and my baby. She was born six years ago, but is only a year old with our travels and is so smart. Don't let the protestors' lies scare you out of your opportunity."

The new ship was a massive Zeppelin-shaped silver double-decker with intricate golden embossing around its working parts. From its balloon body, the sea-green engines hung like cut gems in cages of gold. Steam poured out of the engines as it idled.

"Well played," a man said after the FAMs left the dock and Maggie stood alone.

"Excuse me?" she said, eyebrow raising.

He wore an electric-blue suit and a monocle. He stood next to Maggie looking over the railing toward the tethered ship and did not bother to look up. Some children in pastel outfits ran past them and giggled after stomping a rainbow-painted android toy.

The man's long dark dreadlocks hung from his top hat like thick cords against his tanned white skin. The monocle he wore had an intricate lens and a thick black leather strap decorated tastefully to match his silver ear chains. Maggie assumed the monocle was to support some kind of gadget.

"I heard you with those girls. They're the ones who send their babies to themselves in the future because they can't be bothered now. Those idiot protestors give them doubts, and you don't want to be out of a job, yeah?"

Maggie folded her arms under her breasts, stretching her light green peasant-blouse tight. "Those women care greatly about their children, as do I."

"Right. Your six-year-old that is a one-year-old and brilliant due to the magic of time travel. The math doesn't add up. Where is she, then?" he asked.

He stepped closer to her, and she realized he was younger than she thought. He was mocking her, but he smiled.

"Aren't you sharp?" She allowed herself to smile back.

"That's not what my tutor used to say," he said and raised a soft arched brow. "But, I'm right?"

"You're right. The math doesn't work, and I have no baby. I meant I care about their babies enough to fight lies with lies."

"Do they pay you to lie as a ship worker, or does it just come naturally, Emmy Sanger?" he said, reading the name she had on her obtrusive wet-nurse breast pin. The name she would have given him, or anyone, if asked.

"They only pay me to feed the babies, Mister . . . ?"

"I suppose you can call me Mr. Sharp," he said.

"I've been fighting lies with lies as an added service for a while, Mr. Sharp. You don't approve? I can give you statistics on how the lives of the babies and mothers improve."

"How would I know they weren't lies?" he said and grinned. "So you plan on traveling with babes into the future forever?"

She laughed. "I'm sure you know, we aren't really time traveling. The ship moves faster than light. So time slows down on the inside."

"Don't be so sure of what I know," he said. "My name isn't really *Sharp*. The Zeppelin is slow because it's so fast? I didn't make my money in quantum physics."

Maggie laughed again. That made twice in six years—more than she expected. He had some genuine humility. A rare trait on the ship's upper deck. A live band started loud music for the ship's bon voyage as soon-to-be-passengers danced.

"What did you make your money in?" she asked.

"Manipulation, same as you. Only I build things," he said.

He held out a golden mechanical orb in his palm. Pieces in the back of it, shaped like tiny wings, began to flutter. It lifted off his hand and flew before her face. She held out her palm, and it landed with a gentle tickle. It was a little golden owl with gears for eyes. Not a tiny scrap of metal on it looked aesthetically misplaced in its intricate design. Some people slowed to look. Maggie was glad no one stopped.

"It's beautiful," Maggie said.

She felt her chest tighten. She was always so impressed by mechanics as her training had been mostly theoretical. For the first time she felt that she was possibly in the future.

"If you're looking for a way into the future, don't waste your money on the ship," she said, "All that truly happens is the world moves on without you."

"Maybe I want to be still while all my troubles die," he said.

He held out a palm, and his toy owl flew back to him while his monocle lens rotated.

So, he was a talented inventor who was hoping the ship was his way out of a situation. He probably thought he could get away with anything, once on it, since he wasn't even giving his real name. Men like him were the reason they had security on the ship.

The dock's sound system announced boarding was to begin. "Well, good luck to you," she said as she readied herself to embark.

"Luck would be nice in my situation," he said.

He touched the brim of his hat and left her. She felt pinpricks in her chest begin to rise. Hopefully he was just an enthusiast who paid to see the ship up close, and she'd never see him again. Five days would go by for Maggie on the ship, and when she returned he'd be two years gone, and likely with a new fancy.

The club was called The Stopped Watch, which wasn't an accurate pun. Maggie only came because she'd received some free drink tickets as a staff prize. She looked around at women in heavy pastel make-up and faux East-Indian garb. They contrasted greatly to her own swept up chestnut hair, simple white billowing dress, and black leather corset.

Maggie sat next to a shouting, gin-stinking couple. The slim bustle-dress-frosted-lipstick girl held out her wrist and showed the older man her Cog-Am scar around which she'd had tattooed tiny flowers.

"I had no idea what it was about," the girl said. "Then I found a clue at my house, which led to another and another. It turned out it was a game me and my friends created for ourselves. The prize was finding the final clue, which was a recorder of us saying we were going to create the game! Good fun! But, it is a bit frightful. I really do have no memory of creating it, and I can't ever. Who knows what other things I've done!"

Maggie turned abruptly away from the couple, her mouth agape. The lives of the rich were so different. She was far from anti-Cog-Am, but she didn't believe they should be used for games. That was almost as bad as forcing someone to erase their memories against their will.

She realized that the blue-suited man, the so-called Mr. Sharp, was next to her. She wondered how he could see anything in the dark club through the tinted blue glasses he wore.

"So, what'd you do it for?" he asked as he leaned into her.

"What?" she said.

"That lil' social-itch bitch had her memory erased for fun. What did you want to forget? Your Cog-Am? Long sleeves and cuffs give it away, pet."

He fingered her black leather cuff and pulled on its decorative chain. The smell of fermented honey was on his breath.

"I forget," she said dryly.

"Right, I didn't forget you're a liar," he said right in her ear.

"You can stop calling me a liar anytime." She was happy to yell it over the music.

"Am I brassing you off? You can just drink to forget me. No need for an expensive procedure. I'm surprised they don't have little Cog-Am booths on this Zeppelin nightmare of dimwits."

She planned to say she had tried to warn him about the airship, and to tell him plenty of intelligent people had Cog-Ams, and that they weren't just used to forget. But, Mr. Sharp had taken his glasses off. She had only seen one of his eyes earlier when he had the monocle on. Seeing them both was quite different. They were blue and rimmed with black liner, and they were set on her. His whole face together was like looking at something far too bright for this dark place. The music stopped briefly, and Maggie spoke in the dead space.

"Just—shut up!" she said.

"What will you do if I don't? Suckle me 'til I'm quiet? Do me a favor then, don't wait a half-hour. Do it now, so I get the booze," he said.

Maggie jumped off of her bar stool and went to his. She kissed him on the mouth fully, mashing her burgundy lips into his pale pink ones until he opened them. She could pretend she did it because he understood about lactation and drinking. But, it really was his eyes. Mr. Sharp grabbed her arms and searched her face, his brow crinkling over his aquiline nose. Then he kissed her back with such fever it was as if he had genuine passion for her. But, Maggie knew that wasn't true. They were just strangers on a ship about to leave a bar together for a long grope on their way to a room.

⚜

They swung each other down the halls of halo-gas-lamps. It was nearly a shoving war as their lips and bodies rubbed against each other. She would try to push him back—enough to get her garments aside, enough to get the main event started—but then he would start pushing and pulling her to where he wanted to go.

She gasped as he lifted her up so easily. She wasn't as petite as she once was but she supposed she was still a miniature hourglass woman.

"Don't worry," he said, "no open windows or doors here, so I can't throw you off, as much as I might want."

"You can't shock me," she said in his arms.

"Don't speak too soon. My lactating liar."

They kissed as he carried her into his suite, which was a far cry from the staff bunks. It was the room of a traveler who had two years of money to waste in five days.

"You're not getting any," she said to him. She kicked off her shoes, breathing heavily as his lips found her neck.

"It would seem you're lying again," he said.

"I mean," she said, "you aren't getting any of my milk. If that's what all of this is about. You seem a bit fixated on me, and you know a lot about lactation."

"Oh," he said. "No, I was—was just trying to shock you with the lactation comments, and now it seems I'm the one—"

She laughed too hard to retort and then kissed his sweet stammering mouth. She felt a rush of warmth toward him that wasn't just lust.

Mr. Sharp walked over to the wall and opened his blinds to what the Zeppelin brochure dubbed a Tru-Window, made to look like a view of the ever-changing sky. A faux-sun rose to orange, then burned to white, then receded back to orange before disappearing to blackness and faux-stars. The full rotation took moments and was utterly false. It was seen as a great luxury in the airship, but Maggie personally thought Mr. Sharp was a far better luxury, even if he showed bad taste in paying for a Tru-Window.

She smiled at him across the room. Due to her, his top half was naked now. He was lean and muscled with long dreadlocks hanging over his shoulders. His bright blue eyes looked at her unflinchingly. The orange light danced across the dark stubble on his triangle chin.

Maggie bounded across the room. She jumped on him, expecting to take him down and get his trousers off, but instead he threw her on the bed and within seconds, had all her clothes off like he had skinned an apple. He did this as he kissed her with such fever she didn't know how he breathed.

Maggie had the sweetest struggle to break away through the pleasure in order to please. As the faux horizon went from dawn to dusk, she only got to kiss him a few times before he pulled her on top of him and gave her pleasure like none she could remember. His face, going from dark to orange to white with the window light, showed as much bliss as she felt.

It did have to end, and when it did Maggie shivered into his body and laughed when she felt the cool steel ball of the toy owl roll up her bare back in his hand. The man quickly reached behind him to turn on a soft light and grab his thick strapped monocle. He only took seconds to fasten it on; then the little golden owl chirped and whirred and flew up to Maggie's face as if to say hello. She giggled at his toy. There was night outside for the moment.

"It really is beautiful," she said.

"I'll give you a special one for your baby. I—"

She kissed him quiet. Perhaps she should ask him his actual name.

"I told you, I have no baby. I'm just filled with hormones and milk to care for them."

"That's not all you're filled with. CADD is actually more than a toy. It's a Cognitive Amnesia Deleting Device."

She stiffened and sat up. "Deleting a Cog-Am is impossible!"

"You don't remember meeting anyone smart enough to break one," he said with a smirk.

He rolled his eyes at her as if they were trading wits then made a motion with his head and the owl flew away from her and to the room's desk where it shut itself off. Mr. Sharp took off the monocle.

"I've frightened you. I didn't mean to. Well, I did a bit . . . None of this is going as planned." He sighed.

He had planned this! To frighten the time traveling wet-nurse for some warped political cause, no doubt. Maybe he planned to manipulate her Cog-Am, turn her against all she stood for. She had heard such horrors were possible. Another outsider who thought he knew what was best for women and their children. She pretended to gather her clothes as she looked for the security alarm trigger. When she saw it above the door behind him, she jumped to hit it with her palm.

"What did you do?" His eyes closed and fists clenched.

"It's a silent alarm. Ship security is much tighter than you're led to believe," she said.

"I was led to believe a lot and now—wait? You called security? You do realize you're naked. I'm not going to hurt you, even after all you've done." He laughed at her, but she was far from laughing.

"All I've done," she said. "You people see me as a child abuser because I do this work, so you plan to—what? Abuse me in kind?"

"You really have no idea who I am. Get your clothes on. They'll be coming. Been in this situation before, yeah?" he said as he retrieved his pants from the hand-carved dresser.

"I'm sorry I don't recognize you from whatever misguided movement you're from. I don't often live in the present. But I assure you, I've never been in this situation before," she said.

She slowly stepped away from him, backwards toward the door.

"I did not take this job to shag the rich," she said "I work on this ship to help children and their mothers. Maybe it's you who have me confused with some other pudgy wet-nurse."

She gasped as he pulled her to him, put his lips on her forehead and pulled them off with a smack.

There was a knock at the door. "Security."

"You're not pudgy. You just had a baby." His words came faster now. "But, it was really years ago, and you're keeping her an eternal infant."

"I have no baby!" she cried.

"Maggie," he said, "stop lying!"

"What did you call me?" Her eyes were wide as saucers.

He had called her Maggie. She felt confused and aching and something else, like fear of falling off the ship into the ever-changing sky. All the possibilities swirled in her mind, and they all involved one thing—family, and not her own. She had no more family. And no baby. The rich and powerful Dowds had already taken everything from her when they took their son, and now they wanted the baby she didn't have?

Security pounded on the door. "We're terribly sorry, but you'll need to open the door or—"

"Help!" she shouted, and the door crashed in.

The events happened so quickly, and Maggie dropped to the floor to figure them out. She realized she was still not afraid. She couldn't fear losing what had already gone.

After a flurry of sounds and moving body parts, two security men lay on the ground holding their faces where Mr. Sharp had hit them but somehow managed to remain untouched. Maybe he was an extremely expensive mercenary. It was surely the only explanation, or at least the only one she would accept.

"The baby has to grow up," he whispered as he knelt to where she sat on the floor.

"You are damned good," Maggie scoffed, "The Dowds found a true believer with endless physical skills. Tell me, how much are they paying you?"

"Listen—" he said.

"No! You listen to me. Tell them they won't win this one. They can't. My baby died in the womb."

"What?" he roared.

Maggie's head buzzed.

More security in black-plated armor surrounded the man and wrestled him to the ground, shouting. But, Maggie just kept at him.

"Don't be so distraught," she said. "You've completed your mission."

She tried to stop her voice from shaking. Her brain was filled with foolish ideas. Deleting a Cog-Am *was* impossible—she knew this.

Still she stood over him with pressured speech as security tried to push her back.

"I don't know why they would want my baby now. I was the only one who wanted her. When she was sick inside me I came to this bloody ship thinking it could save her. I'll throw you a copy of the report in your cushy cell to prove she was never born."

"You wouldn't have been the only one who wanted the baby—"

A blow to Mr. Sharp's head silenced him, and they dragged him off.

Maggie screamed.

As she sank to the ground, the remaining Security-bobs asked her questions. They thought the man had hurt the wet-nurse. They couldn't be more wrong. There was really only one man who would have wanted her baby, Dugland Dowd. But his parents had forced him to forget everything he knew.

❦

Dugland was behind the bars of the ship's brig. Even with a black eye and under stark light, Maggie thought he looked pretty. His presence forced color and real light into the white starkness. He was shoeless and shirtless, wearing only his bright blue pants and hanging suspenders.

"I'm not pressing charges. Let him out," Maggie said softly to the ship's bobby, a broad, older man with a white handlebar moustache.

"'Fraid not, Ma'am. This one caused a load of trouble. Maybe next time don't be so quick to push the panic button when you get frisky."

"Leave her alone," Dugland spat at the bobby. Then he looked at Maggie. "So you're here to give me the report on your miscarriage? Tell me, this supposed family I'm working for, do you hate them all?"

Did he really think she still didn't know who he was? Well, she *had* been ignorant so far.

"No, the baby's father—his parents were wrong and awful for forcing a Cog-Am into him so he'd forget me, but they weren't wrong about him being too young."

"Too young—" he cackled, "I heard he was just months shy of being of age and not young of mind, but maybe he was a fool because he thought you loved him. That you—"

"He was too idealistic to see . . ." she began. A chasm of pain opened in her throat.

"You sure you're remembering him right with all you've had erased with that bloody gadget?" he said, pointing to the Cog-Am in her wrist. He folded his arms and looked away.

Maggie couldn't find her voice to explain.

"You should go. Didn't you hear the bobby?" he said. "You're nothing more than a loose wet-nurse."

"He's right," the bobby said as he came to her side. "Move along, lest I put you in there with him."

"If that's what it takes." Maggie stamped the bobby's foot as hard as she could. As he groaned, she raced to the bars and put her hands around them.

"What are you doing—" Dugland scoffed, "There's stubborn and then there's thick."

He approached her slowly and clasped his hands over hers on the bars until the bobby, cursing under his breath, pushed Maggie into the cell. She knew she was risking her job but all she felt was relief not to be dragged away from him again.

Pushing back sobs, she spoke. "I am thick. Just a wet-nurse. I don't tutor prodigies anymore. Do they call him a prodigy now that he's grown up?"

"How would I know what became of a spoiled rich kid you couldn't wait to forget? I'm a hired gun, remember."

"Maybe *you* are the one who's thick," she said. "I remember everything about Dugland Dowd. I just don't remember what he looked like. I programmed my Cog-Am to forget his face."

The bobby shook his head as he closed the door of the cell.

"I bet you wish you could just erase it all except the lesson to never fall in love," said Dugland. He turned away from her and went to the other side of the cell.

"You think that's what I'd wish now?" She sat on a bench and folded her knees to her breasts. It was an action that used to be easier. "Well, I can tell you, back then I was out of wishing fairies, so I went to science. You of all people should understand that."

"Oh, I understand all right," he said, pacing in a small circle. "I understood it all when I deleted my forced Cog-Am. I understood that I had a plan with some-one to overcome mind-rape, but instead, she ran and diddled with her own mind. I've understood for years now how she lied to me!"

"You want the truth? I was a fool!" She stood. "I learned something wasn't right with the baby. I thought I could run to this ship to freeze time to save her. I understand that you're angry but—but did you have to seduce me when I clearly thought you were a stranger?"

He bounded over to her. "Maggie, that wasn't what I intended to do."

Now she was the one who turned away.

"When we docked, two years had passed," she said as she looked through the bars. "You were a twenty-year-old boy who was happy with a twenty-year-old right-sort-of-girl."

The bobby tut-tutted from his too small desk.

"Is that what my mother told you? And you believed her?" asked Dugland.

"What did it matter what I believed? There was nothing I could do," she said.

She would not cry in front of him even if she had to sound bitter. He'd never tolerated her crying.

"I suppose I can see why you'd want to forget," he said, "but—"

"You aren't listening. That's not how I had my Cog-Am designed . . ." she said.

He angrily swiped his eyes with the heel of his hand. Maggie's passion to ex-plain herself suddenly disappeared. She sat on the hard bench again.

"Right. I'm sure you boiled everything down into particles you can't see or touch so you can freeze it all up but still remember. At least it didn't make you frigid."

"'Ey chaser!" As the bobby bolted up from his desk, his white mustache also leapt. "If you were so smart, you'd understand how this ship works. You've had all this time to get over it all. For her it was just a short bit ago. It's much harder on the likes of her."

"Is it?" Dugland asked. "I've been without her twice as long. I'm the one still in love."

"Dugger—" Maggie began. Her voice was so low and shaky that it was drowned out by the bobby's bitter laugh.

"For the love of God, boy!" the bobby said. "She didn't erase you. She's dulled the pain, like I did with my Cog-Am after the war."

"I said before, I only had the visual memory taken." Maggie spoke softly.

Dugland bent down so they were eye to eye.

"Well," he said, "I suppose I can understand that. Physicality and looks were never my strong suits back then. But I've gotten better. You see I've learned to fight."

"That's not true. You were perfect," she said.

She made her eyes go blurry so his face was just a peach blur and a mass of black locks. She remembered a younger version of his lilting voice mocking her own haughtiness.

"Are you so stubborn that you'll even argue about information you had erased from your brain?" he said.

But it was his humor that broke Maggie.

"But, I didn't forget." She sobbed into her hands. She felt him place his hands on the ball she had made of herself.

"I see you remember that if you cry I'll do anything you want. I can forget how to fight, you know. I hear those Cog-Ams can erase things like that."

"Oi!" the bobby said. "You're the worst chaser I've ever seen. Most beg or propose."

"I've already proposed. This is a private conversation between me and my fiancée. Don't you have some drunken deeds to cover up? Bribes to take?" Dugland grumbled.

"Why? You offerin'?" the bobby asked.

❧❦❧

Maggie opened her eyes.

"Told you it wouldn't hurt," Dugland said.

He was bending over her as she lay on the bed. He pulled the golden owl's claws from the inside of her wrist's Cog-Am slit. It felt like a thread of milk being pulled from her arm. The ship was slowing so the orange light in the Tru-Window was programmed to stay longer. Outside, she didn't know if it was sunrise or sunset.

Maggie didn't feel as dizzy as she expected. She touched Dug's face and pushed back the dreadlocks he had acquired. His face looked so angular now. It made him look less trusting. Not that he was ever trusting, but his baby face had made him seem so. Now it was gone. She felt her eyes burn.

"You're putting on pains just to be right," he said, "I know it didn't hurt."

Now he looked like the sweet boy she remembered. He kissed like him, too. He just had sleeker, striped gray pants with the wild suspenders. She pulled away from his lips and it tugged at her more than milk or a memory thread.

"Of course it hurt," she said. "All that lost time. You've caught up with me. You're an old man now, Dugger."

"You prefer me with my bad fashion choices and clumsy baby fat?"

Dugland lifted her easily, showing off. He sat down and cradled her in his lap. Maggie smiled. "You were just a bit pudgy. Now it's my turn."

Her white dress showed sun shadows from the window.

"I want you pudgier. I'll fill you with babies, lady."

"So arrogant," she said. "I'm not going to be one of those wives that sit all day. I plan to work directly with the FAMs now."

"Those women who aren't ready for their babies? Well, I guess if anyone can make them study up and get ready, it's you," he said. "We dock in an hour. The future is coming."

"It's not really the future. We've just traveled to the present so fast it slowed time," she said in between kisses.

"Yeah, yeah. You know I was never good at quantum mechanics. If memory serves, I needed a tutor. Teach me again."

Maggie decided the sun was definitely rising.

ALICE
Morgen Knight

Looking up from where he lay, into leafless limbs, Rob suspected he was dreaming. The sky was blue, for one thing, and he could hear the sweet chirps of unseen birds. The naked sun was off somewhere to his left and a wave of pure white clouds were huddled together to the right. It was too perfect *not* to be a dream. This knowledge had to be kept secret from his broader self. Realizing you're in a dream can bring the whole house of cards tumbling, and he wanted to hold on to this. You don't get to see blue skies anymore. All the clouds are dark, skittering in a mad dash like the rabbit in that Lewis Carroll story. Late! Late! Late!

With her head on his right shoulder, Alice talked about how, when she was a little girl, she'd wanted to grow up and be a writer. A piece of poetry she'd written around the age of ten had gotten published and, from then on, it'd been her dream. She told him about how she'd walk around with paper and pen, writing down ideas or a small detail she felt was important. At some point, life got busy and the dream petered out, all her little story ideas packed up in the vault of her mind. "And they're still there," she said matter-of-factly. "Stacked up in neat rows, some of them running loose like sugared-up children, knocking into shit," she giggled.

Rob smiled while his eyes traced the curve of a branch. It reminded him of a slender arm, the kind exposed by a formal dress, a bit toned. But he was listening to Alice—sweet, foul-mouthed little Alice. He owed that to her. It was something he'd seldom done when she was alive.

Not at first, though. Not before he'd seen her naked often enough to erase the mystery, met her family, and decided exactly how much effort he had to put into this to keep her around. Before that, he'd found her every syllable a new discovery, inspecting it, holding it, questioning it. After . . . there was no reason to lie to himself, he'd fallen into the pattern of letting her words pass over him, his mind filling with the silence between them like a swimmer gasping for air between waves.

"We're like Adam and Eve," Alice said. "A boy, a girl, a tree. Parents of a shitty new world."

"We can't be parents," Rob said. "You're dead. But maybe we're like Noah and his family. Except instead of dying by water, the world died for it." The extent of his religious knowledge didn't extend much further than that. Like most children of broken homes, he viewed all institutions warily, suspiciously fallible.

"Fucking eerie," Alice muttered.

The dream collapsed, and Rob woke with a sudden jerk, banging his knees against porcelain. He was curled in the bottom of a bathtub. His rifle was tucked against his body; the barrel poked down between his bent legs like an android phallus, the butt beneath his chin. The world was a very dangerous place, now. Not as bad as during the dying, or right after (was there ever a positive to say the killing had leveled out?), but you could still get shot for a drink of clean water.

Rob worked his way to his feet. His lower back ached, but that was the price of sleeping in a bathtub. It was the only place he felt safe sleeping indoors. A psychologist would probably have a field day with it. Links to the womb. A locus of yearning for the precious liquid lost. Maybe, if he found a psychologist *really* out there, the porcelain tub was the physical divination of his spirit animal, the turtle! To Rob, tubs were just safe places. It concealed him as he slept and, as a person reared in Tornado Alley, it'd been hammered into him that tubs were the best spot in any emergency to tuck into a ball and kiss your ass good-bye. Earthquake— tub. Nuclear war—tub. It was a tub he'd hidden in as the world had gone to shit. Of course, he'd lined it with couch cushions and pillows. He wasn't a masochist.

What struck Rob as weird was sleeping in people's beds. A bed is sacred ground. People spend a third of their life in one, they dream in them, they make love and share their fears in them. Sleeping in other people's beds was an intrusion, even if the owners were dead.

He left the bathroom, rifle slung over his shoulder, and was stopped by what remained of the rising sun. Most of the east face of this building was gone above the fifteenth floor. He was on the twentieth. The ceiling near the missing wall lacked a section, carpeting from the apartment above sagging down like a dead animal's tongue.

The sky was constantly overcast, but the hues of dusk and dawn filled the sporadic gaps between the monstrous clouds like swipes of high art. Spillman or Tolndover. Rob stood there watching the pink streaks evanesce into a bland white that shot across the landscape in dramatic pulses, reminding him of police search-lights in old prison movies. He didn't know if the sky would ever again be as blue as it had been in his dreams.

When Rob finally turned around, Alice was sitting on the back of the couch, feet on the springs where the removed cushions would have been. "I had a dream with you in it," he said, scratching his thick facial hair.

"Again?" A smile snaked across her face. "Was I doing naughty things?" The ghost Alice in his dreams was never the ghost Alice of awake.

"We talked about biblical stories," he said.

Her face scrunched up in the cutest way. "That doesn't sound like me." She stood. "Do you think it'll rain today?"

"Maybe," Rob said. He wished he had more answers. Who didn't? There were too many troublesome questions running around like orphaned children, the answers that parented them long deceased. The rain, if it came, would be like the blasts of sunlight—sporadic and brief. "I think we'll move on to a different building today." Every night he'd choose a different apartment, moving across the city building by building. There was no hurry, anymore. That life had died of thirst. And he (and Alice) would scour the apartment's cupboards and closets. They usually found canned goods and prescription pills and porn. There was probably a deeper statement about the times they'd lived, in that.

Today's modest banquet consisted of creamed corn, beef jerky, a priceless can of mixed fruit and lightly molded biscuits you could use as a weapon. He drank from a bottle of clouded water, careful to never waste a drop.

"Do you think it's ever too late for a man to find himself?" he asked, wrist-wiping his mouth.

"It's never too late to discover good things," Alice said. "You'd have to be a prick to think so."

Rob ate in silence, looking out at the city through the space of a missing wall. The view was the kind a man could relax and die taking in, wrought of pure destruction.

No one knew how the water became polluted, or contaminated; at least, Rob didn't. The last radio transmission he'd heard had been about a bacterium resistant to this and that, but others were crying out about pollution and Mother Nature finally having had enough of us and . . . did why really matter now? Most of the water in the world would kill you with one drink. It was a horrific way to die. He'd seen it happen, run from it.

Once the sickness had started to spread, the wars began. Not only country against country, but neighbor against neighbor. Streets rallied against streets. The thirsty mobbed rumored sources of clean water, and the atrocities were countless. The clouded sky was the result of superpowers flexing their muscles. China and Russia had both sprinted for the Arctic Circle, wanting what remained of the ice, destroying one another along with it. Pakistan had thrown a few nukes at India. North Korea had lobbed a few of their backyard fusion experiments south, just for the hell of it—everything was going down, why not settle a score or two?

Had America skipped through unscathed? He'd heard that most of the western seaboard was bright enough to read by at night in the Rockies. Who knew how bad it'd gone down in the east.

The poisoned rain had followed, killing plants and people alike. He'd been alone by then (as alone as a man with a ghost can get), drinking from a small stock of bottled water he'd killed a man to get. But over the last months, the rains had changed. The smell was different. What few animals were still alive drank from fresh puddles and survived.

Alice was standing on the far side of the apartment, looking out. The cool wind wrapped sinuous streams around her, brushing her dark hair. Daylight broke distantly through the scattered cracks in the restless sky; narrow sheaves of white light wafted with ephemeral shadows like shifting gossamer drapes. She was utterly beautiful, caught in youth eternal and framed by the dark hues of destruction unfolded. It was the end of this world, and he wished he could hold on to this image of her forever. Even if she wasn't real.

When they left the building later, Alice walked beside him, sometimes talking, sometimes keeping her thoughts inside. In the brief bursts of sunlight, she'd never cast a shadow. Her steps had never made noise. When she yelled, her voice didn't echo off the buildings' indifferent faces, only in the chambers of his mind. But she was there. When they touched, he felt her; when he spoke to her, she responded; when he needed her, she was there. And, yet, he could never settle on her reality. Were all ghosts like this, given to haunt only a few? The shadow in the room that only one sees? Or was she not a ghost at all? Simply a configuration of his addled mind, the brightest star in the constellation of what had been, a dead light to wish upon?

He had watched her die in the bed they had shared. It is so hard to go thirsty when you can smell water that's sitting in the other room. You go crazy, lips cracking like drought-stricken land, blood thick, mind sluggish and *pounding*. The longer it draws on, the stronger the scent of water gets, teasing you, making simple hunger look like pussy problems. But you know it's poisoned. Rob had heard stories of people stuck in life rafts, drifting around the ocean. How, even though all the saltwater could do was kill you more quickly, after a while some would jump in and try to drink the ocean, try to *drown* in it, they were so thirsty.

The water mocks you.

He didn't know where she'd drunk from—they were getting by on small pools of liquid in the bottom of canned vegetables—but he suspected it was the toilet. It had to have been in the middle of the night, while he'd slept. All he knew for sure was that one morning, her skin had been a telling red. Blue, bulging veins could easily be traced across her brow, her arms, her back. By midday, the milkiness had clouded her eyes. All Alice could do was curse and scream. The pain drove her mad. She'd bled all over their designer sheets.

Within forty-eight hours, she was gone, like all the others. Had a part of him felt relief? The screams had stopped. What few supplies they'd had didn't have to be shared.

Rob shook his head, aborting the question. They had found a small patch of only half-wilted, bleached grass near the river. He loved the sound of it, something he'd never been aware of before. They lay there for a while. It was strange that it had taken a fallen world for him to face the fraud of a life he'd pretended to love.

He wished that he could say he'd lain beside her as she'd thrashed in the torment of gripping death. That his comforting had eased her fear and pain somewhat. He wished he could say that. The closest he'd gotten was the doorway. The sickness scared him. Like a child afraid of the dark room, he'd stood there, asking if she were okay, knowing she wasn't.

After she'd died, he'd left their condo.

Their building had been populated by go-getters. Lawyers at the bottom of the ladder, first-year doctors, the young and upwardly mobile. Rob was a broker, stretching his hand up toward the middle rungs, with nice clothes, a leased BMW, a beautiful live-in girlfriend. He'd known it all and had it all, and in the end it was all a handful of dust. How do you drink a gold watch? How do you feel superior when all there is is you? His closest relationship was a woman he'd forgotten he loved. It all seemed pointless, now.

He had grown up somewhat humbly. His dad had been a maintenance man and, for some reason, Rob had been ashamed of this. And the clothes he'd worn. And the limits on life. That's why he'd pushed himself so hard, he figured. The right address, the right car, the right clothes. Be the kind of man others want to be. It was almost laughable, now. It's the people without money that try the hardest to show it off. And just when he'd grabbed what he'd wanted, the world ended and proved all his prizes insubstantial.

Lying on the half-wilted grass, he placed his head in Alice's lap and wept. She stroked his head without a word.

Alice had shown up two days after Rob had abandoned her in the condo. Most people were dead. Those that weren't were violent and paranoid. He'd hidden whenever people came around, gripping the end of a small baseball bat with a trembling hand. From a covered vantage point, he had watched a small war over a hot tub on the fourth floor, next to the gym, after Alice had died. Neighbors that he had known passingly brutally cut one another down. The water was bloody at the end, but the victors had drunk from it deeply then filled their containers.

Rob had been on the brink of suicide by water when she'd spoken. He'd been curled up on the floor of someone else's exclusive condo near the roof. All of his dirty clothes had designer labels; his loafers were Italian leather, and his breath was

Calvin Klein because he'd tried to drink cologne. And then she'd said his name, and it was like being awakened to a new life.

"But you died," he'd said.

"The dead don't always leave," Alice had responded. Smiling, beautiful Alice whom he had held back with his distance and biting criticisms. He had always been afraid that she would see that he needed her more than she needed him. It was a truth that had crawled among his fears like a sole maggot in the dead of night.

Alice had taught him how to get water from a water heater. From a radiator. She had helped him build the distillery he now carried that had saved his life. It was the only thing that could clean the water, a bit of knowledge that came along way too late for way too few. His was small—two metal containers connected by a copper tube. Contaminated water was poured into the first container, capped, then placed over fire. The water boiled, the steam passed through the copper tube and became liquid in the second container, as it cooled. His setup could clean a gallon of water overnight. He'd seen much bigger stills among the larger groups, but Rob preferred the shadows.

They spent the night in another apartment. Rob pulled the cushions off the couch, then read from a book of poetry he'd rescued from a battered store. He'd never been much of a poetry fan before. All the books on his tablet had orbited a central theme: success. But true success lasts, and all of his had proven false.

He read poetry because Alice liked it, because it meant something. Same reason he'd spent two days fixing a truck he'd driven long enough to realize he enjoyed the walking. Alice had said she believed it was never too late for a man to do good things. Rob wasn't sure how much of it this world held, but he wanted to live with substance. He didn't know how far that would go in redeeming him from such a wasted life, but he felt he had to try.

"Bury my body," Alice had said after she'd appeared.

"And then what happens? Will you go away?"

"I don't know."

"Are you even really here?"

"I don't know that either."

He'd buried her in a nice, open park. Her body was wrapped in fine cotton sheets. In the dirt above her, he'd planted an apple seed taken from a looted gardening shop. Then he'd walked around the park, planting seeds. He liked the idea that in some future, some kid might run laughing through a forest of apple trees. Not once would the kid wonder why the trees were here.

That felt substantial.

"Where will we go?" Alice finally asked. They were sitting on the roof of a new building. Behind them, the still had been erected, and fire curled around the bottom of a metal container. In front of them was the doomed cityscape and the distant bend of the river.

"North, I think. Where it used to snow a lot." It was his best plan. "I don't feel hurried," he explained. How much of life had been wasted by rushing? "Do you think anyone else has a personal ghost?" He smiled.

"I don't know," Alice said thoughtfully. "Maybe I'm not a ghost. Maybe this is a dream. Maybe you're in a coma. Maybe you're batshit crazy." She laughed lightly. "Or maybe all that's bullshit, and you're the ghost. I'm simply your guide through the land of the dead."

Rob looked around at the city. It really was beautiful.

SING

Karin Tidbeck

Originally appeared in *Tor.com*, April 2013

The cold dawn light creeps onto the mountaintops; they emerge like islands in the valley's dark sea, tendrils of steam rising up from the thickets clinging to the rock. Right now there's no sound of birdsong or crickets, no hiss of wind in the trees. When Maderakka's great shadow has sunk back below the horizon, twitter and chirp will return in a shocking explosion of sound. For now, we sit in complete silence.

The birds have left. Petr lies with his head in my lap, his chest rising and falling so quickly it's almost a flutter, his pulse rushing under the skin. The bits of eggshell I couldn't get out of his mouth, those that have already made their way into him, spread whiteness into the surrounding flesh. If only I could hear that he's breathing properly. His eyes are rolled back into his head, his arms and legs curled up against his body like a baby's. If he's conscious, he must be in pain. I hope he's not conscious.

A strangely shaped man came in the door and stepped up to the counter. He made a full turn to look at the mess in my workshop: the fabrics, the cutting table, the bits of pattern. Then he looked directly at me. He was definitely not from here— no one had told him not to do that. I almost wanted to correct him: *leave, you're not supposed to make contact like that, you're supposed to pretend you can't see me and tell the air what you want.* But I was curious about what he might do. I was too used to avoiding eye contact, so I concentrated carefully on the rest of him: the squat body with its weirdly broad shoulders, the swelling upper arms and legs. The cropped copper on his head. I'd never seen anything like it.

So this man stepped up to the counter and he spoke directly to me, and it was like being caught under the midday sun.

"You're Aino? The tailor? Can you repair this?"

He spoke slowly and deliberately, his accent crowded with hard sounds. He dropped a heap of something on the counter. I collected myself and made my way over. He flinched as I slid off my chair at the cutting table, catching myself before my knees collapsed backward. I knew what he saw: a stick insect of a woman clambering unsteadily along the furniture, joints flexing at impossible angles. Still he didn't look away. I could see his eyes at the outskirts of my vision, golden-yellow points following me as I heaved myself forward to the stool by the counter. The bundle, when I held it up, was an oddly cut jacket. It had no visible seams, the material almost like rough canvas but not quite. It was half-eaten by wear and grime.

"You should have had this mended long ago," I said. "And washed. I can't fix this."

He leaned closer, hand cupped behind an ear. "Again, please?"

"I can't repair it," I said, slower.

He sighed, a long waft of warm air on my forearm. "Can you make a new one?"

"Maybe. But I'll have to measure you." I waved him toward me.

He stepped around the counter. After that first flinch, he didn't react. His smell was dry, like burnt ochre and spices, not unpleasant, and while I measured him he kept talking in a stream of consonants and archaic words, easy enough to understand if I didn't listen too closely. His name was Petr, the name as angular as his accent, and he came from Amitié—a station somewhere out there—but was born on Gliese. (I knew a little about Gliese, and told him so.) He was a biologist and hadn't seen an open sky for eight years. He had landed on Kiruna and ridden with a truck and then walked for three days, and he was proud to have learned our language, although our dialect was very odd. He was here to research lichen.

"Lichen can survive anywhere," he said, "even in a vacuum, at least as spores. I want to compare these to the ones on Gliese, to see if they have the same origin."

"Just you? You're alone?"

"Do you know how many colonies are out there?" He laughed, but then cleared his throat. "Sorry. But it's really like that. There are more colonies than anyone can keep track of. And Kiruna is, well, it's considered an abandoned world, after the mining companies left, so—"

His next word was silent. Saarakka was up, the bright moonlet sudden as always. He mouthed more words. I switched into song, but Petr just stared at me. He inclined his head slightly toward me, eyes narrowing, then shook his head and pinched the bridge of his nose. He reached into the back pocket of his trousers and drew out something like a small and very thin book. He did something with a quick movement—shook it out, somehow—and it unfolded into a large square that he put down on the counter. It had the outlines of letters at the bottom, and his fingers flew over them. WHAT HAPPENED WITH SOUND?

I recognized the layout of keys. I could type. SAARAKKA, I wrote. WHEN SAARAKKA IS UP, WE CAN'T HEAR SPEECH. WE SING INSTEAD.

WHY HAS NOBODY TOLD ME ABOUT THIS? he replied.

I shrugged.

He typed with annoyed, jerky movements. HOW LONG DOES IT LAST?

UNTIL IT SETS, I told him.

He had so many questions—he wanted to know how Saarakka silenced speech, if the other moon did something too. I told him about how Oksakka kills the sound of birds, and how giant Maderakka peeks over the horizon now and then, reminding us that the three of us are just her satellites. How they once named our own world after a mining town and we named the other moons for an ancient goddess and her handmaidens, although these names sound strange and harsh to us now. But every answer prompted new questions. I finally pushed the sheet away from me. He held his palms up in resignation, folded it up, and left.

What I had wanted to say, when he started talking about how Kiruna was just one world among many, was that I'm not stupid. I read books and sometimes I could pick up stuff on my old set, when the satellite was up and the moons didn't interfere with it so much. I knew that Amitié was a big space station. I knew we lived in a poor backwater place. Still, you think your home is special, even if nobody ever visits.

⁂

The village has a single street. One can walk along the street for a little while, and then go down to the sluggish red river. I go there to wash myself and rinse out cloth.

I like dusk, when everyone's gone home and I can air-dry on the big, flat stone by the shore, arms and legs finally long and relaxed and folding at what angles they will, my spine and muscles creaking like wood after a long day of keeping everything straight and upright. Sometimes the goats come to visit. They're only interested in whether I have food or ear scratchings for them. To the goats, all people are equal, except for those who have treats. Sometimes the birds come here too, alighting on the rocks to preen their plumes, compound eyes iridescent in the twilight. I try not to notice them, but unless Oksakka is up to muffle the higher-pitched noise, the insistent buzzing twitches of their wings are impossible to ignore. More than two or three and they start warbling among themselves, eerily like human song, and I leave.

Petr met me on the path up from the river. I was carrying a bundle of wet fabric strapped to my back; it was slow going because I'd brought too much and the extra weight made me swing heavy on my crutches.

He held out a hand. "Let me carry that for you, Aino."

"No, thank you." I moved past him.

He kept pace with me. "I'm just trying to be polite."

I sneaked a glance at him, but it did seem that was what he wanted. I un-strapped my bundle. He took it and casually slung it over his shoulder. We walked in silence up the slope, him at a leisurely walk, me concentrating on the uphill effort, crutch-foot-foot-crutch.

"Your ecosystem," he said eventually, when the path flattened out. "It's fascinating."

"What about it?"

"I've never seen a system based on parasitism."

"I don't know much about that."

"But you know how it works?"

"Of course," I said. "Animals lay eggs in other animals. Even the plants."

"So is there anything that uses the goats for hosts?"

"Hookflies. They hatch in the goats' noses."

Petr hummed. "Does it harm the goats?"

"No . . . not usually. Some of them get sick and die. Most of the time they just get . . . more perky. It's good for them."

"Fascinating," Petr said. "I've never seen an alien species just slip into an ecosystem like that." He paused. "These hookflies. Do they ever go for humans?"

I shook my head.

He was quiet for a while. We were almost at the village when he spoke again.

"So how long have your people been singing?"

"I don't know. A long time."

"But how do you learn? I mean I've tried, but I just can't make the sounds. The pitch, it's higher than anything I've heard a human voice do. It's like birdsong."

"It's passed on." I concentrated on tensing the muscles in my feet for the next step.

"How? Is it a mutation?"

"It's passed on," I repeated. "Here's the workshop. I can handle it from here. Thank you."

He handed me the bundle. I could tell he wanted to ask me more, but I turned away from him and dragged my load inside.

⁕

I don't lie. But neither will I answer a question that hasn't been asked. Petr would have called it lying by omission, I suppose. I've wondered if things would have happened differently if I'd just told him what he really wanted to know: not *how* we learn, but how it's *possible* for us to learn. But no. I don't think it would have changed much. He was too recklessly curious.

⁕

My mother told me I'd never take over the business, but she underestimated me and how much I'd learned before she passed. I have some strength in my hands and arms, and I'm good at precision work. It makes me a good tailor. In that way I can at least get a little respect, because I support myself and do it well. So the villagers employ me, even if they won't look at me.

Others of my kind aren't so lucky. A man down the street hasn't left his room for years. His elderly parents take care of him. When they pass, the other villagers won't show as much compassion. I know there are more of us here and there, in the village and the outlying farms. Those of us who do go outside don't communicate with each other. We stay in the background, we who didn't receive the gift unscathed.

I wonder if that will happen to Petr now. So far, there's no change; he's very still. His temples are freckled. I haven't noticed that before.

Petr wouldn't leave me alone. He kept coming in to talk. I didn't know if he did this to everyone. I sometimes thought that maybe he didn't study lichen at all; he just went from house to house and talked people's ears off. He talked about his heavy homeworld, which he'd left to crawl almost weightless in the high spokes of Amitié. He told me I wouldn't have to carry my own weight there, I'd move without crutches, and I was surprised by the want that flared up inside me, but I said nothing of it. He asked me if I hurt, and I said only if my joints folded back or sideways too quickly. He was very fascinated.

When Saarakka was up, he typed at me to sing to him. He parsed the cadences and inflections like a scientist, annoyed when they refused to slip into neat order.

I found myself talking, too, telling him of sewing and books I'd read, of the other villagers and what they did. It's remarkable what people will say and do when you're part of the background. Petr listened to me, asked questions. Sometimes I met his eyes. They had little crinkles at the outer edges that deepened when he smiled. I discovered that I had many things to say. I couldn't tell whether the biologist in him wanted to study my freakish appearance, or if he really enjoyed being around me.

He sat on my stool behind the counter, telling me about crawling around in the vents on Amitié to study the lichen unique to the station: "They must have hitchhiked in with a shuttle. The question was from where . . ."

I interrupted him. "How does one get there? To visit?"

"You want to go?"

"I'd like to see it." *And be weightless*, I didn't say.

"There's a shuttle bypass in a few months to pick me up," he said. "But it'd cost you."

I nodded.

"Do you have money?" he asked.

"I've saved up some."

He mentioned how much it would cost, and my heart sank so deep I couldn't speak for a while. For once, Petr didn't fill the silence.

I moved past him from the cutting table to the mannequin. I put my hand on a piece of fabric on the table and it slipped. I stumbled. He reached out and caught me, and I fell with my face against his throat. His skin was warm, almost hot; he smelled of sweat and dust and an undertone of musk that seeped into my body and made it heavy. It was suddenly hard to breathe.

I pushed myself out of his arms and leaned against the table, unsteadily, because my arms were shaking. No one had touched me like that before. He had slid from the stool, leaning against the counter across from me, his chest rising and falling as if he had been running. Those eyes were so sharp, I couldn't look at them directly.

"I'm in love with you." The words tumbled out of his mouth in a quick mumble.

He stiffened, as if surprised by what he had just said. I opened my mouth to say I didn't know what, but words like that deserved something—

He held up a hand. "I didn't mean to."

"But . . ."

Petr shook his head. "Aino. It's all right."

When I finally figured out what to say, he had left. I wanted to say I hadn't thought of the possibility, but that I did now. Someone wanted me. It was a very strange sensation, like a little hook tugging at the hollow under my ribs.

Petr changed after that. He kept coming into the workshop, but he started to make friends elsewhere, too. I could see it from the shop window: his cheerful brusqueness bowled the others over. He crouched together with the weaver across the street, eagerly studying her work. He engaged in cheerful haggling with Maiju, who would never negotiate the price of her vegetables, but with him, she did. He even tried to sing, unsuccessfully. I recognized the looks the others gave him. And even though they were only humoring him, treating him as they would a harmless idiot, I found myself growing jealous. That was novel, too.

He didn't mention it again. Our conversation skirted away from any deeper subjects. The memory of his scent intruded on my thoughts at night. I tried to wash it away in the river.

"Aino, I'm thinking about staying."

Petr hadn't been in for a week. Now this.

"Why?" I fiddled with a seam on the work shirt I was hemming.

"I like it here. Everything's simple—no high tech, no info flooding, no hurry. I can hear myself think." He smiled faintly. "You know, I've had stomach problems most of my life. When I came here, they went away in a week. It's been like coming home."

"I don't see why." I kept my eyes down. "There's nothing special here."

"These are good people. Sure, they're a bit traditional, a bit distant. But I like them. And it turns out they need me here. Jorma, he doesn't mind that I can't sing. He offered me a job at the clinic. Says they need someone with my experience."

"Are you all right with this?" he asked when I didn't reply immediately.

"It's good," I said eventually. "It's good for you that they like you."

"I don't know about 'like.' Some of them treat me as if I'm handicapped. I don't care much, though. I can live with that as long as some of you like me." His gaze rested on me like a heavy hand.

"Good for you," I repeated.

He leaned over the counter. "So . . . maybe you could teach me to sing? For real?"

"No."

"Why? I don't understand why."

"Because I can't teach you. You *are* handicapped. Like me."

"Aino." His voice was low. "Did you ever consider that maybe they don't hate you?"

I looked up. "They don't hate me. They're afraid of me. It's different."

"Are you really sure? Maybe if you talked to them . . ."

". . . they would avoid me. It is what it is."

"You can't just sit in here and be bitter."

"I'm not," I said. "It just is what it is. I can choose to be miserable about it, or I can choose not to be."

"Fine." He sighed. "Does it matter to you if I stay or leave?"

"Yes," I whispered to the shirt in my lap.

"Well, which is it? Do you want me to stay?"

He had asked directly, so I had to give him an answer, at least some sort of reply. "You could stay a while. Or I could go with you."

"I told you. I'm not going back to Amitié."

"All right," I said.

"Really?"

"No."

⚜

I could have kept quiet when the procession went by. Maybe then things would have been different. I think he would have found out, anyway.

We were down by the river. We pretended the last conversation hadn't happened. He had insisted on helping me with washing cloth. I wouldn't let him, so he sat alongside me, making conversation while I dipped the lengths of cloth in the river and slapped them on the big flat stone. Maderakka's huge approaching shadow hovered on the horizon. It would be Petr's first time, and he was fascinated. The birds were beginning to amass in the air above the plateau, sharp trills echoing through the valley.

"How long will it last?"

"Just overnight," I said. "It only rises a little bit before it sets again."

"I wonder what it's like on the other side," he said. "Having that in the sky all the time."

"Very quiet, I suppose."

"Does anyone live there?"

I shrugged. "A few. Not as many as here."

He grunted and said no more. I sank into the rhythm of my work, listening to the rush of water and wet cloth on stone, the clatter and bleat of goats on the shore.

Petr touched my arm, sending a shock up my shoulder. I pretended it was a twitch.

"Aino. What's that?" He pointed up the slope.

The women and men walking by were dressed all in white, led by an old woman with a bundle in her arms. They were heading for the valley's innermost point, where the river emerged from underground and a faint trail switchbacked up the wall.

I turned back to my laundry. "They're going to the plateau."

"I can see that. What are they going to do once they get there?"

The question was too direct to avoid. I had to answer somehow. "We don't talk about that," I said finally.

"Come on," Petr said. "If I'm going to live here, I should be allowed to know."

"I don't know if that's my decision to make," I replied.

He settled on the stone again, but he was tense now, and kept casting glances at the procession on their way up the mountainside. He helped me carry the clothes back through the workshop and into the backyard, and then left without helping me hang them. I knew where he was going. You could say I let it happen—but I don't think I could have stopped him either. It was a kind of relief. I hung the cloth, listening to the comforting whisper of wet fabric, until Maderakka rose and silence cupped its hands over my ears.

I don't remember being carried to the plateau in my mother's arms. I only know that she did. Looking down at Petr in my lap, I'm glad I don't remember. Of course everyone *knows* what happens. We're just better off forgetting what it was like.

⚜

Maderakka set in the early hours of the morning, and I woke to the noise of someone hammering on the door. It was Petr, of course, and his nose and lips were puffy. I let him in, and into the back of the workshop to my private room. He sank down on my bed and just sort of crumpled. I put the kettle on and waited.

"I tried to go up there," he said into his hands. "I wanted to see what it was."

"And?"

"Jorma stopped me."

I thought of the gangly doctor trying to hold Petr back, and snorted. "How?"

"He hit me."

"But you're"—I gestured toward him, all of him—"huge."

"So? I don't know how to fight. And he's scary. I almost got to the top before he saw me and stopped me. I got this"—he pointed to his nose—"just for going up there. What the hell is going on up there, Aino? There were those bird things, hundreds of them, just circling overhead."

"Did you see anything else?"

"No."

"You won't give up until you find out, will you?"

He shook his head.

"It's how we do things," I said. "It's how we sing."

"I don't understand."

"You said it's a—what was it?—parasitic ecosystem. Yes?"

He nodded.

"And I said that the hookflies use the goats, and that it's good for the goats. The hookflies get to lay their eggs, and the goats get something in return."

He nodded again. I waited for him to connect the facts. His face remained blank.

"The birds," I said. "When a baby's born, it's taken up there the next time Maderakka rises."

Petr's shoulders slumped. He looked sick. It gave me some sort of grim satisfaction to go on talking, to get back at him for his idiocy.

I went on: "The birds lay their eggs. Not for long, just for a moment. And they leave something behind. It changes the children's development . . . in the throat. It means they can learn to sing." I gestured at myself. "Sometimes the child dies. Sometimes this happens. That's why the others avoid me. I didn't pass the test."

"You make yourselves hosts," Petr said, faintly. "You do it to your children."

"They don't remember. I don't remember."

He stood up, swaying a little on his feet, and left.

"You wanted to know!" I called after him.

A latecomer has alighted on the rock next to me. It's preening its iridescent wings in the morning light, pulling its plumes between its mandibles one by one. I look away as it hops up on Petr's chest. It's so wrong to see it happen, too intimate. But I'm afraid to move, I'm afraid to flee. I don't know what will happen if I do.

The weather was so lovely I couldn't stay indoors. I sat under the awning outside my workshop, wrapped up in shawls so as not to offend too much, basting the seams on a skirt. The weaver across the street had set up one of her smaller looms on her porch, working with her back to me. Saarakka was up, and the street filled with song.

I saw Petr coming from a long way away. His square form made the villagers look so unbearably gangly and frail, as if they would break if he touched them. How did they even manage to stay upright? How did his weight not break the cobblestones? The others shied away from him, like reeds from a boat. I saw why when he came closer. I greeted him with song without thinking. It made his tortured grimace deepen.

He fell to his knees in front of me and wrapped his arms around me, squeezed me so tight I could feel my shoulders creaking. He was shaking. The soundless weeping hit my neck in silent, wet waves. All around us, the others were very busy not noticing what was going on.

I brought him to the backyard. He calmed down and we sat leaning against the wall, watching Saarakka outrun the sun and sink. When the last sliver had disappeared under the horizon, he hummed to test the atmosphere, and then spoke.

"I couldn't stand being in the village for Saarakka. Everyone else talking and I can't . . . I've started to understand the song language now, you know? It makes it worse. So I left, I went up to that plateau. There was nothing there. I suppose you knew that already. Just the trees and the little clearing." He fingered the back of his head and winced. "I don't know how, but I fell on the way down, I fell off the path and down the wall. It was close to the bottom, I didn't hurt myself much. Just banged my head a little."

"That was what made you upset?"

I could feel him looking at me. "If I'd really hurt myself, if I'd hurt myself badly, I wouldn't have been able to call for help. I could have just lain there until Saarakka set. Nobody would have heard me. You wouldn't have heard me."

We sat for a while without speaking. The sound of crickets and birds disappeared abruptly. Oksakka had risen behind us.

"I've always heard that if you've been near death, you're supposed to feel alive and grateful for every moment." Petr snorted. "All I can think of is how easy it is to die. That it can happen at any time."

I turned my head to look at him. His eyes glittered yellow in the setting sun.

"You don't believe I spend time with you because of you."

I waited.

Petr shook his head. "You know, on Amitié, they'd think you look strange, but you wouldn't be treated differently. And the gravity's low when closer to the hub. You wouldn't need crutches."

"So take me there."

"I'm not going back. I've told you."

"Gliese, then?"

"You'd be crushed." He held up a massive arm. "Why do you think I look like I do?"

I swallowed my frustration.

"There are wading birds on Earth," he said, "long-legged things. They move like dancers. You remind me of them."

"You don't remind me of anything here," I replied.

He looked surprised when I leaned in and kissed him.

Later, I had to close his hands around me, so afraid was he to hurt me.

I lay next to him thinking about having normal conversations, other people meeting my eyes, talking to me like a person.

I'm thrifty. I had saved up a decent sum over the years; there was nothing I could spend money on, after all. If I sold everything I owned, if I sold the business, it would be enough to go to Amitié, at least to visit. If someone wanted to buy my things.

But Petr had in some almost unnoticeable way moved into my home. Suddenly he lived there, and had done so for a while. He cooked, he cleaned the corners I didn't bother with because I couldn't reach. He brought in shoots and plants from outside and planted them in little pots. When he showed up with lichen-covered rocks I put my foot down, so he arranged them in patterns in the backyard. Giant Maderakka rose twice; two processions in white passed by on their way to the plateau. He watched them with a mix of longing and disgust.

His attention spoiled me. I forgot that only he talked to me. I spoke directly to a customer and looked her in the eyes. She left the workshop in a hurry and didn't come back.

"I want to leave," I finally said. "I'm selling everything. Let's go to Amitié."

We were in bed, listening to the lack of birds. Oksakka's quick little eye shone in the midnight sky.

"Again? I told you I don't want to go back," Petr replied.

"Just for a little while?"

"I feel at home here now," he said. "The valley, the sky . . . I love it. I love being light."

"I've lost my customers."

"I've thought about raising goats."

"These people will never accept you completely," I said. "You can't sing. You're like me, you're a cripple to them."

"You're not a cripple, Aino."

"I am to them. On Amitié, I wouldn't be."

He sighed and rolled over on his side. The discussion was apparently over.

I woke up tonight because the bed was empty and the air completely still. Silence whined in my ears. Outside, Maderakka rose like a mountain at the valley's mouth.

I don't know if he'd planned it all along. It doesn't matter. There were no new babies this cycle, no procession. Maybe he just saw his chance and decided to go for it.

It took such a long time to get up the path to the plateau. The upslope fought me, and my crutches slid and skittered over gravel and loose rocks; I almost fell over several times. I couldn't call for him, couldn't sing, and the birds circled overhead in a downward spiral.

Just before the clearing came into view, the path curled around an outcrop and flattened out among trees. All I could see while struggling through the trees was a faint flickering. It wasn't until I came into the clearing that I could really see what was going on: that which had been done to me, that I was too young to remember, that which none of us remember and choose not to witness. They leave the children and wait among the trees with their backs turned. They don't speak of what has happened during the wait. No one has ever said that watching is forbidden, but I felt like I was committing a crime, revealing what was hidden.

Petr stood in the middle of the clearing, a silhouette against the gray sky, surrounded by birds. No, he wasn't standing. He hung suspended by their wings, his toes barely touching the ground, his head tipped back. They were swarming in his face, tangling in his hair.

I can't avert my eyes anymore. I am about to see the process up close. The bird that sits on Petr's chest seems to take no notice of me. It pushes its ovipositor in between his lips and shudders. Then it leaves in a flutter of wings, so fast that I almost don't register it. Petr's chest heaves, and he rolls out of my lap, landing on his back. He's awake now, staring into the sky. I don't know if it's terror or ecstasy in his eyes as the tiny spawn fights its way out of his mouth.

In a week, the shuttle makes its bypass. Maybe they'll let me take Petr's place. If I went now, just left him on the ground and packed light, I could make it in time. I don't need a sky overhead. And considering the quality of their clothes, Amitié needs a tailor.

Contributors

Charlie Jane Anders is the author of *All the Birds in the Sky*, a novel coming in early 2016 from Tor Books. She is the Editor-in-Chief of *io9.com* and the organizer of the Writers With Drinks reading series. Her stories have appeared in *Asimov's Science Fiction*, the *Magazine of Fantasy & Science Fiction*, *Tor.com*, *Lightspeed*, *Tin House*, *ZYZZYVA*, and several anthologies. Her novelette "Six Months, Three Days" won a Hugo award. Website: http://CharlieJane.com

Aliette de Bodard lives in Paris, where she has a day job as a System Engineer. In between programming and mothering, she writes speculative fiction–her stories have garnered her two Nebula Awards, a Locus Award and a British Science Fiction Award. Her newest novel, *House of Shattered Wings*, is set in a devastated Paris where rival Houses fight for influence–and features fallen angels, Vietnamese dragons and entirely too many dead bodies. Website: http://aliettedebodard.com

J.D. Brink - If taking a college fencing class, eating from the trash can, and smelling like an animal were qualifications for becoming a sword-swinging barbarian, J.D. Brink might have been Conan's protégé. Instead he's been a sailor, spy, nurse, and officer in the U.S. Navy, as well as a gravedigger, insurance adjuster, and school teacher in civilian life. His work has appeared in *Pseudopod.org*, *Tales of the Talisman*, *Ascent Aspirations*, and *Cemetery Moon*, and his novels *Hungry Gods* and *Tarnish* have been published by Fugitive Fiction. Website: http://brinkschaostheory.blogspot.com

Leah Brown is a biomechanical engineering student and a fiction writer living in Golden, CO.

Carla Dash resides with her husband and two cats in Quincy, MA, where she video games, teaches English Language Learners, and occasionally squeezes in some writing.

Terry Durbin is a writer of suspense, horror, and other less classifiable fiction. He's a husband, father, grandfather, and proud caretaker to two remarkable dogs. His books *Chase*, *The Legacy of Aaron Geist*, and his short story collection, *Reflections in a Black Mirror*, are available from Amazon. http://www.amazon.com/author/terrydurbin

Keith Frady is a short story writer living in Atlanta, GA. He has been published in *Eunoia Review*, *Gravel: A Literary Journal*, *Drunk Monkeys*, and *Bewildering Stories*. He hopes to write a Batman comic one day, and to publish a collection of his short stories in the near future. Twitter: @Keith_Frady

Hugh Howey is the author of the acclaimed post-apocalyptic novel *Wool*, which became a sudden success in 2011. Originally self-published as a series of novelettes, the Wool omnibus has been a #1 bestselling book on Amazon.com and is a *New York Times* and *USA Today* bestseller.

The book was also optioned for film by Ridley Scott, and is now available in print from major publishers all over the world. Hugh's other books include *Shift, Dust, Sand, The Shell Collector*, the Molly Fyde series, *The Hurricane, Half Way Home, The Plagiarist*, and *I, Zombie*. Hugh lives on a boat that he hopes to sail around the world. Website: http://www.hughhowey.com

G. Scott Huggins makes his money by teaching history at a private school, proving that he knows more about history than making money. He loves writing both serious and humorous fiction. When he is not teaching or writing, he devotes himself to his wife, their three children, and two cats. He loves good bourbon, bacon, and pie. If you have any recipes featuring one or more of these things, Mr. Huggins will be pleased to review them if accompanied by a sample.

Michelle Ann King writes science fiction, fantasy and horror from her kitchen table in Essex, England. Her work has appeared in various venues and anthologies, including *Strange Horizons, Daily Science Fiction*, and *Unidentified Funny Objects 2*. She loves Las Vegas, zombie films and good Scotch whisky, not necessarily in that order. Her short stories are being collected in the Transient Tales series, and she is currently at work on a paranormal crime novel. Website: http://www.transientcactus.co.uk

Morgen Knight is an award-winning horror/thriller author living in Kansas City. She is currently working with her agent on the release of her debut novel. Website: http://morgenknight.wordpress.com

Matt Leivers - When he isn't writing, Matt Leivers runs a small record label. When he isn't doing that, he plays in psych-folk oddbods United Bible Studies. When he isn't doing that, he's an archaeologist. He lives in England with his girlfriend and cats. Visit him on Twitter at http://twitter.com/MALeivers

Dan Micklethwaite does most of his writing in a small, wet town in the north of England. He escapes vicariously via his short fiction, which has traveled extensively and internationally, to such wonderful, exotic locales as *Timeless Tales, Birdville, AE SciFi, BULL, 3:AM, Litro*, and the *Missing Slate*, in whose New Voices competition he was runner-up in 2014. His debut novel, a contemporary riff on Don Quixote set in aforementioned small, wet town, is due for release in 2016. Website: http://smalltimebooks.blogspot.co.uk

Michael Milne is a writer and teacher who lives in Suzhou, China. He teaches little kids all about using periods and capitals and juicy words, so he does that really well. He roams the world looking for the best bowl of noodles.

Mel Paisley is an illustrator, activist, and peddler of strange stories working out of Savannah, GA. Their work centers around using fairytales to open up a dialogue on mental illness that surmounts stereotype while expanding imagination. When not writing or painting, they work as the head publicist for *Douleur Magazine*, scour Wikipedia, and get overly excited about pilfered color swatches and cracks in the sidewalk. They have been published previously in the *Port City Review* and *Psyched Magazine*, and featured in nine gallery exhibitions. Currently, they are working on a novel length illustrated storybook about a boy who's mind takes a walk out of his body and gets pulled through the water of a Holocaust survivor's painting in 1950s New York City. Website: http://melpaisley.tumblr.com

Holly Phillips is Canadian. Some people think that's all you need to know about someone, and in her case this may be true: she is frequently polite, often drinks beer, and will wear a toque if it's cold enough. She's also an omnivorous reader, a hard-core sleeper, and a yoga-mat owner. She hunts lattes with her partner Steven through the mean streets of Vancouver, BC.

Shannon Phillips lives in Oakland, CA, where she keeps four chickens, three sons, a dog, and a husband. Her first novel, *The Millennial Sword*, is about the adventures of the modern-day Lady of the Lake in San Francisco. Website: http://joshannonphillips.com

Kyle Richardson writes about shape-shifters, superheroes, and the occasional clockwork beast. He currently lives in the suburban wilds of Canada with his adorable wife Michelle, their squirmy little son Kai, and an imaginary dragon named Chloe who scorches everything she eats.

He also works as an Assistant Editor at Meerkat Press, where he's constantly impressed by the imaginations of contributing writers.

A. Merc Rustad is a queer non-binary writer and filmmaker who lives in the Midwestern United States. Favorite things include: robots, dinosaurs, monsters, and tea. Their stories have appeared or are forthcoming in *Fireside Fiction, Daily Science Fiction, Escape Pod, Inscription Magazine, Scigentasy*, and *Vitality Magazine*. When not buried in homework, Merc likes to play video games, read comics, and wear awesome hats. Website: http://amercrustad.com

Steve Simpson lives in Sydney, Australia, mostly. He has a paid job but the voices at night tell him to write speculative fiction. He thinks it might be the neighbors. Simpson's hobbies include experiments with negative light and time travel, and research on epileptic seizure detection. Info on his short fiction, poetry, and other random stuff can be found at: http://www.inconstantlight.com

Jody Sollazzo grew up in the suburbs of New York City. She now lives in Northern California with her partner, their dragon-loving daughter, and food-loving dog. She works in mental health, disability rights, and anti-bullying. Always a fan of bad timing, she is also achieving her life long dream of being a writer. Her short stories appear in several anthologies. She is working on a novel that is a role reversal of *Beauty and the Beast* that takes place in a prep school with time-traveling fairies with disabilities. Blog: http://thatdisabledmom.blogspot.com/

David Stevens lives in Sydney, Australia, with his wife and four children, where he teaches law. His stories have appeared in *Crossed Genres, Aurealis, Three-Lobed Burning Eye, Pseudopod, Cafe Irreal*, and elsewhere. Website: http://davidstevens.info

Karin Tidbeck is the award-winning author of *Jagannath: Stories* and the novel *Amatka*. She lives and works in Malmö, Sweden, where she makes a living as a freelance writer. She writes in Swedish and English, and has published work in *Weird Tales, Tor.com, Words Without Borders* anthologies like *Fearsome Magics* and *The Time-Traveler's Almanac*. Website: http://www.karintidbeck.com

Jeff VanderMeer's most recent fiction is the NYT-bestselling Southern Reach trilogy (*Annihilation, Authority*, and *Acceptance*), all released in 2014 by Farrar, Straus and Giroux. The series has been acquired by publishers in 23 other countries. Paramount Pictures/Scott Rudin Productions have acquired the movie rights. His nonfiction has appeared in the *New York Times*, the *Guardian*, the *Washington Post*, the *Atlantic.com*, and the *Los Angeles Times*. A three-time World Fantasy Award winner and 14-time nominee, VanderMeer has edited or coedited many iconic fiction anthologies, taught at the Yale Writers' Conference, the Miami International Book Fair, lectured at MIT and the Library of Congress, and serves as the co-director of Shared Worlds, a unique teen SF/fantasy writing camp located at Wofford College. He lives in Tallahassee, Florida, with his wife, the noted editor Ann VanderMeer. Website: http://www.JeffVanderMeer.com

Michal Wojcik was born in Poland, raised in the Yukon Territory, and educated in Edmonton and Montreal. He has a Master's degree in history from McGill University, where he studied witchcraft trials and medieval necromancers. His short fiction has appeared in *On Spec*, the *Book Smugglers* and *Daily Science Fiction*. Blog: http://onelastsketch.wordpress.com

Victoria Zelvin is a graduate of the inaugural class of Roanoke College's Creative Writing program. She currently lives in Ballston, VA, with her one-eyed cat Leela. She strives to write things that don't make sense, but that are internally consistent in the lack of sense she's making. Website: http://victoriazelvin.com